THE CC

A LE… THRILLER

BOOK 1 OF THE MASON PIERCE SERIES

MICHAEL STAGG

The Concrete Alibi: A Legal Thriller

The Mason Pierce Series, Book 1

For more information about Michael Stagg, go to https://michaelstagg.com

To keep up with the latest information on Michael, Mason Pierce, and other books, sign up for the Michael Stagg newsletter here or at https://michaelstagg.com/newsletter/

Created with Vellum

PART I

1

Molly Danvers was freezing, and the wait outside the Stone Street Cider Mill wasn't helping at all. The only thing that made the cold bearable as she stood there in the falling snow was knowing that her friends were waiting for her inside and that they'd already ordered her a Hot and Hard Cider.

The jury would later learn that it was at this point, while she was waiting in line, that Molly Danvers sent her last text to her father, reassuring him again that she'd made it to the Cider Mill and that she was just fine.

It took ten minutes for Molly to reach the large wooden front doors, and in that time the snow kept falling and more people kept arriving. She was glad she'd left the Dune Sled just before sunset because those who'd stayed to see the last rays of the sun dip below Lake Michigan from their vantage on the great dune bluffs were the ones who were joining the line behind her. She'd gotten separated from her friends on the way over—Ashley had to drive Carly and Sophia because they'd both brought bottles of schnapps to the Big Dune and couldn't hold their booze any more than they could steer a straight sled. No one was ever truly she gave it a quick stir with the cinnamon stick and drank deep, welcoming the warmth as it filled her chest.

The Stone Street Cider Mill had set up three dedicated stations for the hot drinks in the center of the patio, so it wasn't difficult for them to get another round, which Ashley was happy to do. After Ashley returned, the four women staked out a prime spot in the northwest corner next to a propane heater where they had easy access to the drink station without being subjected to the press of people that were beginning to spill from the dining room onto the patio.

The view from where they stood was perfect. Floodlights from the Cider Mill illuminated Lake Lacache, which was frozen and covered in the snow that had fallen steadily for a week straight and was still coming down now. On a clear day from where she stood, Molly would have been able to see across Lake Lacache to the dune bluffs on the other side, which rose between Lake Lacache and Lake Michigan. But it was dark, and it was snowing, so she could only see the big flakes drifting down as far as the floodlights allowed. Still, even then, being able to see the snow falling through the windows on the three sides around them was beautiful and surprisingly peaceful, Molly thought, especially in contrast to the growing noise within.

The patio had become so crowded that it took Sophia twice as long to get their third round of drinks. They'd had space when Molly first arrived, but now they were sharing their space heater, first with a woman waiting on her husband, then with some local guys who looked familiar but whom Molly couldn't place, and finally with three couples in their fifties who couldn't get over how young sledding down a four-hundred-foot dune made you feel.

By the time the girls were ready for a fourth round, the crowd had become too much, and Molly wanted to go. Fair was fair though, and it was her turn, so Molly said she'd buy one last round before she left. Molly's pronouncement was met with outrage and negotiation—Sophia protested that there was no way she could leave so early, Carly said she'd buy the drinks if Molly stayed, and Ashley argued that Molly couldn't leave until she had her t-shirt. But then, in reaction to the look on her face that she couldn't quite hide, the three girls mobilized to keep Molly there just a little while longer. Carly went to the patio drink stand to buy four more ciders, Ashley went back into the dining room to pick up a Dune Sled t-shirt, and Sophia stayed in the northwest corner of the patio with Molly, switching places with her so she could have her back to the outside wall and Sophia could keep the space in front of Molly open so she could breathe.

Molly decided, in that moment, that she was lucky to have three such good friends.

There was a crack, a deep dull thud that felt like it ran right up Molly's legs into her spine. She wavered and lost her balance for a moment, figuring the Hot Hard Ones had a sneakier kick than she'd realized. Then the ground dropped away and Molly was falling and Molly was screaming and she had a vivid look at the surprise on Sophia's face a moment before they hit the ground.

Though she never knew exactly what it was, Molly felt the cold of the snow and then she felt the crush of the concrete and then Molly Danvers felt nothing at all.

2

At six forty-five the next morning, a Sunday, Mason Pierce was parking his truck outside Maggie's Deli when his phone buzzed. He frowned at the number, which he'd only seen once, back when he'd interviewed for his new job. He answered.

"Mr. Freid?"

"Pierce, good, I reached you. Half the firm's not answering yet, all that personal space nonsense."

Mason Pierce didn't follow all that but said, "I'm here, Mr. Freid. Is something wrong for tomorrow?"

"Tomorrow? What the hell's tomorrow?"

Mason cocked his head. "My first day?"

"First...ah, Christ. Have you signed all your paperwork?"

"Yes, sir. Last week."

"So you're officially part of Kramer Burns? You're a working attorney for us?"

"Yes, sir. You hired me."

"Well good news, Pierce. Your first day just got moved up."

"Sir?"

"To today. Where are you?"

Mason looked at the restaurant. "Outside Maggie's Deli."

"Where the hell is Maggie's Deli?"

"Downtown. On Second, near Pine."

"The city, Pierce! What city are you in?"

"Northlake, sir."

"Thank Christ. Listen, one of our clients took it in the shorts last night. I need you to get over there."

"Where, sir?"

"To the Stone Street Cider Mill."

"What happened?"

"Its patio collapsed."

"Oh no."

"Have you heard about it?"

"No, but I haven't checked anything this morning."

"Good, maybe there's still time before all the jackals descend."

"Jackals?"

"Other lawyers. Mounds of rubble mean piles of cash. I need you to get over there right away. How soon can you get there?"

"Twenty minutes."

"Do it. I'm stuck up here in Petoskey with the family, and it hasn't stopped snowing for a goddam week, so it's going to take me until noon to get down there."

"Okay."

"I already sent Hyde Warren, he's the owner, home but the moron didn't call me until this morning, so who knows what his people have told the law already. You make sure none of his employees say a word, you hear me, Pierce? You're the only one who talks to the sheriff until I get down there."

"Right."

"Nothing but concern for the victims and help with the rescue effort but no information about last night or what happened. Are we clear?"

"Shouldn't be a problem since I don't know what happened last night."

"Perfect. And text me a casualty count as soon as you have it."

"People died?"

"They did. And there may be a lot."

"Who?"

"I don't have the faintest idea, but we're going to see their names on court captions soon enough. Get over there."

"Will do, sir."

"And quit with the 'sir.' You're a lawyer, not a waiter. It's Peter."

"Got it, Peter."

"Hold down the fort until I get there."

"Done."

Peter Freid, the managing partner of the new Northlake office of the law firm of Kramer Burns, hung up, and Mason Pierce, its newest associate, caught his breath. Then he hustled into Maggie's to break the news to his cousins.

MAGGIE'S HAD a deli counter along one side and a collection of booths and two-top tables on the other. It was more wood than metal, but the whole front wall was a window to the street, so light poured into what would otherwise be a dark place. He checked the line at the deli counter, then found his cousin Austin waving from a booth on the far wall, his sister Lily smirking in the seat across from him.

Lily Stone had blonde hair like straw that tended to stick in all directions by the end of a workday. She had a strong jaw, a sharp nose, and shoulders widened by swimming, all matched by a swift deliberateness when pouring a seawall, picking a fight, or in this case, sliding her cousin a cup of already-poured coffee.

"Already adopting those soft lawyer ways, I see," she said. "Couldn't pull yourself out from under the blankets?"

Mason shook his head, stayed standing, and grabbed the welcome coffee.

"You don't get to keep lawyer's hours until tomorrow," Austin said. Lily's brother pushed his ball cap back on his curly hair and grinned through a bushy beard. "We get one more day to put those paws of yours to use doing honest work."

Mason shook his head again. "Can't, Austin. Just got a call from my boss. The lawyering starts today."

Austin looked skeptical. "On a Sunday?"

Mason nodded.

Lily didn't look as if she believed him either. "When?"

"Now. I have to get going. I just wanted to let you know."

"Where are you going this early?" said Austin.

Mason wasn't sure how much he should reveal, so he just said, "To an accident site."

"Car?" said Lily.

Mason shook his head.

Austin grinned at his sister. "He's not sure he can tell us."

"Is that how it's going to be now?" said Lily. "Shutting out your own family because of this confidentiality crap?"

Mason thought, then said, "I'm sure you'll figure it out when you see the news later today."

"Later my ass," said Lily, pulling out her phone.

Austin's grin to Mason broadened. "You asked for it."

Mason smiled back. "I did." He quaffed the rest of the coffee and set down the cup. "I have to get going—"

Maggie—yes, the Maggie of Maggie's Deli—came over with a tray bearing three foil-wrapped packages. She gave Mason a smile as she slid the tray onto the table and said, "Here are your burritos, your hot sauce, and god help me, Austin, the blueberry syrup, and don't you dare tell anyone I let you do it."

gency vehicles, and heavy equipment jockeyed and wove around regular cars covered in snow from the night before.

Mason stopped, turned around, and drove his truck a little ways back so he could park on the side of the road. He surveyed the scene, thought for a moment, then pulled an orange construction vest and a hard hat out from the back of the cab. He gave the hot sauce on his sleeve one last wipe, which only served to smear the red wider, put on the hat and the vest, and made his way through the snowy lot.

A blockade, complete with sawhorses and yellow tape, was guarded by two sheriff's deputies doing their best to find room for emergency and construction vehicles. Mason Pierce strode right up to them. One deputy, who was patiently explaining to a civilian woman why she couldn't have access, took one look at Mason and waved him through.

It was the same with the next two checkpoints. Gawkers and busybodies were being turned back as deputies and firefighters allowed Mason to pass. Even when Mason walked up the steps and arrived at the double wooden doors to the Cider Mill itself, the deputy stood aside and kept his eyes on the lot for people who weren't supposed to be there. The vest and hat were part of it, of course. But the real reason was Mason Pierce himself. Anyone who looked at Mason Pierce believed he belonged there.

Mason Pierce was six-and-a-half feet tall and broad enough that his shoulders filled the double doorway as he walked through. As he stomped his work boots free of snow, he removed his hard hat to reveal a shaved head, a once-broken nose, and a resting expression that looked as if he'd woken up that morning chewing glass. In fairness to the deputies, Mason Pierce looked more like a nineteenth-century bareknuckle prize fighter than a lawyer, and his vest only reinforced the story his face seemingly told.

Mason was aware, sometimes acutely, of how he looked because if he forgot, someone usually reminded him. For now, though, he took advantage of it and made his way through the crowd of emergency personnel to the dining room.

Mason entered a large lobby filled with dark wood and clear glass that revealed a cider press and distillery tanks on one side and a large warehouse-style dining room on the other. The room was filled, but what caught Mason's attention was the sheriff talking to a Cider Mill employee.

Mason hurried over to where Sable County Sheriff Sean Sizemore was sitting across a table from a man in a black Stone Street Cider Mill polo shirt. Sheriff Sizemore had dark, slicked-back hair with the first whispers of gray lines. Aviators hung from the front pocket of his brown uniform shirt, and a hat, which his unlined hair showed he never wore, sat on the table in front of him. A deputy was taking notes as Sheriff Sizemore said, "How many people were in here, Wyatt?"

The man in the Stone Street Cider Mill shirt, Wyatt, shook his head. "I don't know, Sheriff. I just don't."

"You were pretty crowded, weren't you?"

"It was Dune Sled weekend, Sheriff," Wyatt said, as if that explained everything.

"Were you charging a cover?"

"We always—"

"—Good morning, Sheriff," said Mason.

Sheriff Sizemore looked up, did a double take. "Mason? What are you doing here?"

"I represent the owner."

"I thought you worked for Judge Roderick?"

"I'm with Kramer Burns now."

"Since when?"

"Since today."

Sheriff Sizemore kept his eyes on Mason, then said, "I'm working here, Mason."

"So am I. I'll sit in on the employee interviews."

"Why would you do that?"

"We need to find out what happened just as much as you."

Sheriff Sizemore pursed his lips, then looked back at Wyatt, the manager. "This was our biggest Dune Sled in years, what with all the snow."

Wyatt nodded. "I believe it."

"How about you? Biggest crowd you've had here?"

Wyatt frowned. "It was big, sure. Ever?" He shrugged.

"What's your max capacity?"

"The county will have records of that," Mason said.

Sheriff Sizemore stared.

Mason shrugged. "No reason to guess when you have access to the exact number."

"Good point. How many people were here last night, Wyatt?"

"I don't know."

Sheriff Sizemore stared at Wyatt now. "We need to know. An exact number. How would we find that out?"

"Well, we could check—"

Mason held up a hand. "I'll confer with my client, and all of his employees, and we'll figure that out, Sheriff."

"Are you obstructing my investigation, Mason?"

"Is this a voluntary conversation, Sheriff?"

Sheriff Sizemore sat back and pointed at the manager. "I asked Wyatt."

"I'm helping Wyatt and his employer get you the most accurate information, Sheriff."

"Are you, Mason?"

"Yes," Mason said and returned the stare.

Sheriff Sizemore stood, picked up his hat, tapped his fingers with it. "All that fresh snow, Mason. It was a record crowd for the

Dune Sled. I'd be willing to bet that it was a record crowd for the Stone Street Cider Mill. Assemble everything you have. I'm going to want the door receipts, bar charges, anything that will tell us how many people were here."

"The t-shirt sales should help with that, won't they?" said Wyatt.

Mason raised his hand, but it was too late.

"Yes, it would, Wyatt. Thank you. That too, Mason. A warrant's on the way."

"I'll be looking for it."

Sheriff Sizemore pointed outside. "The rescue is still active. We'll have investigators here afterwards for a while."

Mason nodded. "I'm sure we will too."

"Stay out of our way."

"Same."

As the Sheriff walked away, Mason turned to Wyatt. "What's your last name?"

"Jenkins. Wyatt Jenkins."

"All right, Wyatt. I'm Mason Pierce, and I'm one of your lawyers."

Wyatt's brow furrowed as he looked up at Mason. "Really?"

"Really."

"I thought you were with the construction crew."

"I'm not. I'm going to be investigating this. Just how busy was it last night?"

Wyatt Jenkins looked around. "We were packed."

"How packed? Not more than in summer, right?"

Wyatt Jenkins shook his head. "In summer, more places are open. Half of the bars on the Bluffs close for the winter."

"So...?"

"So we were packed."

"And the patio?"

Wyatt Jenkins looked down. "The patio was wall to wall."

He choked, then bowed his head and wiped at his eyes.

"What, Wyatt?"

"Callie, our hostess. She was one of them. They found her this morning."

Mason put one hand on Wyatt's shoulder, engulfing it. "I'm sorry."

Wyatt nodded and wiped harder.

"Wyatt, is there any video?"

Wyatt shook his head. "Hyde said he was going to get a security system, but he never did. Is that bad?"

"It's fine."

Wyatt blinked. "Am I going to get fired?"

Mason's mind was on evidence, so Wyatt's question caught him off guard. "Why would you get fired?"

"Because I was the manager last night. I can't get fired, Mason. I need this job."

"I wouldn't think so, Wyatt. It's not like you caused the collapse, right?"

Wyatt shook his head.

"Then let's start getting things together. Are there any employees here?"

"I told them all to go home." He choked again. "The ones I could find."

"Have you been up all night?"

Wyatt Jenkins nodded.

"Then let's get you some coffee and set you up in the office. You can pull the receipts together from last night. Can you hang on just a little longer?"

Wyatt Jenkins nodded again.

The two went back to the little manager's office, and Mason put Wyatt to work assembling the t-shirt sales and the cover charges from the night before. Then, with a last admonition not to talk to the sheriff or anyone else without him, Mason shut the door on Wyatt Jenkins.

He was about to go out and inspect the wreckage of where the patio of the Stone Street Cider Mill used to be when his phone buzzed.

He looked, sighed, and answered.

"Hi, Amber."

"Mason, thank God. I need your help."

4

Every plaintiff's lawyer needs a network to snag clients, and Jerome Baggman had put one together that worked while he slept. Sure, most of his people were in the Detroit area, but injury and money knows no boundaries, so he had people all the way west to Grand Rapids and more than enough up I-75 to Flint and Saginaw but he had less in the far north. Less was not none though, because rich people Up North meant lake houses and water, and lake houses and water meant pontoons and power boats, and pontoons and power boats meant booze. Lots of it. And booze meant business.

Most of Jerome Baggman's network Up North was in more affluent areas like Petoskey and Charlevoix and Torch Lake, so it took longer—until he'd poured his first coffee—for someone to get word to him about the Stone Street Cider Mill collapse, along with the names and addresses of the wife of one victim and the parents of another.

Jerome Baggman, the man who brought the bag to those who've been wronged by the negligence of another, sipped his coffee, fired up his tablet, and spent his Sunday morning learning about some godforsaken place in the upper Lower Peninsula called Northlake.

5

Mason took a breath, then said, "Wherever you are, I can't come get you right now, Amber."

"I know that! I'm in Chicago."

Before he could help himself, Mason said, "I thought you were in Grand Rapids?"

"I don't have to tell you where I am."

"No. You don't. What's going on?"

"I need money. Chicago is way more expensive than Grand Rapids."

"Amber, we've been broken up for more than a year. I gave you everything I had, and then some, to get you started."

"That's the least you could do. You dragged me up to that snowbound, godforsaken place—"

"You wanted to come to Northlake."

"—which completely stalled out my career, so now I need you to—"

This was not the first time they'd had this conversation, or even the fourteenth, so Mason said, "Amber. I'm at work. I have to go. You got all there is."

"That's not true!"

"Goodbye, Amber." Mason hung up.

Mason hadn't even put his phone in his pocket before the first text appeared.

This is serious, Amber texted.

We have a big problem.

You know you have money.

You haven't even tapped your mom's place.

One text bubble after another appeared. Mason's phone was already on silent, but it vibrated again and again and again.

He was about to put it away when he saw a new notification —a call from his boss, Peter Freid. He answered.

"How does it look?" said Peter.

"Bad," said Mason.

"Do we have a final casualty number?"

"They're still pulling them out."

"Alive or dead?"

"Not sure. Hopefully alive."

"Not necessarily. Alive is more expensive. Get to the office. I finally made it through this damn snow, and we need to start setting up our defense."

"I'll get whatever the manager has, then head over."

"You already talked to him?"

"I did."

"Good. Move your ass." The phone went dead.

Mason went back to the office where Wyatt Jenkins had been hard at work pulling together the night's receipts. Mason thanked Wyatt and told him to go home, get some rest, and wait for their call. Then Mason waited as the manager turned off the computer and put on his coat, before walking Wyatt Jenkins out to make sure no one interrogated him again on the way to his car.

Mason felt his phone buzz as he climbed into his own truck. It was the twenty-seventh text from Amber. He turned off his phone and drove to the office he'd never seen.

6

Though Mason Pierce had lived in Northlake for most of his life, there was a simple reason why he'd never seen the office of Kramer Burns—it hadn't existed before that week.

Most of the law firms in town were located in the Old Downtown, by the courthouse and the Public Safety Building. The office of Kramer Burns was out near the big lake, and its driveway was right next to the entrance to the Bluffside Farms Golf and Country Club, a gated community that mixed housing, recreation, and moneyed exclusivity with a grand view of Lake Michigan.

The location told Mason his new firm was going after money, not court cases. Which was hardly a surprise.

Mason parked his F150 next to the two other cars in the lot—a BMW of some sort and a Honda Accord—very much aware that his truck was covered in far more dirt than the other two. Then he walked through the oversized outer doors, past the offices of Siege Tower Financial and through the door at the end of the hall bearing the gold lettering of *Kramer Burns*.

A woman with auburn hair and a bright smile stood behind the marble-topped reception desk. "And you must be Mr. Pierce."

Mason found it impossible not to smile back. "I am."

"I'm Melody Carmichael. Normally, on your first day, I'd get you all set up—Firm ID, laptop, that sort of thing, but I've been told that right now, this is your laptop," she handed him a legal notepad, "and this is your mouse," she handed him a pen, "and I'm to take you to Mr. Freid's office."

Mason took them both and nodded.

"I think, though, that we can make a detour to the coffee station, don't you?"

"I do."

Her eyes twinkled. "It's on the way."

"Is that Pierce, Melody?" came a voice.

"We're coming, Mr. Freid," she called and waved Mason along.

They passed an alcove that smelled of coffee, and, sure enough, Melody ducked in, poured him a branded mug, and said, "End of the hall. Welcome to Kramer Burns."

Armed with paper, pen, and coffee, Mason walked down the hall and through the frosted glass doors.

A man who seemed too young for his thick white hair stood in front of his desk.

"Good Christ, Pierce," said Peter Freid. "I forgot how big you are." Peter Freid strode over and extended a hand.

Mason shook it. "Good morning, Peter."

Peter Freid looked down and cackled. "I forgot about that too. It's like shaking a deer antler."

Mason didn't know much about ski slope casual, but he could see that Peter Freid was wearing it, and he became acutely aware of his own worn work boots, faded jeans, and weathered canvas coat that had been perfect camouflage at the worksite but seemed sorely out of place here. He instinctively looked back and saw that he had, indeed, tracked a few cookie-cutter triangles of dirty snow into his boss's office.

"I'm sorry about that," he said, pointing.

"Is it from the Cider Mill?"

Mason nodded.

"Then don't be. Melody!"

"Yes, Mr. Freid."

"Have custodial sweep up behind Pierce!"

"Yes, Mr. Freid."

"Speaking of work, let's get to it. Sit," said Peter Freid as he went behind his desk.

They did.

Mason felt Peter Freid's eyes on him as he chuckled, then said, "Melody!"

"Yes, Mr. Freid?"

"Tell Detroit we're going to need stronger chairs!"

"Yes, Mr. Freid."

He turned back to Mason. "Alright, Pierce, we were going to spend a couple of days easing into this new satellite office thing, finish setting up the space, then bang around town for a few lunches, but Hyde Warren has got his tender parts in the wringer with this patio collapse, and we have to unwring them. Last I heard, we were at three dead and five injured—"

"Three more ambulances left while I was there this morning," said Mason.

Peter Freid waved. "We'll find out the total soon enough. Listen, this wasn't the plan for how Kramer Burns was going to establish itself up here, but when a patio filled with opportunity collapses into our lap, we're going to take it. Hyde is an old buddy of mine from school, which is one of the reasons we're here in Northlake. He was going to introduce me to some of the players around town, but we're going to go one better—Kramer Burns is going to take care of everything for him on this. Everything. And when the business interests up here see what a goddam fine job we did for him, that's going to open opportunity for you, for me, and for Mother Burns. Understand?"

Mason nodded.

"All right, I seem to remember that during your interview you said you grew up doing construction?"

"I did. Foundations and seawalls."

"Good. You're going to handle that part of the case. You were there today. What do you think?"

Mason thought. "There were a lot of cars in the lot, even with everyone who would have left last night. And we've had an awful lot of snow."

"I think the legal term is a 'shit-ton.'"

"I get the sense that the sheriff thinks the patio was overloaded."

"What does Mason Pierce think?"

"I'm not sure. But it's an old building. And that's a lot of weight."

Peter Freid nodded. "Our engineering expert, Cameron Thomas, will be here tomorrow. Meet her at the site in the morning."

Mason nodded. "I'll let you know what we find."

"I know what you're going to find."

"What?"

"That it wasn't our fault. Keep me updated on how."

Mason opened his mouth, closed it, then nodded.

"Welcome to Kramer Burns."

"Glad to be here."

"All right, go see Melody, and have her set you up in your office."

Mason nodded and left Peter Freid's office.

Peter Freid cackled. "Melody!"

"Yes, Mr. Freid?"

"Tell Detroit we're going to have to widen the doors too!"

"Yes, Mr. Freid," said Melody, then she went about setting up the office of the newest associate of Kramer Burns.

7

Mason spent the next couple of hours getting hooked into the many tendrils of Kramer Burns. Computers and networks and electronic file systems and company phones and tablets and passwords and ID badges and all manner of things that our cave-dwelling ancestors or head-shaking grandfathers would have doubted were really necessary to do "work" but which the modern mega-law firm found to be indispensable.

When they were done, Peter sent Melody home, then came into Mason's office and said, "I want you to stop at Hyde Warren's house on the way home. In between sprints to the bathroom to clean out his pants, he's put together his construction and renovation records for the Cider Mill. Get them, review them, and let's see what we have."

"I'll head right over." Mason stood.

Peter Freid looked up, shook his head, and laughed. "I'll get used to it eventually."

Mason nodded. "I did."

Peter Freid laughed again, slapped Mason's shoulder, and left.

Mason followed him out the door and went to meet the owner of the Stone Street Cider Mill.

MASON'S PHONE buzzed as he parked in Hyde Warren's driveway. Two more texts from Amber. He ignored them and walked up to the door.

A middle-aged man with white receding hair cut short and white stubble on his chin opened it before Mason had a chance to knock. He peered up at Mason through gold-rimmed glasses and said, "Peter said he was sending a lawyer."

"He did."

"You're Mason Pierce?"

"I am."

"You don't look like a lawyer."

Mason chose to interpret that as a comment on his work boots and canvas coat. "I was out at the Cider Mill all day."

Hyde Warren's face fell. "I wanted to go back over, but Peter said to stay away while the sheriff is there."

"Probably a good idea. He was going after your manager pretty hard."

Hyde Warren hesitated, then said, "How many?"

Mason didn't have to ask what he meant. "I'm not sure. Three more were pulled out while I was there this morning."

"Dead?"

"I'm not sure of that either."

Hyde Warren looked as if all of the concrete rubble of the crumbled patio was on his shoulders. "You'd better come in."

He shut the door behind Mason and pulled a box off an end table. "Here are the paper records for the first ten years or so. There's a thumb drive in there with the records since."

"Did you build the patio?"

Hyde Warren nodded. "In 2002."

"Anything since?"

"Just repairs, maintenance, inspections. No problems that I saw."

Hyde Warren's hands shook as he gave Mason the box. "Everything I have is tied up in the Cider Mill."

"I understand, Mr. Warren."

"There was never any sign that anything was wrong. I would've done something if there was!"

"I get it."

"I would never try to hurt someone."

Mason hefted the box. "I'll start sorting through this to prove it."

Hyde Warren caught his breath. "Right. Sorry. Peter said you have construction experience?"

"Some."

"But you're a lawyer?"

"Yes. We have a whole team on it, Mr. Warren. I'm meeting with a construction expert out there tomorrow, and then we'll know more."

"Tomorrow? Okay. I'll wait to hear from you."

Then Mason took the box, thanked Hyde Warren, and went home.

~

MASON PIERCE LIVED in a cottage on Lake Michigan. Tucked away on a gravel road, surrounded by trees on three sides with the neighbors a hundred yards away, you probably wouldn't find it unless you were going there. It had two bedrooms, a kitchen that shared space with the main family room, and a three-season screened-in porch on the back. His house was old, a maintenance nightmare, and in need of more work than his lawyer schedule allowed. There were two reasons he kept it.

The first was right there out the back—Lake Michigan. The house sat a couple hundred feet above the water with a rickety, weathered wood stair that led down to a strip of beach whose width depended on the wind and the water level of the lake.

The second was that it was the only thing he had left from his mom.

Mason wasn't thinking about either of those things, though, as he parked his truck in front of a second building that was too big to be a shed but too small to be a garage and took the box of Cider Mill records into the house. He cleared space at the kitchen table, sat in a sturdy wooden chair, and began to go through the box from Hyde Warren to see what he could learn about the Stone Street Cider Mill.

He found sales documents from when Hyde had bought the Cider Mill back in 2002. The listing pictures showed there was no patio on the back, so he looked to see if there were any plans and eventually found a set of blueprints at the bottom of the box also dated 2002 from a company called Landmark Reconstruction.

Mason spread the blued paper out on the table, fighting the curling edges until he weighed them down with a couple of polished stones he had on a shelf. The plan showed the patio extending out from the side of the Cider Mill supported by concrete piers spaced at regular intervals with the last row to be sunk and anchored right at the edge of Lake Lacache so that a person standing on the patio would only see water. The plan also showed a patio floor of concrete and flagstone. Mason didn't know what kind of underlying structure all that called for but, from his semi-qualified perspective, it seemed like there were enough piers and steel beams to support it.

Still, flagstone and concrete on the floor. Stone and concrete half walls for a rail. That was a lot of weight before a single person stepped foot on that patio. He'd be interested to hear what an expert had to say.

By the time he finished a cursory look, it was late. He packed up the box to take with him in the morning on his first *official* day as an associate of Kramer Burns.

8

Cameron Thomas knew how to handle being jerked around by law enforcement, but that didn't mean that she liked it. It wasted her time.

"I'm sorry, Ms. Thomas," said Sheriff Sizemore. "I can't let you down there."

"*Dr.* Thomas," she said.

Sheriff Sizemore blinked, then smiled. "I don't care if you're a doctor, a lawyer, or an indigenous people's leader. I can't let you down there during an active recovery operation."

"I've been here for two hours, Sheriff." She pointed at the dining room of the Stone Street Cider Mill where deputies, emergency personnel, and construction workers in orange vests milled about drinking coffee. "The active phase seems to have passed."

"It's cold out there, Ms.—*Doctor* Thomas. You'll forgive my men if they warm up after spending all night looking for survivors."

"I'm not minimizing their effort, Sheriff. I'm minimizing your excuse to keep me from doing my job."

"I can't risk adding another casualty to the list by letting you out there right now, Dr. Thomas."

"How long is that list right now, Sheriff?"

Sheriff Sizemore appeared uncertain for a moment, then said, "Six dead. Twenty-four injured."

Cameron Thomas nodded, but she didn't write it down. She'd remember.

"Besides, I need to confirm with the owner that you're actually—" Sheriff Sizemore glanced over her shoulder and stopped. Cameron Thomas turned to see what had distracted him.

A man was walking towards them who was a head taller than everyone he passed. He had a shaved head, a once-broken nose that had healed with a crook, and shoulders as wide as the aisle he walked down. He wore a cheap dark suit and a navy peacoat with his hands stuck deep into the pockets and, to Cameron's eye, looked as if he were there to break legs for a gambling debt that was overdue.

"She can't have access to the property yet, Mason," said Sheriff Sizemore to the man.

The man stopped, and though Cameron looked most men in the eye, she had to tilt her head up to him.

"Dr. Thomas?" he said in a low voice.

She extended her hand. "Cameron. You're Pierce?"

"Mason." His hand engulfed hers, which wasn't a surprise, but it was also rough as sandpaper, which was.

"You're a lawyer?"

His smile faded. "I am."

She smiled. "Peter said you have construction experience?"

"Some." His voice had a rasp to it, as if he'd been yelling or outside all day.

"Good. Then I suppose you won't be totally useless."

His smiled returned.

Sheriff Sizemore stepped forward. "I was just telling *Dr.*

Thomas that she can't have access to the site while the recovery effort is going on."

Just then, a large man with a red face and blond hair wearing a fire rescue uniform walked up, holding his helmet. "That's it for my guys, Sean," he said to Sheriff Sizemore.

Sheriff Sizemore pursed his lips. "Are you sure?"

"I'm going to leave a couple of guys and one rescue vehicle back for the rest of the day, just in case, but we're letting the rest of the boys go home."

"Is the active recovery over now, Chief Hagan?" said Mason.

"I'm afraid it is, Mason," said Fire Chief Hagan.

"It's still an active crime scene," said Sheriff Sizemore.

"Your investigation might be active, Sheriff," said Mason, "but the scene certainly isn't, crime or no."

"I'm going to send investigators in now."

"So are we," said Mason, pointing to Cameron.

"Don't disturb anything."

Mason smiled, and Cameron thought that although it seemed good-natured, on that face it was intimidating. "You either."

"We'll be taking samples."

"Us too."

Cameron raised her hand. "I've worked with police investigators before. We both have an interest in getting it right and in looking for the same thing. There's not going to be a problem. Where's your guy so we can work this out?"

Sheriff Sizemore blinked. "He's coming in from Traverse City."

"Has he left yet?"

Sheriff Sizemore looked at Fire Chief Hagan. "I just learned that the rescue was over."

"So did I," said Cameron.

Sheriff Sizemore pressed his lips together. "He'll be here shortly," he said and pulled out his phone as he walked away.

"Have him come see me so we can coordinate."

Before the sheriff could respond, Cameron turned to Mason. "You know where we're going?"

"I do."

"Show me the way," she said to Mason.

Mason pulled on a dark stocking cap, which only reinforced the appearance that the leg-breaking was about to begin, and led her down a hall to a side entrance.

As they walked, she said, "So you've spent time in the trades?"

"I used to."

"Judging from your handshake, I'd say you still do."

Mason shrugged. "I've been practicing law for a couple of years now."

"Really? I'm surprised we haven't bumped into each other on my other Kramer Burns cases."

Mason's mouth twitched. "I started at Kramer Burns yesterday."

Cameron smiled. "Glad to see you hit the ground running."

"I try. How about you? Builder?"

"Structural engineer. But you can't build a bridge or a tower every day, so I like to consult on cases too."

"Done many?"

"A couple of dozen."

"Both sides?"

She nodded. "The injured and the evil doer."

As they walked down a narrow hall, Cameron noticed that Mason's shoulders alternately grazed the walls with each step. Then he opened the side door to a blast of cold, and they went outside.

Cameron Thomas took a second to survey the wreckage. The exterior wall of the Cider Mill was easy enough to see with its gray stone that rose three stories up to a steeply sloped roof. The glass doors on the middle floor that had led to the patio from the dining room were intact and closed, and the front cellar wall that was built into the steeply sloped shore was visible too.

The slope of the shore, on the other hand, was all snow-covered wreckage. Large, jagged sections of concrete. Twisted rebar. Sections of bent window frames and broken glass with a large section of it covered by the panels of metal roof. A thin section of the patio, next to the wall, still stood; another section sloped down so it rested on the ground. The rest, most of it, was the ruin on the shore.

The steeply sloping ground down to the lake was slick with snow. Cameron found a path made by many boots down the slope and followed it.

"Dress shoe soles are pretty slick," she said.

Right on cue, Mason slipped but caught himself.

"You can wait up top," she said.

"I'm fine. Haven't gotten a close look yet."

Cameron made her way down the embankment until the collapsed patio blocked her path. It had broken into large sections, covering the ground beneath. She picked her way around, being careful not to go under any wreckage.

"Watch out for the rebar," she said.

"Got it."

She stepped around, then squatted down, shooting the beam of a small flashlight under the rubble. "I can't see the steel support beams from here."

She leaned in farther, looking.

"I can't see the piers or the seawall either." She sighed. "I'm going to have to be here with the construction crew when it starts excavating to get a good look. When do they start?"

A man's voice echoed down from the top of the slope. "Hey Lily, did you call for a typist?!"

Mason grimaced, then smiled. "I'll find out," he said, and started back up the slope.

Cameron nodded, then went back to inspecting the wreckage.

9

Mason slipped up the hill, using his hands here and there for balance, to find his cousins Lily Stone and Austin Pierce standing at the top of the embankment wearing orange vests, hardhats, and grins.

"He could be working, Austin," said Lily.

"I don't see how," said Austin. "Do you see any computers down there?"

Mason climbed the rest of the way up the embankment. "What are you two doing here?"

"Has he forgotten who the best seawall company in Northlake is?" said Austin.

"I think he has," said Lily.

Mason looked back down the slope at the snow-covered wreckage of the patio. "I don't think you're going to be able to work on the seawall for a while."

"That's why we're here now, to assess and repair," said Austin.

"And to provide our expertise," said Lily.

"Which is significant."

"And will be included in the bill."

Mason shook his head. "You know I represent the owner, right?"

Lily nodded. "Then you can tell him how important our expertise is."

Mason looked down at where Cameron Thomas was still poking around the wreckage. "Which construction crew is handling the cleanup?"

"Warhelm Industrial," said Austin.

"I didn't realize they did jobs this small," said Lily.

Mason looked at the wreckage. "I don't think this is going to be small."

"Mom missed you yesterday," said Lily.

"I missed being there."

"She missed your dad too."

"Not happening, Lily."

"I know, but you know her."

"I do."

"Mason!" The voice came from down by the wreckage. It was Cameron.

Mason stepped closer to the edge as she yelled again, "Mason!"

"Yeah?"

"I see a leg!"

"Austin," said Mason.

"On it," he said and sprinted toward the equipment.

"Have the sheriff get the life squad," Mason said to Lily, who sprinted away with a thumb raised over her head.

"Coming!" yelled Mason, and scrambled down the embankment.

When he arrived, Cameron Thomas was pulling jagged pieces of concrete out of the pile, clearing a triangular-shaped hole. "We need—"

"—On its way," said Mason. "Where?"

Cameron never stopped throwing pieces as she pointed.

Mason peered into the growing gap. He saw the once-white boot, now gray with dust and clotted blood. He bent down and threw pieces aside with both hands.

The gap grew until the boot became a leg. Later, Mason would acknowledge that he should have waited for the sheriff to assess the scene, and he would agree that Lily and Austin would have only taken a few minutes more to put the crane in place to move all the sections of rubble in a far more safe and effective manner, and he would acquiesce that, given the time that had passed and the lack of movement that he saw that there was little likelihood that Molly Danvers, the twenty-one-year-old junior at Michigan Tech, home for winter break and out with her high school friends, was still alive. But when the boot became a leg, none of that entered Mason Pierce's normally analytical mind.

Instead, Mason Pierce threw six more pieces aside in rapid succession, then reached under the great concrete slab that covered the place where Molly Danvers had spent her last, panicked, painful, awful moments.

"You'll never be able to—" said Cameron Thomas, then stopped as Mason flipped the concrete slab aside, sending it sliding down the embankment.

Then Cameron Thomas and Mason Pierce moved to Molly and, as they agreed they should have known, found that it was too late.

"I TOLD you not to move anything until I got here!" said Sheriff Sizemore.

Austin Pierce did not appear the least bit disturbed by the sheriff's ire. "I didn't."

"I don't see anybody else driving a crane over here."

"You heard me," said Austin.

"It's my fault, Sheriff," said Mason.

"No, it's not Mason," Sheriff Sizemore said. "I know Austin here was driving the crane, and I told him to wait before disturbing this *crime scene*."

Austin Pierce shook his head. "The only crime here is that someone stole your hearing, Sheriff. I. Didn't. Move. The concrete."

"I moved it, Sheriff," said Mason.

Sheriff Sizemore put his mirrored aviator gaze on Mason, then on the concrete slab that had slipped all the way down to the lake's edge. "How?"

Mason shrugged.

Austin Pierce and Lily Stone cackled.

"We thought she might be alive," said Cameron Thomas.

Sheriff Sizemore kept his gaze on the slab, pointedly not looking at where a team of paramedics were gently extracting Molly Danvers from the rubble and slipping her body into a bag. "There was no chance of that."

"We see that now," said Mason.

Sheriff Sizemore held out his hand. "Give me your pry bar. If you find something, you send for me."

"He can't," said Cameron.

"You bet your ass he can, or I'll arrest him right now."

"There's no pry bar."

Sheriff Sizemore stared.

Mason put both hands in the pockets of his peacoat. "I won't disturb anything else, Sheriff."

Sheriff Sizemore stared a moment longer, lamented that he was surrounded by fornicating non-professionals, then went back up the slope.

Austin nudge Lily. "I hear typists get excited when they go outside."

Lily nodded. "Just like dogs. Run around in circles, tear everything up. Rip their pants."

Mason resisted the urge to look down at his now-torn suit pants and said to Cameron, "I need to go back to the office—"

Austin shook his head. "Outside too long already."

Lily grinned. "Probably have to plug him back in to his charger."

"Do you need me?" Mason said to Cameron, ignoring his cousins.

Cameron shook her head. "I'm going to be here for a few days." She handed him her phone. "Put your number in. I'll let you know if I need anything."

Lily Stone coughed. Mason shot his cousin a look, typed in his number, gave Cameron her phone back, then headed up the embankment before his family could do any more damage.

He was just outside the front door of the Cider Mill when he heard the scream. He turned to the cordoned-off area of the parking lot that included reporters, gawkers, and, he now realized, people with hope of word of survivors. He caught a glimpse of the woman running away from Sheriff Sizemore to the ambulance, saw the man follow her, and as he climbed into his truck, heard the keening of Mrs. Danvers as she learned that her daughter had been found.

PART II

10

If you asked people why they trusted Kyle Stewart, they usually couldn't say. There was nothing remarkable about him; he was neither tall nor short, heavy nor thin, handsome nor "aesthetically challenged," as his sweet old Aunt Melanie used to say. He had an easy way of speaking and a better way of listening, and most people found that they had a connection with Kyle, whether it was a person they both knew or a state park they both loved or a restaurant with a dish you just had to try.

Then, there was his name. Kyle Stewart. People just didn't worry about being fleeced or tricked by a guy named Kyle, and they certainly didn't worry that a Kyle was going to beat them within an inch of their life even though Kyle Stewart had, in fact, done all of those things. No, Kyle was the guy from the next street or the next town or the next state who you met by happy coincidence and was glad for it.

Kyle Stewart sat in the parking lot of Wyatt Jenkins' apartment building, checking the scores on his phone. Kyle Stewart found that the beauty of international basketball was that you could bet on it in the mornings, and he had done just that. As he scrolled through the betting app, he saw that he had lost two, won one, and decided to make up the difference with three in-game bets on a fourth. Then he got out of his car and made his way up to the building where Wyatt Jenkins lived.

Rather than go to the building's main entrance, Kyle Stewart stepped onto the small cement pad that functioned as a patio and knocked on the sliding glass door. This was because, Kyle Stewart had found, when you knocked on the patio door, people assumed you had a right to be there, and while they might not buzz you in or throw open a deadbolt, they'll almost always slide the glass door open to see how they could help, especially if it was snowing, as it was now.

Wyatt Jenkins slid open the door. "What's up?"

"Wyatt, right?" said Kyle Stewart.

Wyatt Jenkins wore sweatpants and a Grand Rapids Griffins hockey jersey and had the look of someone who'd just woken up or was deep into a day of *Call of Duty*. "Yeah?"

"I need your help."

"The rental office should be open by eleven." Wyatt Jenkins pointed over Kyle Stewart's shoulder. "Jimmy might be dicking around somewhere, but he's usually here."

"Thanks, no, I mean I need your help in particular."

"Why's that?"

"Because I was told you'd be the man who knows."

"Knows what?"

"How many people were on the Stone Street Cider Mill patio when it collapsed?"

Wyatt Jenkins took a step back. "I don't know anything about that."

"Maybe not exactly, but the man in charge has a pretty good idea, right?"

"I'm not the owner."

"A good manager knows even more than the owner."

"I was told not to talk to anyone."

"Sure. By who?"

"By my boss's lawyer."

"Ah. Your boss's lawyer. What about your lawyer?"

"My boss's lawyer is my lawyer."

Kyle Stewart shook his head. "A lot of people think that. Until it's too late."

"Too late how?"

"Too late when the boss's lawyer blames the employee for the accident."

"I didn't cause any accident!"

"I know that, and you know that, but if he has a choice between blaming you and blaming the boss, who do you think the boss's lawyer is going to pick?"'

Wyatt Jenkins stared. Kyle Stewart waited. He was good at that.

Finally, Wyatt Jenkins said, "It'll be just like Watertown."

Kyle Stewart knew exactly what had happened to Wyatt Jenkins at Watertown, but he said, "What happened at Watertown?"

Wyatt Jenkins appeared to realize he'd spoken out loud. "Nothing. Who do you work for?"

"I'm just helping the families learn the truth. I know you didn't do anything wrong, so that's why I came to you. I figured you'd know the truth of it."

"The truth of what?"

"What happened."

Wyatt Jenkins shook his head. "I don't know what happened, not really."

Kyle Stewart waited.

"One minute I was bringing up our last box of the Dune Sled t-shirts and then there was"—he looked up at Kyle Stewart "—there was a lot of other stuff."

Kyle nodded. “You had to have been busy as hell.”

“Always.”

“No way they pay you enough for all you do there.”

“All I *did* there.”

“They didn’t fire you, did they?”

Wyatt Jenkins shook his head. “No. But we’re not going to be open for a while, and that means I’m not going to get paid.”

“It’s always the working man who gets the shaft.”

Wyatt Jenkins nodded at that self-evident truth.

“And who gets the blame.”

Wyatt Jenkins stopped nodding. But Kyle knew that some truths don’t require acknowledgment.

“You didn’t build that patio, Wyatt, and you weren’t in charge of maintenance. Hell, you’d only been there eight months, right?”

“Six.”

“Six! So you’d never even been there in the winter before, right?”

“No.”

“Or during a Dune Sled.”

“First one.”

“And I’m guessing the manager isn’t in charge of maintenance or contracting for snow removal, right?”

Wyatt Jenkins shook his head. “Hyde handles all the money.”

“I bet he does. And I imagine not much trickles down to the people who actually make it for him.”

Wyatt Jenkins was silent. This time, Kyle Stewart filled it.

“I don’t imagine you got a bonus.”

“For what?”

“For all the extra revenue you generated that night.”

“Not with what happened, no.”

“That’s not your fault, but I guess that makes sense. Instead of a bonus, you probably got paid time off, or a survivor's bonus."

Wyatt Jenkins stared.

Kyle pretended not to notice. "I imagine the counselors Mr. Warren hired for you aren't cheap. You've been through a traumatic experience, all of you."

"There haven't been any counselors."

"None? None at all? Wyatt, I'm not telling you your business, but you need to talk to somebody, man." He shook his head. "After all you went through."

Wyatt Jenkins stared at his stocking feet for a moment, then said, "Callie's funeral is in a couple of days."

"Callie. The hostess?"

Wyatt Jenkins nodded.

"That's horrible. I don't know how you're handling it so well."

"It's not my fault she died."

"I know it isn't. That's why you should tell someone about it."

Wyatt Jenkins cocked his head.

"To make sure the boss's lawyer doesn't say that it was."

Wyatt Jenkins stood there. Kyle Stewart waited, all patience and concern, ignoring the snow that was accumulating on his shoulders.

Then Wyatt Jenkins slid the patio door open the rest of the way, and Kyle Stewart went in.

11

It was snowing the next morning when Mason Pierce went out to the Cider Mill again. He found Cameron Thomas in the dining room, standing off to one side, watching a heated discussion between Sheriff Sizemore and a man with a fierce red beard wearing an orange vest and a hard hat.

Mason joined her. "What's happening?"

Cameron smiled. "Just talking about the weather."

"I have to get in there, Red!" said Sheriff Sizemore.

The red-bearded man, Red, shook his head. "It's not safe, Sheriff. Not in this weather."

"My job is to investigate these deaths."

"And my job is to remove the rubble and rebuild. When the weather clears."

Sheriff Sizemore shook his head. "Have you seen the forecast? It's not going to clear for at least a week."

Red shrugged. "I can't control that."

Construction sites are always loud, and demolition sites more so. There's a rhythm to it, though, a range of clatters and bangs that are expected and that an experienced hand like Mason eventually tuned out.

The screech of metal and concussive bang that shook the window just then was not one of those things.

Red ran to the window, then whirled on the sheriff. "What did you do?"

Sheriff Sizemore looked out the window, then flinched.

As Red cursed him and sprinted out the door, Mason and Cameron moved to the window.

A crane had tipped over and was sliding down the embankment.

"It may be a while before I can investigate," said Cameron.

"Looks that way," said Mason.

~

RED GIBSON, Chief Construction Officer for Warhelm Industrial Services, ran to the top of the slope where his guys were already in motion to save the crane. Fortunately, Red had anticipated the hazard posed by the steep slope, the snow, and the half-cocked sheriff and had anchored the crane with a series of cables that kept it from going all the way into the lake. Still, this was as much of a cluster as Red thought it could be when the sheriff first suggested they ignore the weather.

His boys were already in motion, but Red knew it was going to take a long time and more equipment to recover the crane, and he didn't see any sign that the weather was going to make it any easier.

The sheriff's investigation, and Red's work, would have to wait.

The operator's door, flat up facing the sky, popped open, and a guy with a Yankees cap instead of his hard hat climbed out.

He waved at Red. "I'm okay."

Red cursed and headed down the slope.

WITH THE FALLING snow and tipping crane, nothing was happening at the Cider Mill site, so Mason was on his way back to the office when his Aunt Linda called.

"Mace-honey, I'm sorry, but I can't get a hold of your father," she said.

"You know how he is, Aunt Linda."

"I do, and that's what has me worried. With him being him and with all this snow, well, I think something might have happened."

"I'm sure he's fine."

"Could you please check on him?"

"Sure. I'll stop by on the way home from work."

"You can't go sooner?"

"Actually, I'm working right—"

"—I've been trying to reach him since yesterday."

Mason sighed. It wasn't that far out of his way from the office.

"I'll put eyes on him."

"Oh, thank you. I feel so much better."

"Okay, Aunt Linda. Bye."

So Mason took the detour to his father's house.

WHEN MASON PULLED into his dad's driveway, Jackson Pierce was beating on the plow of his truck with one cane while leaning on the other. He stopped the moment he saw Mason, turned, and—carefully placing his canes so they didn't slip sideways—went back up the porch steps.

By the time Mason climbed out, Jackson Pierce had planted both canes on the porch and was staring down.

"Shouldn't you be working?" he said.

"Shouldn't you be answering your phone?"

Jackson Pierce cursed. "Did your aunt call you?"

"She did."

"Woman won't stop bothering me."

"So tell her you're not dead next time."

"I'm not dead. Go back to work."

Mason glanced at the plow on the front of his dad's truck and could see it was crooked. He could also see that he'd have to work up to mentioning that, so Mason made a show of checking the time. "It's my lunch break."

"Lawyers get those?"

"Never let the man take your lunch."

Jackson Pierce harrumphed in agreement at that statement. He had to. It was his.

"Coffee or beer?" he said.

"Coffee."

"Come on in then," his father said and went into the house without waiting.

~

Jackson Pierce was a big man. Not as big as Mason, but big enough to see he'd contributed. He was about six foot four, though he now stooped to use his canes, and wide at the shoulders, though the green and black plaid flannel he wore billowed with room that was no longer needed. He had shaggy brown hair that was parted down the middle and fell to his shoulders and a long brown mustache that drooped at the edges, giving his face a default frown. His face had the weather and lines of someone who'd spent most of his life outside, but the pallor of his skin said that had been some time ago.

Jackson Pierce moved with a practiced rhythm—using his

canes to get to the cupboard, setting one aside while he grabbed mugs and poured, then pivoted in half turns to deposit them on the round plastic table before grabbing his second cane to take a seat next to his son. He slid a mug to Mason.

"So what are you doing at work?" his dad said.

"You know about the Cider Mill collapse?"

"Hard not to."

"We represent the owner."

"Seems like he's nine different kinds of screwed."

Mason smiled. "My boss expressed a similar sentiment."

"Is it your guy's fault?"

"I'm not sure yet. The sheriff thinks they might have been over capacity."

"That's not good. Collapses aren't pretty things."

His father would know. Mason nodded. "They're not."

"Especially with the snow. Did he clear it?"

Mason realized he hadn't checked to see if Hyde Warren had removed the snow from his roof. "I don't know."

"Seems like you should." His dad sipped his coffee. "That's a lot of weight. A foot of wet snow can run up over forty pounds per square foot. More if it ices up."

"I'll have to remind our expert."

Jackson Pierce snorted. "What do you need a construction expert for?"

Mason smiled. "I can't ask myself questions."

"I wanna say your uncle put a rip rap seawall in there. Did it hold up?"

"I'm sure it did. I wouldn't worry about it."

"Son," said Jackson Pierce, "I'd think by now you'd know that the worst thing that can happen usually does. But that's your uncle's problem."

Mason knew his dad had no reason to doubt that bleak philosophy.

"Want another one?" his dad said.

"No, I'm good." Mason pointed out the window. "Snow's still coming down. Your plow a little crooked?"

Jackson Pierce stated that the plow mounting was the male offspring of a sex worker, then said, "I can get it."

"It's a two-person job. Let's get it on my way out."

So Mason and his dad put their mugs away and straightened the ill-reputed plow, which did indeed require one man to hold the plow while the other straightened the pin.

As he was driving back to the office, Mason was thinking about his dad—about him being alone in a house that wasn't the one Mason had grown up in—when his phone buzzed. Without thinking, he answered it.

"Mason Pierce."

"Mason, it's Sheriff Sizemore. I wanted to catch you at the Cider Mill, but you left."

"Yeah, once things were shut down for the day, I left. What's going on?"

"I'm calling as a professional courtesy regarding your client's surrender."

"Surrender? What for?"

"I have a warrant for Hyde Warren's arrest."

12

Mason paused, then said, "For what?"

"Involuntary manslaughter," said Sheriff Sizemore. "Seven counts."

"I'm away from the office right now, Sheriff. Let me get Peter Freid in on this."

"I don't know Freid, Mason. I know you. If you tell me that you'll have Hyde Warren at my office by 9:00 a.m. tomorrow, then I won't drop a truckload of deputies on his house right now."

"Will he be eligible for release?"

"That's up to the prosecutor and the judge."

"Why are you doing this?"

"Because I know you. And I know Warren too."

"No, I mean, why are you arresting him for an accident? What's happened?"

Sheriff Sizemore paused, then said, "We have a witness from that night."

"A witness to what?"

"Facts that support manslaughter."

"We're going to find out eventually."

"I'm sure you will. So you'll bring Warren in?"

"I'll see that he's there."

"9:01 and the deputies storm his house."

"No need for the blitzkrieg threat, Sheriff."

"A description, Mason, not a threat."

Sheriff Sizemore hung up.

Before Mason could say, "Call Peter Freid," his phone buzzed again. He answered without looking.

"Mason Pierce."

"Ah, Mr. Pierce, this is Corey Wainwright of North Vale Construction. How are you today?"

Mason's attention snapped to the phone and the number, which was identified right there on the screen as North Vale Construction. He silently cursed himself and said, "Good morning, Corey. How can I help you?"

"Mr. Pierce, I'm calling about the lot you and Amber Vincent reserved for our development at Lakeside Vineyard. We've been having some trouble reaching her, so I thought I'd contact you directly."

"I see."

"We're happy to inform you that we're ready to start digging your foundation this spring, so we just need the two of you to make your final payment on your lot and then set up a meeting with our architect to design your one-of-a-kind Vineyard home."

Mason stared at the phone. "There's been a misunderstanding, Corey. I've never agreed to purchase a lot at Lakeside Vineyard."

"I guess there must be, Mr. Pierce. I'm looking at the purchase agreement right here."

"Take a look. I assume my signature isn't on that document."

"Well, it says 'Amber Vincent and Mason Pierce' right here at the top."

"And the signatures?"

"Just a moment." There was a rustling of paper over the phone. "You're right, it does appear that Mrs. Vincent was the only one who signed this, but—"

"It's Ms. Vincent."

"What?"

"It's Ms. Vincent. We're not married."

"Man, broken engagements are the worst. Still—"

"Never engaged, either, Corey. Or common-law spouses or anything else that would make me liable for her contracts."

There was silence on the other end of the line, then, "Uh, so are you and Ms. Vincent still planning to go forward with your agreement?"

"That's not my agreement, Corey. I wasn't aware that Amber had done it."

"Our company entered into this on the assumption that both of you would be responsible for—"

"—Then your company should have talked to me."

More silence, then, "Do you know if Ms. Vincent plans to go forward with it?"

"I don't. We're not together anymore. We haven't been for some time."

"I see. Well, you know the payment is still due—"

"—Not from me, Corey."

"Do you know where I can find Ms. Vincent?"

"I don't. As I've said, we haven't been together for some time. If you'll excuse me, Corey, I have to go."

"Can I just confirm her phone number—"

Mason hung up.

A lot. Amber had gone and signed them up for a lot when he couldn't even pay his student loans. Mason knew he hadn't signed any agreements, and even as casual as Amber was with the truth, he didn't think she'd cross the line into forgery. But he was sure, he was *positive*, that she would have said absolutely anything to get a lot if she wanted it.

And a lot in a place called Lakeside Vineyards sounded exactly like the type of thing she would want.

By then, Mason had arrived back at the office. So he went in to tell Peter the news about Hyde Warren directly.

"INVOLUNTARY MANSLAUGHTER!" Peter's face went red. "How are they going to hit him with manslaughter?"

"The sheriff says he has a witness," said Mason.

"To what? Lighting a fuse on a keg of TNT? Sawing the supports out from under the patio?"

"He wouldn't say."

"Did you ask?"

"Yes."

"It takes a lot to jump from an accident to manslaughter. He must have something."

"So who do you want me to call?"

Peter went from being distracted to focusing on Mason in an instant. "What do you mean?"

"Who do you want me to get on board to represent Warren in the criminal case?"

Peter blinked, then laughed. "We're not calling anybody."

"But this is a serious charge."

"First rule of big firm life, Pierce. Never let a case walk out the door. We're already doing the work on the civil side. We'll handle the criminal case too."

"Who's going to do that?"

"You are."

Mason blinked. "I haven't handled a manslaughter case before."

"No? What were you doing the last two years working for Judge Roderick, picking your nose?"

"No."

"You had dozens of criminal cases come through there, right?"

"Hundreds."

"Judge Roderick presided over dozens of trials?"

"He did."

"As his staff attorney, you did the jury instructions, wrote opinions, supported objections?"

"Yes."

"You didn't sleep through those trials, did you?"

"No."

"Paid attention to how to cross-examine a witness, how to enter evidence?"

"Yes."

"Why you just worked on a whizzbanger of a double murder for that firefighter and the kid, right? The one where the downstate attorney got his client off on both killings?"

"He found the real killer, yes."

Peter dialed in on Mason. "Then, Pierce, you have a better education than damn near any public defender who walks in on the first day. If you're as smart as everyone says you are, you can handle it."

Mason thought. "Will the court let me?"

"What do you mean, let you?"

"Let a first-timer handle a manslaughter case?"

"Fortunately, you'll be working with a former federal U.S. Attorney."

Mason looked blankly.

"Me."

"Ah. I didn't know."

"Clearly. I'll handle the flash, you'll handle the bang, and we'll both make a bunch of money."

"But...what if we lose?"

Peter grinned. "Pierce, the first rule of lawyering—we get paid to try cases, not win 'em."

Mason's confusion must have shown.

"Don't worry, don't worry, we're going to win. This all sounds like bullshit. In the meantime, we don't need another firm mucking around poaching our clients, our hours, and our results. We've got a great opportunity here—let's ride this train to billable hours and victory."

It was an odd speech as rah-rah's go, but Peter certainly seemed to feel it so Mason didn't question him as Peter said, "Go to Warren's house, explain the situation, and have him turn himself in at nine p.m. tonight. The night shift will be on by then, so less eyes to see and mouths to blab. Hopefully, we'll avoid any perp walk footage."

"Got it."

"Get out of here. We have a lot of work to do."

Mason left Freid's office and headed for Hyde Warren's home.

13

Hyde Warren didn't take the news well. Mason had never told someone he was being arrested for manslaughter before, but he had delivered bad news, and it seemed to him that Hyde Warren's disbelief and bargaining stages lasted longer than usual.

Mason had intended to inform Hyde in person, leave, and come back later that night to escort him to the sheriff's office, but Mason saw immediately that neither Hyde, nor his wife Jessica, could be trusted to make rational decisions in the next few hours, so he decided to stay. He encouraged them to go ahead with dinner, declined a plate for himself, and asked if there was a place where he could make a few calls.

That seemed to help. The two of them went back to preparing a meal, which had the look of a sweet nightly ritual, and Hyde pointed Mason to a small study at the end of the hall.

Mason had worked for the previous two years as the staff attorney for Judge Lancaster Roderick here in Northlake, so he knew what was required to bond a person out of jail and knew it could take a couple of days if he didn't do it right, so he picked up the phone to call the chief prosecutor for Sable County, Astrid Olsen.

She picked up. "Mason."

"Hi, Atti."

"I assume this is about Hyde Warren?"

"It is."

"Thanks for reaching out. Have whoever is going to represent Hyde on the criminal side call me, and we'll work through the bond."

"I am. Me and Peter Freid."

A pause. "I see."

"I'm calling to see if we can have agreed terms for bond if he turns himself in."

"It's a multi-death case, Mason."

"True. But he's local—"

"Murders usually are."

"—so everything he has is here in Northlake. He's not a flight risk. It's also not a violent crime—"

"The collapse of concrete is crushingly violent."

"—so he's not a danger to the community. If you agree to standard bond, we'd agree to come in voluntarily for all appearances, including an immediate arraignment."

There was some more negotiation—Astrid commenting on the number of deaths and injuries, Mason countering with cooperation and the corporate nature of the crime, until eventually they agreed on a number for the bond and the turn-in deadline of nine the following morning as Sheriff Sizemore required. They also agreed for Hyde to appear at an arraignment as soon as Judge Roderick scheduled it.

When the details were set, Mason said, "How in the world are you getting to manslaughter on this, Atti? This couldn't have been more of an accident."

"If you actually stick around for the trial, I'll tell you."

"We're in this, Atti."

"To make a quick deal, maybe. Not to try it."

"We'll try it."

"I doubt it. You might stay on the pleadings, but you'll hire someone else to come in at the last minute. It's what big firms always do."

Mason didn't know one way or the other, but now wasn't the time to discuss it. "Peter's tried criminal cases."

"A decade ago? Two? This isn't federal white-collar, Mason."

That angle wasn't getting him anywhere, so he said, "Sheriff Sizemore said you had a witness."

A pause. "Did he now?"

"He did. A witness to what?"

"The circumstances leading to the deaths, of course."

"Which were?"

"Significant."

"Atti."

"Mason."

"Stonewalling didn't help in the Niesen case," he said, and regretted it as soon as he did.

Brock Niesen was a teenager accused of killing a firefighter and a toddler. A downstate lawyer by the name of Nate Shepherd had defended the case against Astrid. And won.

"My disclosures had nothing to do with that."

"Are you sure this witness is telling the truth?"

Astrid Olsen chuckled at that. "Actually, I am. And your client will be sure too."

"Atti—"

"Listen, I'm not getting into it tonight. You have your surrender and bond deal. Take it and go. If you're still around in a couple of weeks, we'll talk."

"I will be."

"It's a lot different in front of the jury than watching from the bench."

"I know."

Astrid Olsen gave a dry laugh. "I'm not sure that you do. Yet. Judge Roderick isn't going to go easy on you."

"That I do know."

"Neither am I."

"I know that too."

"Do you really want to start your career at the Evil Empire with a loss?"

"I just fight the rebels they tell me."

"Talk to you soon, Mason."

They hung up. Mason knew Astrid Olsen was telling the truth—she was going to try to bury him, and his former boss, Judge Roderick, would impartially watch it happen.

If he let it.

His phone buzzed. A group text from his cousin Lily: *We're at The Loon. It's Tuesday.*

Austin followed with a meme of a cat banging a keyboard with the text: *Unless you're busy.*

He ignored them, made a call to a bail bondsman, then went back to the kitchen to check on Hyde.

The ritual of preparing dinner seemed to have calmed him, and his wife insisted that Mason join them, and if the pork chops were a little dry and the asparagus chewy, Mason thought they could be forgiven, all things considered.

He spent dinner telling them what to expect. He helped with the dishes, then helped Hyde Warren marshal the assets he needed to post bond, which turned out to be surprisingly simple. The bond deposit owed the bondsman was an eye-watering number to Mason, but Hyde Warren didn't even blink as he asked if Mason had the bondsman's payment information.

Mason did, and a short time later, he was receiving a call from the bondsman that the funds had been received.

By then, it was time to go, so Hyde Warren kissed his wife goodbye, and Mason took him to turn himself in to face the charge of killing seven of his customers, including Molly Danvers.

~

Peter Freid had been right—it was a good idea for Hyde Warren to surrender in the early evening at the Sable County Jail. The jail sat on the outskirts of town, the night shift of deputies was smaller, and the post-bar closing DUIs hadn't started to arrive yet, all ways to reduce notice for Hyde Warren. Astrid Olsen was as good as her word—she'd told them that she'd accept bond pending arraignment so that when the bond was presented at the end of the process, the deputy accepted it and told Hyde Warren he was free to go so long as he appeared in court when summoned. All in all, Mason thought it went about as well as being arrested for mass manslaughter could go.

Hyde had been in no state to talk on the way to his processing, but now that he knew he wasn't spending the night in jail, Mason thought he could handle a question.

"Hyde, the prosecutor said she has a witness."

"To what?"

"My guess is to over-filling the patio. Did you?"

Hyde looked at Mason and shook his head. "I have no idea. I was mostly with the t-shirts and in the kitchen."

"Could you? Have been over your occupancy?"

Hyde shrugged, which didn't make Mason feel any better at all.

"Do you know who the witness might be that she's talking about?"

"No idea. We had a manager, an assistant manager, and at least twelve wait and cook staff on that night."

"Send me the roster."

"I will. But it could be anybody." Hyde Warren paused. "Anybody except Callie Portman."

Mason recognized the name of the hostess who'd been killed in the collapse.

Hyde Warren turned to him. "I need to go to that funeral."

"I don't think that's a good idea."

"She worked for me since she was in high school."

"Okay.

Hyde Warren leaned back against the headrest. He looked exhausted. "How could they think that I killed them, Mason?"

They didn't say much else on the way home. Mason waited in the drive as Hyde Warren walked to his front door, which was flung open by Jessica Warren, who hugged him then brought him in. As the door shut, Mason checked his phone and saw two more texts from his cousins letting him know they were still at The Loon, which was a very welcoming place for large typists with sausage-sized fingers.

Mason would normally beg off. But now he thought his former seawall crew might actually be able to help, so he headed for The Loon.

14

Kyle Stewart hated video conferencing. Hated it. Nothing was worse than having to be ready to meet someone in person when you weren't actually meeting with someone in person, but Jerome Baggman always insisted on video calls. The man believed that one of his great gifts was being able to read people, and phone calls impinged on that great gift, so video calls it was. Kyle Stewart couldn't argue with Baggman's success—four of the ten highest verdicts in Michigan history would seem to support it—but Kyle knew that Baggman's victories were as much because of the efforts of people like him as any ability of Baggman to "read people."

So Kyle Stewart had prepared as if he were meeting Jerome Baggman in person, and he didn't even mind that Baggman was late since it gave Kyle time to check on his badminton bets.

He'd lost his ass on the Indonesian Masters tournament and saw the Princess Sirivannavari Thailand Masters as his path back. He found that western countries failed to give badminton its due, both as a lightning-fast sport of stunning skill, and as an early morning betting opportunity when football, baseball, and basketball players were still in bed. Westerners didn't know a damn thing about betting it, so with the right betting house, he'd found you could sometimes get odds that an Asian house would never offer.

Good odds could never protect you from huge upsets, though, and Kyle Stewart cursed as he realized that he'd lost, that his badminton hole had just gotten deeper, and that he was good and truly shuttle-cocked.

His phone notified him that Jerome Baggman was waiting. He took a quick breath, and the man himself appeared.

"What do we know?" Jerome Baggman said without preamble. When he wasn't on display in a courtroom, the man was blunt to the point of rudeness. Kyle Stewart didn't mind.

"It looks like Kramer Burns is going to handle the criminal case," said Kyle Stewart.

"Really. Who are they bringing in?"

"All indications are that the Northlake office is handling it."

Jerome Baggman scowled. "All they have up there is Peter Freid and an associate, what's his name?"

"Mason Pierce."

Baggman smiled. "Freid is a talented lawyer, but he hasn't handled a high-profile criminal case in decades. What do we know about this Pierce?"

"Brand new associate. Spent two years working for the judge, Judge Roderick."

"So he's green. Good."

"He's a little older than a new associate. Worked on a seawall crew up here before he went to law school."

"So he knows a backhoe from the hole it makes."

"You'd think."

Jerome Baggman nodded. "Build files on both of them. Prioritize Pierce since he's new." He smiled. "If Freid and this Pierce lose the criminal case, they won't be able to print money fast enough to pay me on the civil case."

"Got it."

Jerome Baggman peered through the screen at Kyle Stewart. "Find me their pressure points, Kyle. Find me their sports books."

Kyle Stewart felt his face flush, and his only hope was that the phone screen was too small for Baggman to see it.

If he did, Jerome Baggman didn't reveal it. Instead, he continued. "And go to this prosecutor, Anna Olsen."

"Astrid."

"Astrid, right. Tell her we'll share the results of our investigation, even our experts, if she seems open to it. Prosecutors are always understaffed and underfunded. It would look strange for a civil attorney to volunteer to help with a prosecution, but sharing investigative resources? Why that will just save the good taxpayers of Sable County money in the pursuit of justice."

"I'm on it."

"I know you are."

Jerome Baggman leaned back. "The Smithfield case settled. Payment won't come through for another thirty days, but I can sport you an advance on part of it. If you need it."

"I don't need it," Kyle Stewart said reflexively.

"Sure you don't. If you want it, then."

Kyle Stewart looked away. "Who wouldn't want money sooner than later?"

"Who wouldn't? I'll have half of your percentage transferred into your account today."

"That's up to you. I can wait."

"Sure you can. Build those files, Kyle. Get me information."

Jerome Baggman was gone before Kyle could say he would.

Kyle stared at the blank screen for a moment before doing some calculations in his head.

The day's badminton matches would be over by the time the money came in from Baggman, so Kyle opened his sportsbook app and checked the basketball schedule for that night.

15

The main tourist strip in Northlake is an area called the Bluffs, a picturesque spot four hundred feet above Lake Michigan that commands a high view of a vast expanse of sand and blue water for as far as a visitor could see. Bars and restaurants, most with glass walls, windows, and decks to take in the lake view, stretched along a scenic strip, with shops and vendors and even a stage or two scattered randomly in between, all designed to put Northlake's best foot forward to its many visitors.

The Loon wasn't one of those places.

Most tourists wouldn't even notice it, which was part of its appeal. The Loon was on the north side of town, on the corner of an intersection of two county roads that it shared with a propane dealer and a butcher shop that specialized in high quality, pasture-raised meats and deer processing. Tourists flew through the intersection without noticing since there was no gas station or dollar store, but a local, or a tourist who was courteous to one, would know that the unlettered painted sign of a bird with a dark head, checked wings, and a white belly was the home of reasonably priced drinks, breakfast skillets served round the clock to accommodate any shift, and a Cajun smoked whitefish that you either had the fortitude for or you didn't.

A well-cared for gravel lot held some cars and more trucks out front. On the inside, a bar ran along the left side and back wall with heavy wood stools bolted in place. There were rows of thick wood tables sitting on thick, x-shaped legs that seated anywhere from six to twelve on heavy wood benches, all of which were sturdy enough to land on and too heavy to lift. Everything—the bar, the stools, the tables, and the benches—was sanded smooth and stained dark so that nicks and skillet burns might be said to add character rather than show wear, but if you said that out loud, Brenda would tell you to get your snotty ass out her place, while The Dean would give you a harsh stare. There was a bar shuffleboard up front, just to the right of the door, and if you're surprised there was no pool table, then you haven't given sufficient thought to improvisational missiles and ready-to-use clubs, which Brenda and The Dean clearly had.

Mason heard a holler from a back table as he came in the door. "Mace!" A man with a bushy brown beard wearing a Northlake Seawall hoodie waved.

Mason waved back at Austin Pierce but headed over to the bar. A woman stood behind it, an empty pitcher balanced on the index finger of each hand. She had salt and pepper hair tied back in a thick braid, pale blue eyes, and a deeply lined face that made it impossible to guess whether she was forty-five or sixty-five years old. Fortunately, from Mason's perspective, she was smiling.

"I take it you'll be refilling your crew," she said.

"I suppose I'd better, Brenda. Thanks."

As she put each pitcher under a tap, one filling with a dark brown, the other a light amber, she said, "How's the new job treating you?"

"Learning a lot."

"Adapt or die."

As the pitchers filled, a woman's voice yelled, "Two's not going to do it, Brenda." Lily.

Brenda raised an eyebrow. "Your cousin's thirsty."

"It *is* Tuesday."

"It is at that. Light?"

"Please."

After Brenda filled a third pitcher with light beer, Mason took all three in one hand and headed over to his cousins and his best friend. The customers he knew didn't pay attention to him or nodded. One group of guys by the bar stared, which Mason was used to, since there was nowhere to hide at an altitude over six and a half feet.

The pitchers were taken the moment he set them down, one into each hand.

"Bronson didn't think you'd make it," said Lily. Her blond hair stuck out in all directions, as it did by the end of every workday, and she grinned at Mason as she refilled her glass.

Her husband, Bronson Stone, sat next to her. He had dark hair shorn close at the sides and a sharp nose. He was all angles and lines, at his jaw, his cheekbones, the cords of muscle in his arms, which created shadows on him that were a degree greater than the light would seem to warrant, making it hard to read his expression. It was only through long practice, developed over a friendship that went back to junior high, that Mason was able to do it.

Bronson shrugged as he poured from the darkest pitcher. "He's got responsibilities now."

"Hey!" said Austin. "I have responsibilities!"

"Zero," said Lily.

"Not a one," said Bronson.

Austin Pierce grinned through his beard and pushed his

Northlake Seawall cap back on his curly brown hair. "You see how it's been, Mace? You leave, and they lash out at me. It's sad."

Mason smiled. "You seem overwhelmed."

Austin raised his mug. "Drowning." He took an enormous gulp. "But my head's above water since you're paying."

"Why's that?"

"You know the rule, last one here pays," said Lily.

"But I wasn't going to come."

"Then you wouldn't have paid." Lily shook her head. "Don't they teach logic at law school?"

Austin shook his head. "Has nothing to do with the job."

Mason sighed but, in fairness, they had him.

Undistracted by his brother-in-law, Bronson Stone said to Mason, "You hear about that crane tipping at your client's place?"

"I was there," said Mason and took a sip.

Lily shook her head. "Took them all day to right the thing and get it back up the hill. You should have seen it. Red Gibson and Sheriff Sizemore really went at it after they finally recovered the crane. Red told him to get his five starred ass off the property and come back when the sun comes out."

"And the sheriff did it?"

"What was he going to do?" said Bronson. "He couldn't investigate anything, so he left."

Austin finished three-quarters of a beer in one long pull, then re-filled.

Mason raised an eyebrow.

Austin shrugged. "They were free. For me, anyway. Besides, we ain't working tomorrow with all this snow. Why so late?"

"Work," said Mason.

"'Til ten? You need to change jobs?"

Mason nodded, then shrugged.

"Word is they might be charging your man with something," said Bronson.

Mason gave his best friend his full attention. "How'd you hear that?"

Bronson Stone shrugged. "There's always talk at a worksite."

"He probably doesn't remember what working's like, Bronson," said Austin.

Mason ignored Austin. "Who was talking?"

"A couple of deputies. One was telling the other that he was on tap to pick up your client if he didn't come in tomorrow."

"Ah."

"Will he?"

"Will he what?"

"Turn himself in tomorrow."

Mason realized that it wasn't exactly a state secret. "He took care of that tonight."

"Why are they arresting him?" said Lily.

"For the deaths."

"They're hitting him for murder?" said Lily.

"Manslaughter."

"Is that any better?"

"Some. Not much."

"What did he do?" said Bronson.

Mason thought. "I'm not sure."

"Seems like his lawyer ought to know that," said Lily.

"I agree."

Austin set his mug down and wiped foam off his beard before he waved and said, "He didn't shoot anybody, right?"

"No."

"Didn't drive a car into a crowd? Release poison gas?"

"Of course not."

He waved. "There you go."

"There you go, what?"

"He didn't kill anybody. Honestly, this law thing isn't that hard." Austin re-filled his mug, then Mason's, and took another swig.

"It doesn't work like that, Austin."

"So how does it work?"

"If Hyde recklessly disregarded a known risk to someone's safety, he committed involuntary manslaughter."

Lily nodded. "Like if he say, over-loaded a patio?"

Austin pointed. "Or didn't clear snow from his roof!"

Mason nodded.

Austin grinned and smacked the table. "Hah!"

"It was the biggest crowd at the Dune Sled ever," said Bronson quietly. "Because there was so much snow."

Mason nodded again. "You see the issue. I could use your help."

"Name it," said Austin.

"Anything," said Lily.

Bronson nodded.

"You're going to be on site once the work starts up again, right?"

Lily, who was the head of the crew, nodded. "Until the wreckage is clear and we can assess the seawall underneath, yes."

"Just let me know what you hear?" He tipped his head at Bronson. "Like tonight."

"Done," said Lily.

"Thanks." Mason finished his beer and held up a hand when Austin went to re-pour it. "I have to be in early tomorrow."

Austin grinned. "Oh, I won't be doing that. Snow day!" He leapt to his feet. "Wait! The mini-tacos!" And he ran over to put an order on Mason's bill before he left.

Austin bumped into a guy wearing a Yankees cap by the bar. Mason watched the man snap his displeasure as beer spilled over onto his hand, saw Austin say something that might, loosely, have been considered an apology, then watched the man snap something again and chest up on Austin, who immediately turned on the guy and yelled, "You wanna scrap? Are we gonna scrap?"

"Ah shit," said Lily.

"Not again," said Mason.

"Let's scrap!" yelled Austin.

"Go time," said Bronson and was already out of his seat.

The three crossed the room as Yankee Boy swung. Austin cackled, ducked it, and barreled into the man's chest.

A second man in a hunter-orange hoodie leapt onto Austin's back. Bronson swept in from the side and knocked the man off Austin's back, which allowed Mason to grab Austin by the belt and the scruff, and throw him aside. Lily immediately grabbed her brother in a full nelson and walked him, bent double, back to the table.

Yankee Boy scrambled to his feet. Mason grabbed him by the front of the sweatshirt with one hand, held the other up, open.

"Hey, hey, hey, hey, hey," said Mason. "He's sorry."

Yankee Boy pushed Mason's hand away. It didn't move.

He tried to push past Mason. Mason held him pinned against the bar and said, "Next round's on me."

Yankee Boy smacked at Mason's unmoving hand again. "Your friend's an asshole."

"My cousin. And sometimes. Please, let me get you a round."

The man struggled again, but when he couldn't move, he eventually relaxed until he nodded. Mason let go and held up both hands. Then he pointed at the bar. "I'll order."

Yankee Boy stared, then nodded. As he and his friends went back to their bar stools, Austin said from across the room, "I *did* apologize!"

Bronson stood next to Mason, shaking his head. "You can't be doing that, Mace."

Mason shrugged.

"You have to let us handle it."

"Next time," Mason said and walked up to Brenda. He noticed the Easton aluminum baseball bat that now leaned on the back side of the bar but didn't mention it as he said, "I'll pick up our tab, Brenda. And theirs."

Brenda handed him the receipt, which she'd already printed. "I included the mini-tacos."

Mason smiled. "I should hope so." Mason jerked his head at the guys at the bar. "New?"

"A crew with Warhelm's outfit up from Chicago. I get the impression one of them just lost his job. Did a crane tip over?"

"It did."

"He's a little raw about it."

"Understandable." Mason paid, leaving double the tip for the aggravation.

Brenda waved the receipt. "Good to see you, Mace."

"You too, Brenda. Best to The Dean."

Then he left.

~

Austin Pierce poured the last of the pitcher into his mug. "We're starting another tab, right?"

"Of course," said Lily. "Here." She took the pitcher from Austin and another back up to Brenda for a refill.

"You need to be more careful," said Bronson.

"Get off my ass," said Austin. "What's the harm in a little scrap?"

"Mason can't do that anymore," said Bronson.

"Can't do it? He might not have left any for us!"

"Austin. Mason *can't* do that, remember?"

Austin frowned, then blinked, then said, "Oh. Right."

Bronson nodded. "Right. So don't put him in that position."

"I won't. I won't."

Lily sat back down, her lips pressed together.

"What?" said Bronson.

"Yankee Boy asked if we were all going to be so brave now that Shrek has left."

"Ah." Bronson sipped his beer, unconcerned.

"Said I better keep control of the little bowling ball and his mouth."

Austin giggled. "Hurtful."

"And?" said Bronson.

"Other things," said Lily.

Bronson scowled. Austin giggled some more.

"Brenda told him to shut his pie hole or she'd drop another crane on his Yankee ass."

Now Austin laughed. "That's the guy?"

"Apparently."

Austin took a big swig then wiped his beard before he smiled at Bronson. "Mason's gone now."

"He is."

"And we aren't lawyers, are we?"

"Definitely not."

"So we can do whatever we want."

"I think Brenda and The Dean would say otherwise."

Austin pointed his mug at Bronson in agreement. "We can do whatever we want *outside*."

Bronson sighed. But he smiled, faintly, when he said, "I suppose."

Austin grinned and didn't take his eyes off Bronson as he yelled, "Lily, did you leave a big *tip*?"

Lily hung her head.

"I couldn't tell. I had to *crane* my neck to see you over at the bar."

Lily laughed as Yankee Boy and his friends turned.

Austin continued to yell. "I had to crane my neck so hard *I fell right over!*"

Bronson sighed. It seemed like a good time to finish his beer.

16

Mason Pierce's memory was excellent, but events that held his career in the balance stayed with him even more. As he drove home from The Loon, keyed up with unspent adrenaline, he forced himself to go through the character and fitness interview again, remembering every word.

"This assault charge was only three years ago," said the man.

Mason sat straight in his chair, careful to keep his hands folded. "It was."

"So you were in law school?" the man said.

Mason nodded. "First year."

The man shook his head and looked back down at the papers while the woman's eyes narrowed. "You understand we have to make a recommendation to the State Bar on your character and fitness to be a lawyer?"

"I do."

"Do you think lawyers should be putting people in the hospital?"

"Ideally, no."

"So you admit your conduct wasn't ideal?"

Mason Pierce shook his head. "I didn't say that at all, ma'am. Lawyers are called upon to deal with conduct of others that is less than ideal all the time."

The man raised his head. "We deal with that conduct in court, not a surgical suite."

Mason smiled. "Ideally."

Mason knew that most people didn't find his smile reassuring, no matter how genuine and friendly it was. He also knew that he would never be able to explain what had happened that night to these two lawyers, and he knew that, after one look at him, they wouldn't believe him anyway.

He smiled and he sat and he waited as the two lawyers from the character and fitness committee decided if they'd allow him to receive his law license. The man shuffled his papers. The woman stared at him. Mason met her gaze. He knew that made people uncomfortable too, but he wouldn't let himself look down. It would make him look guilty. He wasn't.

Finally, the man sighed. "You've left us in a quandary, Mr. Pierce. The charges were dropped, so technically you don't have a criminal record. At the same time, the man you attacked—"

"Allegedly attacked," the woman corrected.

The man rolled his eyes. "—allegedly attacked almost died, and that's a fact."

Mason Pierce didn't respond. He waited.

"We don't really have a choice," said the woman. "Under the rules."

"No, I suppose we don't," said the man. "Given the lack of legal proceedings against you, we're going to recommend that you be approved, Mr. Pierce."

Mason Pierce heard the "but" coming.

"But," the man said, "we're also going to express our concern over *your history and recommend that the State Bar give no further leniency if you have another incident like this."*

Mason Pierce kept his face neutral. "That implies you're giving me leniency now. I haven't violated any character and fitness rules."

"The State has a standard to be a lawyer, Mr. Pierce," said the man. "We're not sure you meet it, but there's no concrete reason to reject you." The man signed a paper and slid it over to the woman.

"I'm going to be on this committee for another five years, Mr. Pierce," she said. "If something like this happens again, I'm going to recommend that the Bar pulls your license. Do you understand?"

Mason Pierce knew what a protest would sound like, so he just said, "Yes."

The woman stared at him a moment longer before signing the paper as she said, "Welcome to the Michigan Bar."

~

EVEN NOW, two years later, Mason Pierce could see that woman's stare and hear her voice. And he knew, because he'd checked, that she still sat on the State Character and Fitness Committee. Not that it mattered. He'd also received the letter they'd placed in his file.

There wouldn't be a second chance.

He shook his head, smiled, and resolved not to be the first lawyer to lose his license over a mini-taco.

17

Kyle Stewart possessed a range of funeral suits and an unerring instinct for which one to wear. His instincts had been right again about the suit for the visitation of Sophia Kern.

He stood off to the side, ostensibly watching the funeral video cycling through pictures of Sophia Kern's young, short life. His dark blue sport coat, gray shirt, and dark jeans perfectly split the middle between the church suits of Sophia's older uncles and parents, the dress pants and shirts of her friends, and the various dress of people on the way home from work, so that there was nothing about him that attracted notice. Further, his spot inside the solemn viewing circle of the video discouraged conversation and, if someone did comment, Kyle could usually deflect it with a comment on the next slide.

The video was cycling through a third time, marked by the reappearance of Sophia waving from atop the horse who was apparently a constant companion, when Kyle discreetly snuck a peek at the betting app on his phone. He was even more discreetly placing a bet on the Giant Slalom at the Alpine Ski

World Cup event in Schladming, Austria, when he saw what he'd been waiting for—Mr. and Mrs. Danvers.

Though he hadn't seen them in person, Kyle Stewart recognized Marty and Faith Danvers right away since Faith had been posting pictures non-stop since her daughter's death. The two slipped in the side door and moved quietly to the back of the receiving line, but their arrival sent a ripple through the people waiting to talk to Drew and Allie Kern. As if by silent command, the crowd parted so that Drew and Allie Kern could see the parents of their daughter's best friend.

Faith Danvers took a step, then stopped and bowed her head, her husband's hand on her shoulder. Allie Kern's hand went to her mouth, then she ran to Faith and threw her arms around her.

Kyle Stewart knew that Faith Danvers had not left her house since her daughter Molly had died. He knew because he'd been unable to catch up with her.

Sorrow resonated off the two bereft mothers at a frequency that was felt rather than heard. Allie Kern had been stoic all day, dealing gracefully with heartfelt condolences and arrogant assurances of where Sophia was now, but Faith Danver's raw grief broke straight through that wall. The two mothers hugged, whispering into each other's shoulders, as their husbands shook hands then stood aside.

It was too much for Marty Danvers. He kissed the top of Allie Kern's head, whispered to his wife, then slipped back out the door.

The rest of the funeral home watched sidelong, pretending to speak to each other or to look at their phones while they were all really watching Allie and Faith. Every one of them.

Kyle Stewart waited. Sophia's video cycled through a fourth time. Allie and Faith continued their embrace, nodding and speaking softly into each other's shoulders.

When they pushed back, Allie Kern wiped the tears from the

corners of her eyes with a tissue. Faith Danvers did not. There were no tears there. Just anger.

Good, thought Kyle Stewart.

Then Allie Kern pointed at Kyle Stewart and said, "That's him."

There was a moment when all eyes in the room followed Allie's finger to Kyle Stewart. He ignored the looks, watched the video, and waited.

As Faith Danvers walked over to him, the focus of the crowd returned to Allie Kern, and then closed back in upon her to share in her grief.

Faith Danvers looked to be in her mid-forties and was youthful enough that she would have regularly been told that she looked far too young to have a daughter in college. Now though, she had black circles under her eyes, circles made darker by her jet-black hair that folded in around her face. Kyle Stewart knew all manner of grief, and he knew from one look at her that Faith Danvers hadn't slept.

And that she was angry.

"Allie says you're going to make them pay," Faith Danvers said.

Kyle Stewart nodded. "I work for the man who will."

"They're saying it's an accident."

"They always say it's an accident."

"I've had four firms email me, three condolence cards, and two flower arrangements."

Kyle Stewart nodded.

"It's obscene."

Kyle Stewart nodded again.

"What makes you any different?"

"I'm not the lawyer, Mrs. Danvers."

"What makes the lawyer you work for any different?"

"None of those things you received were from me."

Faith Danvers' mouth twisted into a sneer that seemed directed as much inward as outward. "I could argue that being here is even worse."

"It would be," said Kyle Stewart. "If Allie hadn't invited me."

"Why would she do that?"

"Because she thinks we can help your family the way we can help hers."

Faith Danvers eyed Kyle Stewart. "And split expenses, I expect."

"Now's not the time to discuss economics, Mrs. Danvers."

"Why the hell not? Losing money is the only thing these people understand."

Kyle Stewart nodded, paused, then said, "Working together helps everyone."

"This Jerome Baggman you work for. He's good?"

"He's the best."

"He's from Detroit. Will he play up here?"

"He'll play anywhere."

"That good?"

"Six hundred and thirty-nine million good."

Faith Danvers waved a hand. "Lawyers always put those career numbers on TV. It's like the billions of McDonald's burgers sold. It's meaningless."

"Last year."

"Last year what?"

"Those were his recoveries last year."

Faith Danvers stared at Kyle Stewart then, not with greed or envy or aspirations, but with sharpening, angry calculation. "So he can take all Hyde Warren has?"

"Whatever the law allows."

"What do I need to do?"

"After things have settled down—"

"Things will never settle down again for my family."

"—we'll need to go over a contingent fee agreement with you and Mr. Danvers."

"Marty will do what I say."

"—and after both of you sign it, Mr. Baggman will get to work."

"Isn't he working already?"

Kyle Stewart smiled. "He is. He'll get to work for *you*, I should say."

"Let's go find Marty. I expect he's in the car." She turned to leave.

"It can wait until after the visitation, Mrs. Danvers."

Faith Danvers turned back on him. "I won't rest until Hyde Warren pays for what he did, Mr. Stewart. And neither will my daughter."

With that, Faith Danvers walked out of the funeral home.

Kyle Stewart followed. He felt the buzz of a notification on his phone.

His bet had paid off.

PART III

18

One month later, Mason Pierce sat in his office with Peter Freid, getting cursed out by the man himself.

"How do we not have access to the site yet?" said Peter Freid.

Mason scowled. "We had two feet of snow followed by three weeks below zero, Peter."

"And?"

"The machines can't operate in those conditions."

"Boyne's been open. Shanty Creek too."

"Those are ski slopes, not accident sites."

"You're telling me weather has been delaying our mass casualty investigation? What are we, an elementary school?"

"The construction company's already lost one crane, Peter. And that was before the icing even happened."

Peter Freid shook his head. "Mother Burns doesn't understand that."

Mason shrugged. "Detroit doesn't have Northlake's snow. Or ice."

"They aren't noticing the weather at all. Do you know why?"

Mason shook his head.

"Because they've crawled so far up my ass that it's a balmy 98.6 degrees to them. We need to get access this week."

"It's supposed to warm up. I'll get out there as soon as the crews can work. Hyde Warren has the construction company on standby."

"Good." Peter Freid waved a hand. "So you got the prosecutor's disclosures this morning. What's the basis for the charges against Warren?" said Peter Freid.

Mason didn't want to say it because it sounded like an excuse, but it was also true. "I haven't read them all yet."

"Are they written in Sanskrit or something?"

"They just came in. It looks like they're angling for overcrowding and failure to clear the snow off the roof."

Peter Freid leaned forward, one hand resting by its fingertips on a stack of papers. "Listen, Pierce, Baggman filed the civil suit today, and somehow, the conflict-less son of a bitch is representing all of the families of the fatalities and all of the injured. He's pled wrongful death, negligence, intentional infliction of emotional distress and all other manner of happy horseshit."

Mason had read the pleading. He nodded.

"Some of it's insured, some of it's uninsured and all of it's bad."

"I understand."

"Good. And since you're busy understanding, then do you understand what it means that Baggman filed suit on the same day you received the prosecutor's criminal case disclosures?"

Mason hadn't thought of it but realized it now. "You think they're working together?"

"Of course the prosecutor and Baggman are working together! And do you know why?"

"To save resources?"

Peter Freid rolled his eyes. "Jerome Baggman doesn't give two shits about conserving resources. He's one of the only plaintiff's lawyers with a war chest so big he won't have to finance a lick of this case because he's smart and he's fiscally conservative and he's focused on getting our nuts in a vice. Do you want our nuts in a vice?"

"I do not."

"And do you know how he's measuring our nuts for a vice by working with the prosecutor?"

Mason nodded. "The burden of proof is higher in the criminal case, so if Atti beats us there..."

"Who the hell is Atti?"

"Astrid Olsen, the prosecutor."

"We're on an 'Atti' basis with her, are we?"

"Most people who know her call her that."

Peter gestured for Mason to get back to it.

Mason did. "So if *Prosecutor Olsen* beats us in the criminal case, the finding will be binding on us in the civil case because the burden of proof is lower in the civil case."

Peter nodded. "Right. There are ways for us to fight it, but we'd be ninety percent screwed, and Kramer Burns has a strict policy against being fornicated unless we're the ones doing the fornicating."

Peter went from nodding to shaking his head so quickly it was like a bobblehead doll. "And of course the reverse isn't true —if we get Warren off the hook on the criminal case, Baggman still has a full opportunity to bang us on the civil side because a jury could find that while there wasn't enough evidence to convict Warren of a crime, there's more than enough evidence to take all of his money. Do you understand?"

"I do."

"So it's our job to keep Hyde Warren from getting convicted of a crime, and then it'll be our job to keep him from getting OJ'ed."

Mason knew he'd regret it but said it anyway. "OJ'ed?"

Peter rolled his eyes. "O.J. Simpson? Being acquitted in the criminal case and then losing everything in the civil case. Don't you follow current events?"

"I don't think I was born yet."

Peter Freid looked at Mason, blinked, then suggested that he was an impertinent hindquarter prone to Oedipal relations.

Mason smiled and shrugged.

"You get the point," said Peter.

"I do."

"So figure out the basis for the manslaughter charges and let's unleash the resources of Mother Burns on this case."

"I will."

"Have you sent the disclosures to Cameron Thomas yet?"

"Melody is loading the materials now. Dr. Thomas will have them by the end of the day."

"Good."

"What does our expert think the cause of the collapse was?"

"She hasn't been able to get access like everyone else."

Peter stood. "You're the construction guy. You need to figure this out."

Mason nodded. Peter left and Mason got to work.

19

The fact that it was unwarranted didn't take the sting out of Peter's rebuke, so Mason grabbed the first box of the prosecutor's disclosures and discovery responses and searched for the basis for the manslaughter charges against Hyde Warren.

Mason had skimmed them as soon as they came in, of course, just to get the lay of the land and to see if he could get a handle on what Atti Olsen was claiming Hyde had done. But when he rushed through it, all he'd seen was evidence of how crowded the Cider Mill had been, so he dove in again and this time examined it all closely.

There were the night's receipts from the dining room, the dining room bar, and the patio drink stations. There was the order for the Dune Sled t-shirts they were handing out. There was the total of the cover charge collected. And there were meteorological records for the amount of snowfall Northlake had experienced that winter.

Then he looked at Astrid Olsen's preliminary witness disclosure. She'd listed a bunch of employees, probably the whole roster. Then she just listed name after name after name after name. There were more than one hundred. One hundred and sixty-eight to be exact. On a hunch, he went back to the first batch of receipts from the dining room bar. Eventually, he matched a name to a receipt. Then another. When he found the third, he realized she'd listed every person who'd used a credit card at the Cider Mill that night.

He frowned, checked the one hundred sixty-eight credit card users against the occupancy limit. The maximum occupancy of the whole restaurant was two hundred and forty-seven, which left more than enough space.

It took Mason another five minutes to realize the problem. The names were only of the people who'd *paid*. Further discovery would certainly show that there'd been plenty more people there who hadn't paid a tab.

That confirmed what he'd guessed—the prosecutor was going to claim that Hyde Warren had overloaded the patio until it collapsed.

Mason went through it all again. Then he picked up the phone and called Cameron Thomas.

"Can I get to the site yet, Pierce?" she said.

"The weather's clearing. Should be this week."

"Then I don't have anything to report."

"I do," Mason said. "The prosecutor's going to claim we exceeded the occupancy."

"Did you?"

"Possibly."

"Not ideal, but okay. We need to figure out the number so I can do my load calculations."

"I understand. They're also going to claim snow added to the weight."

"Did they say that?"

"They included snowfall totals."

There was silence on the other end, then Cameron Thomas said, "The people and the snow might be the precipitators. But that doesn't say what actually collapsed."

Mason scowled. "The patio, right?"

"Yes, the patio collapsed. But what collapsed on the patio and why is what I need to focus on. Did they name an expert?"

Mason leafed through the witness disclosure. "Barry Wasmeuller."

"Ha."

"Ha what?"

"He's a whore. He wasn't bad when he started, but now he'll say anything. For now, I'd guess he's going to support the overcrowding theory, and he'll spread out to whatever else they need. He won't be doing any sophisticated analysis, but he'll be able to respond to whatever we say."

"All right. I'm sending you all of these file materials. What else do you need?"

"I need to get back out there once we can get on site."

"I'll go out and take a look today. I'll text."

"I'll plan on coming out tomorrow unless I hear otherwise."

Mason didn't know if the weather would warm enough to work, but he also knew that everyone was done waiting without trying, so he said, "See you tomorrow."

As soon as Mason hung up, he checked the efile, saw Melody had uploaded them all, and sent them to Cameron.

He was thinking about the best way to tackle the occupancy issue, a way that he could use easily at court, when he received a call from prosecutor Astrid Olsen.

"I told you we want access to the site when your client's construction crew starts working."

"Good morning, Atti."

"You heard me."

"What makes you think my client's crew has started working?"

"One of the deputies saw trucks out there last night. There are more there this morning."

"It's barely fifteen degrees out."

"Warm enough, apparently."

"I'll find out what's going on."

"You should *know* what's going on, Mace."

"Still working on that first cup of coffee, Atti?"

"Are you really staying on this case?"

"I told you we are."

"Then you need to work with me on access. And we should probably coordinate with Baggman."

"Why would I do that?"

"Because if we don't, he's going to be banging around messing up both of our cases. The man's a blunt instrument."

"It seems to me you're already working with him."

"I have an obligation to conserve the state's resources."

"Uh-huh."

"And it will complicate our lives less."

"If you want less complications, dismiss these ridiculous charges."

It was barely above zero outside. The other end of the line still got colder. "Seven people are dead, Mace."

"It was a horrible accident, Atti."

"That your client was responsible for."

"I've gone through your disclosures, Atti. I see a Dune Sled weekend and snow."

Silence.

"What I don't see is a murder weapon. And I don't see malice or reckless disregard or even negligence."

"Your client packed the Mill until it collapsed."

"That's it? That's your case?"

"That's enough. I want to have access to the site as soon as you do."

Astrid Olsen hung up.

Mason stared at his phone for a moment then sighed. He was going to have to stop at home.

He wasn't dressed nearly warm enough.

20

Northlake sits right on the coast of Lake Michigan, and although that vast blue water creates a temperature buffer that allows for some of the best apples and cherries in the country, it also creates massive amounts of lake effect snow, and if you happen to combine that lake effect with a polar vortex sweeping arctic air down from Canada, what you get is snow then bitter, freezing cold that will immobilize any project you're unfortunate enough to have started outside.

The investigation and removal of the Stone Street Cider Mill site had been paralyzed for weeks for just that reason. On that day, though, the temperature was finally rising into the twenties and, if it wasn't exactly sunny, the sky made it appear that sunshine was possible and not just some legend told by nostalgic ancestors.

There was still wind, because there always was, so Mason pulled the hood of his canvas coat up over his stocking cap and dug his gloved hands deeper into his pockets as he looked down at the snow-covered site. The snow was thicker than it had been the last time he'd been here, so that what he knew were jagged corners of concrete, broken sections of roof, and twisted sections of rebar looked like rolling mounds of snow that an enterprising kid could turn into an ice fortress.

There was one spot where that illusion didn't hold. On the far-right side, down by where the slope met the frozen surface of Lake Lacache, the snow had been uncovered, the concrete rubble exposed, and excavation getting under way. Trucks and heavy equipment were clustered at the top of the slope with workers hopping in and out, climbing up and down, shouting and gesturing, to get things going.

Mason walked over, noting that all the vehicles bore the logo of Warhelm Industrial Services. With instincts developed from growing up on sites just like it, Mason homed in on the foreman, marked by an orange hardhat and a glorious red beard, who seemed to be alternating between shouting at people live and over a radio.

"Look at it, Manny, it's a goddam sheet of ice," he said into the radio. "I want every single man hooked up to safety lines... Yeah, I know it's a pain in the ass, but so's an OSHA investigation. And I better not have to tell you that I want all the equipment anchored."

The red-bearded man caught Mason's eye as he approached, nodded acknowledgement, then said into the radio, "I know he was a jack-stick, that's why I fired him. Don't repeat his mistake. You take orders from me, not the sheriff. Red out."

The man shook his head, lowered the radio, and said, "Go see Duffy for your rigging. No one goes down unless they're hooked up to a line."

Mason shook his head. "Not here for Warhelm. I'm Hyde Warren's lawyer. Mason Pierce." Mason extended a hand and the man shook it.

"Red Gibson." Red Gibson squinted. "Mason Pierce. You Jack Pierce's boy?"

"I am."

"And he let you become a lawyer?"

"He had some things to say about it."

The smile vanished from Red's beard. "How's he doing? Heard he was walking again."

Mason nodded. "With a little help."

"Can't imagine that improves his mood."

Mason smiled. "It does not."

"My best to him."

"I'll tell him."

"I take it you're here to coordinate all the legal stuff?"

"I am. Looks like you can finally get going on the cleanup?"

Red Gibson nodded. "Inspected it myself last night and got the green light this morning."

Mason watched as, right on cue, five men went down the slope, attached to safety lines. "I've got an expert coming out tomorrow who'll want to watch. And test."

"We won't be moving anything until then. Get him on our insured list."

"Her."

Red Gibson stared at him. "Lawyers never make things easy."

"So I've been told. The other side—the prosecutor, the families' lawyers—they're going to be looking for access too."

"We've done that before. Same process for them."

"I'll get you an approved list. No one else comes in."

Red Gibson nodded. "None of them, including you, are to be down there. We'll categorize the wreckage and are taking it offsite. You people can do your investigating there."

Mason nodded. "Once everything is gone, we'll need a chance to look at the ground and the seawall before the new construction starts."

Red Gibson took a deep breath. "I'll talk to Hyde—"

A voice cracked over the radio. "Duffy to Red. We need you down here."

Red Gibson looked at Mason. "We done?"

Mason nodded. "Thanks."

"Get them on the insured list or they're not coming in. Use the regular office number."

Mason nodded again.

"On my way," Red Gibson said into the radio and walked toward a crane.

As he watched three more roped men go down the slope, Mason's phone buzzed. The office.

"What's up, Melody?"

"Oh good, Mason, hi. I have Amber Vincent for you."

Mason took a deep breath, then said, "Fine, put her through."

"No, Mason. She's here."

"At the office?"

"Yes. Do you want me to set up an appointment?"

Mason looked at the sky. "No, Melody. I'm at the site. I'll head back now."

"I'll let Ms. Vincent know."

"Thanks." Mason thought, then said, "Why don't you have her wait in my office?"

"She's actually speaking to Mr. Freid now. I'll show her in there when they're done."

"Thanks," said Mason and hurried to his truck.

21

There was a brief period, about the length of the drive from the Cider Mill to the office, when Mason let himself imagine that Melody had successfully invited Amber to wait in his office. He even allowed himself the briefest fantasy of slipping into the office, nodding at Melody, who discreetly pointed the way, and quietly entering his office and shutting the door behind him to find out why Amber was there.

The reality when he walked through the main office door, though, was exactly what he knew it would be. Amber stood in the center of the reception area, laughing at something Peter Freid had said, one hand on his arm. Melody sat behind the reception desk, a wry smile on her face as she presented the situation with one hand in the universal gesture that said, "Here you go."

"And I must say I've gotten used to the Miracle Mile being right there," Amber said.

"A bit of a change from Northlake, was it?" said Peter.

"Only if you enjoy civilization," said Amber.

"The Bluffs seem nice," said Peter.

"The Basic Block?" said Amber, shaking her head. "The apple pickers certainly seem to think so."

And there was the woman Mason knew.

"Northlake's not so bad," he said.

Amber Vincent's face brightened as if she hadn't already noticed him come through the door. She said, "Hey, Handsome," let go of Peter's arm, and walked across the room.

Everything about Amber Vincent was extra. Her hair and nails were extra-long, her skirt was as extra-high as her shirt was extra-low, and all of it was extra-tight in a way that accentuated every other extra thing about her. The extra was impactful enough through the filters of a social media platform or the dim lights of a club. But in person? Combined with the extra attention she gave with those extra dark eyes? Well, it could be devastating, especially when brought to bear on you for the first time.

As Peter appeared to have learned.

Amber gripped his shoulders and leaned up for a kiss. Mason presented his cheek, acutely aware of Peter's combination of wry amusement and slack-jawed disbelief. He and Amber seemed like an odd match, he knew. But the simple fact was, Mason attracted attention and Amber welcomed it. Everywhere he went and in everything he did, there was no hiding for Mason, and the fact that Amber not only attracted that attention but basked in it had provided Mason with a welcome relief from a pressure he hadn't even known was there. The realization of the depths to which she needed that attention had come later, along with other realizations for both of them that had left their relationship in tatters. A relationship that Mason had thought was long behind him.

Amber took Mason's jaw, turned it, and gave him a kiss on the lips and a smile. "I missed you."

Melody's exhale of disapproval was faint, but audible.

"You didn't tell me you were coming."

"I thought I'd surprise you."

"I'd have met you."

Amber stepped back. "So considerate. But then I wouldn't have seen your office and met Peter here."

Peter smiled as Amber pointed at him.

"He was just telling me all about your new firm. Did you know that you have offices in eight states?"

"I do."

"And that you're one of the biggest firms in Michigan?"

"Yes."

"Such an amazing opportunity that they're opening an office right here in your own hometown." Her eyes narrowed. "You didn't even have to move."

Peter cleared his throat. "The home office is giving it a shot, anyway. They always wait to see if an office is profitable before leaving it open permanently."

"That only makes good sense, Peter," Amber said, not taking her eyes off Mason. "Not much sense in spending all that time doing something if you don't make any money."

Amber stayed close to Mason, too close to be comfortable for a new acquaintance or an ex-girlfriend.

Mason took a slight step back. "If you focus on good work, there'll be enough money."

"Spoken like a true master of *a trade*." Amber smiled.

"Here, why don't you come into my office—"

Amber didn't move. "Your own office, even. So much better than that old rickety desk in the courtroom. Peter was telling me about all the benefits associates at your firm have. Signing bonuses, clothing allowances, performance bonuses, all on top of a six-figure salary? Peter said it's quite a package."

"I'm sure he did. Shall we?" Mason didn't touch her, but he put one hand behind her and gestured to his office with the other.

"No need to manhandle me, Handsome. Not yet, anyway." She turned back to Peter. "It seems I'm being sent to the office. Maybe I'll see you later?"

"I'm sure," said Peter as Mason ushered Amber Vincent into his office and closed the door.

"Are you sure about that door, Handsome?" she said. "Your boss might get the wrong idea."

"There's no chance of that," Mason said.

Amber grinned. "There is if I start moaning."

Mason stood on the far side of his desk. "Are you going to make me crack the door?"

"Oh, Mason. I can't make you do anything." She sat, crossed her legs. "Unless you'd like me to try?"

Mason sat. "Nothing's changed, Amber."

She looked around. "It seems to me that quite a bit has changed since I saw you last."

"You mean after you left me?"

"I left Northlake, Mason. Not you."

"We both know that's not true."

"There're no opportunities here for me, Mason."

"Never said there were."

"Yours have certainly picked up. Do you think you'll move to Detroit?"

"No."

"Then you'll need a house."

"I have a house."

She smiled. "Not that's fitting for a prominent associate with a major law firm though."

"I'm not buying the lot, Amber."

"What, are you going to entertain clients at your mommy's shack? Sorry, *cottage*."

Mason stared.

Amber didn't care. "If you want these people to take you seriously, you can't be living in a tiny house that you drive to in a dirty pickup."

Mason wasn't going to outline it—the student loans, his own rent, his dad's situation, and the money that had gone to her credit card bills when he'd been working at the Court that had prevented him from saving anything at all. Amber knew about it; she'd complained about it often enough when they had been together. So instead, he said, "Anything else?"

Amber's face softened. "The builder is going to sue me, Mason."

"I imagine they will."

"I don't have enough to pay them."

"Then I suppose there's nothing to get."

"I can't afford a lawyer."

"They are expensive."

"Will you defend me?"

"I can't."

"You're just going to let them abuse me?"

"I'm not letting them do anything, Amber. I'm not part of this."

"Oh yes, you are." She gave Mason a wicked smile. "I bet Peter would represent me."

"No, he won't, for the same reason I can't. You're going to say I'm part of this deal. I'm not. That puts us on opposite sides, so I can't represent you, and neither can my firm."

Mason watched the shift he knew was coming. Amber was quick, she was cunning, and she had a lightning-fast instinct for the path of least resistance to getting her way. "I suppose we *are* on opposite sides, since you put me up to this."

"How's that?"

She flipped her long hair back over one shoulder in a gesture she never made, raised her voice an octave, and said, "I don't know anything about contracts. I just did what my super-smart lawyer boyfriend told me to do and signed the papers myself."

"Why would he tell you to do that?"

She batted her eyes. "Why, to get a better deal, of course."

Mason shook his head.

"And why would you do that?"

Amber put her hands on her crossed knees and looked down, avoiding eye contact, her voice now soft. "Because he scares me when he's mad."

It was a display he would have totally fallen for two years ago. He knew strangers would now. Still, Mason said, "Not going to happen."

Amber looked up, the fear washed away by a flash of anger.

"I put you through law school! I stood by you when you were slogging away at that stupid court job making dick-all when you should have been going after something like this!" She raised both hands to his office. "And now that you finally have it, you turn me loose? No way!"

Mason nodded. "I met you the month before I graduated law school when you thought I was a pro football player. You moved up here at the end of the summer and left one month after it got cold. And somehow, in that short time, you managed to incur a debt up here that I didn't know about and that I'm not going to pay."

Amber's anger became a sneer. "You need to be a man and take care of this."

"Guess I'm not man enough for you, Amber."

"That's why I'm gone."

"Sure."

Amber stood. "This isn't over."

"I'm sure it's not."

Amber turned and left, leaving the door open. He saw the

instant change as she waved to Melody and cheerfully called a goodbye to Peter on the way out the door.

Mason was returning his attention to his less complicated problem of handling a multi-fatality patio collapse when his phone buzzed. It was Cameron Thomas.

"We have a problem," she said before Mason could speak.

"Just one?"

"For the moment."

"What?"

"You know how the Cider Mill's total capacity was two hundred and forty-seven?"

"Yes."

"The patio has a separate max occupancy. It's only one hundred."

Mason cursed.

"Exactly."

"We don't have an exact number yet, Cameron, but I think there were definitely more than one hundred people out there."

"Maybe," said Cameron. "But it's still bothering me. That number of people still shouldn't have been enough to cause a collapse out of nowhere. I need to see the site right away."

"I was out there today," Mason said. "They were starting removal."

Now it was Cameron's turn to swear. "You didn't let them, did you?"

"I don't know that I could've stopped it. But I think it was mostly setup today."

"I need to be there when they start. I'm driving up tonight."

"That'll take you—"

"Five hours, I know. But I need to be there when they get going."

"Meet me at Maggie's at six. We'll go over together."

"Maggie's?"

"A deli nearby."

"I'll find it."

"In the meantime, I'll go see Hyde tonight."

"Why?"

"It sounds like I need to know if he shunted people out to the patio on purpose or if it just happened."

"All right. I'll see you tomorrow at six."

Mason hung up, sent a text, and headed over to see Hyde Warren.

22

A month with multiple manslaughter charges hanging over his head had not been kind to Hyde Warren, but then again, you'd probably worry about someone who seemed fine with it. His face was pale, the white stubble on his chin was longer, and his gold-rimmed glasses didn't hide the dark smudges under his eyes as he opened the door. "Come in, Mason," he said.

"Thanks."

As Mason stepped in, Hyde Warren looked over his shoulder and said, "We can just pop into my study here—"

"—Is that him?" said Jessica Warren from around the corner.

Hyde Warren shut the front door gently and guided Mason with a hand on the back toward the pair of glass doors just off the entryway.

"Hyde?"

Hyde Warren didn't speak.

"Mason, is that you?"

Mason stopped. Hyde continued to push on his back, but Mason didn't move.

"It is, Mrs. Warren," he said.

Hyde shot him a panicked look and kept pushing toward the library.

"Stop it, Hyde," said Mason.

Hyde looked down and nodded, just as Jessica Warren came around the corner. She wore loose-knit pants and a knee-length sweater against the cold, and she swept right up to Mason in a neat billow of loose wool and graying hair as she said, "I told you last time, it's Jessica. Are you staying for dinner?"

"No, ma'am. I just need to meet with your husband for a moment. Am I delaying it?"

"Nothing that can't be kept warm." She glanced at Hyde with a frown that was more concern than disapproval. "I don't suppose you've come to tell us this is going away."

"No, ma'am, I haven't."

Jessica Warren shot him a look. "Honest to God, Mason, the 'ma'am' is worse than the 'Mrs. Warren.'"

"Sorry, ma—Jessica."

"I imagine this is a private meeting?"

"It is."

"I'll be right there, Jess," Hyde Warren said.

"You'll be there when Mason says you're done, Hyde." Jessica smiled and rubbed her husband's shoulder. "It'll all keep."

"But the carrots need to be—"

"The carrot will get the julienning they deserve this time, not the one my distracted husband gave them last week. I'll be here when you need me."

"We won't be long, Jessica," Mason said.

"Take as long as you need," Jessica said and went back around the corner with a swirl of sweater.

Hyde gestured, without touching Mason this time, and the two went into his office. Mason noted that, though she was gone, Hyde seemed calmer from his wife's recent presence and made a note of it for trial.

"So what's going on?" Hyde Warren said.

"We have an issue," said Mason, and just like that, Hyde Warren's remnants of calm were gone.

Panic flashed across his face. "What?"

"You know your total occupancy for the Mill is 247."

"I do."

"Do you have a separate occupancy for the patio?"

"Yeah, we went round and round with the inspector about that."

"Why?"

"No one can keep track of what room people are in. We had a single limit for years, but then, out of the blue, a new inspector insisted on a separate limit for the patio and made us add an exit and an emergency stair. Cost me sixty grand."

Mason scowled as he recalled the building paperwork and the dates. "So you built the patio in 2002?"

"Right. And it was fine for fifteen years, and then all of a sudden the new inspector's crawling up my ass and said we had to reconfigure our exits and put a separate occupancy number on it."

Mason could see he was in trouble on the occupancy, so he switched to intent.

"The night of the collapse, did you tell any of your employees to send guests out to the patio?"

"No. I was busy moving t-shirts and restocking the bar."

"All of them?"

"What do you mean?"

"The bar in the dining room and the ones on the patio?"

"They all need booze."

Mason thought, nodded, then said, "When did you set up the drink stations on the patio?"

"The night before."

"And the space heaters?"

"Same. Why?"

"Were you worried too many people would be out there?"

Hyde shook his head. "It was going to be in the teens that night, Mason. I don't care how many heaters I put out there; people would get their drinks and come back inside."

Mason nodded. "Did you tell your employees to limit how many people went out there?"

"Why would I do that?"

"To make sure you didn't exceed the occupancy limit."

Hyde's eyes widened. "I'm sure they knew."

"How? Did you tell them?"

Hyde's eyes darted before he said, "It's posted on the wall out there. They'd have to know. What does all this have to do with my case?"

"I think they're going to say that you consciously disregarded the risks of an over-filled patio."

"That's crazy!"

"I want you to think, Hyde. Did you tell anyone, anyone at all, to funnel customers to the patio?"

"No, I told you, I was too busy. I wasn't even out there by the end of the night."

"How about snow removal? Who was in charge of that?"

Hyde frowned. "Did someone fall in the parking lot too? We have a plow guy who takes care of that..."

"No, I mean for the roof."

Hyde's frown deepened. "Snow removal for the roof? Why would I do that?"

There was Mason's answer, but he had to be sure. "Did you ever remove the snow from your roof at the Cider Mill?"

Hyde shook his head. "The roof didn't collapse; the patio did. Why does that matter? Was I supposed to do that too? How many things do they expect me to do just to sell some cider, for Christ's sake?"

Right then did not seem like the time to explain load distribution to Hyde Warren. Mason had his answer. Any snow that had fallen that winter was likely on the Mill's roof the night of the collapse.

Mason spent a little more time with Hyde, explaining the court process and reassuring him that they were doing everything they could. In the end, returning to the kitchen with Jessica seemed to do more for him than anything that Mason said.

When he left, though, Mason had his answer. Although Hyde hadn't tried to hurt anyone, he'd paid no attention to any potential hazard created by the number of people on his patio or the snow on his roof.

With enough outrage from, say, seven dead and two dozen injured, Mason thought it might be enough for manslaughter.

23

Kyle Stewart didn't know his way around Northlake yet, but he had an unerring instinct for sports bars with lots of TVs and Keno, and he had found just such a place in The BeachHead. The BeachHead was a typical northern bar on the inside—a lot of blond wood, TVs of different shapes and sizes, and a couple of keno screens announcing a constant stream of winners. There were tables in the center and a bar along one side, and there was even a glass wall on the west side that gave a clear view of Lake Michigan.

Kyle Stewart didn't notice any of that just then though because at that exact moment, it appeared that the second string of a Big Ten favorite was about to give up a twenty-three-point half-time lead and fail to cover a twelve-and-a-half-point spread.

A scrub on the losing team launched a half-court shot at the buzzer.

Swish.

An eleven-point win. Which was another way of saying a loss.

Kyle Stewart looked up at the ceiling and decided now

would not be the time to check his sportsbook balance. Instead, out of the corner of his eye, he saw the Keno screen flash. He took out his ticket and watched the winning numbers flash.

Fifty dollars. It wasn't a Big Ten bet by any stretch, but it was a victory.

A woman came in and sat a couple of seats down at the bar, but Kyle Stewart barely noticed her as he held up the ticket and said, "Chris, got a winner here." The bartender came over and took the ticket. He stopped on the way back at the woman, who ordered a vodka soda. She still wore her long winter coat and was resting her forehead on one manicured hand so that her long hair hid her face.

The bartender put the vodka soda in front of the woman, who ignored it. Then he ran Kyle's ticket through the scanner and said, "Cash out or re-bet?"

You never know if you're on a hot streak unless you bet, so Kyle said, "Let it ride, Chris."

The woman raised her head, took her drink, and gave Kyle a faint smile. "Winner?"

Her eyes were dark brown and bigger than he expected.

Kyle Stewart nodded.

"I'm glad," she said. "At least someone is."

"Split the ticket, Chris," said Kyle before he realized it.

"No, no," said the woman, holding up one hand. "I didn't mean it like that."

Kyle shrugged. "Maybe you were lucky."

The woman shook her head and looked back down at her drink. "Not recently."

Chris slid one ticket in front of the woman before giving the other to Kyle.

"I don't know how to play," she said.

"They'll put the new winning numbers up in a few minutes. That screen over there."

The faint smile again. “Thanks.”

Kyle motioned for another Old Fashioned for himself but didn’t offer to buy one for the woman. Then, though it was painful, he watched the recap of the basketball game until, mercifully, the station switched to the second game of the doubleheader. He still didn’t say anything.

“You don’t look like you live here,” the woman said.

Kyle Stewart smiled on the inside. “What makes you say that?”

“The shoes.”

Kyle raised an eyebrow.

The woman pointed one long nail around her vodka tonic. “You can’t buy them at any store within one hundred miles of here and, even if you ordered them, someone who lived here wouldn’t wear them this time of year because the snow and the gravel and the salt would destroy them in two weeks.” She smiled fully now. “And those shoes aren’t brand new, but they also aren’t damaged, so…” She smiled, shrugged, and sipped.

Kyle studied her. “Seems I need to work on my camouflage then. Thanks.”

“Vacation?”

“Work.”

The woman turned on her stool to face him. “What do you do for work?”

Kyle thought, then said, “I’m a troubleshooter.”

“That’s pretty vague.”

Kyle shrugged. “Problems can be that way.”

“And you fix them?”

“I try.”

“For who?”

“Businesses, law firms, investment firms. Whoever needs it.”

She snorted. “How can you work with lawyers?”

Kyle smiled. “I take it you’ve had a problem one?”

The woman nodded. "My ex."

"A lawyer?"

She nodded. "He's being an asshole."

"Lawyers can be exceptional at that."

The woman finished her vodka tonic as the screen behind the bar flashed. Kyle pointed. "Time to check our tickets."

"How do we do that?"

Kyle slid his ticket over and pointed. "Watch which numbers come up there and see if you have any on your ticket." She leaned over, looked at his, looked at hers, then looked at the screen.

"I have that one!"

Kyle nodded.

"And that one!"

Kyle smiled as the woman won a two hundred dollar payday. Kyle hit for another fifty.

The woman brightened as Kyle told her she was a winner. Then her face fell. "Wait, this should have been yours."

Kyle shook his head. "I gave it to you."

"What do we do now?"

Kyle motioned to Chris. "Chris here will cash it for you."

Chris came over, took both of their tickets.

"I'll take another vodka tonic," said the woman. "And please give ..." She looked at him.

"Kyle."

"Kyle, another one of his."

"Not necessary," said Kyle.

"It's the least I can do. We're winners!"

Chris took both tickets. "Cash?"

Kyle smiled. "Let it ride, Chris."

The woman looked at Kyle.

He shrugged. "You don't know if you're on a hot streak unless you bet."

Her eyes widened. "I like that. Let it ride, Chris!"

"You got it," said Chris with practiced non-judgment.

The woman slid over a seat and removed her winter coat to reveal a skirt that seemed too short and a blouse that seemed too thin for a Northlake winter before she extended her hand. "I'm Amber."

"Nice to win with you, Amber."

"That's about the nicest thing anyone has said to me today, Kyle."

Kyle nodded. "The whole ex-thing?"

She nodded. "But let's not ruin our luck with talk of lawyers."

"I like your instincts."

Chris returned with two drinks and two new tickets. "Can I get you some menus?"

Kyle remained silent.

"I could eat. How about you, Kyle?"

He looked at her.

She looked back from under long eyelashes. "Deciding if I'm trouble, Mr. Shooter?"

"Not at all. You definitely are."

Amber smiled. "It's nice to meet someone who's good at what they do."

Kyle smiled. "Two menus, please, Chris."

Once they'd ordered dinner—blackened whitefish for him and a Michigan salad for her (featuring dried cherries, walnuts, and blue cheese, with a vinaigrette, if you've never been)—it only took Kyle a few minutes to figure out that he'd hit a longshot. There really weren't that many lawyers in Northlake, and there was a grand total of one who was a massive six-and-a-half-foot tall Cro-Magnon man. Amber didn't get too specific about her problem—she was really very good at this too—but, like most, it clearly centered around money, and that was something Kyle knew how to address. After she lamented the high prices in Chicago, he mentioned that he had friends there who complained about the same thing, that it was a dog-eat-dog world to fill their clubs.

Amber, in turn, pushed him on what brought him to Northlake. When he said, reluctantly, that he was doing some work on the patio collapse, she noted that, coincidentally, her ex's firm was working on just that case.

Finally, after their last Keno ticket had inevitably lost and nothing remained of their food but a crusted edge of whitefish and a few blue cheese crumbles, Kyle mentioned that he knew owners in Chicago who were always on the lookout for influencers for their clubs and online campaigns. Amber thought that sounded promising. Amber mentioned that she'd just met a man, a lawyer but a decent-seeming one, not like her ex at all, who might know things that were interesting to people who shot trouble. Kyle thought that sounded promising but didn't want her to go to any trouble. Amber smiled and said that's the last thing it would be, and the two gave a toast to an unexpressed understanding.

Soon after, Kyle said he had to leave for an early morning of work. Amber seemed surprised because Kyle knew she'd been expecting an offer to continue their discussions elsewhere. Kyle also knew that he wasn't going to be getting anywhere with Amber that night, and he thought he detected the slightest disappointment from her that she didn't get to be the one to tell him so. Still, a last mention of the Chicago contacts cleared that up and, when they parted at the door, she thanked him for an unexpectedly lovely evening and even took him by the shoulders and kissed his cheek.

As he watched her get into a sports car that was far too low for a Northlake winter, Kyle Stewart thought again that you never know if you're on a hot streak unless you bet.

24

When Mason walked into Maggie's at 5:50 a.m. the next morning, he found Cameron Thomas sitting in a booth, which was good, with his cousin Austin Pierce, which was decidedly bad. Austin was talking, waving a foil-wrapped breakfast burrito for emphasis, while Cameron sipped her coffee and listened.

"So what did he do?" said Cameron Thomas around sips.

Austin's grin only got bigger when he saw Mason approach. "He stood there, big as a mountain, all stony-faced." He pointed his burrito. "Yep. Just like that!"

"I don't think Dr. Thomas is interested in old stories," said Mason.

"Of course she is! Aren't you, Dr. Cammie?"

Mason winced but, as always seemed to be the case with Austin, Dr. Cameron Thomas smiled. "I think I am."

Austin chuckled. "So I say, because of course I'm there with him, and Bronson and Lily too, I say to these non-union boys, most of them over thirty if they're a day, I say, 'Well, it seems to me that you boys want to scrap.'"

Mason sighed, left them, and got in line, which was mercifully short.

"Good morning, Yousef," said Mason to the man behind the counter.

Yousef smiled. "The lawyer has arrived, Chad."

The man at the grill, back to them, raised both spatulas like a runner taking the starting blocks.

"One or two?" Yousef said.

"One," said Mason.

Yousef frowned. "I'm hurt."

"I'm behind a desk now, Yousef."

"Double Egg, Double Ham, Double cheese, peppers, hot sauce, wrap, hot," Yousef called and Chad's spatulas were off to the races. After another assurance to a skeptical Yousef that he simply didn't need the same amount of fuel that he had when he was laying cinder block and building seawalls, Mason moved down the line to the register and Maggie.

"Having a crew reunion?" Maggie said, smiling.

"A happy coincidence."

Austin's voice carried to them. "And I said, 'No, no, put him down!'"

Mason winced. "Or a coincidence anyway."

Maggie looked sly. "It *is* a good story."

"Not one that people from the firm need to know."

Maggie made a point of leaning to the side so she could see around him. "I don't know. Your co-worker seems to be enjoying it."

"She's an expert."

"At what?"

"Structures."

"Then she's been on worksites before. I wouldn't sweat it."

"Have you met Austin?"

Maggie handed him the foil-wrapped breakfast and an extra-large coffee. "Are you hiring a lot of experts?"

"Just Dr. Thomas so far. Why?"

"There was a man asking after you a few days ago."

Mason tilted his head. "Did he say why?"

"Said he knew you were working the Cider Mill case. Then wanted to know all about you."

Mason scowled. "Like how?"

"That you're from here, that you worked construction, that you'd worked at the Court. He was more saying it than asking it, but I think he was looking to me for confirmation. It started to get a little creepy."

"Yeah?"

Maggie nodded. "I think he could tell too. As soon as I started shutting down, he apologized and waxed on about the pastrami being the best he'd found up north."

"Which is true."

"Undeniably. But also as creepy as the questions."

"What did this guy look like, the one who was asking?"

Maggie frowned, then bit her lower lip. "You know, I don't know that I can say. Average, I guess. Pleasant. Sorry."

"No, thanks. There's a lot going on right now."

She smiled. "We miss you in the mornings. Lawyers need to eat too, you know."

"I'll do better."

Austin's voice boomed over to the register. "And then he just picks up the whole thing. With one hand."

Mason sighed, pointed over his shoulder. "I have to—"

Maggie grinned. "See you."

As Mason walked over, Austin kept going. "Now this thing weighs a hundred pounds if it's an ounce, and Mason just flips it over—"

"Dr. Thomas and I need to go, Austin."

Austin ignored Mason and held his burrito straight out in front of him. "Then just steps over the guy, a full-grown man, mind you, and walks over to the scaffold and starts picking up cinder blocks two at a time and setting them over his head on the scaffold floor for his dad to lay."

"His dad was there?"

Austin grinned. "The whole time. Just watching it all from up top on the platform as he finished a row. Ol' Uncle Jackson has had enough now though, so he just turns and says to the guy, 'Tell your boss that as soon as your union cards come through you're welcome on the site.' Then he looks down at Mason and says, 'If you're done screwing around, we're behind.'"

Austin grinned. "The guy got up, watched Mason loading those cinder blocks four at a time, and left. Didn't hear a peep out of them for the rest of the job."

"And you said you all were how old?"

Austin cackled again. "Fourteen."

Mason saw Lily and Bronson at the door. "Looks like it's time for you to go, Austin."

"So it is." Austin wiped his beard with a napkin, crumpled it up with his foil, and said, "Nice to meet you, Dr. Cammie. You in town for a while?"

She nodded. "Probably."

"Then make sure he brings you to The Loon on Tuesday nights. We'll be there."

"She's going to be pretty busy, Austin," said Mason.

"Wouldn't miss it," said Cameron, smiling.

Lily Stone opened the door wearing her yellow work vest over her canvas coat and pulled her hood down to reveal her straw hair sticking out even more than usual. She accepted a coffee from Austin with a nod of thanks and said, "Change of plan, brother. Still too crappy to start on the Rileys' seawall, so

Dad subcontracted us out to Warhelm's group to help with the Cider Mill clean-up."

"Looks like we're all headed to the same place!" said Austin.

"Hi, Mason." Lily looked at Cameron. "Who's this?"

Austin cackled. "I'll explain on the way."

25

"The Cider Mill site is opening up today," said Kyle Stewart. "You need to get your people up here."

"Why am I just hearing about this now?" said Jerome Baggman.

"Because it's just happening now."

Jerome Baggman stared through the screen.

"My contact got canned when he dumped a crane," said Kyle.

"So get a new contact."

"I'm working on it. Meantime, the weather broke two days early, and the company decided it could start."

Jerome Baggman nodded. "The criminal pretrial is tomorrow. I'll call Olsen and make sure she pushes for a quick trial."

Kyle Stewart pressed his lips together. "I don't think that's likely with the weather delays."

"If you don't push, nothing happens. What have you learned about the defense team?"

"Peter Freid, former US attorney turned senior partner whose hard-driving days are behind him. From what I can see, he agreed to go north and set up this satellite office so he could be near his vacation home in Petoskey. I think he wants to make this office a go and ride the profits into semi-retirement."

"I know Freid. Old and tired works for me with opposing counsel. How about this Pierce?"

"Local guy who worked—"

"—Yes, construction and for the judge. What do we *know* about him? Where are the pressure points?"

Kyle Stewart thought, then said, "Money."

"Money? He's working for Kramer Burns!"

"He's got a boatload of law school debt."

"What lawyer doesn't?"

"His dad fell off a scaffolding and hasn't worked since."

"That's something."

"He lives in a tiny place he inherited from his mom, but it looks like his ex-girlfriend might have signed papers to build a house, which she's not able to do without him paying for it."

"Glad to hear someone else has ex problems. Okay, so there's enough floating around out there that might make him vulnerable, but that doesn't seem like any more than normal."

Kyle Stewart paused. "There's one other thing, but I'm not sure how it helps."

"Let's hear it."

"He was involved in an assault case when he was in law school."

"Someone beat him up?"

Kyle Stewart shook his head. "Have you seen him?"

"Pierce? No."

"No one beat him up. Three guys wound up in the hospital, and one almost didn't' make it."

"So he did it?"

"Looks like it, but no charges were filed even though the guys were hurt pretty bad."

"Where did it happen?"

"Up here."

"Home cooking?"

"I'm not sure."

"Find out." Jerome Baggman looked thoughtful. "So aggressive enough or angry enough that he can go off. I can work with this. Keep an eye on the Cider Mill today until our people get there, then watch the pretrial tomorrow."

"Will do."

"This is big enough, Kyle, that I want you to push. I need all the information you can get me."

"Push what, exactly?"

Jerome Baggman paused, then said, "Everything."

26

The Sable County courthouse was an old-school edifice with a sleek modern interior. On the outside, it was four stories of limestone and granite topped with a copper-domed circular tower, the kind that would never be built today because of the cost of the materials and the sheer number of skilled stoneworkers you'd have to find. Inside that ornate stone was a state-of-the-art facility with security scanners, gleaming floors, and screens outside each courtroom declaring the judge and the day's schedule.

Mason had left a little extra time to get there since he knew he'd run into folks on the way up to Judge Roderick's courtroom. And he did—Max at security, Kara from the clerk's office, and Francine from maintenance all said hello, all wondered how things were, and all professed to miss him, though Francine admitted that was in part because, with him gone, she now had to use a stool to pull paper towel racks off the top shelf. Mason found that he missed them too, missed the larger group of folks he ran into on a daily basis.

Good company doesn't pay the bills, he could hear his dad say as if he were standing right there.

Mason came to the screen that identified Judge Roderick's courtroom, saw *State v. Hyde Warren* first up on the docket, and went in.

He couldn't help himself—he looked at his old desk first and saw that it had been moved to the center of the window and that a thirty-ish woman sat there, squinting through leopard-print glasses, typing. She kept going as Mason walked through the swinging gate and up to the rail that marked the area for court personnel.

He waited another moment as she kept going, then said, "Mason Pierce here on the Hyde Warren case."

The woman started at his voice, then squeaked and rolled her chair back when she saw him. Then she put her hand to her heart and laughed, "The judge told me, but my God!"

Mason smiled. "I didn't mean to startle you."

"How in the world could you come up here that quietly? You'd think it'd take a tugboat or something." She pressed her lips together and jerked her head. "Sorry. I blurt."

"Not necessary. I apparently creep." He extended a hand. "Mason Pierce."

"Duh." She bit her lip, nodded, and said, "Holly Gorman. I've heard all about you."

"Don't believe it."

"Do you know I had to order a new chair?"

"Yeah?"

"The springs were totally shot, poor things. Look at you."

Mason nodded. "My apologies to the springs."

Holly Gorman tapped her screen. "How did you get the daily sort on the auto docket to work?"

"It doesn't."

"It doesn't?"

"Not that I ever found. I had to do it by hand."

"That's stupid." Holly winced again. "Sorry. Not you. It."

"I agree."

"Here for the Warren pretrial then?"

"I am."

"Will Mr. Freid be here?"

"Just me. And Mr. Warren."

"That's okay this time, but Judge Roderick will require lead counsel to be here for the final pretrial."

"Okay."

Holly Gorman looked up. "You knew that, didn't you?"

"I did."

"Judge Roderick will see you as soon as...there's Ms. Olsen."

Astrid Olsen stepped through the swinging gate. Mason had known her for years since they'd both grown up in Northlake, and though they hadn't known each other well in high school—they were separated by a couple of grades and several social circles—Mason had come to know her far better when he worked for Judge Roderick since Astrid Olsen was the chief prosecutor for Sable County. She seemed the same—white-blond hair pulled back in a long braid and one of her many pale blue suits that he believed was a conscious decision to accentuate disconcerting pale blue eyes. But where those eyes had always held a warm greeting for him when he'd been working for the judge, they were wary now.

She nodded. "Mason."

"Atti."

She looked around. "No Freid?"

"Just me today."

"When are you two substituting out?"

"We're not."

Astrid Olsen stared at him, then shrugged. "Your funeral. Or your client's anyway. Speaking of which, where is he?"

Mason checked his phone. "Just got through security, on his way up now."

"Hi, Holly," Astrid said. "Is the judge ready for us?"

"As soon as Mr. Warren gets here. It'll be out here, though. On the record."

Mason raised an eyebrow. "Not in chambers anymore?"

"Not for this case. And not with you on it." Holly bit her lip. "Shoot."

Mason smiled. "Makes sense."

Hyde Warren bustled into the courtroom, followed by a man who quietly took a seat in the back row. Mason excused himself, went to meet Hyde, and guided him through the gate to the defense table.

"I'm sorry it took so long; I had a pocketknife," said Hyde Warren.

"You're fine. We're just going to set dates today. You won't have to say anything unless I tell you to."

Hyde Warren scowled. "Then why am I here?"

"Because it was a condition of not keeping you in jail."

Mason knew it was a mistake as soon as he said it. A wave of stuttering panic visibly swept over Hyde. Some clients needed to be reminded of the threat of looming incarceration; Hyde Warren did not, especially before a court appearance in which Mason wanted him calm. He spent the next minute speaking in hushed tones, calming him like he would a dog who'd heard the delivery truck in the driveway, until they were cut short by the entrance of Judge Roderick.

Judge Lancaster Roderick was in his late forties with a thick head of hair so brown that it was almost black and brown-framed glasses that jerked and bobbed when he spoke. "Two of my favorite people," he said. "But why don't you identify yourself and your party for the record."

Astrid Olsen for the State and Mason Pierce for defendant Hyde Warren, did.

"Well, we have ourselves a little reunion here, don't we?" said Judge Roderick. "Ms. Olsen, how are you?"

"I'm fine, Your Honor."

"And I see you haven't shrunk any, Mr. Pierce."

"I have not, Judge."

"Did Holly tell you she had to replace the springs on your chair?"

Holly Gorman blushed and looked down.

"She mentioned it, Judge."

"She does have a tendency to do that. Fine attorney. I'd say she has big shoes to fill, but I imagine that's not the compliment I'm intending where you're involved, so we'll just say she's hit the ground running."

"I'm glad to hear it."

"So," Judge Roderick settled back in his chair. "Let's get to it with this thing. Before I waste anyone's time, Ms. Olsen, are you going to be filing any nonsense that I can't be impartial in this case since Mr. Pierce is appearing for the defendant?"

"I am not, Your Honor."

"Good. Mr. Pierce, is that because you're going to be stepping away from this case for new counsel or is Ms. Olsen just that convinced of my impartiality?"

"Neither Mr. Freid nor I is stepping away from representing Mr. Warren on this, Judge. I can't speak to Ms. Olsen."

"That's probably best. Ms. Olsen, this is your shot. Ask me to transfer the case, and I might consider it now if you have a good reason. I won't if you do it down the road."

Astrid Olsen gave Mason a sideways glance before she said, "The State is satisfied with the case as it currently sits, Your Honor."

"Peachy," said Judge Roderick. "Let me fill you two in on some of the ground rules then. All pretrials are going to be on the record, just like this. This is as bad a tragedy as we've had here in a while, and everyone, you two included, deserves a clear record of what's gone on. Objections?"

A couple of "No, Your Honors."

"Good. Now you two are good at what you do, so I assume you know that there's a whole bunch of civil cases based on this incident too?"

A couple of nods.

"And if I'm not mistaken, Mr. Pierce, your office is defending those too?"

"We are, Judge."

"And the bulk of the civil cases are being handled by the office of Jerome Baggman out of Detroit for the families. Ms. Olsen, have you been in contact with his office?"

There was a moment of hesitation before Astrid Olsen said, "We have, Your Honor."

"Good. I'm presiding over those too, so we're not going to have all sorts of separate discovery fights on this. I expect you two to cooperate with the civil discovery process; am I understood?"

A couple more of "Yes, Your Honors." Then Astrid Olsen said, "Along those lines, Your Honor, we need to have access to the property."

"You certainly do. Mr. Pierce?"

"The weather made it inaccessible for a while, Judge."

Judge Roderick picked up a stack of papers and waved it around. "This is from Mr. Baggman demanding access and retention of evidence. Do you have similar thoughts, Ms. Olsen?"

"We filed a motion to join, Your Honor."

"Why aren't you giving them access, Mr. Pierce?"

"The defense doesn't control the weather, Judge."

Astrid Olsen looked over her shoulder. "It's my understanding that the defense has started construction work today, Your Honor."

Judge Roderick looked at Mason.

"There has been some preliminary work, Judge. The site's dangerous right now."

Judge Roderick scowled. "I know it's dangerous, Mr. Pierce. Seven people died there."

There was a discussion then, about the State's interest in investigating, about the families' rights to discovery, about Mr. Warren's rights to fix his property, and about everyone's safety. In the end, they agreed that what was being removed was trash and that it would all be stored off-site at a warehouse, the expense of which would be taxed as costs in all the cases.

That led to an argument about who was in charge of access and coordinating all of the many parties' desires to view, test, photograph, and otherwise clamber all over the stuff. Judge Roderick listened for about five minutes before he raised a hand and said, "Yeah, I'm not dealing with that. I'm going to appoint a special master from the local bar who's going to oversee that aspect of discovery. You can chew his, or her, ear off about it."

Before they could respond, Judge Roderick pointed at Mason. "Who's running the salvage operation?"

"Warhelm Industrial Services, Judge."

"Fine. Every single piece of that patio is to end up in the warehouse, got it?"

"Yes, Judge."

"And nothing is to be disposed of until the special master signs off."

"Fine."

"Objections, Ms. Olsen?"

Astrid Olsen looked over her shoulder again. "No, but I assume Mr. Baggman might want to weigh in at some point."

Judge Roderick waved the papers again. "I've heard his opinions. He'll be fine."

He set the papers down and said, "Now, that leaves us with scheduling. How far out are we looking?"

Astrid Olson said, "We're ready as soon as the Court is, Judge."

"Really? Seems like there's a lot to do, and you haven't done any of it."

"We'll be ready."

Judge Roderick turned to Mason and said, "Mr. Pierce?"

"Whatever's good for the Court is good for us, Judge."

"Do you like chicken for breakfast, Holly?" said Judge Gorman.

"Not really, Judge."

"Well, too bad, cause we're getting a game of it this morning. Set them up with a speedy trial date. The two of you work with Holly and back out all of your other deadlines. Then I suggest you two get going. It seems like you have a lot of work to do."

With that, Judge Roderick rose and left. When he was gone, Holly Gorman said, "This is going to be a mess."

She put a hand to her mouth and blushed. "I mean, how does late spring look for the two of you?"

27

"A special master?" said Peter Freid. "Why would he impose a special master?"

Mason explained the dynamics of the pretrial to Peter and Judge Roderick's impatience with managing the site.

"How long will it take to clear all that stuff from the site?" Peter asked.

"Two, maybe three weeks to move it off site, if the weather holds."

"Fine. Anything else?"

Mason thought, then said, "You might want to check in on your buddy. He was struggling today."

Peter sighed. "Hyde always was the nervous type. Knows how to make money but frets all the way to the bank. I'll go see him. You get down to the site and tell Thomas what's going on."

~

MASON FOUND Cameron Thomas standing at the top of the slope talking to Red Gibson, the man in charge for Warhelm Industrial Services, and an older man in a shiny parka with fur lining around the hood. The Warhelm construction crew was swarming up and down the slope behind them, starting the removal and disassembly of the already-disassembled patio.

"My boss said we start clearing today," said Red Gibson.

"You can't do that!" said Shiny Parka.

"You already said that," said Red. "But unless you have an order in your pocket, get out of my way."

"What'd I miss?" Mason said to Cameron Thomas.

"The foreman wants to do his job, and the plaintiff's expert doesn't," she said.

Shiny Parka looked at Mason and said, "Bringing one of your goons over here isn't going to intimidate me! You cannot move that debris!"

Cameron smiled at Mason. "I think you just got promoted to goon."

"Dammit," said Mason. "I was holding out for thug." He turned to Red Gibson. "Remember me?"

Red Gibson nodded. "The Pierce kid, sure."

"I just came from court. The Judge gave us some orders."

Red's beard jutted. "I have my orders too, Pierce."

"From Mr. Wilhelm?"

Red Gibson nodded.

"Could you call him for me? I'll explain it to him."

"He doesn't want to hear excuses from me," said Red Gibson. "He wants me to do my job."

"Tell him that the customer's lawyer would like to speak with him."

The foreman stared at him a moment, then pulled out his phone.

"Why are you listening to him?" said Shiny Parka.

"Because he represents our customer," Red said, punching numbers. "And he's polite."

Cameron gestured to Shiny Parka. "Barry Wasmeuller,

Mason Pierce. Mason, Barry is working with the State and the families."

Mason held out his hand.

Barry Wasmeuller kept his hands in his shiny pockets. "I won't be intimidated by you."

Mason cocked his head, pulled back his hand, and said, "You mentioned that."

They all fell silent as Red Gibson spoke. "Mr. Warhelm, it's Red, out at the Cider Mill site...No, not yet, there' are a couple of things going on. Hyde's lawyer wants to talk to you...I know, I know, but it's the Pierce kid, and I thought you might want to talk to him...No, the other one, Jackson's boy...Right."

Red Gibson nodded and held out the phone to Mason.

"Mr. Warhelm? It's Mason Pierce."

"So you're Jackson's son?"

"I am, sir."

"Give him my best. What's going on at my site?"

"There was a hearing this morning, sir. The Court appointed a special master who's going to supervise the investigation of the accident site by all of the parties."

"What does that mean for my company?"

"Can you delay for a day while we put things in place?"

"I'd rather not. You know how schedules are when you're working against the weather."

"I do. I think the Court is going to insist."

"Do you have a solution for me?"

"Do you have a line on any warehouses we could use?"

John Warhelm chuckled. "I have a line on a warehouse you can rent."

"I think if I can get both experts to agree on a categorization system, we can get things moving."

"I'm not interested in having my boys waiting while 'experts' prove it to each other, Mason."

Mason looked at Cameron. "At least one of them is practical."

"Idle hours erode profit, Mason. You know that."

"I do, Mr. Warhelm. But an agreement will move things along faster than waiting for a special master to sort it out."

"That sounds practical. Can you get an agreement done in three hours?"

"I think so."

"Then do it in two. Unless I have a court order delivered to me before then, Red will start the backhoes."

"We can do that."

"Good. Then tell Red to give the boys a long lunch and come back ready to work through dinner. I'll send him the warehouse location."

"Yes, sir. Thanks, Mr. Warhelm."

John Warhelm paused, then said, "I'm glad to hear that you're practical. A lot of people could learn from that."

Then he was gone.

Mason gave Red Gibson his phone back and relayed Warhelm's message. Then he turned to Cameron and Wasmeuller and said, "We've got two hours to work this out before Red starts hauling stuff away."

"Fine," said Barry Wasmeuller, "let's go inside."

"Seems to me we need to be out here so we can see what we're talking about," said Mason.

"I agree," said Cameron.

As Barry Wasmeuller objected, more to the cold than the task, Mason's phone buzzed. A text from Austin Pierce.

Bring Dr. Cammie to The Loon tonight.

Mason thought, then typed. *Maybe. If I see her.*

She's right next to you, asshole.

Mason looked around. Austin and Lily waved from a few machines over.

Mason shook his head, typed, *We'll see how work is.*

Lawyers aren't supposed to lie, came the reply.

Mason sighed and made a show of putting his phone in his pocket. He missed the last thing Cameron said, but in reply, Barry Wasmeuller stuffed his hands farther into his shiny parka. "Fine. Let's get on with it."

"Good," she said. She pointed at Mason's pocket. "Problem?"

He glanced over at where Austin and Lily were laughing as he put away his phone.

"We'll see," said Mason.

28

When she walked into The Loon, Cameron Thomas didn't see Mason, which was strange because he'd been right behind her. She was halfway toward sliding into a long table to wait when a call of "Dr. Cammie! Dr. Cammie!" came from the back.

A familiar man with a broad grin and a thick beard waved.

She headed back. "Austin, right?"

Austin Pierce grinned some more. "First guess even! This is Lily and that's Bronson and that's your seat." He pointed to an open spot next to Bronson.

"I'm supposed to meet Mason."

"Which means you're meeting us."

Cameron smiled and sat.

Austin slid a glass forward and gestured at two pitchers. "We have an array of selections for you this evening. Light or Dark?"

"Dark," she said without hesitation.

"An excellent choice." Austin poured. "Madam will be most pleased."

"Hungry?" said Bronson next to her.

"Starved."

"The Dean is here tonight, so I'd suggest the skillet."

"The Dean?"

"Brenda's husband."

"I'm sorry, Brenda?"

"They own the place. That's her there."

"The Dean's here?" said Lily.

"In back," said Bronson.

"I didn't think he worked Tuesdays."

"Brenda said they switched things around."

Lily frowned. "Since when?"

"Since Tuesdays became a little more animated."

"Pfft," said Austin over his beer. "We handled it."

Bronson shrugged. "I think that's the animated she was talking about."

Austin was all innocence. "I apologized!"

Lily smirked. "So well that Mason had to bail your ass out."

"I handled it!"

"Mason and I handled it," said Bronson and took a drink. "You got duck-walked by your sister."

Austin waved him off. "She surprised me."

"How did Mason bail him out?" Cameron said to Lily.

Lily grinned. "Oh, when this moron was getting jumped, Mason went over and—"

"—diffused the situation with a few calm words," said Bronson.

Lily twisted her smile at her husband. "Don't cut me off, Corporal."

"Don't talk out of school, Foreman."

Austin rolled his eyes. "You see what it's like, Dr. Cammie? Both of them flaunting their titles at every opportunity." He waved a mug at Bronson. "This one's always on about serving in an engineering company of the National Guard, while this one," the mug came back around to Lily, "won't let a moment go by without letting you know she's the *Foreperson* of our crew, while those of us who are the salt of the earth just go about actually getting the job done without a peep of complaint."

"I didn't say I was a corporal," said Bronson.

"And I didn't say I was the foreman," said Lily.

"See! You just did it again!" Austin grinned then took a big swig. "See what I'm dealing with here, Doctor?"

"I do," said Cameron. She looked around. "That skillet sounds like the thing. Is there a server?"

Austin barked a laugh. "I'll order it." He grabbed an empty pitcher and headed up to the bar.

"So what took so long to get started today?" said Lily.

"Organization."

"Of rubble and scraps?"

"Of a crime scene," said Bronson.

"Exactly," said Cameron.

Lily scowled. "So don't you just make a grid of the site and then put the rubble in corresponding sections in the warehouse?"

Cameron stared at her, then laughed. "Yes. That's exactly what we do."

"So what took little lord Shiny Parka so long to agree to that?"

"It wasn't his idea."

"So what? Nothing else makes sense."

"He got there. Eventually. Fortunately, Mason was smart enough to keep our meeting outside. The cold finally persuaded him."

Austin returned with a full pitcher, slid over the bench to sit down, and poured. "Skillet's on the way, Dr. Cammie. Mason is too, right?"

"He should be. He was right behind me."

Cameron took the beer Austin offered her, sipped, then said, “So, you’re usually a seawall crew?”

Lily nodded. “Just on loan for this rubble clearing contract. We’ll repair the seawall after if there’s any damage.”

“Once it thaws,” said Bronson.

Lily nodded. “It’ll be awhile yet.”

“And Mason was part of your crew at one point?” said Cameron.

“’Til he got soft,” said Austin.

Cameron nodded, then pointed at Austin. “So you’re a Pierce,” then pointed at Lily, “you were a Pierce,” then pointed at Lily and Bronson, “and you two are married. I take it Northlake Seawall is a family company?”

“It is,” said Lily.

“It was,” said Bronson at the same time.

Both stopped.

Bronson gestured, and Lily said, “Mason’s dad and our dad started the company, years ago, building cinderblock foundations. Dad and Uncle Jackson had a disagreement about how the company should be run and split up. Uncle Jackson and Mason kept doing cinderblock work, and our dad started the seawall company.”

Cameron raised an eyebrow. “Mason left his dad’s company to work for yours?”

Lily shook her head. “No, Uncle Jackson had an accident. His scaffold collapsed on a job, and his spine was injured. He recovered enough to walk with his canes, but his time laying foundations was done, so Mason came to work for my dad.”

“As a summer job or something?

Austin barked a laugh. “No.”

“Well, he’s a lawyer now, so it couldn’t have done it that long.”

Austin smirked. "You may have noticed that Mason is a bit large."

Cameron nodded.

"He started working with his dad when he was eight. He's worked for his dad or my dad since, well, a couple of months ago."

Cameron stared.

"I don't mean playing on the job site and hanging out with dad; he did that back in kindergarten. I'm talking about moving block, pushing wheelbarrows, all that good stuff."

"How'd he get away with that?"

"Uncle Jackson? By the time Mason was eight, he was the size of a small man, so no inspector would notice unless he looked real close under the ball cap or heard his squeaky voice. By the time he was thirteen, he was already bigger than most guys, so it wasn't an issue."

"But school?"

"Oh, he went. Never missed a day. Then straight to work after."

Cameron Thomas sipped her dark beer as she digested this new information. "Did you all start working then too?"

"Some," Lily said. "But the three of us didn't go full time until after college."

"Or high school," said Austin. "Elitist."

"But not Mason?"

"You remember the 2008 housing collapse, right?"

Cameron nodded.

"Mason didn't have time for anything except school and trying to help Uncle Jackson keep his company afloat."

"What about your dad's company?"

Lily grinned. "The beauty of seawalls is that Lake Michigan keeps eroding shoreline regardless of the economy. And the richer the client, the more likely they've put their house in front of a view that's trying to destroy it. We were fine. Uncle Jackson and Mason were still doing foundation work though, so they were scraping by for a little while. They were just getting back on their feet when Mason's mom got sick, and not too long after that, Uncle Jackson had his accident. Mason couldn't run things all on his own and take care of them and take online college courses, so they folded up Uncle Jackson's business, and Mason came to work for us."

Bronson filled his glass. "After Mason's mom died, he went back to school full time to finish up and joined us on weekends and breaks."

"Even through law school?"

Bronson nodded. "And when he was working for the court. It wasn't 'til he joined the big firm that he figured he'd have to spend all his time doing that."

Cameron did the quick math. "So he's been on worksites..."

"This'll be twenty-two years."

"How can that be?"

Austin shrugged. "These things add up when you start at eight."

"Two spicy skillets, one pizza, one Rueben wrap," called Brenda from the bar.

"A spicy skillet?" said Cameron.

Austin grinned. "You look like you can handle it."

"I'll help you," said Bronson, and the two went up to the bar to get their dinner.

"How'd he end up in law school?" said Cameron.

"Not sure on that one," said Bronson. "You'll have to ask him."

"I would," said Cameron Thomas. "But where is he?"

29

Mason was following Cameron Thomas out of the parking lot at the Stone Street Cider Mill when his gas light came on. He cursed his absent-mindedness, especially when he remembered it had come on for the first time on the way there. He saw the taillights of Cameron's car continue on down the road as he took a left, then a right, to get to Buddy's, the nearest gas station.

He shot Cameron a text saying he'd be right there and re-sent the address just in case. Then he got out and started pumping.

A truck pulled up behind his to wait. The other side of the pump was free, but Mason didn't really pay attention since he knew how tight it was to move a long truck around in Buddy's lot. When a second truck pulled in and hemmed him in from the front, though, they had Mason's attention.

A man got out of the front truck, a white GMC Sierra like you'd see on any construction site. Because the truck was facing him, there was no license plate.

Mason glanced at the truck behind him. It turned on its

brights. The driver's door opened, then the passenger side, letting out the blare of music, but no one got out.

Mason put his back to the pump and kept squeezing the handle to keep the gas flowing.

The man who got out of the front truck had a Tigers ball cap on with the old English D. He was bundled against the cold in a canvas coat with a hooded sweatshirt underneath, and thick yellow leather work gloves, one of which held a Busch Light tall boy.

"Almost done?" English D said.

"Soon," said Mason.

The man nodded, threw his head back and drained the can before tossing it in the garbage can by the pump. He reached into his pocket, pulled out another one, and peeled off a glove to crack it.

"You coming from the Cider Mill site?"

Mason stared for a moment, then nodded.

"Lot of work there." It was more a statement.

"There is."

"They hiring?"

The pump kept clicking. "Check with Warhelm's foreman."

The man smirked, took another drink. "That's too bad. Red doesn't care for me much."

"Hard to believe."

The man pointed around his tall boy. "Your clothes aren't very dirty for someone working on a site."

Mason smiled. "Yours are for someone who wasn't."

English D pointed around the tall boy. "You're one of the lawyers, aren't ya?"

The pump clicked off. Mason held it for a moment longer, decided against using it for anything other than filling his tank, and replaced it on the pump.

"Yeah, you are," English D said, taking another drink. "Seen your picture on my phone. Helping that murderer."

Mason pointed. "I need you to move your truck."

"Know who can't move? My cousin."

Mason stood there, silent.

English D went on, waving the can. "She's laid up, pins in her leg, all suspended from a harness in one of those contraptions so that she can't even get out of bed to pee. Said she probably won't walk right for a year and even then she won't be able to stay on her feet for a whole shift. Meanwhile, the hospital is running the meter, charging her every day to wipe her ass. The murderer going to take care of that?"

"I'm sorry to hear about your cousin," said Mason. He jerked a thumb over his shoulder. "You can fight your friends for the pump now."

Right on cue, the music shifted, and Kid Rock let loose with a Bawitdaba from the speakers of the second truck.

English D shook his head. "Not going to fight them."

The boys behind him got out of their truck. One wore a Yankees cap and had the faintest hint of green around one eye.

Mason smiled. "Wow. Did a crane fall on you or something?"

Yankee Boy glanced at his buddy on the other side of the truck, then scowled.

One thing about being on a worksite from the time you were young, you get a sense of when people are spiraling up into it, whether it's yelling at the foreman, snapping on a co-worker who's pushing a joke too far, or deciding it's just time to get even, say, after you and your buddy's got your ass whooped, and you later find a member of the crew that did the whooping out pumping gas alone.

So Mason was ready when he turned back to English D to find a punch already on its way. Mason jerked his head back, caught English D's hand by the wrist, pulled him forward, then grabbed the back of his head and slammed his face against the side of his truck.

Then he held it there.

The man yelped, then tried to pull back his head. Mason kept the man's face pressed against the truck and checked on Yankee Boy and his friend, who'd stopped, uncertain.

"Buddy installed cameras, you know," said Mason. He ignored English D struggling to pull his head back and focused on the other two.

They stopped, looked around.

"There, above the pump," said Mason. "And there, at the door."

English D struggled. Mason pushed. English D yelped.

"I'm sorry about his cousin, and I'm sorry about your ass-beating, but I'm just filling my tank here."

English D kicked at Mason's leg, but he had no leverage, what with his face smushed against the truck. Mason lifted his leg out of the way, then stomped on English D's other foot with a boot heel.

English D cried out.

"Why don't you boys move your truck?" Mason said. "Then I'll let your friend go, and we can all get back to work."

They hesitated.

Mason pushed.

"Gah!" said English D. "Do it."

Yankee Boy and Driver got back in their truck.

Mason gestured to shoo. The truck backed up. Once it did, Mason let go of English D, who'd been pushing up so hard that he tumbled back. He put a hand on his cheek, jumped into his truck, and peeled out.

Mason waited, watching them go. Then he checked the side

of his truck and was disappointed to see he'd put a dent in it. He sighed, climbed in, and put his truck into drive, anxious to get to The Loon.

There was an explosive pop, and he instinctively ducked, looking for a shooter. Instead, when his head went level with the dash, he saw the low-pressure lights for his two rear tires.

He swore, got out and checked. They were both flat. A couple of feet behind them, he found three triangular pieces of metal, the kind where there was always a point sticking up no matter what.

It appeared he hadn't won after all.

Mason was halfway to his spare when he realized the obvious problem. He only had one.

He pulled out his phone and looked up the number for Tate's Garage.

~

KYLE STEWART WATCHED it all unfold from the McDonald's parking lot across the street. It hadn't been hard to goad the guys, to needle the one's wounded pride and to inflame the other's anger and to console them all with a twelve of tall boys.

It hadn't gone how Kyle had hoped. He'd hoped there'd be a fight and that Mason Pierce would clean house on these half-drunk buffoons.

Right on camera. Which would create something that the State Bar would be very interested in and give them leverage when they needed it.

Pierce hadn't taken the bait though, and Kyle would be hard pressed to spin what Pierce had just done into an assault. But Rome wasn't built in a day, and neither were Kyle's plans. At least one of them had remembered to use the caltrops, the novelty item he'd given them that had been used to disable cavalry horses and combat Jeeps for centuries.

Two flat tires were infuriating enough to evoke a tantrum in many people. Pierce appeared to be handling it, which didn't worry Kyle either.

Most people could handle the first thing.

30

"Sorry I missed you last night," Mason said over the phone the next morning.

"Sorry I couldn't wait," said Cameron. "I was beat."

"It's just as well then. I didn't get there for another forty-five minutes after you left."

"You still came?"

"Old tradition. Last one there buys."

"Ah. How's the truck?"

"It was just the tires. Tate's will have new ones on them later today."

"Bad luck."

"Something like that." He thought about telling her about the scuffle but instead said, "How's the setup there?"

"This Warhelm guy came through. I expected a small warehouse, but an airplane hangar is even better."

"Dr. Thomas! Dr. Thomas!" a voice yelled in the background.

Mason smiled. "Is that Wasmeuller?"

"I think it's a good thing the court imposed the special master, Mason. First load's here. I'll call you later today."

"Thanks. And sorry to have left you with Austin and the Stones."

Cameron laughed. "Don't apologize. They were very entertaining. Especially Austin."

"He does like to talk."

"I didn't mind. I heard some stories I'm sure I wouldn't have heard otherwise."

"Dr. Thomas!" shouted Barry Wasmeuller again.

"See you this afternoon," said Cameron, and hung up.

As soon as he did, Peter stuck his head into Mason's office.

"How are you doing?" he asked.

Mason raised an eyebrow. "Excuse me?"

"Don't feel special; I've been designated as your firm mentor. It means that I have to tell Mother Burns that I've checked in with you."

"Oh, everything's fine, Peter, thanks."

"Melody got you all signed up for our health insurance and those things?"

"A few weeks ago, yes."

"You got your signing bonus?"

"I did, thanks."

"Don't thank me, thank the Ponzi scheme of billable hours that feeds our existence. Did Melody tell you about all of our internal programs?"

"Internal programs?"

"Like the clothing allowance."

"You did actually, yes."

"And the down payment program?"

Mason shook his head. "I don't remember that one."

Peter leaned back. "Mother Burns knows how hard it can be to put together a down payment on a house, especially with student loans being what they are these days. We'll match what you put toward your first down payment with an interest-free loan."

"Doesn't that still count as a loan when the bank's figuring out your debt?"

"If a less sophisticated firm had developed the program, maybe. Not the way Mother Burns does it."

Mason didn't like the sound of that at all, but he said, "I'm not in the market right now, but I'll keep it in mind."

"Mother Burns likes its attorneys to put down roots in the community. Helps with business and stability for the firm."

"Good."

"I'm just saying, that option is there if you want to get started on a house here."

"Like I said, I'm all set right now, Peter, but I'll remember it."

Peter stared, then waved, "All right. My mandated duty is done. How's the site management going?"

Mason's phone buzzed.

"That's Cameron now," he said.

Peter gave the okay sign, then waved, and left.

"You need to get out here," she said.

"Already?"

"Already. I think I know why the patio collapsed."

"What was it?" said Mason.

"I'm acting very casual right now walking over to the coffee station. When you get here, meet me there." She hung up.

Mason stared at his phone, got up, and walked out.

~

NORTHLAKE MUNICIPAL AIRPORT was one of those small airfields you find in rural areas, designed for crop dusters, recreational planes, and private aircraft for rich folks looking to get away. There were only seven hangars at NMA. Two belonged to John

Warhelm, and one of those had been cleared, for a fee, to house the wreckage of the Stone Street Cider Mill patio.

The hangar was filled with men and equipment. Mason detoured around a front-end loader that was carefully dumping a load of concrete into a large, taped square and made his way to the very back of the terminal where he found a table with three tall, brown plastic coffee dispensers. He filled a foam cardboard cup, capped it, and made his way over to where Cameron Thomas stood, sipping her own coffee, staring at the equipment.

She nodded to him. She started to speak, but when she had to shout her hello, she stopped and pulled out her phone. Mason got a text a moment later.

Grid B-2. Tell me what you see.

Mason raised an eyebrow.

Don't want to prejudice you.

Mason nodded.

But make a show of looking at row A first.

Mason nodded again and headed over.

He saw that there was a huge grid marked out on the floor with duct tape and that each square was labelled with a letter and a number.

The first row, Row A on the grid, apparently, looked to be mostly metal roof panels. It made sense; the roof would have been on top and would have been pulled off first before the cranes could get to the wreckage beneath. Mason took his time walking down the row, stopping to look at each numbered square, taking the occasional picture with his phone.

When he got to Row B, the wreckage turned to concrete. He could see parts of what had been the stone patio floor and the stone railing, much of it still in large pieces. When he got to B-2, it took him a moment before he understood what he was seeing.

It was the fragments of a concrete pier that had been used to support the patio on the shoreline below. It was split longways in several sections, and some of those sections were split and crumbled and broken again.

Mason was looking at a pier failure.

He stared at it for a little bit, but he didn't take a picture, and he didn't stare for long. Instead, he moved down the rest of row B, which included another pier that was mostly intact. By the time he was done, they'd brought in a few squares of material on row C, so he strolled past that, which mostly looked to be concrete flooring and a steel support beam. When he saw the state's expert, Wasmeuller, paying attention to him, Mason made a show of taking pictures of the steel beam from several angles. Then Mason pocketed his phone, went back to the coffee station to re-fill his cup, and wandered back over to the side where Cameron Thomas stood, watching.

"Is that our source of the failure?" said Mason behind his cup.

"Looks like it to me," said Cameron, doing the same.

"Which pier is it?"

"Right-front corner as you're looking at the lake. What did you notice?"

"Besides the failure?"

Cameron Thomas nodded.

"Is there something I should see?"

Cameron sipped, then said, "Something you *don't* see."

Mason Pierce frowned, then headed back to the grid.

He went to the steel beam in row C he'd taken pictures of before and stood next to Barry Wasmeuller, who was now scraping the beam for samples, taking pictures, and measuring while muttering words like "torsion" and "flex." Mason made a point of watching him until Wasmeuller was looking over his shoulder and hiding his notebook as he wrote. Mason stood a while longer, then walked back to the B-row, and wandered past the fragments of the failed pier, with its jagged, multiple breaks, including the ones that ran longwise right down the middle.

He'd like to think he'd have noticed it on his own, but Cameron's hint made it easy. He didn't even pause at the pier as he walked back to Cameron.

"There's no rebar in the failed pier," he said.

Cameron nodded. "Not a lick."

"That would let the column shift."

"Sure would. Especially after more than twenty years."

"I'm surprised it lasted that long."

"Me too."

Mason thought. "That doesn't get us all the way off the hook."

Cameron nodded again. "We still have to figure out why it collapsed."

"But it certainly gives us something to talk about. I'll find out who built it."

"And I'll dive into the engineering part of it, figuring out the forces that would cause the failure. But first I'm going to have some fun and distract Wasmeuller as much as I can."

Mason smiled. "He seems very focused on the beam."

Cameron laughed. "It was hard not to notice the large man hovering over it."

Mason shrugged. "It could have been faulty."

Cameron set down her cup. "Well, it seems you have some history to research, and I have a beam made of red herring steel to test."

"Pleasure, Cameron."

"Same, Mason."

As Mason walked to the hangar door, he heard Barry Wasmeuller squeak, "Well you'll just have to wait until *I'm* finished taking samples of the steel."

Mason smiled and left.

PART IV

31

Three weeks later, everyone involved in any aspect of any case involving the collapse of the patio of the Stone Street Cider Mill was gathered in Judge Roderick's courtroom. Prosecutor Astrid Olsen was there on the criminal case, Jerome Baggman and three other lawyers whose names Mason didn't catch were there representing the victims and victims' families on the civil cases, while Peter Freid and Mason were there to defend it all.

Judge Roderick listened from the bench as Jerome Baggman said, "This is an outrageous attempt to delay my clients' rightful recoveries, Your Honor!"

Judge Roderick looked amused. "Seems like you're skipping a few steps there, Mr. Baggman."

"Steps I can only take when we try our case against Mr. Warren and his LLC."

Judge Roderick shook his head. "You can't stop the defense from bringing other responsible parties into the civil case, Mr. Baggman."

"I can when it's a defunct entity, Judge! Defense counsel is just trying to create a straw man to shift responsibility off of their client. They can't blame an old construction company for the collapse."

"That's exactly what we're allowed to do, Judge," said Peter Freid. "The Civil Rules allow us to designate Potentially Responsible Parties and have the jury decide if their negligence caused any part of plaintiffs' damages. That's what we're doing."

"How convenient," said Jerome Baggman.

"I don't think the negligence of those companies was convenient at all," said Peter Freid. "For your clients or mine."

"You're just trying to shirk your responsibility to the families!"

Peter shrugged. "I'm allowing the jury to allocate responsibility according to the law."

Judge Roderick raised his hand. "Save it, counselors. You've got a year to fight about it in discovery. Defendant's proposed PRP designations are allowed, and you'll have ample opportunity to study it some more. The question that concerns me more is how we're going to handle this in the criminal cases. Ms. Olsen, what's the State's position?"

Astrid Olsen stood. "Your Honor, counsel's attempt to shift blame for the collapse to a defunct corporation should not be permitted by the Court. The manner in which a concrete pier was constructed isn't relevant to Mr. Hyde's actions, and those of his employees, the night of the collapse."

Judge Roderick nodded. "Mr. Freid, I've read your brief, but take me through the parties you're looking to identify again."

"Mason Pierce is running point on that, Judge," said Peter. "Do you mind if he addresses it?"

"Not at all. Let's hear it, Mr. Pierce."

Mason stood. "Your Honor, the Stone Street Cider Mill was originally built in 1923—"

"—You're blaming people from over a century ago?" said Jerome Baggman.

"Wait your turn, Mr. Baggman," said Judge Roderick.

"Sorry, Judge. Mr. Pierce's audacity is matched only by his height."

"Mr. Baggman."

Jerome Baggman raised a hand and sat back.

When Judge Roderick looked back at him, Mason continued. "The Stone Street Cider Mill was built back in 1923. Our client bought the Cider Mill in 2002 to turn into a distillery, restaurant, and bar open to the public. Because the building was so old, Mr. Warren hired a company that specializes in restoring historic buildings called Landmark Reconstruction."

Judge Roderick was writing. "What year was that?"

"2002-2003, Your Honor."

"Who built the patio?"

"Landmark Reconstruction was the general, Judge. But they were a company that specialized in restoring historic buildings—"

Judge Roderick looked up. "The Cider Mill is historic?"

"The stonework exterior was considered to be a classic design. And the...clientele in the 1920s and 1930s generated some historical interest."

"During Prohibition?"

"Yes."

"Would that clientele have come from Chicago and Detroit?"

"I wouldn't put rumors on the record in a hearing, Your Honor."

Jerome Baggman snorted.

Judge Roderick stared.

"Sorry, Judge," he said. "Allergies."

"We have Benadryl in the holding area, Mr. Baggman."

"I do believe they're under control now, Judge."

"Proceed, Mr. Pierce."

Mason checked his notes. "The general contractor, Landmark Reconstruction, was a downstate company. They hired a local business, Corwin Concrete, to pour the piers that supported the patio."

"Piers?"

"Think of a thick square column, Judge. In this case, it was made out of concrete with a stone facing on the outside that matched the stone exterior of the Cider Mill itself. Other contractors worked on the patio, but it's the support piers that we're concerned with."

"And why is that?"

"Because it is our belief that one of the support piers was improperly constructed and failed, causing the patio to collapse."

Jerome Baggman snorted again.

Judge Roderick rolled his head. "You'll also find that our holding area has an excellent air purification system, Mr. Baggman."

"Not necessary, Judge."

"You seem to be having trouble with our dust."

"I believe I'm on top of it now."

Judge Roderick turned back to Mason. "So your firm wants to name the general contractor, Landmark Reconstruction, and the sub, Corwin Concrete, as potentially responsible parties in the civil case?"

"Right."

"You know there's no such designation in a criminal case."

"That's correct, Your Honor, but we do intend to point to their negligent workmanship as the cause of the collapse."

Jerome Baggman coughed in a way that sounded very much like "convenient."

Judge Roderick let that one go. "Ms. Olsen, what is your response?"

While Jerome Baggman had been coughing and commenting, Astrid Olsen had been still, but now she said, "Judge, this case has nothing to do with a twenty-three-year-old construction project. It has to do with Mr. Warren's criminal conduct in the days and hours leading up to the biggest mass casualty event in Northlake's history."

"The case has to do with the collapse of a patio, Your Honor," said Mason. "And what caused it."

Astrid Olsen kept her focus on the judge. "Judge, this case will be hard enough to keep orderly as it is. Mr. Pierce should not be permitted to come in blasting finger guns in every direction except his client."

Judge Roderick rocked back in his chair. "I think our metal detectors will keep out any inappropriate guns, Ms. Olsen. And Mr. Pierce certainly is allowed to show that the patio collapsed as a result of something other than his client's conduct. Of course, it has to have been completely separate from his client's conduct in order to exonerate him, but there you go."

When Jerome Baggman started to speak again, Judge Roderick raised his hand and said, "I've heard enough. If you want to keep the evidence out, Ms. Olsen, you can file a motion, but based on what I've heard today, it's coming in. As to the civil case, defendant's notice to designate potentially responsible parties is allowed, and plaintiff's motion to strike the notice is denied. Mr. Baggman, you can join those potential parties into the case if you want or try them in abstentia. Which is it?"

"We just learned about them from Mr. Pierce's motion, Judge, so I don't know that we've decided yet. I think we'll have to do a little checking of our own."

"All right. You know the response time. Follow it."

"Will do, Judge." Jerome Baggman talked to the judge but was staring at Mason as he spoke.

"It's been a delight," said Judge Roderick, and they were dismissed.

As Mason gathered his things, Astrid Olsen came over. "Are we really going to go through this song and dance with the old companies?"

Mason shrugged. "That's up to you, Atti. Are you still going to bring this case?"

Astrid Olsen raised her chin. "The voters have made their opinion clear. Someone has to pay for this tragedy."

Mason pointed to where Jerome Baggman was talking up another lawyer. "Your civil shadow seems to be handling the *pay* part."

"There are greater obligations than money, Mason."

Mason nodded. "Yes, there are. And that means that if you continue with this, we'll be putting on evidence regarding the true source of the collapse."

"The source is your client's greed and negligence."

"I guess we'll see."

Astrid Olsen looked up at him, her ice-blue eyes a little icier. "Then let's talk to Holly about the schedule."

They went over to where Holly Gorman was typing at her station behind the second rail.

"We need to confirm our expert disclosure dates in the criminal case on the construction issues, Holly," said Astrid.

As she stared at the screen and hit keys, Holly said, "The Judge thinks it's a crap defense."

She whirled to Mason, eyes wide behind her leopard-print glasses. "Shoot."

Mason smiled. "It gets easier, Holly."

Holly looked up. "I hope so."

After they set their expert deadlines, Mason said, "Should I tell Peter to expect an offer?"

Astrid stared at him for a moment, then looked away. "Not that you're going to like."

Mason waited.

"I have to attach death to the charge. And I can't reduce the number of counts."

Mason nodded. "That's going to be a problem then."

"The sentence after he's found guilty will be worse."

"If you can show he did something, sure."

"I will." She made a point of looking at the defense table. "Besides, I don't think your client's going to hold up that long."

Before he could stop himself, Mason looked back to see Hyde Warren twisting a piece of paper into a long tube and shredding the end.

"He's better off than he'd be in prison," he said.

Astrid Olsen shrugged. "We'll see."

Then she gathered her things and left.

Mason went over to Hyde.

"So are they going to dismiss the case?" Hyde asked.

"No, Hyde."

"But it's not my fault! The judge said he was letting evidence in that the construction company screwed up the pier!"

"He's just going to let us present the evidence, Hyde. A jury still has to decide fault."

"It's not mine!"

"That's what we're trying to show."

Mason looked down at the table, now covered with tiny specks of shredded paper. "Let's get going, Hyde," he said, and began sweeping the specks into his hand.

Hyde noticed the paper flecks and winced. "Sorry."

"No worries," said Mason and lightly clapped the paper into a garbage can.

"Bravo, Big Boy," said a voice behind him.

Mason turned as Jerome Baggman continued. "I knew Pete would be pulling out all the stops on this one, but digging up a three-decade old construction job? That's some legal excavation right there."

"Can I go now?" said Hyde Warren.

"Go ahead, Hyde," said Mason. "I'll call you."

As Hyde Warren scurried out of court, Jerome Baggman watched him go like a hungry hawk, before turning back on Mason. "But Lord Above, who knew he'd enlist a bulldozer with a law license. Where'd you play ball?"

Mason picked up his file. "I didn't."

"C'mon now, don't be modest; a man your size had to have played ball."

"No, Mr. Baggman, I didn't."

"Well that's a damn shame and a waste besides. And it's Jerry." Jerome Baggman extended his hand. Mason took it.

"Oh, hey, ow!" said Jerome Baggman. "No need to squeeze there, Big Boy."

Mason had done no such thing.

Baggman removed his hand and shook it. "That's quite a grip there. Grew up squeezing a shovel instead of a pen, then?"

Mason stared. "Something like that."

Baggman nodded. "So you know your way around a worksite?"

Mason shrugged. "Just finding my way around a courtroom, Mr. Baggman."

"Oh, it seems to me that you've found that, Big Boy. Naming defunct construction companies and subcontractors who are just minding their own business, not knowing that you're accusing them of murder thirty years after they were anywhere near the same Cider Mill that your client walks into every day? I think you've found your way just fine."

Mason decided this conversation wasn't going anywhere and made to leave.

Jerome Baggman put his hand on Mason's arm.

"You're local, am I right? So you probably know which

companies are still around, still employing folks? And which ones can be blamed without bothering a local, northern soul."

"The permits and the contracts say what they say, Mr. Baggman. Not me."

"Do they now? Well, we're still waiting on that discovery. Your boss going to give it to me?"

"I'm sure he will."

"Yes, yes, I'm sure ol' Pete is just banging away at those documents every night. Or at something anyway." Jerome Baggman grinned in a way that sharpened his eyes. "I look forward to working with you on this one, Big Boy."

"We'll talk soon, Jerome."

"Friends call me Jerry."

Mason's phone buzzed. He wouldn't normally check it in court, but now seemed like a good time.

He read the text from his dad. *Your place open? I need to borrow your multi-meter.*

"I'm sorry, Jerome. I have to go."

Mason texted his dad that he'd meet him there and left.

32

A lot of people's connections to gravel roads come through romanticized country songs describing a return home or heading to the singer's favorite fishing hole. That can be true enough in the summertime, or even in the fall, but in late winter, when the ice melts, they can become a treacherous obstacle course of jagged potholes and ruts of mud that will guide you right into the deepest one.

Jackson Pierce found himself in just such a predicament. He'd been on his way to his son's house and had just turned off the paved state road onto the gravel township road when he banged into a pothole that hadn't been there when the road had been covered in snow for the last four months.

He cursed and he slammed on his brakes and turned into the skid, but some damn computer in his damn truck thought it knew better and pumped the brakes for him so that he skidded into the snowbank of plowed snow that was too high to have melted but now had a nice hard outer ice coating that smashed his right front headlight.

Mason's road was usually pretty quiet, and it was just then, for which Jackson was grateful. Once he was stopped, he turned off the truck, caught his breath, then climbed out to survey the damage.

That process, climbing out and going around to the right front side, took far longer than Jackson Pierce would admit to, but he managed, pulling his canes off of the front passenger seat, then using them for a base before he hopped down. The truck was too high really for his current state, but he'd be damned if he was going to sell it, just like he'd be damned if he asked for a ride. And if you were going to drive yourself, Jackson Pierce knew that dealing with flats and hazards was the price you just had to pay.

Jackson had been using the canes for some years now, so knew he had to keep the canes close to his sides, straight up and down, so that they didn't shoot out sideways and send him ass first into the snow. The road wasn't hard to navigate because the snow was packed firm, but when he came around to the right side, it was deeper and one look told him that while the snow would hold his canes, he'd never be able to lift his feet high enough to shuffle through it.

Jackson Pierce didn't swear out loud, but he mentally cursed all construction scaffolds straight to hell, a message he sent several times a day. He was going to have to get the right front bumper out of the snowbank, and he was going to have to change the right front tire, and he was going to have to do it in that order.

He caned his way back around to the driver's side door and hauled himself in, fairly easily because he still had full use of his massively strong shoulders and arms, for which he was thankful. He then spent the next fifteen minutes rocking the truck back and forth, gunning it in low gear and reverse, changing the wheel angle, before getting out again to see how he was doing.

That gave him a thought, because Jackson Pierce was a practical man who'd spent his life finding practical solutions. He couldn't walk through the snow, but he could drop into it from above, so he got back in his truck, scooted across to the passenger side, opened the door, and dropped down, canes and all. The snow sank to the tops of his loosely laced work boots, but now he could see that the underside of his bumper was hung up on a ridge of ice in the larger snowbank where the plow had thrown the snow.

Jackson grinned, tossed one cane onto the passenger seat, got down on one knee while holding onto the running board, and dug out the underside of his bumper with the straight handle of his other cane, using it like an ice pick to knock it away piece by piece.

It took a while and Jackson broke a sweat, which anyone who's lived up north will tell you is a bad idea when you're working in the cold, but he kept chipping and he kept grinning as he broke away the nasty frozen stuff that had reached out to grab his truck.

When he saw space between the bank and the bumper, he reversed his cane, pushed himself back up, and pulled himself back into the cab. Three revs of the engine, back-forward-back, and he was free. He told the snowbank both that it couldn't hold Jackson Pierce and that it could go fully and completely impregnate itself, then caught his breath for a moment before he started his next job of changing the tire.

That made him realize his next problem, which you've probably already foreseen but which he hadn't thought of because, in fairness to Jackson, he'd been preoccupied with chipping his truck out of an ice bank with a cane.

His spare was mounted under the truck.

It had been some time since he'd had to change a tire, so he'd forgotten that you had to unwind it from underneath instead of just pulling it out of the bed. He should have remembered because the last time he'd done it had been on this very same road. Mason's mom had been diagnosed then, and it wasn't good, and she'd become obsessed with leaving the old cottage to Mason. They'd argued on the way—him telling her that they could both leave it to Mason in thirty years, her saying his head was in the sand; him snapping back that she had to think positive—and sure enough, he'd hit a pothole and flattened the tire.

But that had been before the scaffold, and his legs, had failed him. He'd changed the tire easy that day, quick enough that his wife was able to pick things right back up when he was done—that she wasn't being negative, she was being realistic, and the sooner he was too, the better off they'd all be.

Jackson Pierce pushed away all those things that had nothing to do with getting him off this icy road and climbed back out of the truck.

He pulled the jack and tools out from under the seat, keyed open the little hole next to his license plate, then juggled the canes so he could assemble the irons to lower the spare. That proved tricky—it would have been easier if he could kneel and turn the irons with both hands, but he couldn't and still hold his balance—so he bent double, canes in the crotch of both shoulders, and spun the irons 'til the spare hit the ground.

Now you may have noticed that during all the time that Jackson Pierce had spent freeing his truck so far, not another car had passed. That didn't surprise him. This particular section of road only served the eight houses on the bluff, including Mason's, and at least half of those weren't occupied in the winter. Last he'd heard, there were a couple of other diehards like Mason, but a cold winter day with wind screaming off the Big Lake was plenty reason to stay inside, so Jackson wasn't surprised that no one passed and, more importantly, he didn't think to take any measures to warn anyone that he was there, other than his hazards, which weren't facing traffic since his truck was turned sideways from revving himself out of the snowbank.

Instead, Jackson was focused on pulling the spare tire out from under the truck bed with the handle of one cane, and on lining the jack up with the frame, which he had to get down on his hands and knees to do in order to keep his balance. That's when he realized that positioning the jack was one thing, and accomplished easily enough, but turning the tire iron to raise it was going to be something else entirely.

Jackson Pierce stared for a good bit, added winding a jack to his list of things that could go self-fornicate, then resigned himself to sitting ass deep in the snow, legs extended in front of him under the truck, so that he could keep his balance as he wound the jack.

He cackled once when the jack grabbed the right spot on the frame, cackled again as the truck began to lift, and crowed that a motherless whore of a pencil pushing jack designer wasn't going to keep Jackson Pierce from changing his own goddam tire, canes or not.

He was still like that, sitting flat on his butt between the truck and the snowbank, canes beside him, legs extended, when the car flew round the curve, blared its horn, and slammed its brakes into a sideways skid right at him.

Jackson Pierce had time for one more curse.

33

Kyle Stewart knew that breaking into a house was always a gamble. Everyone knew that it shouldn't be occupied when you do it, but owners can return unexpectedly, friends can drop in for a surprise visit, or a mom could be worried that junior wasn't eating enough. Add to that nosy neighbors, hidden alarm systems, and sleeping dogs, and you find that even an empty house carries risk. Further, even if you were in and out clean, you had to be careful not to leave anything behind since a phone, a tool, a fingerprint, any of those, could point back to you and send you off to Jackson State Penitentiary.

Kyle Stewart supposed that if he were caught up here, he'd be sent to the Central Michigan facility, or worse, to Baraga Maximum Correctional in the Upper Peninsula, but the end result would be the same and one that he wasn't interested in. That's why he'd been so careful to manage the downside risk on this particular break-in.

The victim lived alone.

The victim worked long hours, and simple surveillance had revealed that he was regular as a cuckoo clock—out the door at

5:45 a.m. and rarely home before 8:00 p.m., and usually later now that he was busy.

No dog.

No neighbors to speak of. He supposed a boat could conceivably see the house but, from this height above the lake, the boater would need binoculars and have to be looking right at it. Kyle had checked three times now, and he couldn't see the neighboring houses through the bare trees, which wasn't a surprise since it was a quarter of a mile in each direction and one of those was a vacation rental that wasn't occupied right now.

All that led Kyle Stewart to conclude that a break-in was worth the risk and that the middle of the afternoon was the best time to do it.

Because there was so little traffic on the road, Kyle Stewart knew that if a neighbor saw a strange car, they might just remember it, so he'd purchased a food delivery app magnet to slap on the side of his car, which worked just as good as an invisibility cloak and was cheaper besides.

That left the house itself, which posed absolutely no challenge to him. It was a rickety little cottage, at least seventy years old, with no security other than a deadbolt on the door and the surrounding woods, neither of which created an obstacle of any consequence.

No, Kyle Stewart knew that, as far as break-ins went, this was as low risk as it got, like making a straight bet on a Big Ten football team against some small I-AA school. Sure, Michigan might blow it every once in a while against an Appalachian State, but you could usually count on the payout.

What made this break-in even more attractive was that, while the risk was low, the potential reward was Kentucky Derby longshot high. Jerome Baggman's patio cases were worth seven figures at least and probably eight, especially if that owner got sent off to jail first. Kyle Stewart worked on a percentage, a small but significant percentage, of the recovery, which would clear up an awful lot of sportsbook accounts and leave money to make money afterwards. While that sort of arrangement was frowned upon by the State Bar Association and so not committed to writing, Kyle knew that Jerome Baggman was as good as his word—so long as Kyle delivered the goods.

So, with the odds of success stacked in his favor and the potential reward measured in stacks of cash, Kyle Stewart broke into Mason Pierce's house right there in the middle of the afternoon.

No doorbell camera, no alarm, just a deadbolt that was soon turned. Kyle Stewart moved from room to room, which didn't take long since it was a just a little two-bedroom, one-bath with a great room, a galley kitchen, and a screened-in porch that ran the length of the back with a view of the lake. The inside was neater than the outside would indicate, which made his job that much easier.

It wasn't long before Kyle Stewart had tapped into the wi-Fi to intercept what went through it and placed two listening devices which, given how small the house was, would catch just about everything that was said. He was going to go then but realized this setup allowed for a bonus device, and soon he had a small camera hidden in the second bedroom which, it looked to Kyle, functioned as an office. The lack of clutter made hiding the camera a little trickier, but not much, and he soon had the camera placed so that it had a view of whatever was on Mason Pierce's desk, including his computer monitor.

The timer in his head was sounding now, and while Kyle's instincts were sometimes wrong on the over/under, they were never wrong about when it was time to go. He took a last look around for signs of his presence; found none. The wi-Fi he used would just look like a neighbor had added it since it was named with the rental's address. With that, Kyle Stewart left, even taking the time to re-lock the front door deadbolt on the way out.

Jerome Baggman had a reputation as a good legal mind and a great performer, but even more, he was a meticulous planner who left nothing to chance. Now, assuming Pierce worked at home, which almost all attorneys did, Baggman, through Stewart, would get advance warning on what Pierce knew about the case. If they were lucky, they might even uncover something personal that they could work with. And every morsel of information put Kyle Stewart that much closer to his payday.

Kyle Stewart hopped into his car and backed out the two-track driveway to the gravel road. As he started down the sloppy, snowy road, he checked his phone to see if the Wi-Fi monitoring was active. There was a satisfying "ping" as his phone indicated that all was as it should be, and Kyle Stewart grinned before he tossed the phone on the passenger seat and looked up to put both hands on the wheel.

A GMC pickup was ass-out in the road, blocking most of it with its oversized bed. Kyle Stewart cursed, slammed on the brakes and swerved, but the tail end of his SUV broadsided the back of the truck's bed, slamming it back into the snowbank on the far side.

Kyle Stewart cursed again as his car skidded to a stop just beyond the truck. He stayed in his car, looking in the rearview.

The truck was now pressed against the snowbank. Its hazards were blinking.

Kyle didn't see anybody.

He cursed careless hicks who left broken-down trucks on roads, then took off before the owner returned.

He cursed again when he realized he wouldn't be watching any basketball that night.

He had a car to dispose of.

34

Mason was driving home to meet his dad when his phone buzzed. It was Cameron Thomas.

"How'd the hearing go today?" she asked.

"The judge allowed us to identify Landmark Reconstruction and Corwin Concrete in the civil case."

"Was that in doubt?"

"Not really. The prosecutor's going to give us asses and elbows in the criminal case, but it'll come in."

"Good. That's why I'm calling."

Mason frowned. "Is there a problem?"

"No. Yes. Well, maybe."

"Ah."

"No, there isn't a problem because my theory still holds—there was no rebar in the support pier and that caused the collapse."

"Okay."

"Yes, there's a problem because I've just figured out that the support pier might have been tampered with."

"Tampered with? Like someone's been messing with your investigation?"

"No. Like someone took a jackhammer to the pier."

"What?" Mason was so focused on understanding what Cameron was saying that he nearly missed his gravel road. He hit the brakes and slid to make the turn. A curse slipped out as the cab of his truck fishtailed.

"I know," said Cameron.

"No, it wasn't that; I just almost missed my street. How can you tell it was a jackhammer?"

"You've used one?"

"Sure."

"You know when you split concrete, you leave marks before the concrete actually splits?"

"Right."

"Those are here."

"How many?"

"Enough to be pretty sure that's what I'm looking at."

Mason thought about what it took for him to wield the big two-handed jackhammer to take out a patio or an old seawall. "That would be awfully hard to do."

"What's that?"

"Lift a big jackhammer up and drive it parallel into a standing support pier."

"True. But there's no reason that a person couldn't have used a handheld, or even a hammer and chisel, I suppose, but that would be slow work."

"Fair. I was just thinking about what I'd used before."

"There are plenty of tools that'll go straight into a pier."

"Did someone do that?"

"It looks like it to me."

"How so?"

"You know how the piers are square forms filled with concrete with a decorative stone exterior on the outside?"

"Yes."

"The marks are in the outer stone. It looks like it split the mortar and the seams in places."

"Couldn't the collapse have done that?"

"It's possible. But it seems pretty even. And the marks are right next to the seams, like the hammer blade was slipping into the weak spot."

Mason drove, thinking.

"How sure are you?" he said.

"I want to test some more. But pretty sure."

"That leaves another question."

"Seems like more than one."

"True. But the biggest one for me is why would—*Holy shit!*"

"Mason! Are you okay?"

"Call you back, Cameron. Bye!"

Mason slammed on his brakes, flung open the door, and ran to his father's truck.

LATER, Mason knew that it had only taken him seconds to get to his father's truck, but at the time he felt like he was caught in a slow scan of the whole scene. The hazards blinking on the truck. The big dent on the left rear driver's side of the bed that hadn't been there before. The empty driver's seat.

It took Mason a moment to notice that the truck was jammed into the snowbank and a moment more to see the tire iron loose at his feet.

Mason ran around to the front of the truck.

And saw one of his father's canes.

"Dad!"

"About time," came a voice from under the truck. "I'm freezing my ass off."

Mason walked around the far corner. "Dad?"

Jackson Pierce was jammed between the front tire and the snowbank. He looked up, his long hair hanging down over his eyes. "I thought you were coming right home?"

"Are you all right?"

"I told you, I'm freezing my ass off!"

"I mean, are you hurt?"

"Everything hurts, but no more than usual." Jackson Pierce looked up through hair lank with snow. "Actually, I take that back, I'm numb."

Mason's heart sank. "Your spine?"

"No, not my spine, you moron. I'm lying in snow!"

"I'm going to call 911—"

"—The hell you are. Move this truck and help me get up."

"Hang on."

Mason went around to the back to get a better look. From there, he could see that the bed of the truck had swung around and plowed up a small wall of snow that had trapped his dad between the truck tire, the small wall of snow, and the bigger snowbank. He saw small trenches on top of the snow that he figured were from his dad's other cane. If he had full use of his legs, his dad probably would've been able to force his way out. Since he didn't...

"Let me move the truck," said Mason.

"That's what I said!"

It took five minutes to dig out around his dad and get the truck moved without crushing him, and another five more to get him into the cab and convince him to stay there while Mason went about changing the tire. Jackson Pierce rolled down his window and yelled instructions for five minutes before Mason suggested he roll it back up and use all that hot air to get warm.

They were engaged in this free exchange of ideas when a white SUV rolled up. Mason straightened from where he was hunched over the jack while Jackson, after a look of defiance at Mason, rolled down the window.

A blond woman in a ski jacket stepped out of the car.

"Cameron?" said Mason. "What are you doing here?"

"When a friend says, 'Holy shit' and hangs up on you when he's driving, I take an interest."

Mason came around the truck as she walked over. Before she got there, Jackson Pierce opened his door and climbed out. Mason noted that he left his canes in the cab and stood there, holding the door for support.

"How'd you know where to go?" said Mason.

"You said you almost missed your street."

Mason nodded. "Cameron Thomas, Jackson Pierce."

There was a tricky moment where Jackson had to let go of the door to shake Cameron's hand, but his dad's pride and the fact that he didn't need to walk to do it held him upright.

"Your hand's freezing," said Cameron.

"Been working on the truck for a bit," Jackson Pierce said.

She eyed him up and down. "You're soaked."

Jackson Pierce shrugged. "It's a nice day. Seemed a shame to stay inside."

Cameron craned her head around the truck, then said to Mason, "You going to take all day to change that thing?"

Mason opened his mouth, closed it, then said, "Apparently."

"How about some coffee?" she said to Jackson Pierce.

Jackson gripped the door and shook his head. "I don't want to go while he's—"

"—We're not leaving him unsupervised," said Cameron. "I've got a thermos in my car."

Jackson Pierce glanced into his cab at the canes that were lying there like a nest of snakes. Then he straightened, grabbed one, and said, "Sure."

"Mind if I take your arm?" Cameron said. "Almost went flat on my ass when I got out."

Jackson Pierce looked down at her through that lank, snow-matted hair, and shook his head. "I have spine damage, not brain damage."

Cameron Thomas took his other arm in both hands, supporting them both. "Well, you're standing out here soaking wet when there's coffee in the warm car over there, so I'm not convinced."

Jackson Pierce stared, then chuckled. "I suppose you're right."

The two of them made their way to Cameron's car, striking up a conversation about how much longer it took this generation to change a flat on the way. After she saw Jackson to the passenger side, Cameron Thomas said, "Get a move on, Pierce. We have a lot to talk about."

35

Not long after that, Mason Pierce unlocked his front door and led his dad and Cameron Thomas into his place. He'd left it in moderately good shape and, if it wasn't spotless, it wasn't embarrassing either.

His dad, on the other hand, was doing his best to be obstinate. Mason had front stairs, so Jackson was forced to break out both canes, but Cameron seemed to have found his sense of humor and, if most of that was directed at Mason, it at least got his dad into the house without a scene.

Showering and changing clothes was another matter though. Jackson Pierce's clothes were soaked through, and though he said he was fine, he was shivering despite Cameron's coffee. Finally, after shaming him for dripping all over everything, Mason convinced him to shower and change.

Mason found him some clothes that would fit, left them on his bed, and left his dad to it before going back to see Cameron, who'd found the coffee and was making a pot.

"Thanks."

She waved him off. "He okay?"

"Seems to be."

"He said he worked construction?"

Mason nodded. "Foundations and masonry mostly."

"Accident?"

"Scaffolding collapse a few years back."

"Seems pretty independent."

"That's an understatement."

"Is he improving?"

"That's as good as it's going to get."

"That's tough."

Mason nodded. "On his pride as much as anything."

Cameron Thomas smiled. "I got that impression."

The two sat at the kitchen table as the coffee percolated in the background.

"So we were talking about support piers," said Mason.

"We were," said Cameron. "Someone took a jackhammer to the one that collapsed."

"And you're sure?"

She opened her phone, scrolled, handed it to him.

Mason saw the wreckage of the pier lying on the floor of the airport hangar.

"See the marks there, and there?" said Cameron, pointing.

Mason nodded. "Those are pretty distinct."

"And see the fracture here?"

Mason nodded.

"See this center area here looks like collapse, there's crumbling and breakage. But right above and right below it, you have these clean break lines and marks from the hammer before it slipped into the seam."

Mason stood, grabbed two mugs, and poured coffee as he said, "All right, I'm convinced, someone jack-hammered cracks into the pier."

Cameron nodded. "That's what I thought too."

Mason handed her a cup. "So someone tampered with the pier. To bring it down, maybe?"

Cameron shook her head. "I don't know, Mason. No one would be stupid enough to jackhammer out a support pier that was supporting tons of stone over their head, would they?"

Mason warmed to the idea. "Maybe they just weakened it. They take a handheld jackhammer and split the seam in the stone facing, then split a seam along the concrete, not enough to bring it down, but enough to get it started so that the pier will collapse eventually."

"Mason, a collapse like that would take months if you think you weakened it enough for weight and slippage to do it. Years if you were just waiting for water and ice to do the job." She shook her head. "It doesn't make any sense."

Mason and Cameron sat there, staring at the picture on Cameron's phone. The more he stared at it, the more Mason was convinced that Cameron was right—the marks were made from a jackhammer and that the jackhammer had caused a split at the bottom of the support pier.

"It was a rescue site, you know," Cameron said finally. "They might have had to get through it when they were trying to get to folks."

"I suppose." Mason wanted to believe he'd found evidence of sabotage, but Cameron's skeptical expression said it all. Finally, though, he said, "You're probably right. It doesn't make sense that someone was trying to bring it down. I just saw it and thought maybe..."

Cameron nodded. "I get it."

Mason pointed at her cup. Cameron nodded.

After he refilled it, Mason said, "Let me ask you this—does it change what we said in court today?"

"What do you mean?"

"This support pier still wasn't constructed properly, right?"

Cameron nodded. “There was no rebar in it. That left it vulnerable to collapse.”

“Regardless of any jackhammering?”

“Correct.”

“Would the collapse have happened anyway? Without a jackhammer’s help?”

“Yes. Eventually.”

“So there’s no question in your mind that Landmark Reconstruction and Corwin Concrete screwed up this pier, right? I can still point to that?”

“Why are you two talking about Corwin Concrete?” said Jackson Pierce.

36

Jackson Pierce stood scowling in the doorway of Mason's room, long hair wet but now combed, swimming in one of Mason's flannel shirts as he leaned forward on both of his canes.

That set off a scurry from Mason and Cameron, as they brought him in, sat him down, and filled a large mug of coffee. The color had finally returned to Jackson's face, and though the snow-time under his truck had clearly tired him, his eyes were sharp as he said again, "Why are you two talking about Corwin Concrete?"

"It's part of the case we're working on, Dad," said Mason as he and Cameron sat back down.

Jackson frowned as he took a sip of coffee. "This is good. You must have made it." He said the last to Cameron.

She smiled and nodded.

His dad turned back to Mason. "How could Corwin be part of your case? That outfit closed up shop years ago."

"They built the piers on the Cider Mill patio."

"When was that? The aughts?"

Mason nodded. "'02."

Jackson nodded.

"Makes sense. They were involved in all the big projects up here then. Trying to blame them for your client's problem, are you?"

"Not exactly," said Mason. "We think there's a problem with the way they built one of the piers."

Jackson smiled. "And you're going to blame them for it?" He sipped his coffee in victory.

"We're going to bring it up, yes."

"What'd they do?"

Mason thought about how much he could tell his dad, then said, "Corwin Concrete didn't put any rebar in the support pier that gave way."

"That's no good."

"It's not."

Jackson looked at Cameron. "I assume you're the one who figured that out?"

Cameron shrugged. "It's my job."

"What's this one for then?" Jackson jerked a thumb at Mason.

"Paying my bill." She smiled when she said it.

Jackson Pierce smiled back. "Sounds like money well spent." He sipped his coffee. "Not putting the rebar in, that doesn't sound like Corwin."

"No?"

Jackson Pierce shook his head. "The owner, Kent Corwin, was a real son of a"—he stopped, looked at Cameron, then said—"was a stickler for that kind of thing."

"A real son of a bitch?" said Cameron.

Jackson smiled. "The worst. He'd have his guys' asses in a heartbeat if they cut corners on a job, especially something crucial like this."

"Did you and Uncle Troy ever work there?" said Mason.

"No, no. But it's a small construction world up here, word gets around."

Mason thought for a moment, then said, "If he was so good, why did the business go under then?"

Jackson scowled. "It didn't. Pretty they sold it. Probably made a good bit on it too."

Mason frowned. "I didn't see any successor corporations in the research. I just saw that the business was wound up."

Jackson shrugged. "That sounds like legal work."

"It is," said Cameron.

"It appears I made a mistake introducing you two," said Mason.

"A decent lawyer probably could have figured that would be the case," said his father.

Mason sighed. Cameron smiled.

Jackson Pierce waved a hand. "Anyway, I know some of the guys who worked there have had five or six different company names over the years."

"Not that unusual in construction," said Cameron.

"No. But I've never heard anyone complain about the quality of their work. Prices for sure, because they were always high, but never the product."

Mason nodded. "You've given me some work to do."

"Is that what you call it?"

Mason stared. Jackson smirked.

"Some research," said Mason.

"That sounds more like it."

Mason decided two could play that game.

"So how'd you get stuck under your truck?"

Jackson Pierce looked down and grunted.

"No," said Mason. "I think I need to know."

His dad scowled at him under that long hair before he said, "You know how your road turns to crap in the winter?"

Mason nodded. "It'll hang you up if you're not careful."

"I was careful! But I hit a damn pothole anyway, and it slid me sideways into the snowbank. I was able to get unstuck, but my tire was flat, so I changed it."

Mason cleared his throat.

"I was in the middle of changing it when some moron came barreling down the road and smacked my bed. Spun the truck right around and trapped me against the bank."

"How long were you like that?" said Cameron.

Jackson Pierce shrugged. "Not too long."

"You were pretty wet," said Mason.

Jackson glanced at Cameron, then shrugged again.

"You could have called the garage, you know. Or me."

"Why would I do that?"

"No reason. We should file a police report. Did you see anything?"

Jackson shook his head. "I was half under the truck at the time. Barely saw the car."

"It was a car though?"

"I think so."

"Color?"

"Blue. Maybe dark green."

"See a license?"

"Yes, as a car plowed into my truck while I was lying under a jacked-up wheel, I made a point of noting the license plate before I rolled away."

Mason thought this was far easier on the cop shows.

"Anything at all you can remember?"

His dad actually did appear to give it some thought. "It had a delivery decal on the side. Grubdash? Doorhub?"

"I don't know that those are things, Dad."

"Well, there was a thing on the side, and I had a moment to be surprised."

"Why?"

"Because it only took him a second to hit me!"

"No, I mean, why were you surprised?"

"Oh, because I thought you said the rental was closed for the winter, and you know that Mrs. Roth isn't going to order out. I thought maybe you'd beaten me here and had gotten something."

"You're right on both. They must have been going to one of the other houses and turned down the wrong lane."

"Speeding because they went the wrong way," said Jackson. "Figures."

He stood.

"Where are you going?" said Mason.

"All that's made me hungry."

"I can make something," said Mason.

"Hell no, I need some real food. I'll stop at Dawn's Break on the way home."

"Sure?"

"I said it, didn't I? Besides, sounds like you two have some 'work' to do." He nodded to Cameron and smiled. "Although in her case, it actually is."

"Nice to meet you, Mr. Pierce," said Cameron.

"Jackson, please. And don't hold my son's manners against me."

She smiled. "I won't, Jackson."

Jackson Pierce gathered his canes and with a minimum of fuss and grumbling, no doubt due to Cameron's presence, made his way to the door. He'd almost gone when Mason remembered, "Wait, the multi-meter!"

"Oh, right," said Jackson Pierce.

There was a delay as Mason ran over to his outbuilding, rummaged through his tools, found the multi-meter, and brought it back. Jackson grumbled his thanks as he put it in the pocket of his flannel jacket, then shuffled forward with both canes on the snowy steps.

"Be careful driving, Dad."

"Go to hell, Son."

Mason smiled, waited until his dad made it to the truck, then shut the door.

He turned back to see Cameron Thomas smiling.

"You two are a lot alike," she said.

"Bite your tongue."

37

Kyle Stewart had planted more snooping devices than he could count. He'd never had one pay off so soon.

He hadn't gotten home until after midnight, a consequence of having to drive far downstate to someone he could trust to dispose of his car and give him a new one. The first thing he did when he got back to his rented apartment was check the video and sound of Mason Pierce's house, more to make sure it was all working than anything else. What he found were two large sound files and one video file that were going to slingshot him toward his next payday.

It took him a moment to sort through who he was listening to, but eventually he figured out that the voices were Pierce, his father, and his expert. By the time Kyle could identify the voices, they'd dropped their whole defense causation theory right into his lap. Even the dad had something to add, giving him a little history on the concrete company that he could give to Baggman.

He was completely thrown to learn that Pierce's father had been under the truck he'd hit. Kyle hadn't seen the old man at all and was wondering whether that was a loose end when the old man answered the question for him—he hadn't seen a thing.

The only thing that could link Kyle to the accident was the car itself, and that was now long gone.

By the time the old man left, Kyle was having trouble containing himself. His minimal risk had already generated an outsized reward, and he was on his way to a massive payday.

The second sound file wasn't relevant to the case but was just as interesting. The Thomas woman wanted to know about the house which, having been in it, Kyle knew was no big deal at all and just designed to keep the conversation going. Pierce responded with the only thing that made any sense, it was a work in progress whose real value was its location on a rare private section of the bluffs overlooking Lake Michigan.

The recording stopped then for a time; it turned out the two of them had gone out in the cold to gaze at the Big Lake with the woman oohing and ahhing about the view of the sunset over the ice when they came back.

When they made another pot of coffee, Kyle thought things might get really interesting, but Pierce and the expert kept it to one cup before she left. So no, he didn't get anything so good as the defense lawyer sleeping with his expert witness, but Kyle knew that was just being greedy after all of his other good fortune that day, like complaining about not covering one spread when you've hit seven others. They hadn't done anything inappropriate, no, but that didn't mean that Kyle hadn't discovered all sorts of personal information that might be useful later —that the house was an old cottage that had belonged to his mother, that she'd wanted to pass it down to him after she'd died, that the father had refused to sell it to pay for medical bills, hers or his, to honor her wishes, and that Pierce was working on improvements one small step at a time, limited by his student loans and spare time.

Kyle ignored the woman's words of encouragement—they weren't relevant. What was relevant was all the pressure points the conversation revealed—a young lawyer drowning in student loans, living in a sentimental shack, keeping an eye on a disabled father, and telling a beautiful expert witness all about it.

Some days were just your days, and Kyle Stewart knew better than to question it. Instead, he followed his rule to always play out the hot streak.

It was after midnight in Michigan, sure, but that meant late afternoon in New Zealand, which meant he still had time to place a rugby bet and a couple of prop bets besides. And, since he was just that hot, he doubled it because you never win big unless you bet big.

Then he downloaded his findings onto an encrypted drive to have it personally delivered to Jerome Baggman.

38

Mason grabbed Peter Freid as soon as his boss sat down at his desk the next morning, which wasn't as soon as Mason would've liked, so that he could tell him everything he'd learned. He told him, again, about the rebar that was missing from the pier, but also about the reputation of Corwin Concrete for doing topflight work which made the failure unusual. When Peter asked how Mason knew that, he didn't tell Peter it came from his father—instead he said it was from his construction connections, which seemed to be all the explanation Peter needed. He told Peter about the jackhammer marks, which Peter immediately dismissed as being from the rescue. Mason didn't tell Peter about his father's near-miss or that he'd spent a lot of time with their expert Cameron Thomas last night. He wasn't embarrassed about it, but just then it really didn't seem like it would help.

Peter Freid took it all in and made a point of taking the first sip of the coffee he'd been pouring when Mason had cornered him to talk. He winced.

"Melody?!"

"Yes, Mr. Freid."

"Pierce here has made my coffee cold."

"You should drink faster."

"Or I could give my wonderfully competent assistant an even higher performance rating."

There was a loud sigh. "How about you, Mr. Pierce?"

"No thanks, Melody. I have my Yeti."

"Can you bring another one in tomorrow?"

"Maybe."

Peter Freid harrumphed. "Practical, like always."

Melody came in with a new cup of coffee for Peter and took the old one.

"You're a lifesaver, Melody."

Melody raised her nose. "Why, look at Mr. Pierce, sitting there with coffee that's still piping hot even though he arrived at…7:30, Mr. Pierce?"

"7:00, Melody," said Mason and took a sip from his Yeti.

"You'd think a big firm could spring for thermal cups, wouldn't you?"

"I'm happy to do it on my own, Melody."

"I don't know; seems like a corporate branding opportunity."

Peter waved a hand. "All right, you two. Melody, order us all one of those thermal whatsits and have the firm logo slapped on them. We can't have Pierce out in public with that beat up one anyway, looks bad."

"What a good idea, Mr. Freid."

"And bill it to Mother Burns."

"Of course, Mr. Freid."

Peter came back to Mason. "This bit about Corwin Concrete being sold instead of going belly up is interesting. We just stopped the corporate research when we saw the company was dissolved"—Mason knew that by "we" Peter meant "he"—"I'll have a corporate associate down in Detroit research what happened to it. If someone's out there holding Corwin Concrete's liabilities, we want to know about it."

"I can do that."

"No, I want you to keep focusing on the blue-collar end of this."

Mason kept the wince off his face at that description, and Peter continued. "You've got to figure out how the faulty construction fits with this jackhammer business. I need that to make sense."

"I'm on it."

39

Later that afternoon, Mason was staring at his computer, reading an article about the friction coefficient of asphalt shingles versus metal roof panels when his phone buzzed. He scowled when he saw it was Austin Pierce, not because he was unhappy to hear from his cousin, but because it was unusual.

"What's up, Austin?" he said.

"That's what I was calling to ask you," said Austin. "Is everything okay with your dad?"

His dad had seemed okay when he'd left Mason's house, so he said, "More or less. Why?"

"I ran into him at the auto shop today. I'm getting a new tow package put on the truck because I've got my eye a new boat this year and it's going to be heavier than the last one, so I need a bigger trailer and GMC has a new package that will let me—"

"—Austin?"

"Yeah?"

"My dad?"

"Oh, right, so he was there too, and he was all fired up

because he came in for a new tire, and they told him that his front suspension was shot or something."

"Yeah, he hit a pothole last night out by my place. I'm not surprised."

"Well, he was letting the clerk have it pretty good, which didn't seem like him. I mean, it seemed like him but a more full-on Uncle Jackson than just some blown suspension, if you get me."

"I get you."

"Kinda seemed like one more thing he couldn't fix right now."

"I think you nailed it, Austin."

"Anyway, it was going to take a couple of days; they're all backed up over there, so I gave him a ride home."

"Oh, I appreciate that, Austin. Thanks."

"So that explains how he met Dr. Cammie then."

Mason shook his head at the name. "He mentioned her?"

"Said something about a fine-looking woman who knew more about construction than his son and his friends combined, which I'm just realizing was a shot at me too. And as I was driving him home!"

"Sounds like he was a little out of sorts."

"Got that right. Just thought you might want to check in on him."

"I will, thanks."

"If you're busy with that case, I can give him a ride back to the shop when the truck's ready."

"Thanks, Austin, that would help."

"I tried to get him to go to The Loon with me for dinner, but he wouldn't bite."

"Thanks for trying anyway. Hey, while I've got you, I need a second opinion on something."

"I'm disappointed I'm not the first."

"I'm the first."

"Aren't we cocky this afternoon."

"If you were going to weaken a concrete support pier, what would you do?"

"Weaken it? Why the hell would I want to do that?"

"Humor me."

"Doesn't seem very funny."

"Austin."

"I'm serious, Mason. Why would I weaken it? I'd just knock the damn thing down or I'd shore it up."

"Just say you wanted to weaken a pier so it came down—"

"That's not safe at all."

"What would you do?"

"You lawyers think of the dumbest shit. Is it still supporting whatever it is it's supporting?"

"Yes."

"Like, say, a stone patio?"

Mason paused. "Something of similar weight."

"You really went to school for this?"

"Austin."

"I stand by what I said. If I didn't care when it came down, I'd destabilize the ground around it, especially if it were, say, on a steep shoreline. But then I build seawalls for a living."

"What if you were going to attack the pier itself?"

"The pier that's holding up a structure as heavy as a stone patio?"

"Yes."

"While it's still holding up that structure?"

"Yes."

"First, I'd go to my shrink appointment to get on top of the death wish I had."

"That's not helpful."

"Neither is the question, Mason. Come on, why would I want

to weaken the thing that's holding up the thing that's going to crush me to death if it fails? It doesn't make any sense. If I want to take it down, I hire a demolition company and stand two blocks away while they blow it with a charge or I smash it with a wrecking ball or whatever it is that they swing at this shit."

"But if you were working on the pier itself, it'd be a jackhammer, right?"

"A handheld demohammer, I suppose, or a sledge and a chisel if there were cracks to work with, but I'd probably need a saw for the rebar."

"What if there was no rebar?"

"On a support pier? Then there's no way in hell I'm standing underneath the patio—sorry, something that weighs as much as a patio—if there's no rebar in it because that thing could go with any swing I take. Are you really getting paid for this nonsense?"

"I really am."

"Then the next round at The Loon is definitely on you. I gotta run. Don't worry about your dad's truck; I'll take him in when it's ready."

"Thanks, Austin."

As they hung up, Mason decided that Austin was right. Annoying as all hell, but right. Sabotaging the support pier with a jackhammer or chisel while the structure was intact didn't make any sense. But the marks were there all the same.

So he was missing something.

"The home office found what you were missing," said Peter Freid as he walked into Mason's office.

Mason looked up as Peter dropped a manila folder on his desk.

"What's this?"

"That," he pointed as he plopped into a chair, "is the corporate history for Corwin Concrete."

Mason opened the folder and saw a series of Secretary of State filings. "What's it show?"

"A dead end."

"How so?"

"Your construction contacts were right—Corwin Concrete didn't go belly up, its assets were sold to a construction company called Northern Lakes Construction, leaving the liabilities behind in the now defunct shell of Corwin Concrete, which was wrapped up and dissolved in early 2010. So different history but the same result."

"How so?"

"The important thing for our finger-pointing purposes is that the liability of Corwin Concrete for its faulty construction of the support pier didn't follow its assets to Northern Lakes Construction; that liability died with the husk of Corwin Concrete in 2010, so there's still no existing corporate entity that we can go after."

Mason looked at the Secretary of State sheets, thought, and had to agree that Peter was right.

"You're right."

"I know."

"That was fast."

"They put one of the Detroit business associates on it. Kind of a tool, but he knows what he's doing, with this kind of thing anyway."

"So where does that leave us?"

Peter gave him a finger gun. "Back where we were—you figuring out a way to get Hyde off the hook for this." Then he stood and left.

Mason felt no closer to a defense, but he did feel as if Hyde was growing closer to a life in Baraga Maximum Correctional every day.

40

Jerome Baggman received a call from Kyle Stewart that night. Baggman listened as Stewart outlined everything—the lack of rebar in the pier, the evidence of use of a jackhammer, all of it. Greed dripped from every word Stewart spoke. Jerome Baggman didn't judge Stewart because he felt the same way, but there were two differences between them. First, Jerome Baggman would never be so obvious; his avarice would be cloaked in justice and accountability for horribly wronged families.

And second, he would never bet his hard-won resources on anything he wasn't in complete control of. Which was another reason why Kyle Stewart, though repugnant, was vital.

Jerome Baggman let Kyle finish, then said, "Is there anything to this sabotage theory?"

"Not that I can see," said Kyle.

"What do Pierce and Thomas think?"

"They don't see anything yet either."

Jerome Baggman was very careful how he asked the next question because it was always important to keep the proper distance from people like Kyle Stewart. "Do you anticipate being able to stumble upon similar information in the future?"

"I can almost guarantee it."

"Good. And the faulty construction claim against Corwin Concrete, you said we know the basis for it now?"

"Yeah, they're going to claim that there was no rebar in the support pier and that's what caused it to collapse."

"Hmm. Twenty-three years later."

"Right."

"That's it?"

"That seems to be all they have."

"That's not very much."

"I didn't think so either."

"But it's best to know these things in advance. Keep me informed."

"You know I will, Mr. Baggman."

Jerome Baggman waited. He knew this would be the time, right now. The payday on this case was looking huge and getting bigger by the day. Kyle Stewart would either ask for an increase in his percentage, in which case other measures would need to be taken, or he would take the safe bet on what was becoming sure money, and provide another tidbit of information.

There was a pause on the other end of the line. Jerome Baggman continued to wait.

Then Kyle Stewart said, "There's one more thing that might be useful."

Jerome Baggman smiled. "What's that, Mr. Stewart?"

"Cameron Thomas, the expert, was at Mason Pierce's house pretty late last night."

"Was she now? Interesting."

"Nothing inappropriate seemed to happen, but..."

"Now Mr. Stewart, you know I'm not interested in anything that couldn't be observed from a public place."

"There aren't many houses out Pierce's way, Mr. Baggman, and it's the only house at the end of the drive she turned down."

"I see. And once there, I suppose anything could have happened. Or nothing at all."

"Who's to say?" said Kyle Stewart.

"Who indeed. Thank you, Mr. Stewart. If you send me your hourly bill for expenses, I'll pay it in the usual way tonight."

"Thanks, Mr. Baggman. I'll talk to you soon."

"I certainly hope so."

The two hung up, and Jerome Baggman acted on what he'd learned.

~

On the same night, the head of Kramer Burns, Jacqueline Wilbane, was talking to the partner in charge of its newest branch office, Peter Freid.

Jaqueline "Jax" Wilbane had been the head of Kramer Burns for almost seven years. To lead a firm like that, there were certain things you had to possess—a degree from a top-ten law school, a commanding appearance, a deep knowledge of the law with the creative juice to find solutions—and sprinkle all of it with a willingness to work day and night for the good of Kramer Burns.

Jax Wilbane checked all of those boxes, but that wasn't why she'd been in charge for the last seven years. No, Jax Wilbane led Kramer Burns because she was very good at making all of them money, partners and clients alike.

A new branch office represented a dramatic chance to grow or shrink the pie, so she was more than happy to take a call from Peter Freid that night despite the hour. She listened to Peter Freid's update on the progress of the Northlake office in general and of the Hyde Warren case in particular.

"So do you think you'll be able to tie the collapse back to this Corwin Concrete company?" she asked.

"It's looking that way. But the company's gone, so there won't be a pot of money there."

"Insurance?"

"We're checking, but minimal. They had a claims-made policy and didn't buy a tail."

"Meaning the collapse wouldn't be covered."

"Right."

"Successor companies?"

"Dead ends after an asset sale to a company called Northern Lakes Construction."

Jax Wilbane considered that for a moment, then said, "Were we right about Pierce?"

Mason Pierce had been a topic of vehement discussion among the Kramer Burns hiring group.

"He's as advertised. Some rough edges but there's a smart lawyer under that mountain."

"Can he handle the pressure?"

"We're about to see."

"This is a high-profile case, Peter."

"I'm aware of that, Jax."

"It's even getting play down here."

"I have a computer."

"The way we handle this is going to reflect on us as a firm."

"Trials do that."

"No, results do that. And your result up there is going to be vital to the Firm's interests in Northlake."

"I am nothing if not a steward of the interests of Mother Burns."

Jax Wilbane hated the term, but it was too ubiquitous to stop, so she no longer tried. Instead, she said, "Keep it in mind. And keep me informed."

"Always. Take care, Jax."

"Good night, Peter."

Jax Wilbane stared at her phone. Peter Freid was infuriating, but he was also immune to pressure, which made him a fantastic trial lawyer and the perfect partner to start the new office up in Northlake. Jax Wilbane chuckled. It also didn't hurt that Northlake was far away from his partner's wives.

Jax Wilbane was all about solutions.

PART V

41

For the next ten days, Mason and Peter Freid worked long hours getting ready for the trial date that was approaching, fast, until Peter made a point of telling Mason that he wasn't coming in on Easter Sunday and Mason should do the same because they probably weren't going to find another day off until they were done.

Which meant Mason had no excuse not to go to his Aunt Linda's for Easter lunch.

Mason's relationship with his Uncle Troy and Aunt Linda was complicated. Uncle Troy was his dad's brother and Aunt Linda had been his mother's best friend, meaning many of Mason's childhood memories were of both of their families together. A business dispute, and life, had broken that extended family apart.

As soon as they'd obtained their journeyman's cards, Troy and Jackson Pierce had started a masonry business together specializing in cinderblock foundations for homes and small businesses. As the business grew, Uncle Troy had wanted to take on debt to expand the business, while Jackson Pierce had wanted to stay debt-free and fill their niche. They'd eventually split, with Uncle Troy purchasing equipment and forming Northlake Seawall while Jackson Pierce kept laying cinderblock walls.

When the housing collapse sent the brothers' fortunes in opposite directions, Aunt Linda and Mason's mom had made it manageable, pulling the families together for holidays and birthdays and kids events in ways that the brothers had to attend and at least pretend to get along.

But then Mason's mom had fallen ill, and a year after that, a loose scaffold had failed Jackson Pierce. Mason's father was forced, by his injury and the gravity of his wife's condition, to accept Aunt Linda's support for his wife but not, under any circumstances, Uncle Troy's money even when the time came for hospice and Jackson Pierce couldn't afford the care his wife needed.

A dynamic that had been fragile became untenable for Mason's father. Mason thought for a time there might be a reconciliation after his mom passed, but he soon realized that it had burned a sense of failure and shame so deeply into his father's core that Jackson Pierce could not now bear to be around his brother or his wife's best friend.

Aunt Linda had always treated Mason as one of her own and, after his mom had passed, she'd wanted to step into that role more often, and with more force, than Mason really wanted. But he supposed that was what mothers did too, so though he didn't always welcome it, he appreciated where it was coming from.

To his credit, Jackson Pierce didn't begrudge Mason his brother's family. He'd actually suggested that Mason go work for his Uncle Troy once his own business had collapsed with his spine, and Mason never had to hide that he'd gone to see Uncle Troy or Aunt Linda or Lily or Austin. But if there was a way to bring Jackson and his brother back together, Mason couldn't see it.

Mason carried all that, along with some deviled eggs, to his Aunt Linda's house on Easter Sunday.

"Mace-honey, get in here!" said Aunt Linda as she opened the door.

Aunt Linda was tall, her hair red with strands of white just beginning to show, and a beaming smile. Mason bent down so she could hug him.

When she pulled back, Linda Pierce said, "Young man, have you gone clothes shopping?" she said.

Mason smiled. "They didn't like work boots at the firm."

"I approve! So handsome."

That was another indicator that Aunt Linda had stepped into a mom role. Mason was many things; he knew handsome wasn't one of them. "Thanks, Aunt Linda."

"And eggs too! Wonderful. Come in, we're almost ready. Your cousins are in the sunroom with your uncle."

"Do you need any help?"

"Don't you dare! Your cousins have told me how much you've been working." She paused and patted his chest. "Your mom would be so proud."

Aunt Linda did that a lot. Mason still wasn't used to it.

"Go see them."

With the explosive growth of Northlake Seawall, Uncle Troy and Aunt Linda had bought a house on the Bluffs looking down on Lake Michigan. Northern Michigan being what it was, they'd built a sunroom facing the lake, with a window-filled view that protected the toasty watcher from what were harsh elements a good part of the year. It was spectacular.

Mason found Lily and Austin sitting in overstuffed chairs with his Uncle Troy standing to one side.

"Mace!" said Austin.

Lily gave Mason a hug.

"Where's Bronson?" Mason asked.

"Guard training weekend."

"On Easter?"

Lily nodded. "The CO screwed up and was looking at last year's calendar. They gave people permission to opt out, but you know Bronson."

Mason smiled. "I do."

Uncle Troy came over and shook his hand. He looked down. "Hmm. They starting to get soft from pushing those papers?"

"Not yet."

"Soon, though I bet. How's indoor life treating you?"

"Fine, Uncle Troy."

"Well, if this law thing doesn't work out, you know we always have a spot for you at Northlake Seawall."

"Jesus, Dad," said Lily. "Why don't you just say you hope the house doesn't slip into the lake?"

"Never happen with our seawalls, Lily-Pad."

"Why jinx it?"

"No such thing."

Troy Pierce was a little shorter than his wife but wide, like his son, with pale hair the color of his daughter's. His fair skin had the lines and freckles of someone who'd spent years in the sun, his cheeks had taken on a permanent red hue, and he had the overall look of a man who'd once worked hard but whose sharp edges had been blunted by prosperity.

Uncle Troy pointed at Lily and Austin. "The kids said you've been busy on the collapse case."

Mason nodded.

"It was a damn shame. What are they saying Hyde did?"

"Overloaded the patio 'til it collapsed."

"That seems like it'd be hard to do."

"I agree."

Uncle Troy appeared to be celebrating the Lord's resurrection with a bloody mary. He gestured to Mason, who shook his head, then stirred his drink with a celery stalk, and said, "You'd think those piers would still bear the load, even if they were a few people over."

Mason nodded. "They're going to argue the weight of the snow put it well past that."

"When was the last time he cleared it?"

"August."

"Ah. You got a weight estimate?"

Mason shrugged.

Uncle Troy smiled. "Secret trial stuff?"

Mason smiled.

Uncle Troy grunted, stirred, then sucked the juice out of the groove of the celery stalk. "Austin said something about a support pier being screwed up?"

Mason looked at his cousin, who quickly looked down at his own drink. Mason did a quick calculation—they'd already identified the potentially responsible parties in open court, so there was no harm in getting Uncle Troy's perspective.

Mason nodded. "I think Corwin Concrete might not have put rebar in the pier that failed."

Uncle Troy frowned. "Interesting. I suppose that could cause a failure, especially if it's had twenty years to settle."

"Dad thought that didn't seem like a mistake they would make."

"Corwin Concrete?" Uncle Troy grinned. "No, not at all. Old man Corwin was a real prick about standards."

"Dad said the same thing."

"Your dad's right once in a while. When was the project?"

"2002."

Uncle Troy nodded. "That might explain it. That's right around when old Kent Corwin died."

Mason remembered the corporate research the firm had

done. “Is that why the business was sold? Because the owner died?”

Uncle Troy nodded. “Boating accident. Every rich asshole who can afford a boat thinks they can take it out on Lake Michigan. Maybe the Cider Mill project was going on then. It would explain the slip in standards.”

“I didn’t realize that. Who took over?”

“I wanna say his son gave it a go, but he didn’t last too long. He was more interested in veterinary school or something, if I’m remembering it right. I know he sold, but I don’t remember to who now.”

“Huh,” said Lily from the couch. “The son didn’t want to run the business? Interesting.”

Uncle Troy’s face turned dark. “The Corwin boy was too busy sticking his hand up dogs’ asses to develop business skills.”

“Too bad.” Lily shook her head. “If only there had been another child who had developed all those skills. A daughter maybe.”

“Maybe.” Uncle Troy drained his bloody mary. “Or maybe if the old man had lived longer, the boy would’ve developed a sense of responsibility for the business.”

At that moment, Austin had his head tilted back with a long thin glass at his lips, trying to tease an olive out from between the ice cubes with his tongue. He glanced over, saw his dad looking at him, lowered the glass with a grin and said, “Not a chance, Dad.”

Uncle Troy waved the empty glass. “You just need experience.”

“I have more than enough experience. Just put me behind a backhoe.”

“No, experience *leading*.”

“Who wants that aggravation?” Austin jiggled an ice cube into his mouth. “No, what the company needs is a more reliable leader than me. Someone who, oh, I don't know, grew up in the business and leads the best crew." He smiled at Lily, who smiled back.

"Oh?" said Uncle Troy. "Is Mason leaving the law?"

Lily's smile faded.

"No," said Mason. "And if I did, I still wouldn't be as good a crew leader as your daughter."

Uncle Troy shook his head as he poured another drink. "Until she has kids, maybe."

The grooves of this conversation were well-worn. But Mason still couldn't resist. "Taxes done yet, Uncle Troy?"

Uncle Troy grimaced and shook his head. "Just heard from the accountant. Going to be paying a fortune."

"Big year?"

"Biggest yet."

"Even with me gone and Bronson called up for two months?"

"Three," said Austin.

Uncle Troy scowled. "We were lucky."

Mason nodded to Lily. "Lucky to have a good crew leader running things, for sure."

Aunt Linda, through fortune or instinct, reappeared. "Time for lunch. Troy, would you cut the ham?"

Uncle Troy harrumphed and went off.

Austin stared at Lily for a moment before he said, "You know he's an asshole about this, right?"

Lily's face didn't change as she shrugged, then nodded.

Austin leaned forward. "No one could have done what you did last year."

Lily pressed her lips together. "That Corwin kid may have had it right—I'd probably get more thanks out of a...cat's ass?"

"Dog's ass," said Mason.

"That."

"We're your dog's ass," said Austin, putting an arm around her broad shoulders.

Lily stared at her brother, then cracked up.

"I'm serious. We appreciate you, Mason and me."

"I know, I know."

Lily gave Austin a half hug back, pushed him off, then the three cousins followed Uncle Troy to Aunt Linda's lunch.

42

While lunch at Aunt Linda's had been delicious, the downside was that it was liable to put Mason straight to sleep, so he decided to stop on the way home for a coffee.

It being Sunday, Maggie's wasn't open, so he detoured a mile out of his way to a gas station he figured would be open, Easter or not. His gamble paid off when he saw the neon open sign, and he parked his truck next to the station.

A familiar car at the pump, a BMW SUV, caught his eye, as did the man filling the tank. Mason detoured over and was almost on top of him when he said, "Hey, Peter."

Peter Freid about jumped out of his skin, although it seemed to Mason that the jump came not from his voice, but from seeing him. Unfortunately, Mason was used to that effect—people expecting one thing and getting another—so he really didn't think anything of it.

"Mason, hey," Peter said, checking the gas.

"Thought you were out of town?" said Mason.

"Just got back," Peter said. "Needed a quick fill up and I swear this is the only place open."

"It might be."

Mason didn't hear the pump click, but Peter stopped filling up and racked his pump, looking into the station as he did.

"Did you go anywhere special?" Mason asked.

"Just downstate. Well, I'll see you tomorrow. I'd say bright and early but that will be you, not me."

Mason nodded. "See you then. Happy Easter."

"Yeah, right. You too." Then Peter Freid nodded and climbed into his car.

Mason walked to the station. As he came to the door, a woman was exiting, so Mason opened it and stood to the side.

"Thanks, Handsome," said the woman as Mason realized it was Amber.

"Sorry, Amber, didn't see your car," said Mason.

"No, you didn't," she said and kept walking.

Right around to the passenger side of Peter Freid's SUV.

It took Mason a moment to realize he was just standing there as Amber Vincent climbed into Peter's car. The moment she shut the door, Peter took off.

Mason went in to get his coffee. It wasn't until he programmed in "House", then "X-Large," then "Fill 'er Up!" that he began to laugh.

~

BY THE TIME Mason arrived home, he discovered he didn't care about what he'd seen. If you'd asked him a month earlier, he'd have been pretty sure that was true, but the fact was, you never know until you get hit smack in the face with it, and now he had. As he thought about it, he really wasn't sure who he was rooting for in that scenario, but he figured they'd both get exactly what they wanted, and deserved.

He did make a mental note, though, about what it told him about Peter.

He put thoughts of Peter and Amber aside so he could work. What Uncle Troy had said that day was interesting—he hadn't realized that Kent Corwin had died around the time of the patio project and Peter hadn't mentioned seeing anything about it in the corporate research, so Mason decided to take a look.

The obituary for Kent Corwin was harder to find than he expected. People were still getting their newspapers delivered in the early 2000s in northern Michigan, and it didn't appear that *The Northlake Ledger* had any electronic presence to speak of back then, which also wasn't unusual. Eventually, though, he found a post from the Corwin family foundation on the twentieth anniversary of Kent Corwin's death, which linked to a pdf of what the front page of the newspaper had said.

Mason scanned it. The usual things—successful businessman, beloved father, avid fisherman who would be dearly missed. He was survived by his spouse, a son and two daughters, and three grandchildren.

Two things caught Mason's eye. The first was the year—2002. The same year that they'd built the patio, which explained why, with the turmoil, the construction standards had slipped.

The second was the final quote from the oldest son, Kevin Corwin. "We're going to miss him terribly. He always said he wanted to go out on the big water with a pole in his hand, but we just wish it hadn't been so soon. We're devastated, but we're going to do our best to run things the way he would've wanted."

Mason thought for a moment, then pulled up the electronic file of the corporate research Peter had done. He found a notice of stock transfer in 2003 to Kevin Corwin, which must have been when the son officially took over. The documents the firm had assembled to show the asset sale were more subtle, and Mason had to say that he was reluctantly impressed with whoever had done it back in Detroit. They'd found UCC filings on equipment, a property transfer deed on an office, and a line of credit, along with a few other smaller things that sure seemed to indicate that the assets of Corwin Concrete had been sold to North Lakes Construction in 2004. Then there was a series of filings and documents where Corwin Concrete gave all of its creditors notice that it was wrapping up its business and dissolving. A few creditors even seemed to have taken advantage of it and sought payment but, by the mid-2000s, Corwin Concrete was no more.

The Detroit office had gone one more step, finding that North Lake Construction had sold in 2009 to a company called Lakeside Contractors, but they hadn't gone any farther than that since the assets were the only thing that were moving there, not the responsibility for construction of the patio, which had died a dusty corporate death five years before.

Mason knew from experience that court documents were often the bricks but rarely the mortar that held a story together. He thought. There weren't that many vets in the Northlake area, and his cousin Austin was on his second Great Dane, so he picked up the phone.

"Mason!" Austin said. "I missed you too!"

"Who do you take Miggy to?"

"Dr. Kevin. Did you finally get a dog?"

"No, no."

"Too bad."

"Kevin Corwin?"

"What other Dr. Kevin would it be?"

"Just checking."

"You didn't get a cat, did you?"

"No."

"Are you thinking about a dog then? I know some great—"

"—No. It's for work."

"Miggy," Austin switched to a baby voice. "Tell Uncle Mace that he's boring."

A deep bark.

"Good boy," said Austin. "This isn't for work, is it?"

"Maybe."

"You make me sad. Be at The Loon Tuesday?"

"I'm probably out for the next couple of weeks."

"I suppose that means you'll be keeping Dr. Cammie away?"

"She'll be busy too."

"We need to get you back in balance, man."

"Working on it."

"No, Miggy, dammit! Drop! Sorry, Mace, gotta go!"

Mason smiled as Austin hung up to reap the whirlwind a two-year-old Great Dane can cause.

Then he looked up the information for Dr. Kevin Corwin, Northlake's finest veterinarian.

43

Mason didn't think there was any chance he'd be able to see Dr. Kevin Corwin on Easter Sunday, but it turned out that a chamber of commerce Easter Egg Hunt, complete with live rabbits and chicks for petting and adoption, also attracted the town's best vet. Northern Michigan being what it was, it was too cold to do it outside, but the Northlake Library, which came complete with a greenhouse arboretum, was happy to oblige.

There were more cars there than Mason would have expected, further indication that there was a whole world out there that he didn't know existed. As he was going in, most of the traffic was coming out, consisting mostly of families with young children holding baskets filled with plastic Easter eggs, candy, and, occasionally, a parent holding a cage with two rabbits.

As Mason held a door open for one such family, a little girl, probably no more than four, pointed up at him and said, "An ogre, Mommy. Like the cartoon."

Mommy, a young woman with her arms full carrying a newborn and a diaper bag, absently said, "That's nice, sweetie."

Then she said, "Thank you," raised her eyes to Mason, and went white. "I'm so sorry."

Mason nodded to the mom but said to the girl, "Watch yourself, Donkey!"

The girl giggled and trotted away. The mother told her to wait and sped after.

Mason Pierce, ogre at law, went in.

The library was emptying out, but Mason saw a small cluster of people still at the back and headed over. There, a penned-in area held rabbits, though not many, with a stack of wire mesh cages stacked behind.

An older woman was speaking to a middle-aged man who was holding two rabbits in his arms. "We really can't thank you enough, Dr. Kevin," the woman said. "Kids don't seem to care that much about eggs anymore, but the rabbits were a hit."

"No problem at all, Evelyn," said Dr. Kevin Corwin. "They enjoy the play and we were able to place a few with families that can actually take care of them."

"Evelyn," came a voice. "The food truck vendor needs to be paid."

"Will you excuse me, Dr. Kevin?"

"Of course."

"Next year?"

"You bet."

Dr. Kevin, a stocky man with short black hair turning white, placed the rabbits he was holding in a crate, then turned to catch one of five still scurrying about. He bent over stiffly, and the first one dodged his attempt.

"Give you a hand?" said Mason.

"Love it," said Dr. Kevin, wincing as he straightened and put one hand on his back.

Mason stepped over the knee-high fence and scooped a rabbit up in each hand. Dr. Kevin saw him and laughed. "I don't think I've ever seen one look so small." He opened the door of a crate. "Here you go."

Mason gently placed one in, then the other.

"Don't suppose you're looking to adopt?" said Dr. Kevin.

"I'm afraid not."

"Kids here then?"

Mason bent and scooped up a third rabbit. "No, actually I was hoping to catch you real quick."

Dr. Kevin made a face similar to when his back had pained him. "I'm sorry, but you'll need to make an appointment for your pet."

"Oh, no, no, I don't have a medical question. It's a building question."

Dr. Kevin eyed him. "You're a builder?"

"Used to be. Not anymore."

"Should've guessed. My family's been out of that game a long time, Mr. ...?"

"Pierce. Mason Pierce."

Dr. Kevin scowled. "There was a Pierce who ran a foundation company a while back. Jason maybe?"

"Jackson. He's my dad."

"Jackson, right." Dr. Kevin loaded a bunny into a crate. "How's he doing?"

"Fine, thanks," Mason said because he knew Dr. Kevin was just trying to occupy the time collecting bunnies. "I had a question about your dad, actually."

Dr. Kevin glanced up. "Really? He's been gone a long time."

"That's what I understand. Boating accident?"

"Man loved to fish."

"I'm sorry."

Dr. Kevin shrugged. "He pushed it one too many times on the big lake. It eventually catches up."

"Did you run the business after?"

"For a year or two, while I was finishing up school." He lifted the bunny by the scruff and smiled. "But the bunnies were calling, so I sold it to one of our foremen once I was done. All for the better."

"Do you remember who was running the day-to-day back then?"

"Back when?"

"After your dad passed."

Dr. Kevin set down his bunny crate and turned, his eyes hard. "Why would you want to know that, Mason?"

"I'd like to talk to him about a project they were working on."

"Back in the 2000s?"

"Yes."

"And what project would that be?"

There are a whole bunch of reasons why it's not a good idea for a lawyer to lie to a potential witness. There's also the objective right and wrong of it, which was why Mason said, "The Stone Street Cider Mill project."

The kind man who gave bunnies to children was gone. What Mason saw then was the man who steeled himself to put down a dog when it was time.

"Are you related to the lawsuit?" said Dr. Kevin.

"I represent the current owner."

"So you're looking to blame my family for what your guy did?"

"I just have some questions about the project and I'm not sure who to ask."

"Well, unless you have a Ouija board, you're going to have a hard time asking them." Dr. Kevin started stacking cages. "My dad was running that project when he died. After that, one of our foremen finished it. He'd only been on the job a few years, and I remember he and I were scrambling because a couple of brothers, Troy and Jackson Pierce, were trying to steal a bunch of our jobs once they heard my dad was dead. Even got a few, if I remember right. So I don't really know what was happening at all of our worksites because I was just trying to pass organic chem and keep our family's business afloat while the coast guard searched for my lost father. And your family, Mason Pierce, made that a whole lot harder. Now if you don't mind, hand me that last rabbit and screw all the way off."

Mason scooped the rabbit up with one hand and did.

As Dr. Kevin Corwin latched the last crate, he said, "It took me a lot to get out of that business, Pierce, and I wrapped it up tight so that I wouldn't get dragged back in. If you're looking for money, or a landing spot for blame, there's nothing there. Keep me and my family out of it."

"Thanks, Dr. Kevin. Sorry to bother you."

"No. You're not."

As Mason left the Northlake Library with the last of the bunny-bearing children, something Dr. Kevin had said registered with him, and he decided he had one more place to go. So Mason got in his truck and drove around to the back lot of the library. Then he sat there and waited until Dr. Kevin had loaded his remaining rabbits into his minivan and left.

Then Mason drove around to the front lot and went back inside.

44

A woman Mason recognized from a moment before was standing in the foyer, directing a young man to straighten the children's section from the Easter whirlwind that had struck it.

"Excuse me, Evelyn?" said Mason.

Evelyn pressed her lips together, looked at Mason's chest, looked up, and narrowed her eyes. "You can load the tables through the back?"

Mason blinked. "Excuse me?"

"Aren't you here to pack up the rental tables?"

"No, sorry, I had a research question."

Evelyn shifted focus with her error. "We're about to close. It's Easter."

"That's why I'll be fast."

Evelyn exhaled, inhaled, and said, "How can I help?"

"Do you have the archives for *The Northlake Ledger* here?"

"We do."

"Are they available online?"

"Not yet, no. We've been working on digitizing them, but the grant funding was terminated."

"Are they available here then?"

"Yes. Chase, please show this gentleman the archive terminal."

Chase, looking elated at having been freed from the wreckage of the children's section, smiled. "Right away, Evelyn."

"We close in half an hour," Evelyn said to Mason.

"Yes, ma'am."

Chase showed Mason to a row of study carrels in the back of the library. Chase placed his hand on a terminal. "This is hooked right up to the library's system. Just put your library ID in, and it will let you look."

Mason winced. "Um, Chase, it appears that I need to sign up for my card."

"The woman who does that isn't here today. You'll need to ask Evelyn."

"Could you log me in, just for today?"

Chase looked uncertain.

"Please. I need to check today, and I get the impression that Evelyn's a little distracted."

Chase glanced over his shoulder as if he were at an info drop for Russian agents, then typed at the computer and said, "More than a little. Promise to sign up this week?"

"Yes."

One more tap. "There. That's my ID; don't screw me over on any searches."

"Done. Thank you."

Chase nodded and slipped away, to Mason's amusement, in the opposite direction from the children's section.

Mason had the date of the Kent Corwin obituary. He opened the Northlake Ledger files for 2002, went to June, then scrolled to a couple of days before.

It didn't take much looking. The front page read, *Local Business Leader Still Missing.*

The subtitle is what caught his attention:

Search for Kent Corwin takes grim turn.

Mason scanned the article.

U.S. Coast Guard and the marine division of the Sable County Sheriff's office continued to search Lake Michigan for Northlake businessman Kent Corwin. In a press briefing after a third day, Sheriff Sam Sizemore acknowledged that the focus of the search had changed from a rescue to recovery.

Although reluctant to acknowledge that reality, and continuing to express hope for the family, Sheriff Sizemore eventually said, "We all know the temperature and violence of Lake Michigan. His time of survivability in the water would be hours, not days, so we are hoping to find that he managed some way to escape it and has just been unable to communicate with his family yet."

Kent Corwin, owner of Corwin Concrete and a pillar of the north Michigan building community, took his boat out on Lake Michigan three days ago shortly before an evening storm and did not return.

Mr. Corwin's boat was discovered capsized on a shoal along the shoreline just north of the Bluffs the next morning, unmanned. The Sheriff again warned local residents to use caution during storms on the big lake before stating that the search for Mr. Corwin will continue.

He scrolled forward a couple of days. It was easy to discover what had happened. The search was called off, and Kent Corwin was officially declared missing but presumed dead.

In the abstract, there was nothing unusual about this tragedy. Lake Michigan had been called the most dangerous lake in the United States, and not a summer went by without the lake claiming swimmers in riptides or ships in storms. Its clear bottom was littered with canoes and sails and steamers and diesels that had tried to cross it since man had first seen its beautiful blue horizon.

What was interesting to Mason was that he could see how this—the search, then the uncertainty—would have disabled the concrete business, how distraction then a gap in leadership could lead to a slip in standards on a job.

That seemed like a flavor that might matter, subtly, to a jury. If he could get it in, of course.

The original article had said that Sam Sizemore had been the sheriff back then.

Mason decided to see if Sean Sizemore, the current sheriff and Sam Sizemore's son, worked on holidays.

45

When the dispatcher told Mason that Sheriff Sizemore was off that day, Mason thought he'd have to wait to see him. Then, from his days at the Court, he remembered Sheriff Sizemore describing his church's production of an Easter passion play, complete with lights, sound, and a cable-enhanced Christ ascending into heaven. He recalled Sheriff Sizemore talking last year about how he was humbled to play Peter and that he certainly did not deserve all of the praise that had been heaped upon him for his portrayal since he had just fed off the rest of the cast, although some did say that Marty Pickett's Judas had fallen a bit flat that year.

So, knowing that there was no stage that Sheriff Sizemore didn't like to be the center of, Mason parked in the lot of the mega-church off the highway, which was unsurprisingly full that night, and once folks started streaming out, made his way in through the five-doored glass entrance and waited by the lobby coffee bar.

Sheriff Sizemore came out of the auditorium soon after, shaking hands, saying thanks, and smiling to all involved. He was in civilian clothes, though his aviators still hung from his shirt pocket and his slicked-back hair was unmussed as ever.

Mason hung back but, as always, his head and shoulders revealed him despite the crowd. When Sheriff Sizemore inevitably noticed Mason and nodded, Mason gestured that he'd like to talk. Sheriff Sizemore held up a finger, nodded, and accepted more kudos.

Eventually, the congregants dispersed, and Sheriff Sizemore came over. "Mason! I didn't know you came."

"I was a little late."

"I hope you enjoyed the production."

Mason pointed. "Your congregation certainly did."

Sheriff Sizemore scowled. "Did you even go?"

"Easter traffic was heck."

"What do you want, Mason? I don't have any leads on the car that hit your dad. He really couldn't give us anything besides a food delivery service that doesn't exist."

"No, it's not about my dad's accident. I know you're looking."

"Has he paid his tax bill then? You know I can't do anything if the treasurer has me execute the forfeiture."

This was the first Mason had heard of any tax lien. "It's not about that."

His eyes hardened. "We're not going to talk about Hyde Warren's trial. I feel bad for him, but my office is going to testify to exactly what we found."

"It's not that either, Sheriff. It's about a case your dad worked on."

Sheriff Sizemore blinked. "What?"

"The Kent Corwin accident back in 2002."

"You came here for that?"

"I just learned about it."

Sheriff Sizemore shook his head. "We've been working on

the play all day, Mason. I'm starving, and there's a potluck in our fellowship hall. We can talk about this some other time."

"Did they ever find him?"

"The Lake doesn't always give up its dead, Mason."

"Did your dad file the petition for the declaration of cause of death?"

"Why do you care?" Sheriff Sizemore's eyes narrowed. "Wait, Corwin ran a construction company, didn't he? Does this have something to do with the Cider Mill case? I told you I'm not talking about that."

"I just wondered if your dad found the body."

"You're the lawyer, Mason. Look up the cause of death petition. I'm going to go eat. Next time, come to the service."

With that, Sheriff Sizemore turned and followed the few remaining stragglers to the fellowship hall.

Mason exited the church, contemplating the mystery of an empty grave.

46

Red Gibson hung up his phone, got up, and poured himself a glass of bourbon. It was from one of those boutique Kentucky outfits on the Bourbon Trail, the kind that distilled a limited amount and sold it for a fortune but, once he'd found it, Red had decided that he liked it and, as the Chief Construction Officer for Warhelm Industrial Services, that he could afford it.

He poured it neat without bothering with the amaretto that night because he didn't want to wait to drink it. Not because he was afraid or nervous or steeling himself, but because he found that his best ideas came up when the warmth of the bourbon was going down and just then he wanted to think. So he drank and he stared at his phone and he thought.

He hadn't heard from Kevin Corwin in a long time. Years, now that Red counted, and the fact that he'd called at all showed just how spooked the good doctor must have been.

A lawyer showing up unexpected is never a good thing, and Red had to admit that the Pierce kid was more intimidating than most. Dr. Kevin had said Pierce had been asking about the Cider Mill project, and now Kevin was worried that somehow this all was going to blow back on him. Red had tried to calm him down and told Dr. Kevin to remember what a stickler for details his dad had been. There was no reason to think that the Pierce kid, even if he were as smart and slick as he was big and bald, would be able to pin the collapse on the Corwin company. And even if he did, the Corwin family business had been wrapped up years ago when Dr. Kevin had sold and they'd buttoned things up tight as a drum.

That's when Dr. Kevin had mentioned the part that led to Red's second bourbon. The Pierce kid had been interested in who was running the Cider Mill project after his dad died. Dr. Kevin hadn't told him, but he wanted Red to know in case the lawyer decided to bother him too.

Red Gibson had thanked him, then spent time assuring Dr. Kevin that he didn't need to worry—there was no way Dr. Kevin was personally responsible for what had happened in his dad's business all those years ago. But construction made Dr. Kevin jumpy; he'd never had instincts for it the way he did with animals, so it had taken a while for Red to talk him out of his nervous spiral. By the end of the call, though, Red was pretty sure he'd derailed it. Even though he was nervous, Dr. Kevin was smart, and the truth of what Red told him seemed to get through the fog of his panic—this was not Dr. Kevin's problem.

It was Red's.

He'd been the one in charge of the Cider Mill project after old man Corwin had gone missing in the big lake. Any screwup there would eventually fall on him.

Red took his time with a second bourbon, pondering the warmth in his chest and the ideas in his head, considering what, if anything, he needed to do next. Fortunately, his current job had given him a first-hand look at the patio when they'd cleared the rubble, and he hadn't seen any evidence that they'd screwed up the old job.

Still, old man Corwin had drilled into Red that no detail was too small to double-check, so when Red decided he needed to make a call himself, he also decided that he needed to check something first.

So Red Gibson finished his Kentucky bourbon.

He went and checked something.

Then he made a call.

~

WHEN KYLE STEWART finished telling Jerome Baggman what Mason Pierce had been doing for the last few days, Jerome Baggman said, "So you're saying there's nothing new to report?"

Kyle Stewart looked at the ceiling and shook his head before he said into the phone, "That's not what I'm saying at all."

"So Pierce went to the son of the former Corwin Concrete owner and checked into his death at the library and on his home computer—"

"And with the sheriff."

"And *maybe* with the sheriff, which you can't know for sure because I assume you haven't done something foolish like trying to surveil a church or a sheriff's office—"

"Of course not."

"So our construction worker is doing some historical research, but it doesn't matter. I've had associates on it, believe me, and the corporate trail runs cold after Corwin Concrete—there's no way to get money out of the dissolved entity, a successor entity, the estate of Kent Corwin, or the good Dr. Kevin Corwin. And once we determine there's no money there..."

"I know, you don't want to waste resources on it."

"That's not a profitable way to practice."

Kyle Stewart knew Jerome Baggman was right—there was

no money in going after Corwin Concrete. But Kyle didn't understand what Mason Pierce was doing, and every sharp knows that when you don't understand something, you shouldn't bet. And if you've already placed your bet when something unexplained happens, you better get it explained damn quick so that you can hedge if you need to.

Jerome Baggman filled the silence. "At the same time, I can't have Kramer Burns pointing the finger at an empty pot. Is that still their strategy?"

"Looks like it."

"From both sources?"

"Yes."

"And it's still just a faulty construction claim?"

Kyle Stewart paused. He was known for only giving reliable information, and he'd found that even when he couched things with "possible" or "maybe," people, and especially lawyers, tended to forget qualifiers when they were looking for someone to blame down the road.

"That was a long pause, Kyle."

"Freid mentioned something to Amber Vincent that suggested there might be something more."

"What?"

"It's not confirmed."

"I understand."

"I'm reluctant to mention it."

Jerome Baggman sighted. "We're ten days out from a criminal trial that could lock down an eight-figure payday, Kyle. Spit it out."

"Freid mentioned that there was evidence that the support pier had been tampered with."

"Tampered with? How?"

"He didn't say."

There was one good thing about working with Jerome

Baggman—he surfed a sea of ambiguity every day, and he didn't rail at incomplete information, especially when Kyle had told him that he only had incomplete information.

"I need to know what that's about."

"I'll find out."

"Good. Update me mid-week?"

Kyle had hoped to get until the end of the week, but things always happened faster as they approached trial. "You got it."

Jerome Baggman left the encrypted app. Kyle did too, then went back to trying to make his boss's job of extracting millions easier.

~

SHERIFF SIZEMORE BROKE down the last chair, placed it on the full cart, then waved off the custodian and pushed it to the storage area himself.

New acquaintances were always surprised that Sheriff Sizemore, with his slicked-back hair, ever-present aviators, and clear taste for the spotlight, was the last to leave events like this. People who knew him, though, came to rely on it so that when a problem came up, they automatically thought that "Sean's still here," and sought him out, a thought they carried with them, consciously and unconsciously, to the polls ever since he'd run for his father's office.

His father, the first Sheriff Sizemore, had taught him that, the value of becoming indispensable and reliable in places with a lot of voters, especially voters who were vocal in their support like those here at the church where he was storing the last of the overflow chairs from the Easter potluck.

His father had also taught him to close cases; the quicker, the better. And to do that, you needed to do your job, fully and with complete focus, close the book on it, and move to the next one with the same energy. Which meant you didn't have the time or capacity to think about cases in the rearview mirror.

He'd been a deputy when Kent Corwin had gone out night-fishing like an idiot right before a storm. Old man Corwin was a jackass, but an important enough one that Sheriff Sizemore remembered that his dad had taken charge of the investigation and supervised the marine units personally. Once they'd found the wreckage of the boat, it didn't take a detective to figure out what had happened—just one more rich asshole who thought that the laws of nature didn't apply to special people like him, the kind they rescued from deep water and sand dunes, without fail, every year.

No, it hadn't taken but a couple of days for his dad to solve that one, and Sheriff Sean Sizemore probably wouldn't have remembered it at all, except that it was the first time in his new career that he'd been involved in the process of declaring somebody dead. Normally, the family was the one who pulled the trigger on that, but you can't consider a case closed when someone is missing, and his father had hated loose ends, so he'd had Deputy Sean Sizemore go to the prosecutor and to the court and present evidence of the boat wreck, so that, on exactly the sixty-third day after Kent Corwin had gone after salmon without checking his weather radar or the sky itself, the court declared Kent Corwin dead and the first Sheriff Sizemore closed another case.

That recollection alone was more time than Sheriff Sean Sizemore liked to spend on closed cases, especially those that weren't his.

So he locked away the last cart of overflow chairs into the dark storage area of his church and gave it no more thought.

47

On the Monday morning after Easter, Mason was in the office by his usual time at seven. Melody was in as always at eight-twenty, offering a sunny hello and a thanks for starting the first pot, which Mason always felt guilty about since he'd drunk half of it by then. A little after nine, he heard the door and Melody said, "Good morning, Mr. Freid. How was your holiday?"

"Dandy, Melody. Is Pierce here yet?"

"In his office. Would you like some coffee?"

"Not just now, thanks."

Peter Freid walked in. "Working on the case?"

Mason nodded. "My direct of Dr. Thomas."

"I can give you an expert outline. Qualifications first, then straight to the point."

Mason nodded.

"What is your point?" asked Peter.

Mason ticked them off on his hand. "There weren't enough people on the patio to collapse it. The prosecution can't establish the weight of the snow beyond reasonable doubt. The pier collapsed due to a structural failure."

Peter nodded. "Then get the hell out."

"Got it."

Peter hesitated a moment, then plopped down in a chair. "Listen, about yesterday—"

Mason waved. "Everybody needs gas, Peter."

"It's not serious."

"It's not my business one way or the other."

"She's going back to Chicago soon."

"Really, Peter, I don't care."

"Didn't you date for a while?"

"We broke up months ago."

"But if she came back here—"

"It was permanent."

Peter stopped then and straightened a wrinkle on his pants that wasn't there. "We're all grown-ups. I just would have said something instead of just running into each other like that."

"Northlake is a small place."

"I've learned. So—"

"—So the most uncomfortable thing for me about this situation is this conversation."

Peter looked relieved. "Then it's over."

"Good. There's something else."

"About?"

"The case."

"Shoot."

So Mason recounted what he'd learned the day before—about Kent Corwin's death, that he'd died in a storm and was declared dead a couple of months later, about Dr. Kevin trying to run the business then selling it. He hesitated then, but then figured Peter had to know, so he told him about his own father and uncle had been competitors of Corwin Concrete, and how Dr. Kevin was still irritated about it.

Peter Freid frowned as Mason told him about Kent Corwin's

death. The frown grew as Mason told him about Dr. Kevin, until finally when he was talking about his father and uncle, Peter cut him off and said, "Jesus Christ, Pierce! Did you waste the whole weekend on this shit?"

Mason stopped.

"You've got a theory against Corwin Concrete, right?"

Mason nodded. "They didn't use rebar in the support pier, so it failed."

"What the hell does the death of the owner have to do with that?"

"The owner had a reputation for being a stickler for detail. This would help explain how that error could have occurred."

"We don't care how the error occurred! All that matters is that it did. Let the prosecutor try to explain it away. We're just in there flinging doubt at the wall to screw up her case."

"I was trying to turn square corners with the jury."

"This ain't a foundation, Pierce! The prosecutor's the one who has to turn square corners. Our job is to go in there and knock her case off its...now's the time for you to give me the construction term."

"Footers?"

Peter nodded. "Knock it right the hell off its footers. Get it?"

"Got it."

Peter stared at Mason for a moment. "I can see you're uncomfortable."

Mason shrugged.

"Why?"

Mason thought for a minute. "Because the pieces don't seem to fit."

Peter's irritation dissipated. "This isn't a wall, Pierce, it's a case. It's not our job to make the pieces fit together. It's our job to make sure they *don't*."

Mason stared.

Peter said, "If we have to go down this construction road, we're the guys with a wrecking ball. Every time Prosecutor Olsen or that prick Baggman stack a brick, we knock it down. That's it. You with me?"

"Yeah, sure."

"Focus on the Thomas exam."

"Got it."

Peter Freid stood. "We're only two weeks out. Plan on meeting with Thomas this weekend to nail down her testimony."

"Will do."

"And you'll be at the pretrial Friday with me."

"I was planning on it."

"Good. Did you buy the trial suits like I told you?"

"Last week, yes."

"I figured. I heard there was a run on catamaran sails."

"Work on that one long?"

"Just came to me. I'm quick like that."

"Amazing."

Peter left with no evidence of the awkwardness he'd professed on the way in.

Mason went back to work building his exam of Cameron Thomas.

PART VI

48

Early Friday morning, Cameron Thomas walked into Maggie's Deli. She'd arrived in Northlake late the night before and had forgotten to eat, so the smell of baked goods and coffee as she stepped through the door was delightful. A pleasant man named Yousef welcomed her, confirmed that they did indeed have a fruit and yogurt parfait, then convinced her that an apple Danish would be the perfect accompaniment. She moved down the line to the register where a woman with short dark hair and a charming smile gave her coffee and took her cash.

As Cameron Thomas waited for her change, she said, "Has a man named Mason Pierce been in yet?"

The woman's smile faltered, and Cameron couldn't help but notice the woman's glance go up and down her before she said, "Does he know you're looking for him?"

"He told me to meet him here."

The woman's smile returned. "Then he'll be here. I'm surprised he's late."

"I'm twenty minutes early."

"You must be here on the case."

"I am."

"We've had a lot of that this week." The woman pointed. "That's his table over there. When he sits anyway. I'm Maggie, if you need anything while you wait."

Cameron Thomas nodded and said, "Thanks, Maggie, I will," and as she went over to her table, she pretended she didn't notice Maggie's inspection.

She was partway through her parfait and considering giving in to the Danish when Maggie brought over a foil-wrapped package and a large coffee. Maggie's smile had fully returned. "I remember now. You're one of his experts, right?"

"I am."

Maggie set the foil and the coffee on the table. "So you don't have to wait to get started when he gets here."

"Thanks, Maggie. I'm sure he'll appreciate it."

At ten minutes before their meeting time, Mason Pierce walked through the door, along with a growing breakfast crowd. Cameron would expect someone that big to barge or shamble or plow into the room, but she realized she was being mentally lazy, which she abhorred. Instead, she noticed how careful he was, how he stepped aside and turned and waited to make sure he didn't jostle or bump anyone.

As he let a woman in front of him and stepped into line, Cameron raised a hand, then raised the foil package, which was hot to the touch. Mason waved and smiled, which changed his blunt, broken-nosed face completely, then gently tapped the woman's shoulder and squeezed out of line.

"Sorry, I'm late," he said.

"I'm early."

Mason pointed at the foil. "How'd you know?"

"Maggie thought it would save time."

That smile again. "She would."

He took the lid off the coffee, poured it into a thermal cup, then picked up the foil. "Do you mind?"

She gestured. "I'm halfway done."

As he unwrapped, he asked about her travel and her hotel and all the usual things so as not to seem rude before he got to what was on his mind. "You said on the phone that there might be a problem with the calculations."

Cameron Thomas nodded. "The lack of rebar definitely weakened the support pier."

"But?"

"But I can't say for certain that it caused the collapse."

Mason took a bite of his breakfast burrito, his heavy brow furrowed. "Can you say that it probably caused the collapse?"

"I can say that it probably contributed to the collapse."

Mason shook his head. "They'll kill us with that." He winced. "Sorry, bad choice of words."

"I realize the problem. That's why I called you. I'd like to do some testing on the composition of the concrete itself, see if there are any other issues we can attribute to the original builder, but I know we're getting so close that it might not be admissible."

Mason shook his head. "Don't worry, they were in such a hurry to try Hyde Warren that they didn't require expert reports."

"So I can do it?"

"Test away. At the very least, we'll be able to use it in the civil case."

"Everything still in the hangar?"

"Rubble galore."

"Dr. Cammie!"

Cameron Thomas looked up and saw Austin Pierce barreling over, a Northlake Seawall hat pushed back on his curly head, grinning through his thick brown beard. "Mason didn't say you were back! Are we going to The Loon tonight?"

Cameron couldn't help but smile. "I'm afraid this is a working trip, Austin."

"Bah, don't listen to this guy. There's always time for drafts and mini-tacos. How else are you going to live?"

"I told you I wasn't going to be around much until after the trial, Austin," said Mason.

Austin raised his chin. "I was talking to Dr. Cammie, not to my cousin."

"I'm afraid the same goes for me," said Cameron.

"Boo." Austin plopped down in the seat next to Mason, bumping his shoulder. "Stay on your side, Tiny."

Mason bumped him back but then turned sideways in what looked like an unconscious gesture. This left his breakfast burrito undefended, which allowed Austin to reach over and take a bite.

"We were just talking about the lack of rebar in the support pier," said Cameron.

"Cameron," said Mason.

"I'm investigating by talking to a witness who worked at the site."

Mason hesitated, then nodded.

"When you were clearing the rubble, did you notice anything else that would have contributed to the instability in the pier?"

"Hmm. My brain lacks sustenance."

Mason sighed, gestured.

Austin picked up the burrito and took another bite. "Not when we were clearing it, no. It was still frozen solid. But remember December this year, Mace?"

"Not especially, no."

Austin shook his head. "That's right, you were an inside dog.

It froze and thawed like a b—, it froze and thawed a lot. We must have had three or four rains and freezes. Made it impossible to work."

"Muddy?"

Austin nodded. "That and the temp change destroyed the gravel roads. Looked like bombs went off with all the potholes. It was doing the same thing to shorelines. There was an awful lot of ground moving."

"What about at the Cider Mill?"

"No idea. Wanna go see?"

Mason shook his head. "I have a pretrial this morning."

"Play hooky."

"I don't think my client accused of manslaughter would appreciate that."

"How about you, Dr. Cammie?"

"I have to get the testing samples out before the weekend," she said. "How about after work?"

Austin frowned. "But that means I'll have to go to work."

"It does," said Mason, smiling.

"Balls."

"Indeed."

Austin sighed and popped the last bit of burrito into his mouth. "Fine. Call me."

Two more lime green Northlake Seawall shirts caught Cameron's eye as Lily and Bronson came over.

"Ah, the lovebirds have left the nest," said Austin. He waved a hand. "Welcome."

"Stuff it," said Lily.

"Because you're my sister, I'll pass on the obvious opening there. Morning, Soldier Boy."

Bronson nodded. "Ready? We have to be there by—"

Austin rolled his eyes. "If you tell me the military time that we're expected at the job site, I'm going to scream."

Bronson looked around, then closed his mouth.

"He really did it last time," Lily said to Cameron.

Austin grinned.

"That's all right, we have to go too," said Mason and stood. "I have to get to the pretrial."

Cameron stood. "I'll go to the hangar to get the samples, then meet you at the site after."

"Perfect."

"Can I go to the hangar too?" said Austin.

"No," said Mason, Lily, and Bronson.

49

Judge Roderick looked over his glasses. "Mr. Pierce, does Mr. Freid intend to grace us with his presence today?"

Before he could help himself, Mason looked over his shoulder. Astrid Olsen was sitting at the prosecutor's table, with Jerome Baggman in the row right behind her, but Peter Freid was not in the courtroom.

"I believe so, Your Honor, yes."

"Where is he then?"

"I'm sure he's on his way."

"Ms. Gorman, do we have a full docket this morning?"

Holly Gorman squinted through her leopard-print glasses at her computer screen. "We do, Judge."

Judge Roderick nodded. "Let the record reflect that all parties are represented by counsel for this final pretrial, Astrid Olsen for the State, Mason Pierce for the defendant. Also present is civil counsel Jerome Baggman. Absent is trial counsel for the defendant, Peter Freid. Ms. Olsen, is this case proceeding to trial?"

"Yes, Your Honor."

"Are you seeking to modify the charges prior to trial?"

"No, Your Honor. We will be proceeding with seven counts of involuntary manslaughter."

"Have you made a plea offer?"

"We have, Your Honor. If the defendant pleads guilty to all seven counts, we will recommend a concurrent sentence to Your Honor."

"Your response, Mr. Pierce?"

"We have rejected that, Judge."

"Basis?"

"There's no incentive to accept such an offer, Judge. They haven't reduced the base charge, and at my client's age, one manslaughter sentence is the same as seven. As Ms. Olsen is aware."

"Ms. Olsen, do you intend to offer a reduced charge?"

Astrid Olsen glanced over her shoulder. "No, Your Honor."

"All right then, you know the drill, counselors. You're first up...Ah, Mr. Freid. Welcome to your proceeding."

Peter Freid hurried up the aisle. "My apologies, Your Honor. I—"

"Mr. Pierce can fill you in on what you missed, Mr. Freid. Trial date is confirmed ten days from today. Ms. Gorman, do we have their trial briefs and jury instructions?"

"Yes, Judge," Holly Gorman said.

"Do you want to work the weekend before trial, Ms. Gorman?"

"No way!" Holly Gorman blushed. "I mean, I'll do whatever you say, Judge."

"Me neither, Ms. Gorman. Objections are due Tuesday, Counsel. Be here at eight on the morning of trial and we'll issue any rulings to get things rolling by nine. And I expect you two to call each other before you bother me with disputes. Understood?"

"Yes, Your Honor," said Mason, Peter, and Astrid. Jerome Baggman just smiled.

Judge Roderick pulled out a black three-ring binder. "I also received this from the State." He dropped it with a thud. "Tell me you're not planning on calling one hundred and seventy-eight fact witnesses, Ms. Olsen."

Astrid straightened. "Your Honor, we've obtained affidavits from one hundred and seventy-eight people who have attested that they were on the patio the night it collapsed. We have a right to—"

"You have a right to one day of testimony on that, Ms. Olsen. The affidavits will serve for whatever other point you're trying to make."

"But, Your Honor—"

"One day. Anything else?"

No one said anything.

"Then I'll see you all—"

Jerome Baggman leaned forward and whispered to Astrid Olsen, who nodded.

"Your Honor," she said. "How would you like us to handle the transfer of the patio evidence from the hangar to here?"

"Just how much evidence do you plan on handling, Ms. Olsen?"

"Not too much. A representative sample of some of the sections to help the jury understand the expert testimony."

"Didn't I appoint a special master on that, Ms. Gorman?"

"You did, Judge."

"Contact him then; he'll arrange transport with the sheriff's department."

Mason Pierce stood. "When will that be, Judge?"

"Whenever the special master says, Mr. Pierce. Why?"

"We're completing our investigation."

Jerome Baggman made a tsking sound and shook his head.

"Well, I certainly don't want pieces of concrete and steel cluttering up my courtroom before trial. Is the weekend before agreeable to everyone for transport?"

A chorus of "Yes, Judge."

Judge Roderick smiled. "See how easy that was? Coordinate the time and items with the special master and look over his shoulder all you want, but, just so you know, he has my utmost confidence. Anything else?"

This time, the silence stood.

"Good. See you in ten days. Ms. Gorman, warn the special master they're coming."

They all stood as Judge Roderick left. Once he did, Peter said, "What testing?"

"Cameron Thomas is in town. She's running some final tests."

Peter Freid shook his head. "And her meter, I suppose."

"We need to nail down the support pier failure."

Peter shook his head. "I told you, Pierce. We aren't building foundations—we're knocking them down."

"Just getting a bigger wrecking ball, Peter."

Jerome Baggman looked at Mason, then he motioned Astrid over and whispered in her ear, nodding his head as he did. Then he pulled back, looked at her, and nodded again.

"I agree," said Astrid.

Jerome Baggman smiled. Then he said, "Last-minute scramble, Big Boy?"

"Just some finish work, Jerome," Mason said, and left.

~

THERE WEREN'T many cars at the Cider Mill when Mason arrived, which wasn't a surprise. Although Hyde had reopened the distillery and bar, the site of the largest mass-casualty event in the history of Northlake wasn't much of a place for a night on the town or a lunch with friends. Those that did wander in were usually from out of town.

As Mason parked, he was surprised to see a Northlake Seawall truck among the vehicles. When he came around the side of the building to the shoreline, Austin Pierce was there, talking to Cameron Thomas.

"What are you doing here?" said Mason to Austin.

Austin grinned through his beard. "Helping you and Dr. Cammie."

"I'd love to hear how."

"Dr. Cammie recognizes a seawall expert when she sees one."

Mason looked at Cameron, who shrugged. "If I have to add soil shifting to my model to explain the collapse, I thought it best if the information didn't come from the defense attorney."

"I'm not sure the defense attorney's cousin is any better."

"Can't you just say the top seawall expert in Northlake?" said Austin.

"That would be your sister."

"The second best then."

"That would be your brother-in-law."

"Northlake's seawall bronze medalist?"

"That's me."

Austin grinned and pointed. "Northlake's third-best *active* seawall authority."

"There you go. How'd you get away from number one and number two, by the way?"

"I am out getting sandwiches."

"We best get down there and take a look then."

Mason, Cameron, and Austin made their way down the slope. The rubble had long since been cleared, so what remained was the original rip rap seawall of large rocks, small rocks, and fill. They slid their way down to where the collapsed support pier had been.

The three of them checked the area, Austin kicking dirt and rock, Mason picking up stray rocks and small concrete fragments, Cameron staring.

"It's hard to tell after all of the excavation," said Cameron.

"You can see some things," Austin said. "See that groove?" He pointed up the slope.

Cameron nodded.

"That's from runoff. And it's running right toward where the column was, here."

"It disappears before that," said Mason.

"Duh," said Austin. "The excavators would have scraped it away. But you see down there by the waterline it picks up again."

Mason squinted, tracked the two lines. "It might have run by the support pier."

"The grounds a little loose," said Cameron. "But that could just as easily be from the removal."

"You're not looking, Mace," said Austin.

"At what?"

"Have you been an inside dog that long?"

Mason stared at the rip rap. He stared at the groove and the footer and the surrounding rocks. He didn't see it.

"What am I missing, Austin?"

"Bark to be let out."

Mason stared.

Austin laughed and raised his hands. "Okay, okay. No need to get all glarey. Look at the dirt between the big rocks."

Mason nodded. "I see it."

"Exactly, Mace," said Austin. "*Look at the dirt between the rocks.*"

Mason swore.

Austin grinned. "Who's a good boy? You are."

"What is it?" said Cameron.

"So to prevent soil erosion beneath the rocks, you have to install a granular layer or a fabric before you put on the larger rocks," said Mason. "If you don't, the ground underneath can wash away. One way to tell if that's happening is if the large rocks on top start to get buried in the soil that was underneath."

Cameron stared. "There's a lot of dirt around these rocks."

Mason nodded. "I didn't notice at first because it was covered in snow when the site collapsed. But these large rocks shouldn't have this much dirt between them." He shook his head. "I should've noticed right away when we walked down there."

"Woof," said Austin, still grinning.

"So if the soil was eroding, that would have caused more stress on the pier, right?" said Mason.

"Maybe." Cameron squatted down and stared at the footer. "It could have exerted pressure or shifted the ground. Since there was no rebar in the pier, it would be more susceptible to cracking and failure."

Mason turned. "Austin, can you step away for a minute?"

Austin pushed his hat back and frowned.

"Inside dog stuff," said Mason.

He pulled his hat back down and grinned. "I'll be up the hill when you need me." He scrambled up the slope with an agility that was surprising for his girth.

Mason turned back to Cameron. "Does that give you the instability that you need?"

"It might," said Cameron. "But the real question is, does it help your defense?"

Mason thought it through. "So if the seawall wasn't installed right, I don't think Hyde Warren would have known. He would have relied on the contractor. It would be one thing if it was obvious, but we're talking about a fine layer of filter material or fabric buried under tons of big rocks that then had a stone patio built over it. I don't see how Hyde *could* have known."

Mason was quiet for a moment. Cameron waited as Mason fought through his natural instincts to remember Peter's description of his job.

"If we can show that the construction company didn't do its job when it built the pier and the seawall company didn't do its job when it built the seawall, I think it becomes a lot harder to blame Hyde for the deaths."

"If he overloaded the patio, he'd still be considered a cause though, wouldn't he?"

"Definitely in the civil case. But in a criminal case, I think it's a lot harder to lock a guy up if there's a bunch of other reasons why the person, why the *people*, were killed."

Cameron nodded.

"Do you think we can go farther?" asked Mason.

"How much farther?"

"Can we say that the pier wouldn't have collapsed if the pier and the seawall had been built properly?"

"I couldn't testify to that when it was just the missing rebar. I'll have to dig in to see how much soil has eroded to know for sure."

"We'll need to check the seawall to see if we're right first," said Mason. "I don't think it's worth our time if they built the seawall correctly. The real benefit to us in the criminal case is if we can show a whole bunch of other people caused this."

"Makes sense. How do we do that?"

"We'll need to excavate a part of the seawall to see if there's a filter layer or fabric underneath. We don't need much, but we'll have to be careful not to disturb the structural integrity of the whole wall."

Cameron shook her head. "Where are we going to find someone to do that on a Friday afternoon?"

Mason smiled. “Sounds like a job for the third-best active seawall builder in Northlake.”

“Are you two about done?” Austin yelled.

Cameron smiled back. “I’m not done taking the samples from the pier. I still need to get that in before the weekend.”

“And I’ll need to find out from Hyde who built the wall.”

“I’m getting hungry!” said Austin.

“And probably pick up some sandwiches.”

50

"Where have you been?" said Peter Freid as Mason walked into the office.

Mason stopped, stared. "Really?"

Peter appeared to realize the hypocrisy of the comment but then barreled on. "I understand that, but we have work to do."

"I was doing it. I was out at the site with Cameron Thomas."

Peter scowled. "I thought she was doing following up testing on the concrete?"

"We found a new lead."

"Which is?"

Mason told Peter about the potential soil erosion at the site and the possibility that the contractor hadn't installed the seawall properly.

It took a couple of questions, and he had to explain what granular filter and nonwoven geotextile fiber were, but once he understood what Mason was talking about, Peter got the legal ramifications right away. "We might be able to blame a second person? That's perfect! That's using that big, beautiful noggin' of yours like a wrecking ball. When will we know if they screwed it up?"

"I've got someone looking at it tomorrow."

"Perfect. Who was the original contractor?"

"I was just going to check."

"Well, go, go! And let me know when you do."

Mason ignored Peter's slap on his shoulder and went to his office, then shut the door as Peter was telling Melody how smart he'd been to hire the big bastard.

He started to look for the box Hyde had given him but then remembered that it was all in the efile. He did a term search for "seawall" and found three documents in the file, one of which was the contract.

Mason opened the document. And stared.

A second later, his phone buzzed. Austin.

"Hi, Austin."

"Hey, Mace, about that indie job you offered me at the Cider Mill tomorrow? I can't do it."

"What happened?" although Mason knew exactly what had happened.

"I told Dad I might need to use an excavator tomorrow. He said no problem. Then he asked me for what job, so I told him. And he blew his shit."

"Because Northlake Seawall did the original install?"

"You already knew? Jesus, Mace, you could have saved me an ass-chewing!"

"I didn't know; I just found out myself. Sorry, man."

Mason's phone buzzed. He looked.

"Looks like I have an incoming ass-chewing myself," he said.

"Good luck, Cuz," said Austin, and hung up.

Mason stared at "Uncle Troy" on his screen. He took a breath and answered.

"Hi, Uncle—"

"This is how you treat family?" Mason held the phone away from his ear. "You're going to pull us into your pigsty of shit?"

"Uncle Troy, I didn't know—"

"How many companies build seawalls in Northlake, you dumbass? Six? Seven? You didn't think to see if it was your family's company before you accused it of mass murder?"

"I wasn't going to accuse anyone of murder, Uncle Troy."

"What a fucking lawyer thing to say. No, you're going to say our shitty workmanship killed seven people. That's way better! I think I'll put that on our ad flyer next month!"

"Uncle Troy—"

"How did someone so stupid even pass law school? I expect this kind of stupid shit from my brother, but you're supposed to be the smart one! What a crock of shit!"

"Uncle Troy, I'm sorry. I already told Austin not to come tomorrow—"

"No, you didn't! I did! He's not digging up our work, and neither are you."

Mason took a breath. "I have to, Uncle Troy."

"What? What do you mean you have to?"

"I have to find out if the wall was causing erosion under the pier."

"You mean you have to see if your uncle screwed up a wall. I'll save you the backhoe rental, Mason. I didn't. I used fabric on that just like I do on all the jobs and have since I started this business."

"I understand, Uncle Troy."

"So you won't dig it up?"

Mason paused. "I didn't say that."

"You ungrateful little prick. I kept your family afloat. My wife kept your life afloat. And your first big case, you dump on us? What the hell is wrong with you?"

"I'm not going to dump on you, Uncle Troy. But I have to investigate my case."

"Don't come around anymore, you short-memoried shit."

"Okay."

Uncle Troy hung up. Mason's heart was pounding as he stared at the screen. He barely had time to catch his breath when Peter Freid came in. "So who was it?"

"We have a problem."

"What's that?"

"The seawall company, it's my uncle's."

Peter Freid frowned. "That is a problem. Does your family have an ownership interest?"

"I just told you; my uncle owns it."

"No, I mean, you, your mom, or your dad."

Mason didn't hold the mom thing against him. Instead, he just said, "No."

"Is that the place you worked while you were at the court?"

"And before, yes."

"Still getting checks from them?"

"No."

"And you're too young to have been working for them when the patio was built, right?"

"Right."

Peter broke into a grin. "Then there's no conflict. No problem at all."

"But it's family, Peter."

"That'll make your argument even more effective! Reluctant and all that. It's actually better this way."

"Peter, I can't do that to my family."

Peter's eyes narrowed. "I told you it's not a conflict. The firm will say the same."

"It's not a technical conflict, maybe, but it's an actual one."

"The firm won't agree."

Mason shrugged, then stared.

Peter didn't back off. "We have a guy who trusts us looking at the rest of his life in prison, Mason. You've met Hyde. No way he makes it. We owe him a duty to do everything we can. And the next associate I put on this case will."

Mason snorted. "The next associate won't know rip rap from hip-hop."

Now Peter stared.

Mason thought, then said, "If the wall's made properly, this isn't an issue, right?"

Peter thought. "True."

"Then let me find out, and then you and I can decide whether to have this fight."

Peter didn't look convinced.

Mason anticipated Peter's next argument. "I'll do it with Cameron so you know what I say is true."

"I trust you, Mason. Ish." He stared at Mason, then said, "I want to know by the end of the weekend."

"I'll do the initial dig myself to make sure it gets done."

"Fine."

Then without another word, Peter Freid left, and Mason hopped online for last-minute excavator rentals.

Peter didn't say anything to Melody this time as he passed.

51

On Saturday afternoon, Kyle Stewart was deep into a playoff basketball game in both attention and cash. He was monitoring the score on TV, the individual stat lines on his tablet, and his in-game bets on his phone when his phone screen shifted to an incoming call from "The Baggman."

Kyle cursed when he lost track of the bet that was about to post and frowned when he realized who it was because it was unusual for Jerome Baggman to contact him off schedule. He answered through the encrypted app.

"What's this new defense Kramer Burns is making?" said Jerome Baggman.

"What do you mean?" said Kyle Stewart, his mind still half on his bets.

"That's not the way the flow of information is supposed to work, Mr. Stewart."

Kyle forgot all about the game.

"Of course not, Mr. Baggman. If you could tell me what prompted the call, I'll address it."

"I understand that Mason Pierce is out there on a Saturday afternoon just nine days before trial, operating an excavator on the seawall. What is he doing?"

Kyle had put two systems in place to monitor developments: the electronic ones at Mason's house and the human one with Peter Freid. Neither had given him any inkling of this.

More importantly, something outside of his control had informed Jerome Baggman.

"I'll find out."

"You don't know?"

"Not yet."

"So that's a no?"

"It's a not-yet. How did you hear?"

Silence at the other end of the line. Then, "You should know by now that I leave very little to chance, Mr. Stewart. And I know you know all about hedging. In fact, some would say you're an expert at it."

Kyle literally broke into a cold sweat—the back of his neck tingled, he shivered, and four beads of sweat broke right at his nondescript hairline and trickled down each temple—because he knew what that meant.

Baggman had someone else on the case too.

"I'll have the answer for you right away."

"Someone will," said Baggman.

Kyle Stewart pressed his lips together.

"And someone will get a bonus on this case. In direct proportion to their contribution."

Kyle knew that Baggman would pay him for his time. But time didn't pay the bills. Or his bets.

Bonuses on eight-figure settlements did.

"Understood," said Kyle Stewart.

"Good. I look forward to hearing from you."

The call ended, and his betting app popped back up.

He'd lost every prop bet during the call, and he was now underwater on the spread. *Goddam three-point shots.*

Kyle left his rental and went to see what he could find out.

He lost the rest of his bets on the way.

52

There's nothing worse than trying to do a job with the wrong tool, especially when you know how easy it would be with the right one. Mason cursed, again and finally admitted to himself that it was futile.

He'd planned on having Austin's help to excavate a section of the seawall to check for erosion protection. More importantly, he'd planned on using one of Northlake Seawall's excavators. His discovery that Northlake Seawall had installed the seawall and his conversation with Uncle Troy made it clear that wasn't going to happen. So Mason had been left scrambling to find a piece of equipment he could rent, on a Saturday, with no reservation, that he could haul behind his own truck, that would do the job. He wound up driving to Traverse City to a big box store that rented tools and equipment and picking up a mini-excavator that he suspected wasn't going to be big enough but, with trial almost a week away, felt obligated to try.

It wasn't big enough. The arm wasn't long enough to reach where he needed to dig from the top of the Cider Mill's slope, the bucket wasn't wide enough to manage the large stones that made up the top of the rip rap, and the treads weren't sturdy enough to risk rolling down the steep slope, unless he wanted to end up with a mini-excavator in the lake. He tried to access the seawall from different parts of the slope, he tried to reach down far enough from the top, and he even tried to move some of the rocks farther up, but the mini-excavator was meant for backyard tasks, not major construction, and after a couple of hours, Mason knew he had to give up.

So Mason loaded the mini-excavator back on his trailer and headed back to Traverse City. He hurried to make it back in time to avoid wasting the Firm's money on a second day of rental charges, especially since he knew he was going to have to hit the Firm with a bill for a full-blown commercial rental Monday morning when those kind of rental businesses were open.

The time wasted on the drive, and on the failed attempt, was bad enough. What was worse, though, was that he still didn't know if his uncle's company had installed the seawall correctly.

~

THE SUN WAS low when Mason got home, the temperature pleasant, and there was little wind, all of which was rare enough at this time of year, so that when Mason unhooked his trailer and stowed it, he decided to sit outside to think. So Mason walked through the three-season room on the back of his small house, leaving his phone on an end table, out the screen door, and down the narrow path worn by his feet to the landing at the edge of the bluff.

The landing wasn't much, just a plain twenty-four by sixteen deck of weathered cedar, with a couple of plastic chairs and one sturdy wooden Adirondack. The structure wasn't the point, though. The view was.

The deck, and the edge of Mason's property, sat at the top of a bluff looking down onto Lake Michigan. It wasn't so high here as it was at *The Bluffs*, maybe two hundred feet above the lake, but it still offered an uninterrupted view of the vast expanse of Lake Michigan. A wooden stair, complete with two landings on the way, led down to the beach at the water's edge. The width of the beach depended entirely on the lake's level—a couple of years ago, the water had pounded right up to the bottom of the stairs, while a few years before that, the strip of sand had easily been fifty yards. This year, the beach was somewhere in between and more than wide enough to enjoy a spot in the sand.

Mason wasn't interested in heading down today, though. No, today, he pulled the heavy wooden Adirondack over, centered it on the deck, and sat. Then he watched as the sun, probably three orbs above the water, sank into the lake. Which, in a nutshell, was why he'd never sell the place and never move into some subdivision, however upscale it was.

As the sun set, Mason wasn't sure what he was going to do about Northlake Seawall. He knew he was going to rent an industrial-sized excavator on Monday and then learn whether his uncle's company, his former employer and lifeline, had installed the proper drainage under the seawall. If he had, it wasn't an issue. But if Uncle Troy had cut corners or messed up or forgotten, Mason's firm owed it to Hyde Warren to bring it up. And that was a problem.

If Northlake Seawall was mentioned in the manslaughter case, it would be added as a potentially responsible party in the civil case. That might get it joined in the civil suit. At the very least, the jury would allocate fault to his uncle's company, putting a specific percentage on the amount of responsibility his uncle bore for the deaths and injuries. Even if a judgment was never sought against Northlake Seawall, the publicity would be ruinous. It could kill the company, which Mason realized was a bad choice of words even as he thought it.

Peter Freid had been right—Mason didn't have an actual

legal conflict that would disqualify him or the firm from pointing the finger at his uncle's company, a company that also employed Austin and Lily and Bronson. But he had a personal one, a moral one, of whether he would ruin everything his extended family had worked for on the off chance that it would keep his client out of prison.

There was no question he wouldn't participate in the civil case if this is how things shook out; that went without saying. But he couldn't back out of Hyde's criminal case—not now when they were so close to trial and with Mason being the one who knew all of the technical elements of the case. Hyde, and his firm, were counting on him.

The sun had dropped another orb's worth, and Mason was no closer to a solution when he heard a car pull up. He frowned as a door slammed. He listened, but didn't hear the car leave, like it would if it were a delivery.

He was watching the sun sink while waiting for the car to start again when he heard a voice.

"Mason? Mason!"

Cameron.

"Back here!" he called as he stood. He started to walk back toward the house when Cameron came running around the side of the house.

That sells it short. She was sprinting.

"Cameron! What's wrong?"

"You're not answering your phone."

"I just set it down a little bit ago—"

She waved him off. "Doesn't matter. I was collecting samples for the testing on the support pier—"

"I thought that was yesterday?"

"I didn't finish after our detour to the site with Austin." She paused. "What did you find, by the way?"

"Nothing."

"How can that be?"

"Wrong equipment. I'll have to try again Monday."

"Right." She shook her head. "Anyway, I was taking samples of the support pier and breaking a piece off when I found this."

She held up a plastic bag.

"What is it?"

Cameron handed it to him. Mason took the bag, smoothed it out, then held it up against the dying light. "A ring?"

Cameron nodded. "I can't tell the base metal yet—gold, sterling silver, some alloy, I don't know, but the important thing is that it resists corrosion in concrete."

Mason looked closer. "Looks like a class ring."

Cameron nodded. "Uh-huh."

"Okay. So someone's ring slipped off into the mix. I mean, not a great idea to wear something like that on a worksite, but it happens."

"Look closer."

Mason raised an eyebrow at her. She waved again for him to look.

Mason pulled the plastic bag tight so he could read the name of the school circling the gem.

United States Naval Academy.

He scowled, flipped the ring to its side.

1970.

"Didn't you say the owner of Corwin Concrete was a military guy?" Cameron said.

"C'mon," said Mason, and they hurried inside, ignoring the last of the sunset.

53

Mason pulled up the obituary for Kent Corwin on his computer in the spare room. Along with his status as a prominent businessman, avid fisherman, and devoted father, it listed his many accomplishments.

Including graduating from the US Naval Academy in 1970.

"Hello, Sailor," said Cameron, reading over his shoulder.

Mason started clicking screens.

"What are you looking for?" she said.

"The dates of the Cider Mill job."

He pulled up the bid, the schematic for the patio, and the billings and wrote down the dates on a Post-it. Then he clicked back to the obituary and pointed at the screen.

"He went missing right in the middle of the project," said Cameron.

"Looks like it." Mason sat back and thought.

"What happened to him?"

"According to his son and the court documents, he got caught in a storm while he was fishing on the big lake and drowned."

"Did they find his body?"

"Nope. Just the boat."

Cameron sat down now, and the two of them stared and thought.

"He might have just lost the ring, taken it off, knocked it into the concrete mix," said Cameron. "Something like that."

"True. Weirder things have happened on a job site. Except..." Mason trailed off, thinking.

"Except?"

"Here. You know how this works, but look." Mason's fingers flew over the keys and he pulled up a schematic diagram of a support pier. "They used solid forms for the support piers, right?"

"Right."

"With crisscrossing rebar for support. You've been able to see that in the other piers, yes?"

"Yes."

"So the pattern of rebar they used takes up a lot of space, right?"

"Not really."

"No, I mean, with rebar crisscrossing inside of the form, there isn't room for anything inside the form except for concrete, is there?"

"That's true. What are you saying?"

"I'm saying, that with the rebar in place, there isn't room inside the form for a body."

Mason hit a button, and the rebar disappeared from the schematic. "But if you take the rebar out?"

Cameron stared. "Look at that. Concrete casket."

"Yep."

"But who would do that?"

Mason shook his head. "No idea. But that doesn't matter yet."

"It doesn't matter that there might have been a dead guy in the support pier?"

"No, it doesn't matter who put it there. First, we have to figure out if it matters for the stability of the support pier."

Cameron was with him now. "Having a support pier with no rebar is one thing. Having a support pier with no rebar and a large man-sized air pocket with no concrete is a whole other level."

"Would that make it unstable enough to collapse?"

"It very well might be. I'll do the math tonight."

Mason nodded. "If the math works out, then we can go on to the next problems."

"Which are?"

"Well, first of all, we don't have a body."

Cameron smiled. "There's that."

"So we would have to prove that there was one, and I doubt this"—he held up the baggie with the ring—"is going to be enough."

"That's just it, there's not enough..." Cameron stopped. Her eyes widened. "There's not enough material."

"What do you mean?"

"I mean, there's not as much concrete there."

Mason shook his head. "Sorry, still not getting it."

Cameron leaned forward. "I've analyzed all of the support piers. It's how I knew that the others had rebar. Parts of those were broken by the collapse too, but there are still big sections that are intact."

Mason nodded.

"So I have a good sense of how large each of them was, how much concrete there was. And I'm telling you there's less concrete there for the one that failed."

"Is that because it broke into more pieces and was scattered about or put in the wrong grid?"

"That's what I'd been assuming, but now...,"

Her eyes widened. "Mason, the jackhammer marks. We've been thinking about them all wrong. They weren't made *before* the collapse—"

Mason got it immediately. "They were made *after*! Somebody knew what was in that pier—"

"—and they took it away."

They both sat there, thinking, 'til Cameron said, "We could be wrong—"

"—But we're not. It all makes too much sense."

"So what do we do? Call the Sheriff?"

Mason shook his head. "Not yet."

"Don't you have to?"

"Because we found a ring? I don't think so. The rest is guesswork. Good guesswork, but guesswork. Here's what we do. You do your calculations and see if this makes a difference for our case. If you can show, mathematically, that a concrete pier with a Kent Corwin-sized hole in it was more prone to failure, that goes a long way toward our defense."

"*If* we can show there was a body-sized void in the pier."

"Right. So you do the calculation. Can you get it done tomorrow?"

Cameron nodded.

"Good. Monday, I'm going to keep doing what I was doing—I'll rent an industrial-sized excavator and see if Uncle Troy put erosion barrier down."

"Does it matter?"

"Not if he put it down."

"So isn't it a waste of time?"

"No. First of all, if it's there, it eliminates Northlake Seawall as a cause of the collapse and, selfishly, helps repair my relationship with my uncle. I hope. Second, though, I'm willing to bet that me banging around in an excavator is going to attract the attention of the state and Baggman, who are going to wonder what the hell I'm doing. And that's going to free you up for your investigation at the hangar."

"Which is?"

"To go through every bit of the pier and see if you can find anything else like this." He jiggled the ring-bag. "Clothes or shoe fiber, bone, anything that would support our theory that there was a body in there."

"And so we can prove it's Kent Corwin?"

"I don't really care about that. Any body will do. But I'd say this ring puts us a long way there."

The two thought for a moment before Mason said, "We can't tell anybody until we figure this out."

"No? Why?"

"Think how desperate we look if we're wrong. The state will argue that we'd say anything to get Hyde off the hook, and the perception wouldn't be wrong."

Cameron shrugged. "You're the lawyer."

"Let's not even tell Peter until we have a better handle on it."

"Career preservation?"

"A little. He already told me to drop this once."

"No problem."

"Cameron, this is really well done. You may have saved him, Hyde."

"We've got a long way to go."

"We do. Still."

Cameron smiled. "Thanks."

"Dinner?"

"Starving."

With that, Mason whose cupboard was light but not bare, made some cast iron chicken thighs with peppers, onions, and rice, while the two mapped out what was next and guessed about what they might find.

~

By the time Kyle Stewart returned to his apartment that night, he'd had it. He'd followed Mason Pierce all day, most of which had been spent banging around at the Cider Mill in a mini-excavator that was clearly too small for the job. It took Pierce an hour longer than Kyle to figure that out, and Kyle was forced to watch as the big attorney loaded the too-small excavator back onto the trailer and was forced to follow him back to Traverse City in case he detoured somewhere on the way. Then Kyle had followed Pierce back to his street but, since it was a semi-deserted gravel road with only a few other houses on it, Kyle didn't dare follow him in for fear of attracting attention. The only upside was that he knew Pierce wasn't going anywhere; he was too much of a creature of habit, so Kyle knew that, now that Pierce was home for the evening, he was staying there.

Kyle took his time going home. He ordered some takeout and went to place another bet while he waited, only to be reminded that his account was empty. He checked his emergency fund, which he was surprised to find was also empty until he remembered the basketball opportunity he'd pursued the day before.

It was against his rules to tap into his emergency fund, and it was certainly against his rules to tap into his second emergency fund, but the call from Baggman had him shook and by the time his Szechuan beef was ready, he'd transferred the money and placed three bets. Then he hopped in the car and hustled home.

Though he wasn't expecting to hear anything, he turned on the live feed of the devices in Pierce's house. And was astounded by what he heard.

A body. The two voices were talking about a body.

He dropped his takeout and hit the volume on his monitor, and isolated to the camera in the spare room. He recognized the back of a blond head as Cameron Thomas, the expert. She was leaning over Pierce's wide shoulder. His bald head was blocking the monitor screen. Kyle turned the volume all the way up.

They were talking about a body being in the support pier.

He didn't dare move. He strained and he listened and he watched, his Szechuan beef forgotten.

The more they talked, the more it became clear that they didn't have a body; they had a clue that a body had been there. Several times, the woman tapped something, the clue, on the desk but Kyle couldn't see it and, while he was listening, she never said what it was.

Kyle's ears perked up when the Thomas woman said she'd start looking for more evidence first thing in the morning and then Pierce said he'd see what he could find out too, though he didn't say how or what.

Then they agreed on an important thing—they weren't going to tell the Sheriff about their suspicions, and they weren't even going to tell anyone in Pierce's firm, which meant they certainly weren't going to tell the prosecutor. Instead, they'd investigate and see what they found and then see if this all was something they could use.

The two left the spare room with the camera. Kyle turned the volume down for the spare room mic and up for one of the hidden main room mics. Pierce's voice garbled by a tapping noise, then sizzling. Kyle realized the man was cooking.

Pierce came closer to the microphone, and the noises changed to serving and eating and their conversation became markedly less interesting as the Thomas woman asked Pierce about what projects he planned to do next with the house, followed by a discussion of what type of wood or composite would work best to replace the rickety stair down to the beach. His interest came back for a moment when they cleaned up, as he wondered if more than dinner was coming, but there would be no free show that night as he heard the Thomas woman say it was time for her to go.

When the Thomas woman had left and the sounds coming over the mic were just those of Pierce cleaning up, Kyle opened his software so that he could watch and listen to what had happened before he came home, to see what he'd missed.

What he got was a notification that his file was corrupted.

He re-opened, re-booted, re-everything'd.

File corrupted.

He didn't waste time cursing out temperamental tech. He'd heard and seen enough live to know what was going on.

The Thomas woman had found evidence of a body in the pier but not enough to use. Yet. She was going to look for more tomorrow morning. Kyle didn't know whose body it was, and he didn't care. What mattered to him was that he'd found out that they were planning to ambush the prosecutor, and so by extension, Jerome Baggman, with it.

He'd been lucky. And any head coach will tell you that luck is when preparedness meets opportunity. Like when you put a hidden camera in opposing counsel's house and monitor it.

Kyle also knew that you never mess with a hot streak, so he did three things.

He finished every last bite of the ice-cold Szechuan beef because it was going to be a long night.

He placed five bets that would cover the overnight action and exhaust most of his second emergency fund.

And he left to see if he could get into the evidence hangar before the Thomas woman got there.

54

Mason went to the office first thing Sunday morning. Being eight days from trial, he knew Peter Freid would make an appearance too, but he also knew Peter would be late and he wanted to have the run of the place before Peter arrived.

Mason checked the efile then confirmed with the physical documents that Kent Corwin's "boating accident" had happened right in the middle of construction of the Cider Mill patio. He couldn't tell the exact date the support piers had been poured, but he had a range, and it bracketed the date Kent Corwin had disappeared.

Mason made copies of the documents he would need to prove the dates at trial, marked them as exhibits, then put them all, including the originals, in a folder marked "Patio Construction," and put it in his desk.

There are so many things to do before a trial that one of a lawyer's most important skills is to prioritize what needs to be done and ignore what doesn't move the needle. Mason knew that he didn't need to solve the potential murder of Kent

Corwin, or even prove that it was Kent Corwin's body that was in the support pier—what he had to prove was that there was a body in there and that the presence of the body had de-stabilized the concrete construction. So he only allowed himself half an hour to look into the corporate history of Corwin Concrete again.

Kent Corwin went missing during the Cider Mill patio construction. Sixty-three days after the discovery of his boat, he was declared dead from a boating accident. Kent's son, Kevin Corwin, had taken over Corwin Concrete and was the sole owner during the time the patio was being finished. Kevin Corwin then sold the assets of Corwin Concrete to Northern Lakes Construction, which allowed him to continue on the path to becoming Dr. Kevin, beloved caretaker of pets and rabbits. And a few years after that, Corwin Concrete had been dissolved.

Detroit's corporate research hadn't gone much farther than that because they'd only been tracing corporate liability. Now, though, Mason was looking for a motive for murder, so he traced the sale of the assets of Corwin Concrete from Northern Lakes Construction to another Michigan company, who sold it to an Illinois holding company, which in turn was owned by a Delaware company that looked to have changed hands twice.

Once he got to that stage, two things set off the trial clock in Mason's head. First, access to the Delaware records were behind a paywall that required a corporate account and second, it was going to take more time than he currently had to dig deep enough to find out who the people were behind the Delaware company, which wouldn't necessarily be a public record.

He thought, reconsidered, then reconsidered again before sending an email to Peter showing him the results of the corporate research and asking him if Detroit could run to ground the owners of the Delaware company.

Then he set it aside and started constructing a line of cross-examination for the plaintiff's construction expert if it turned out there had been a body in the support pier.

~

WHEN CAMERON THOMAS keyed in the security code and entered the hangar, she was surprised to find a deputy sitting there on a metal chair behind a card table, sipping coffee.

"Good morning," she said.

"Sign in," said the deputy.

"This is new."

The deputy shrugged. "Sheriff wanted to tighten things up before the trial."

Cameron nodded and signed in. She appeared to be the first one that day. She was glad she'd come in early so that there'd be no one else here, and she was relieved that was in fact the case.

She set up at one end, away from the segment of the grid she was interested in, and prepared to collect more samples.

Now that Cameron knew what she was looking for, it was easy to see that there wasn't enough material for the support pier that had collapsed compared to the other piers. She'd attributed it to the pier falling apart and just losing material at the site and in transport, but she saw now that simple waste didn't account for it all.

Since no one was here but the deputy, Cameron started with the collapsed pier. She found the sections with the jackhammer marks, a jackhammer she now believed had been used to split part of the collapsed pier open after it had collapsed. Sure enough, it appeared that marks were on a section of pier right below the part that had crumbled in the collapse.

Cameron glanced at the door, then moved deliberately. She

used a small, high-intensity flashlight to check the surfaces, then put it on a little stand so that she could use both hands. She turned concrete pieces over, then set them aside. Then she pulled out a small geo pick and, with the care of a paleontologist who has discovered the tip of a triceratops horn sticking out of limestone, began to chip away at the concrete just below the jackhammer seams.

She kept picking along the same line. She didn't find anything.

The hangar door opened, and a man walked in. The echoes of the vast room made it hard to understand what he said, but Cameron didn't need to hear him to know she wanted to divert him from where she was looking, so she put down the concrete fragment she was working on and pushed other fragments in the grid around, like rolling concrete dice.

As one of the fragments tumbled away, she froze. It was right there, sticking out of the top. Barely. But it was there. She kept her face impassive as she took the concrete fragment, which looked like it had fibers sticking out the top, and put it in a gallon plastic baggie. Then she added a couple more concrete fragments that would, if held properly, cover the fibers.

Then, though she knew it was a mistake, Cameron glanced at the door.

The man was staring at her. He smiled and waved.

She didn't know him. She nodded and looked back down as he made his way over.

Cameron took the geo pick, and with a swift *rap-rap*, split off two more fragments from the same area. She put each in a gallon plastic bag, put all the plastic bags in a bigger canvas tote, then moved to another section of grid. She immediately struck off a random fragment and was bagging it when the man came up to her.

"Hard at work already?" he said. He was an average guy, a little shorter than her, with a pleasant smile and an easy air.

"Can't work all day unless you start in the morning," Cameron said.

"Don't you know it. You here for the defense?"

Cameron raised an eyebrow.

"Hey, hey, we're just the help, right? I thought I recognized your name from the sign-in sheet, is all. I'm an outside contractor the special master hired to help with the inventory." He shook his head. "Not that I've ever seen an inventory situation like this. Jesus, it's big." He glanced at the concrete in her hands. "What are you doing?"

"Taking the last of our samples for lab analysis."

The man nodded. "You going to be able to get it done in time?"

"I think so." Cameron smiled. "If I can finish my work."

The man laughed. "Right, right, don't mind me. I've got my own work to do. Just make sure you check out where you're taking things from with Eli over there."

"Will do."

"Happy sampling," said the man, and wandered away.

Cameron watched him go, then deliberately went to five more grids, took a small sample of concrete, bagged them, and put them in her tote. After forty-five minutes, she felt like she'd made a good enough show and headed for the door.

The man, who was writing on a notepad at the other end of the grid, waved. She nodded back.

She went to Deputy Eli at the door. Together, they went through and identified each grid that she'd taken a sample from, which Eli noted in a separate log. Cameron held her breath as he briefly inspected each bag, then exhaled as he put the bags back in her tote and went back to whatever he was doing on his phone.

Cameron Thomas thanked him and left, quickly.

She had another sample to inspect.

~

Kyle Stewart took his time after Cameron Thomas left, walking slowly around the entire grid, making notes that were nonsense on his pad as he went.

Eventually, he came back around to Deputy Eli's station. "How long are you here for?" he asked.

Deputy Eli shook his head. "Seven P."

"Yikes. You closing it up then?"

"No. Well yes, it'll be closed, but we've got another guy coming in then."

"24/7 for concrete, eh?"

"Sheriff Sizemore says it's a big enough case to be worth the overtime."

Kyle Stewart nodded. "The special master feels the same. Speaking of which, did you log what the expert took?"

"Is that what she is?"

Kyle nodded.

"I wouldn't mind a direct examination myself."

Kyle gave a neutral smile that Deputy Eli took to be supportive as he handed Kyle the log sheet. Cameron Thomas had taken one sample from five different sectors.

And three from one.

"Good work," Kyle said. "I just need to check one more thing, and I'll be out of your hair."

Deputy Eli took his log sheet back and waved.

Kyle Thomas walked back to the grid sector where Cameron Thomas had taken three samples. He made a fake note, took a video on his phone, and moved the concrete around.

He didn't see anything. He certainly didn't see a body. He just saw concrete. He took a couple more pictures for good measure, said goodbye to Deputy Eli, and wrote his time out next to the illegible signature he'd used to sign in.

He didn't like to provide incomplete information, but he knew he had a call to make.

JEROME BAGGMAN LOVED WAFFLES, usually with strawberries or peaches if they were fresh and in season. He loved them enough that he only ate them on Sunday, because his Italian suits wouldn't allow him to eat them every day, so he viewed Sunday mornings as a treat, an indulgence that he afforded himself and allowed himself to enjoy.

When he ended his encrypted call with Kyle Stewart that morning though, his waffles were forgotten. He sat there, still, his waffles cooling, his syrup congealing, as he decided what to do next.

Stewart's first tidbit made sense. The defense might try to argue that the seawall was constructed improperly, that the ground had eroded under the pier and had caused the collapse. The associate, Pierce, had been banging around all day yesterday at the site and was going to bang around some more with bigger equipment tomorrow. Jerome Baggman wasn't worried about that. He would be ready for it, sure, would accuse Hyde Warren of trying to shirk his responsibilities and blame others, and he might even be able to bend that around into another failure on Warren's part, that he failed to notice the very ground itself washing away. That would be easy enough to deal with.

The second one, though. The second one was a problem. If it was true.

Stewart said there was a body. A body in the support pier. Or at least the defense thought there was. Or that there had been because there was no body there now. Which was an issue all to itself.

Jerome Baggman could not imagine the loop that claim would have thrown Astrid Olsen for, or even him for that matter, if they'd been blind-sided by it at trial. If the defense could prove that there had been a body squirreled away in the concrete, that would have the jury thinking all sorts of things but least of all that Hyde Warren was totally and egregiously at fault for the collapse. Their attention would be redirected toward this possible murder when Jerome Baggman needed them focusing their outrage on Hyde Warren and dispensing punishment in the only way that careless rich people understand, taking their money.

Stewart hadn't been sure yet. He only knew that Pierce and Thomas thought that there might have been a body in there and thought they had evidence that might prove it. Baggman had told Stewart that his bonus depended on him getting real sure, real quick. He hadn't told Stewart that he was pleased because Jerome Baggman knew that Stewart did his best work when he was hungry and desperate, but the fact was, this warning was key. Warnings gave him time to prepare.

He set up a meeting with his own expert, Barry Wasmeuller, so he could get him ready to address the issue of just what a dead body could do to the structural integrity of a support pier. He texted an associate to put together a motion to exclude undisclosed evidence but didn't tell her what that undisclosed evidence was.

And he put his own team on finding out just who this mysterious body might belong to. Because Jerome Baggman believed in knowledge and he believed in leverage, and he knew, if there actually had been a body in that concrete, that meant there was someone out there who didn't want it to be found.

And that person would want this information suppressed even more than he did.

The waffles were ruined by the time he was done, and he resolved to fix that with a double portion.

Next Sunday.

55

It took Mason until almost noon on Monday to move enough rip rap with the industrial-grade excavator to get down to the grade level of the seawall, below the large rocks. When he had cleared a section the width of the bucket next to the foundation of the collapsed pier, he turned off the excavator and climbed down.

He'd just landed on the ground when he heard, "Hey! Who the hell are you?"

Mason turned around to see a man with a hard hat, vest and a fierce red beard slipping down the slope. He recognized Red Gibson, the construction supervisor who'd managed the clearing and salvage operation.

Mason stood straight and tilted his hard hat back to show his face. "It's Mason Pierce, Red."

"Jesus H., Pierce!" he yelled as he slipped the rest of the way down. "I've been getting calls all morning about an unscheduled unit banging around out here. I had to come all the way in from Manistee."

"Sorry, Red. The owner said I could check—"

"I don't give a good goddam what Warren said, Pierce. We're

the ones who're bonded to work this site, including the rebuild, so no one's operating machinery here without my say so."

Red Gibson had a salty stare honed from decades of supervising sites just like this one. He put that stare on Mason, and said, "Do you even have your operator's permit for this thing?"

"I don't need one for a unit this size, Red."

Red Gibson rolled his eyes. "Not for the state, no, but I do for my insurer."

"I'm not your employee."

"But you're on my site, so it's my ass in the sling! Don't f'ng lawyer me on this, Pierce. You know you owed me a call at least."

Mason thought, then said, "I suppose I did. Sorry."

That seemed to startle Red, who stopped mid-curse. "Well, okay then. What the hell are you doing?"

"Our expert noticed that there was a lot of soil up in the rip rap and thought it might be a sign of erosion. I wanted to see if the contractor had put geofabric or stone down."

Red Gibson stared at him for a moment, then chuckled. "You know who put this seawall in, don't you, Pierce?"

"I do now."

Red grinned. "How'd your uncle take that?"

"You know Uncle Troy?"

"I do."

"Then you know."

"I do. We've been on a lot of the same jobs. That kind of mistake wouldn't be like him."

"No, but still."

"What's the answer?"

"I was about to find out."

"Let's look then."

Mason hadn't wanted company for this part, but he really couldn't complain—Red Gibson did have a stake in this, both from the operation side but also from the fix-it side. If they were going to rebuild, he had to know if the seawall needed to be redone too.

They walked, carefully, on the rough stone wall down to the section Mason had cleared. Red got there first and squatted at the edge of the dig, reaching into the gap. Mason came up behind him and looked down.

He exhaled with relief as Red Gibson said, "Leave it to your Uncle Troy to double bill the shit out of this." Fine, granular stone was under the rip rap and Red had pushed even some of that aside to reveal the geofabric underneath.

His uncle had done everything he was supposed to. If there was any erosion, it wasn't because the seawall was built wrong.

"Overkill to put both in, but it sure as hell wasn't going to erode. Why did you think that was a problem?"

"I told you, because of the soil in the rocks."

Red looked around. "It's not that heavy."

"No, but the pier did collapse."

"It did at that." He pointed. "But not because of erosion. Any other ideas?"

Mason didn't see a reason not to tell Red—they'd already revealed the reason for joining Corwin Concrete, and here was a chance to get a free expert opinion from Warhelm Industrial Services' Chief Construction officer. "There wasn't enough rebar in the pier."

"Oh?" Red frowned. "That's strange. Still, a pier like this should have held, even without the rebar."

Mason nodded. "That's why we were focused on the erosion. That would explain it."

"Except there isn't any. So guess it's back to being overloaded, eh?"

Not the opinion Mason was hoping for. "Maybe so." He held up his phone. "Do you mind? I need to show our expert that the fabric is there."

"Fire away."

Mason took a few pictures for Cameron, then said, "All right, Red. I'll get this filled in and be on my way."

Red Gibson shook his head. "The hell you will, Pierce. You're going to get the hell out of here, and I'm going to fill it back in."

"No, Red, I—"

"Do I really have to explain workplace safety and liability to you, Pierce?"

Mason stopped. "I suppose not, but the excavator—"

"—I'm not going to use this rented piece of crap. Have your guy pick it up, and I'll backfill this with our equipment."

Mason wanted to argue, but he actually thought that Red was right. Plus, he was only a week from trial and the clock was ticking. "Are you sure?"

Red nodded. "Tell Warren that Warhelm Construction will handle it. As part of our deal."

Mason shook Red's hand. "I will. Thanks."

"Don't come out here again without calling."

"Understood."

With that, Mason climbed back up the slope, called the rental company to let them know he was done, and placed the excavator back up in the parking lot where the rental company could get it. Then he hurried back to the office.

~

RED GIBSON WATCHED the Pierce kid go. Then he stared at the gaping wound in the seawall and considered all the Pierce kid had told him. The kid was right; a lack of rebar wasn't necessarily enough to cause a collapse and the measures underneath the seawall were certainly enough to prevent erosion, at least the kind that could cause the collapse.

Red wondered if the Pierce kid had another explanation for

what could have caused the collapse. That wasn't clear to Red—the boy was being a little slippery about it, like lawyers always were, but he didn't get a clear indication that the Pierce kid knew what the problem was.

From what he'd heard of him, though, and what he'd seen, Red Gibson figured that the kid would keep looking for the answer. Which made Red Gibson wonder if the Pierce kid would find it.

There would be people who would want to know about that, but there were also things that needed to be done first. So Red went back to the headquarters of Warhelm Industrial Services—not to the fancy offices where they met with investors and business owners to plan multi-million-dollar projects, but to the yard where they kept the equipment and trucks and tools that really made the place hum. There he procured an excavator of his own, towed it out to the site with one of their trucks, and filled the hole in the seawall that the Pierce kid had made. As the Chief Construction Officer, this wasn't a very efficient use of his time, and it took longer to tow the machine there than it did to fill in the hole, but he knew that one question he would get is whether the seawall had been restored to normal and whether all was as it should be. And he knew the only way he could guaranty it with the certainty that would be required, today, was if he did it himself.

After he repaired the seawall, he inspected the site. The big rocks that constituted the top layer of rip rap were back in place and looked solid. Red Gibson spent extra time combing the entire area around where the support pier used to be, and he didn't see anything that wasn't as it should be, but he checked it a second time anyway. Satisfied that the site was ready for a new patio, if Hyde Warren stayed out of jail long enough to build it, Red Gibson returned the excavator back to the Warhelm Industrial yard.

It was almost five by that time, and he knew he needed to check in on his crews out at the Northlake Commons project, but he had to make one detour on the way. He drove to Warhelm Aggregate and Recycling, scanned his card at the security gate, and drove through the automatic gate. He ignored the roads to the massive pits that produced the gravel and sand for Warhelm Industrial jobs and drove to the other side of the facility where the crusher was located.

As he parked just far enough away so that he could watch the crusher operate, Red was amazed again at his boss's foresight. When the housing economy had collapsed in '08, anyone who was involved in any kind of building business was screwed, and, even though it tended to handle commercial projects, Warhelm Industrial Services was no exception. So his boss had looked for opportunities to keep men busy and to capitalize on others being over-extended. This aggregate operation was one such opportunity, and his boss had snatched it up the moment it had become available. North Michigan had a decent amount of construction, but it also had miles and miles of gravel roads, which all had to be maintained. His boss had bought the operation, along with the right to maintain those roads, keeping some of his own men busy in the process until things picked up, which of course they did.

And when business had picked back up, his boss had added the concrete recycling operation. He sold the recycling to customers as being good for conserving raw materials, decreasing landfill waste, and reducing the cost for the base layer under the gravel on all of those roads. Citizens liked the former, the county commissioners liked the latter, and his boss liked having a road business that was a reliable, steady earner and locked up a part of his construction supply chain to boot.

Red Gibson watched as big chunks of concrete, torn out from old buildings or old roads or old foundations, were dumped into the crusher's maw, pulverized, then came out the conveyor on the other side as manageable stone-sized fragments of concrete perfect for roadway base. And the beauty of the crusher was that it had a magnet belt, so you didn't have to worry about rebar or other types of metal getting mixed in with your recycled aggregate. As the machine crushed the concrete and pushed it forward, the big magnetic strip pulled the rebar out, if rebar was what you were worried about, and shunted it to the side, making it easy to dispose of.

The magnets only pulled out metal, of course. The crusher wouldn't sort out softer refuse, especially refuse that was already coming apart. It wouldn't have to. It would crush it, chop it up along with the concrete material and spit it out into the aggregate pile on the other side.

Red Gibson watched the crusher work, putting thousands of pounds through its jaws just this afternoon. Since the year had started, it had processed hundreds of thousands of pounds of concrete, the jagged, dusty, constant fragments acting like a sandblaster scraping the inside clean of anything but dust day after day after day after day.

At 5:30 on the dot, the crusher stopped and the operator climbed out. He saw the logo on Red's truck and waved. Red didn't know him, but running the crusher was a dusty, noisy job, which Red knew well, so he waved back with respect to the man who was doing it for Warhelm Aggregate and Recycling on that particular day.

Red Gibson looked at the result, at the fine uniform pile of aggregate on the other side, aggregate that Warhelm trucks spread regularly on the county roads outside Northlake, gravel roads that grew pitted and pot-holed from the freeze and thaw of ice every winter, roads that Warhelm Road Works repaired each year. Red looked for another minute before starting his truck up and driving out of the yard.

It took Red a little longer than usual to get to the Northlake Commons project from there because he took one more detour. He drove out along Old Mission Road, beyond the old drive-in, onto a gravel road Warhelm Road Works had repaired just that spring. This hadn't been just a pothole-filling fix. No, Warhelm Road Works had added a whole new base layer of recycled concrete aggregate first, then coated it with a layer of fine gravel.

Red Gibson drove slowly along Old Mission Road, but he didn't have to. The road was smooth and fine. Dusty too, of course, but gravel roads always were. There was always a price to be paid for the material you chose.

When he arrived at Northlake Commons, he didn't go in right away. Instead, Red Gibson made a call and reported on what he'd learned, and seen, that day.

56

"What did you learn?" said Peter Freid as soon as Mason walked into his office after he left the Cider Mill site on Monday afternoon. "Did your uncle's company screw it up?"

Mason shut the door behind him. Peter rolled his eyes. "Well?"

"No, they didn't."

Peter sat back in his chair. "Convenient."

Mason shrugged. "Facts." He pulled out his phone, opened the photos, and set it on Peter's desk. "That's the hole I dug. That's the granular filter layer, and that's the geofabric underneath."

"And that means?"

"That means the seawall install was by the book. Actually, he only had to use one of those, so he over-protected against erosion."

"Was there any erosion there?"

"Not that I could see, no."

"So how do you explain all the dirt in the rocks that got you all excited in the first place?"

"It's hard to say. Could be wind and waves, although Lake Lacache never gets that high. Dirt blowing from the dunes maybe? I'm not sure. What I do know is that there wasn't any erosion there to cause the collapse."

"So we're back to the lack of rebar."

Mason nodded.

"And you said Cameron Thomas was a little iffy on that?"

"She's most of the way there. She's doing some testing now to get the rest of the way."

"Are you going to be able to get her over the finish line?"

This was the moment. This was when Mason knew that he should tell Peter what was going on, that he and Cameron were tracking down a theory, a theory involving a dead body, that might explain the collapse.

But he didn't.

It might have been because he'd just given Peter a theory that hadn't panned out, a theory Peter had made Mason act on before they'd confirmed it was true so that he'd screwed up his family in a way that was going to be hard to come back from. It may have been because he knew this was incendiary, so that there was no way he was saying anything to anyone until he and Cameron had nailed it down. It may have been all of those things.

But the real reason, that he later admitted to himself, was that this would have required him to trust Peter and, just then, Mason didn't trust Peter at all. And yes, Amber was a big reason why.

Mason had been honest with Peter and with himself—he didn't care for Amber anymore. He really didn't mind, in the abstract, that Peter was seeing her. But Peter couldn't possibly know that yet; they didn't know each other well enough, and just as clearly, Peter didn't care. Hence the trust issue.

"I'll get Cameron over the finish line," Mason said. "I'll be working with her more tomorrow."

"There's no room for guessing on this, Pierce. We open in a week."

"I understand."

"Unless you've stood there before God and the jury with your ass hanging out, I don't think you do. Are you going to leave my ass hanging out, Pierce?"

"No."

Peter stared at Mason. When Mason just stared back, Peter finally said, "All right. You're taking the cross of their expert, Wasmeuller, the direct of Dr. Thomas, and I may have you take witnesses where they're talking about stresses on the structure, like people or snow."

"Got it."

"I'll open, close, and take the rest. Are you ready?"

"I will be."

Peter shook his head. "Then you definitely haven't tried a case before. You always run out of time. Get back to work."

Mason started to leave when Peter said, "Oh, hey, did you tell your family that we wouldn't be naming them yet?"

"No."

"Good. Hold off."

"Why?"

"I'm sure the prosecutor saw you digging around out there. Let them worry."

Mason doubted that Astrid Olsen was worrying about it, but he also didn't think two weeks would make Uncle Troy forgive him any faster, so he said, "Okay."

And though Peter was probably right, this directive didn't make Mason trust him anymore.

He worked until Peter left at eight. Then Mason worked some more.

It was eleven p.m. when he left and locked the office door.

57

When people told Kyle Stewart that they were having "a case of the Mondays," he wanted to slap them in the face and ask which one was worse. Today, however, he was undeniably having one.

He'd spent half of Monday morning at the Cider Mill site watching Pierce monkey around with a big excavator, digging a hole. The thing about watching someone else dig in the morning is that the digging is incredibly boring, and the European soccer leagues are playing so Kyle passed the time by alternating between watching Pierce dig and losing half of his second emergency fund on an impossible set piece off a corner kick.

After Pierce left the Cider Mill, Kyle had gone over and struck up a conversation with the equipment rental company agent and a Warhelm construction worker, who said this had all been about some dumb ass erosion measures check and cursed lawyers for their soft-handed stupidity.

Kyle had gone back to his apartment then and done everything he could that afternoon to retrieve the corrupted video and audio files from Pierce's house so that he could hear the beginning of the conversation between Pierce and Thomas about the body. He needed something on in the background, so he put on the World Badminton Tour. By the end of the afternoon, he knew that the audio and video files he wanted were gone for good, along with the other half of his second emergency fund.

He needed to think and to think he needed to bet, but his funds were tapped so he pulled some credit, not too much, just enough to prime the pump to get back on track, and thought while he had some slow and easy twi-night baseball on in the background. He lost a couple of bets, but by the time he was done, he knew the next avenue he needed to pursue, so he called Amber Vincent to tell her, but she didn't pick up.

He was able to distract himself for the first half of the evening. There was playoff basketball going and he rebooted all of his systems to make sure the file corruption problem was fixed so that soon he was listening in Pierce's living room and had the camera recording in the spare room and, although Pierce wasn't there, it would be ready to go when he was.

By the time Kyle had lost the first playoff game and bet the second, he was getting antsy. He texted Amber once, then again at half-time but got no response. He supposed that might be good news, but he couldn't sit still any longer, so he got in his car and drove by Peter Freid's house. The lights weren't on, but that might also explain why Amber wasn't answering. He texted again, didn't get a response, and so drove to the condo where he knew she'd been staying.

That light was on, which still didn't mean anything, but the shadow crossing the gauzy shade did, so he turned off the radio, with his team covering the spread with four minutes to play, went up to the door, and knocked.

Amber Vincent opened the door, still dressed for an evening

out, and rolled her eyes as soon as she saw him. "Can't a girl even unwind after a hard day?"

"You didn't reply, so I thought I'd make sure everything was okay."

Amber laughed. "What a sweet little fib that is. Well, you're here now, so go ahead and ask."

Kyle looked around. "Can I come in?"

Amber pouted. "I don't think a lady inviting a stranger in after-hours is very safe, do you?"

Kyle took a deep breath, then said, "What can you tell me? What does he know?"

"He knows I'm delightful and I'm charming and that I'm far out of his league, although he likes to pretend it's the other way around."

"Did he say anything about the case?"

She made her eyes wide, then blinked. "What kind of companion would I be if I wanted to talk about work when a man was trying to unwind from a stressful time?"

"Amber."

"And trials are stressful, aren't they? I've never been near one, but those movies always show people all wound up and twisted over the tiniest things, so it would seem to me that when someone finally has a free moment that's the last thing he would want to talk about."

"So you didn't learn anything?"

"Of course, some people think 'trialing' is very, very impressive and that you must be very smart and clever and handsome to make a jury believe you, so they just can't help talking about it."

"What did he say?"

"Did I hear a 'please' in there?"

Kyle inhaled, paused, and said, "Amber, could you please tell me what Peter Freid said about the case today?"

Amber laughed as she reached out and touched Kyle's arm. "I thought you'd never ask, Kyle. They were checking to see if the land washed out from under the concrete support so they could blame the seawall company, but it was a dead end."

"What else?"

"What do you mean, what else? That seems like a lot."

"Did he mention anything else he was investigating?"

Amber gave him a wicked grin. "He was certainly investigating something."

"No, with anything undermining the supports."

"He was definitely trying to undermine my supports."

"Like a body."

Amber laughed. "You guessed it! That's exactly what he was investigating."

"Amber."

"*Kyle*."

Kyle stared.

"My God, you're as bad as he is. No, worse, because Peter does like to have fun. For a lawyer, anyway. More than the last one certainly." Amber waved a hand. "Anyway, no, he didn't mention anything about a body. He was occupied with one."

"Well, next time ask—"

"There's not going to be a next time, Kyle."

Kyle froze. "What do you mean?"

"I mean, I'm leaving for Chicago tomorrow. I've had about as much Northlake as I can stand, and I have a couple of gigs that are starting to heat up."

"Amber, you can't just—"

Amber's look went from playfully wicked to ice cold. She pulled up to her full height, which was just north of Kyle's, before she said, "I can't?"

"But you agreed to help me."

"I have. For weeks. A lot longer than I should have. I'm

leaving tomorrow, and you're going to give me those club contacts you promised."

"I said I'd give you those at the end of the case."

"You did not, and you'll give them to me now."

"I don't know that I agree."

Amber stared a moment longer before her sly grin returned. "Suit yourself. I'm sure Peter would be interested to know how interested you are in him. And Mason, well, he doesn't like to hear from me anymore, but I think he'd make an exception for this. So I'm going to leave in the morning. And if I have those club contacts from you when I go, then neither you, nor Peter, nor Mason, is going to hear from me again."

"And if I have trouble finding them?"

Amber leaned forward and put one manicured finger, gently, on Kyle's chest. "I think your subconscious found exactly the right word to describe what you'll find."

Kyle smiled. "Do you really think Peter is going to believe some woman who jumped into—"

The smack was as fast as it was unexpected. The pain in Kyle's cheek was still making its way to his brain when Amber smiled, straightened, and said, "Don't be rude. And be sure to look me up next time you're in Chicago. Bye."

Amber Vincent closed the door.

Kyle Stewart stood there for a moment, his cheek stinging, then walked back to his car, calculating odds as he went. He took a pad out of his car, wrote three names and numbers on the paper, then went back and slipped it under the door.

When he started the car, the satellite radio showed him the final score of the game, a score in which the team he'd backed failed to cover. So Kyle Stewart, putting a hand to his cheek, now knew the answer and had to change his mind.

A case of the Mondays was worse.

58

Two days later, Mason was working at his desk when Cameron Thomas called.

"The lab report is back on the material I found," she said.

"Just a second," said Mason and closed his door. "What is it?"

"Leather. They think."

"What do you mean?"

"I mean, they're almost certain it was leather, but it's been encased in concrete for almost twenty-five years, so it's pretty broken down."

"I don't suppose there's any chance we could get DNA from it?"

"That's not my area."

"Oh."

"But I asked my lab guy."

"And?"

"Not a chance. It's way too degraded. There's barely any leather there, let alone something to be scraped from it."

Mason thought. "Could we say what it's from? Like to argue that it was from shoes or a belt?"

"There's really no shape left, Mason. It could be from a worker's gloves or a bracelet just as easily as it could be random trash like a suitcase tag or a dog leash."

"So it's no help."

"Not without something else, no."

Mason tapped the desk. "Our rebuttal exhibit list is due today."

"What does that mean?"

"It means I have to list the Navy class ring if we're going to use it."

"So list it."

"We're going to look bad if we can't link things up."

"Isn't that a risk you have to take?"

"Maybe. I've generally listed all of the items contained in the hangar, which provides a little bit of cover, but I'm going to have to disclose the ring if we're going to rely on it to say Corwin's body was in there. Right now, without more, they can just as easily say he dropped it."

"Well, the leather isn't going to get us there."

"Okay."

Mason thought. "You still have the ring?"

"I do. In Evidence bag G-4, 23."

"I'm going to need it."

"Why?"

"Because I'm going to see a vet."

~

AN HOUR LATER, Mason was sitting in the waiting room of Northlake Veterinary Clinic next to two dogs and a cat. Cameron had fought to come with him, but he'd argued he couldn't have two potential witnesses meeting beforehand, so she'd relented and given him the evidence bag with the ring.

One by one, the animals went in until finally, twenty minutes after the last one, a Great Pyrenees, the tech came out and said that Dr. Kevin would see him.

She led Mason to a pet examination room where Dr. Kevin was occupied with disposing of a Pyrenees-sized poop.

"I'm pretty sure I said I wasn't interested in talking to you," he said as he scooped a hunk up with a poop bag.

"You did."

Dr. Kevin slowly tied off the poop bag, dropped it in the garbage, then turned his back on Mason to wash his hands. "But you said it was about my father, so you have one minute."

Mason handed him his own bag. "Is this his?"

Dr. Kevin glanced at him, then made a point of pulling a few paper towels to dry his hands before he leaned over and looked at the clear plastic bag in Mason's outstretched hand.

He dropped the towels and snatched the bag. "Where did you get this?"

"Is it your dad's?"

Dr. Kevin pulled the bag open.

"Please don't take it out," Mason said.

"Why?"

"It might be evidence."

Dr. Kevin pressed his lips together, but he resealed the bag and pressed it tight to get a better look, then turned it from side to side.

"It's his Naval Academy ring. Where did you get it?"

"Did he usually wear it?"

"Yes. Where did this come from, goddamit!"

"From the Cider Mill worksite."

Dr. Kevin stared at the ring, then stared at Mason. "How can that be?"

"I was hoping you could tell me."

Dr. Kevin turned the ring over in his hand. "I'm sure he was out there. It was a big job."

"Sure."

"But I feel like I would have heard about it if he'd lost it."

"It mattered to him?"

"He took off his wedding ring sometimes. He never took his academy ring off." He looked up at Mason. "Can I keep this?"

"I'm sorry, right now it's logged as evidence. As soon as the trial's over, though. You're sure it's his?"

"Positive. See, 1970 was the year he graduated. And that's the color of the metal and the gemstone. It's his."

Dr. Kevin's reluctance was obvious when he handed the ring-bag back, but he did. "When will the case be over?"

"A couple of weeks. I'll be sure to let you know what's going on."

Dr. Kevin shook his head. "I'm certain I'd have known if he'd lost it. He'd have bitched to me or certainly to my mom, who would've told me." He looked at Mason. "Don't ask. She's passed."

A realization crossed his Dr. Kevin's face. "Evidence. Why do you care about this ring?"

Mason thought, then said, "We're checking everything that was found in the concrete at the location. This was one of the things."

His eyes hardened. "So you're back to blaming my dad's company."

"I thought that, if this was your dad's, you'd want to know."

"I did. I do. And I want that back."

"I understand."

Dr. Kevin's eyes lit up, and he pointed. "Red would know."

"Red?"

"Red Gibson, my dad's foreman. He'd know if Dad lost something at the site. Especially this."

Mason scowled. "Red Gibson of Warhelm Industrial Services?"

Dr. Kevin shook his head. "I don't know where he works now."

"Stocky guy. Red beard?"

"Like the name. And yes."

"Red worked for your company at the Cider Mill job?"

Dr. Kevin's eyes went cold. "I don't know. He worked a lot of jobs for my dad. Your minute's up."

Mason nodded. "Thanks."

"Don't call me again until you're giving that back to me."

"I can't promise that, Dr. Kevin."

"Then I won't answer, Mr. Pierce."

MASON FOUND Red Gibson back at the Cider Mill worksite. The second Red saw Mason, he frowned. "How are you going to screw up my site today, Pierce?"

"Nothing with the site today, Red. I was looking for you."

"There were no problems with the excavator pickup."

"No, I know, thanks. I had a question."

Red Gibson looked at the empty site. "I'm busy."

"I can see that. I didn't know you worked for Corwin Concrete."

He scowled. "I've worked a lot of places. Why?"

"Kevin Corwin told me to talk to you."

Red's face softened. "What does Dr. Kevin need?"

"He said you might know something about his dad."

"What's that?"

"Did you know Kent Corwin was in the Navy?"

Red Gibson grunted. "Everybody knew the Commander was in the Navy."

"The Commander?"

"Talk to the old man enough and you got a lecture on the discipline of the sea." Red Gibson scowled at him. "What's this about, Pierce?"

"Dr. Kevin said his dad wore a Naval Academy ring?"

Red Gibson shrugged. "Okay."

"He said you might know if he'd lost it? At a site?"

Red Gibson put a hand to his beard. "You know, I do remember him saying something about that. I think it was the day after he lost the keys to his truck. No, it was the day before he dropped a twenty but the week after he left his thermos at home."

Mason shrugged. "Apparently, it was important to him. Dr. Kevin thought you might know."

"I don't."

"Okay. Thanks."

Mason walked back toward his truck.

"Why was he asking about it?" said Red.

Mason kept walking. "Because I found it."

"Where?"

"Here." Mason stopped. "Did you work on this site with him?"

Red shook his head. "I was running a project in Petoskey when he died. Had to supervise both sites after he was gone."

"That explains why you wouldn't know then."

"You've worked a lot of sites, kid?"

"I have."

"You know it's a bad idea to wear bulky rings when you're working with rebar and tools. One catch and..." He made a popping sound and gestured at one hand. "Finger's gone. Wouldn't be surprised if he took it off if he was pitching in."

Mason held up both ringless paws. "Old habit. And why I still have ten. Thanks, Red. It was a long shot. I'll tell Dr. Kevin."

As Mason went back to the truck, he thought about what to do. His rebuttal exhibit list was due today. He had the ring that he'd found in the support pier, but he had nothing to show that a body had been in there, a body that would have destabilized the concrete. Without more, the ring wasn't enough and, if he was able to get it in at all, the state could explain it away as having been knocked into the concrete mix accidentally. The judge would never let him use it as proof, on its own, that the body of Kent Corwin was in that support pier.

As he pulled out of the lot of the Stone Street Cider Mill, Mason wasn't sure what to do. He had until he got back to the office to decide.

IN HIS DECADES supervising construction projects, Red Gibson had learned to confront problems as soon as they developed. Rust or rot or an unstable foundation never self-corrected; they only got worse.

He'd also learned never to just pass a problem upstream. If you tell your boss about a problem, you damn sure better be ready with a solution, or better yet, tell them that the problem has already been fixed.

Of course, sometimes speed was more important than a solution. If the problem was big enough, if it jeopardized the whole project and then some, the people in charge needed to know lickety-goddam-split, solution or not.

After his drive down Old Mission Road the other day, Red had believed that there wasn't a problem at all. Now, as he watched the Pierce kid drive away, he decided there might be a big one. So he pulled out his phone, made a call, and laid it all out.

Then he offered a solution.

59

Mason was halfway back to the office when he realized he had another resource he hadn't even thought of using. He cursed, then said to his truck, "Call Dad."

Jackson Pierce answered. "Aren't you working?"

"I am. That's why I called. Did you and Uncle Troy ever run into Kent Corwin on any jobs?"

"Here and there. Why?"

"Did you know he was in the Navy?"

"Yeah."

"How?"

Jackson Pierce chuckled. "All you had to do was talk to the guy. It would come up. What's with the history lesson?"

"Did you ever see him wear a Naval Academy ring?"

"Every time he chewed somebody out."

"What do you mean?"

"I mean, he'd cuss and he'd hold out his fist with that damn thing on the end of it and say that meant he had standards and you'd better have them too or he'd toss your ass overboard right into the unemployment line."

"So he wore it on the job?"

"Every time he was bitching at someone, anyway."

"Interesting. Red Gibson said it'd be silly to wear a big ring when you're working and I have to agree with him."

"What's Red Gibson got to do with it?"

"Nothing. I was just talking to him about it at the site. Okay, Dad, thanks, I—"

"—You're not mixed up with Red, are you?"

"No, not me. He's supervising construction for my client, for a rebuild."

"Gotcha. But you're not involved with that?"

"No. Why?"

A pause, then, "I just would have told you that his outfit is a stickler for terms is all. But it doesn't sound like your problem."

"No, good to know though. I'll tell my client."

"If he's dealing with Warhelm Industrial, then he probably already knows."

It wasn't hard for his dad to start rolling about local construction, so Mason tried to divert him. "I'm going to be out of commission for a couple of weeks here with this trial. If you need anything, Austin and Lily will be able to help."

"Why the hell would I need anything?"

"You know, like if you get stuck under a truck in a snowbank."

Jackson Pierce told his son to self-copulate.

"I'm just saying, it could come up."

"I'll be fine."

"I'll check in."

"Not necessary."

"Then I'll just do it for fun. See ya."

When they hung up, Mason was almost to the office and he'd decided—he'd list the ring but include it with a variety of other things that had been found at the site and some generic descriptors like "anything embedded in any piece of concrete recovered from the scene at any time." That should give him the cover to use the ring if he found anything more to indicate Kent Corwin's body had been in there.

He parked and went in to draft his rebuttal exhibit list.

THE SOLUTION to hiding the ring was right there in front of Mason, but he didn't realize it until he sat down to do the rebuttal exhibit list. He had been looking at the ring by itself, as the only item they'd found inside the support pier. Once he looked at the whole site, though, at the entire scene of the patio collapse, he realized the area had been littered with items. Purses, glasses, wallets, coats, all manner of things you'd expect to find in a bar on a Saturday evening were there and many of them had been itemized, so it wasn't difficult to make sure the ring was on the long list of items recovered at the site, then reference the list of items itself in his exhibit disclosure.

His initial satisfaction with his solution and excitement at solving the problem dissipated as he scrolled through the list, which then became oppressive as he realized the sheer number of items.

A knit mitten. A money clip. One phone after another, many so damaged as to be unrecoverable.

Those weren't the only things that were damaged. Ski sunglasses (cracked). Thermal vest (torn). Hoop earring (bent). Multiple drink glasses (broken).

Like the glasses, there was plenty of restaurant equipment listed too. Silverware (multiple). Propane heaters (bent). High-top tables (multiple). Speakers (x3).

There was one more thing that caught Mason's eye. It took a moment, but the weight of it caught him off guard. It was the shoes. Snow boots and sneakers, loafers and hiking boots, there were dozens of them found at the scene. Numerous shoes that had come off when people fell or when they struggled to get free or when they were pulled, some dead, some injured, some alive, from the freezing wreckage of the Stone Street Cider Mill patio.

The weight of what he was doing dropped full onto Mason's shoulders. He blinked as he adjusted to it, acknowledged it, and finished his rebuttal exhibit list that now included a Naval Academy ring, year undesignated, found in evidence grid B-2, Evidence Bag G-4, 23.

~

TWO DAYS WENT BY. The state didn't object or react at all.

60

When Mason went into Maggie's early on the Friday morning before the trial, the Northlake Seawall crew was already there.

"Lily," said Austin Pierce as Mason stepped into line behind them. "What's the point of getting one of those cushy office jobs if you're still going to be up with the common man?"

Lily Stone shook her head. "Management types never know what they're doing, Austin. You know that."

Mason nodded to Bronson Stone. "See you still haven't found a decent crew."

Bronson shook his head. "The labor market's tight, Mason. Have to make do with what I have."

"I'd ask where you're working today, but I'll just look for a house falling into the lake," Mason said to Lily.

Lily patted his shoulder. "Going outside twice in one day? Seems like a lot."

They all paused to order from Yousef, cheer on Chad's dizzying spatula work, and order their coffee from Maggie herself. When it was Mason's turn, she held out a hand for his

Yeti, then filled it from a carafe as she said, "So is your trial about to start?"

"Monday. Why?"

"Seems like the circus has come to town."

"How so?"

She popped the lid back on. "A reporter was in yesterday. And some new lawyers showed up."

"How did you know?"

Austin cackled. "It ain't hard to tell."

Maggie smiled. "Actually, it's not. One was complaining that there were no good hotels here, and the other wouldn't stop talking about what a good deal she negotiated on a lake house rental."

"Could you tell where they were from?"

"Downstate. I got the impression it was the Detroit area, but I couldn't say for sure."

"That would be Baggman's group then."

"Baggman?"

"The guy who's handling the civil suits."

Maggie looked down. "There were some other folks too."

"Oh?"

"Molly Danvers' grandparents."

"Oh."

"And Sophia Kern's older brother."

"Right."

"And Callie Portman's aunts."

Mason took his Yeti and his breakfast wrap and the information from Maggie. They seemed heavier than normal. He nodded. "A little sooner than I expected. Sounds like you may want to stock up the next couple of weeks."

"Maybe so. You need anything?"

"I don't want to put you to any trouble. Sounds like you're going to be busy enough."

Maggie smiled. "Existing customers come first."

"Do you deliver?"

"You know we do."

He held up the foil wrap. "Can I order breakfast for three to the office for a couple of weeks?"

"Where is it?"

He told her.

"Easy."

"Let me get some orders then, and I'll email you."

Maggie lifted her chin. "We have an app, you know."

Mason smiled. "I did not. I'll send the first one through."

"My God," said Austin. "These office guys never stop yapping. It's like they get paid by the word."

Mason thanked Maggie and turned back to Austin, who had his cap pushed back and was already half-way through his first breakfast burrito.

"These things take planning, you know," Mason said.

"There was less planning with the pyramids," said Austin around a mouthful of eggs.

"Take it easy on him, Austin," said Lily. "He probably has people who usually order it for him."

Bronson straightened his National Guard cap, his face serious, like always. "You going to be out of commission for a couple of weeks?"

"Pretty much."

"You need any help looking after anything? Your place? Your dad?" Bronson had been deployed several times for disasters in the U.S. and once overseas for a year. He was highly attuned to help from family when he was gone.

Mason smiled. "I'm not going to the Middle East. Just the courthouse."

Bronson shrugged. "Unavailable is unavailable."

"I think I should be good. I'll let you know if something comes up."

"Especially with Uncle Jackson," said Austin. "I'm overdue to harass him anyway."

"Thanks," said Mason, and checked his phone.

"Did he just time-check us?" said Austin.

"He's really very busy," said Lily.

"I'm serious," said Bronson. "Let us know."

"Yes, I did. Yes, I am. Yes, I will. Don't fall in the lake."

With that, Mason left the three of them at Maggie's, a place where they had all met for breakfast since they'd started working together as teenagers, with no idea that it would be for the last time.

PART VII

61

Three days later, Mason Pierce was sitting at the counsel table with Peter Freid and Hyde Warren when Prosecutor Astrid Olsen walked up to the lectern to give her opening statement to the jury. She wore her trademark pale blue suit, and her white-blonde hair was tied in a braid so tight that it seemed to pull her shoulders back.

Mason had watched Astrid Olsen prosecute dozens of cases when he'd worked for Judge Roderick, and he'd told Peter exactly what to expect. She would be precise and methodical, ticking off each element of the crime and the proof she'd use to establish it, and though it would be dry and delivered without drama, it would be effective because each word would have the ring of truth.

Astrid Olsen put her blue gaze on each juror before she said, "Molly Danvers came home from college to join her friends at the Dune Sled. Molly met up with Sophia Kern and Carly Franklin and Ashley Trent, and spent the afternoon sledding and snowboarding on the most snow that had fallen on Northlake's Big Dune in over thirty years."

Astrid Olsen paused.

"They thought they were lucky."

Peter Freid glanced at Mason, raising one eyebrow, but Mason was focused on Astrid as she continued.

"So the most snow that's ever fallen on the Big Dune turned into the biggest Dune Sled that we, the people of Northlake, have ever hosted. And that man, Hyde Warren"—she pointed—"did everything he could to take advantage of it, to pull every last person, and every last nickel, into his place—the Stone Street Cider Mill."

"Molly Danvers went to the Cider Mill that night with her friends. You'll hear from Carly Franklin that they picked the Stone Street Cider Mill because it was having an all-night happy hour for their specialty cider drink, was giving away free merch, and because 'everyone was going to be there.' Molly was the last one to arrive, and when she did, it took a while to meet up with her friends for two reasons. First, because the parking lot was so full that she had to park back on the street. And second, because once she'd parked, she stopped to call her dad, Marty Danvers, to let him know that she'd made it from the Big Dune because he'd been worried about her driving in all that snow."

Astrid Olsen paused then and looked at a couple sitting in the front row, directly behind the prosecutor's table, next to Jerome Baggman. Astrid didn't introduce Marty and Faith Danvers. She stared at them, Marty looking straight ahead at nothing, Faith holding a tissue in both hands but looking directly at the jury, her eyes welling but not weeping.

Mason glanced at Peter, who was too good a trial attorney to frown, but he saw his agitation in the three times he tapped his little finger on the table. This opening was nothing like what Mason had said Astrid would do, nothing like what Peter had prepared to address.

Astrid continued, "Marty and Faith Danvers were glad to hear that their daughter was safe. But of course she wasn't. She wasn't safe at all. But Marty and Faith Danvers didn't know that, and Molly Danvers didn't know that, and neither did Sophia or Carly or Ashley or anyone else who was in the Stone Street Cider Mill that night. That realization wouldn't come until later."

Astrid Olsen stepped to the side. "It took Molly Danvers a little time to find her friends because the main dining room of the Cider Mill was packed. It was packed with free t-shirts and discounted drinks and hundreds of people getting warm from the biggest, best, most snow-packed Dune Sled in years. Molly made her way through the crowd to the patio, which was open to relieve the congestion but also to hold three more drink stations so that Hyde Warren could make even more money. Molly found her friends in the northwest corner, next to a gas heater with a beautiful view of Lake Lacache, so they staked out that corner, and they talked and they laughed and they warmed themselves at the heater and they took turns getting drinks, because the patio was getting crowded and they didn't want to lose their prime place, a place right at the far corner of the patio protected on two sides from the crowd that was getting bigger and bigger as people tried to escape the crowded dining room."

Mason checked the jury. They were locked in on Astrid's story.

"Then Molly decided it was time to go, but the girls agreed they would get one more drink and their souvenir t-shirts before they left. Then they made the second most fateful decision of the night. Carly went to get the drinks. Ashley went to get the t-shirts. And Molly Danvers and Sophia Kern stayed right there on the corner of the patio to save their spots."

Two jurors looked back at the front row. Mason followed them.

Faith Danvers reached out and took her husband's hand, who covered it with his own.

"Then the patio collapsed. Because Ashley was in the dining room getting a t-shirt, she wasn't injured. Or I should say, she wasn't physically harmed by the collapse itself, though she was bruised and sprained an ankle in the rush for the door. Carly Franklin was at a drink station on the patio but closer to the dining room entrance. Her legs were crushed in the collapse, and she may never walk again."

Astrid paused again before she said, "And Molly Danvers and Sophia Kern, at the farthest corner of the patio at the highest distance above the ground, immediately above the concrete support pier that collapsed that night, fell through the floor and were crushed by the concrete that went with them. They were killed, but we don't know when. We don't know how long it took."

Astrid Olsen stepped back a little way from the jurors now.

"We're going to prove all of that to you with records and eyewitness testimony. We're also going to prove to you that this collapse was Hyde Warren's fault, that Hyde Warren showed a conscious disregard of the risk of serious harm to the many customers he lured to the Cider Mill with free merchandise and cheap drinks, that he showed a conscious disregard for their safety when he ignored basic maintenance on the Cider Mill, and that he showed a conscious disregard for safety rules and measures designed to keep something like this from happening, all so that he could squeeze every last penny out of every last customer for his business."

"I mentioned that the second most fateful decision the girls made that night was deciding to stay for one more round. But the first was that they trusted Hyde Warren. They trusted that his business, the Cider Mill, was a safe place for them to be. That it was a safe place to meet. That it was a safe place to share a drink. That it was a safe place to call your parents and tell them that you're okay."

Three jurors looked to the Danvers.

"But it wasn't," said Astrid. "There was nothing safe about the Stone Street Cider Mill that night. Not the structure, not the management, and not the decisions Hyde Warren made. It wasn't safe at all. It was the site where seven people were killed and twenty-seven were injured. And at the end of this case, we're going to ask you to hold Hyde Warren responsible for the lives he took. Molly was just one of them. But there are many more."

Mason thought she was done, but then Astrid Olsen looked at him, not at Hyde Warren but at him, and said, "They're going to try to confuse you. They're going to tell you that the collapse is someone else's fault, an old company that conveniently doesn't exist anymore. They're going to tell you freeze and thaw cycles are unpredictable and that no one could have known that the patio was on the verge of collapse. They don't have to tell us everything they're going to say before trial, so who knows what incredible reason they'll invent for why the patio collapsed."

Astrid Olsen turned to Mason and pointed. "They've even hired a construction worker, that man right there, Mason Pierce, to sell it to you, to lend credibility to their outrageous theories."

She turned back to the jury. "It's all window dressing, all designed to distract you from the facts. Hyde Warren was reckless, and seven people died. And for that reason, at the end of the case, we're going to ask you to find him guilty of seven counts of involuntary manslaughter. Thank you."

Astrid Olsen returned to her seat. She glanced at Jerome Baggman, who gave her a faint, but serious, nod.

Mason felt the heat rise to his face along with the jury's stares. It wasn't just that Astrid Olsen had called the jury's attention to him; it was that she'd hit the main points of Peter's opening, right down to his folksy introduction of Mason to the jury.

Mason watched as Peter Freid sat there, legs crossed, tapping that little finger.

"Mr. Freid?" said Judge Roderick.

Peter Freid looked up. "Thank you, Your Honor." Peter shot Mason a dark look, away from the jury, and stood, buttoning his coat. He walked straight over to the jury, flipped one hand at Astrid Olsen, and said, "That certainly was a compelling story Ms. Olsen told. It always is anytime someone passes, but when it's someone young and vital like Ms. Danvers, when a family, when parents, lose their child, it's more horrible than anyone should have to bear. And the fact that there are seven deaths here? That's just about incomprehensible. We've never seen anything like that in Northlake, not this century, anyway, and probably well into the last. And it's only natural when something that bad, that disastrous, that awful happens, to look for someone to blame so that it all makes sense."

Peter Freid pointed at Astrid again. "That's what Ms. Olsen has done here. She's filed charges against Hyde Warren, blaming him for an unforeseeable collapse, trying to make sense of it all by hanging seven manslaughter charges on him. But, compelling as it was, Ms. Olsen and the State of Michigan don't get to just come in here and tell you the story of Molly Danvers' life that was tragically cut short. Ms. Olsen has to carry the burden of proof, a phrase I don't think she mentioned a single time in her opening. She's supposed to tell you how the evidence will prove, beyond a reasonable doubt, that Hyde Warren killed seven people that night. She didn't do that this morning, and we don't think she'll be able to do it over the next week either. We don't think she'll be able to do it because we don't think the evidence shows it. We think they're going to show you inconclusive social media videos, ambiguous weather reports, a well-travelled expert who will imply it's Hyde Warren's fault, but that doesn't meet their burden, their burden of proving beyond a reasonable doubt that Hyde Warren consciously disregarded a great risk of bodily harm to the people in his restaurant."

"Now I'll be asking some questions of certain witnesses and yes, my associate Mason Pierce, who I will confirm for you right now got those callouses on his hands from hard work that had nothing to do with a law degree, will ask some too. And the way you'll know we're on the right track and that the State lacks evidence for their case is when they fall back to how tragic this terrible accident was. Because it was. It was horrible. It was something that neither the Danvers, nor the Franklins, nor the Kerns, nor any of the other families should have had to bear. But that doesn't mean that Hyde Warren is the cause. So when Ms. Olsen talks to you about the tragic consequences of the Cider Mill patio collapse, I ask you, please, as is your duty, to listen for the evidence that Hyde Warren caused it. Because we think you're not going to hear any, and certainly not evidence beyond a reasonable doubt. And, at the end of this trial, when Ms. Olsen hasn't met her burden, we're going to ask you to render a verdict of acquittal in favor of Mr. Warren. Thank you."

Peter Freid sat down.

He didn't look any too happy with Mason as he did.

62

Peter didn't say anything to Mason until they were back at Peter's office that night.

"That was nothing like you said, Pierce," Peter said as the two sat. "What the hell happened?"

Mason shook his head. "Atti's never opened like that, Peter. Not that I've seen."

Peter raised an eyebrow. "Have you seen *Atti* out and about in Northlake recently?"

"Not really, no."

"No chance, off-the-cuff conversations?"

"What are you saying, Peter?"

"I'm saying she knew exactly what my open was going to be, so I had to change it on the fly."

Mason's face was stony. "No, Peter, I haven't seen Atti or talked to her out and about since this case started. Have you?"

"Ms. Olsen and I are not acquainted socially, no. I suppose it wasn't that hard to figure out what I was going to say, but still, watch it out there. A small town has eyes. And ears."

"True," said Mason. "You never know who you're going to run into at the gas station."

Peter Freid stared at Mason. Then he laughed, a little longer and a little harder than Mason expected, but it seemed genuine. "No, I suppose you don't. I sit before you duly chastised. And with an explanation. Baggman."

"Yeah?"

Peter nodded. "I've tangled with him a few times. He's all stories all the time. That open had Baggman all over it."

"I was surprised you were able to pivot that quickly."

Peter grinned. "That's trial work. Have to be ready when things don't go to plan."

"It was impressive."

"I also cheated. It was the same kind of open I did the last time I tried a case against him. Once I realized what had happened, it wasn't hard."

"Should I ask?"

"I won. But he had a shit case. This one's different. Which brings us to tomorrow. Olsen's leading off with a bunch of fact witnesses. I'll take a couple to start, then you're going to take over."

"Really?" said Mason.

"Really. I don't want your first time with a live witness to be their expert, so let's get you up there and used to it tomorrow."

"Okay. Who's it going to be?"

Peter shrugged. "Who cares? Listen, Olsen is going to truck a bunch of people up there to say two things. First, how crowded it was—how they couldn't get a drink, that it was a long line for the t-shirts, whatever. Don't fight any of that. Your question is —'Mr. Bystander, you didn't count how many people were in the Cider Mill that night, did you?' And the follow-up is—'So you have no idea exactly how many people were there, do you?'"

Mason wrote. "Got it. What if they say they do?"

"Well, there's no way they could, so make them look like an idiot."

Mason couldn't argue that point, so he said, "And the second?"

"She's going to ask witnesses to talk about how horrifying it was, how scared they were, how so many people were injured."

"And the response?"

"Sympathy. And then you say—'Mrs. Bystander, you don't know how the support pier broke, do you? You didn't examine it or perform testing on it, did you? You didn't count the number of people or weigh the snow on the roof, right? So you don't know what caused the collapse, do you?'"

"There's no reason they would have done that, though."

"Of course not. The point is that we remind the jury every time that none of these witnesses have specific evidence. It's all general impressions."

"But what if they do? Have specific evidence?"

"Then you're going to have to neutralize it."

Mason could tell he wasn't going to get any more specific guidance than that, and Peter confirmed it when he said, "All right, I have to give an official report to Mother Burns." He waved a hand. "Go bill."

Mason was halfway out the door when Peter said, "Hey, where was that breakfast from?"

"Maggie's."

"That deli with the hot little number behind the register?"

"I don't know that she'd appreciate that description."

"Sure, she would."

"I know I don't."

"Jesus, Pierce. Just hold the peppers and the righteousness for me next time? Please?"

"Sure."

With that, Mason went to work to prepare for his first witnesses as a trial lawyer.

63

It was after eleven that night and Mason knew that he should go to bed—Judge Roderick had always said that rest and sharpness was just as important as preparedness when you were trying a case—but he wanted to go through his cross-exam outline one more time before he turned in. So he was sitting at his desk in the spare room planning how he would react to testimony about overcrowding when his phone buzzed. He answered.

"Cameron?"

"There's a tooth!"

"What?"

"The lab found a freaking tooth in the concrete!"

Mason sat up. "Explain."

"You know how I sent chunks of concrete to the lab for testing, chunks from the support pier?"

"Right."

"One had the disintegrating leather that we couldn't use."

"Still with you."

"I sent a couple more chunks along with it, and when they

were chipping the chunks apart to get samples to test, they found a goddam tooth!"

Mason's mind raced. He looked again at his outline. "An awful lot of people were hurt or killed in the collapse, Cameron. How do we know that the tooth doesn't belong to one of them?"

"Because it was embedded in the concrete, Mason! Not loose with the sample or loose on the ground; the concrete had formed and hardened *around* it. That means it was there when the concrete was poured!"

"Which would support our body in the pier theory."

"That's what I'm trying to tell you!"

Mason nodded. "Does your lab in Chicago do DNA testing? So we can prove it was Corwin?"

"No."

"All right. I think it's time to let everyone in on this. Can you get it?"

"The tooth? I'll pick it up tomorrow."

"Good. Bring it to my office. I'll be in trial, so give it directly to our receptionist Melody, tell her it's for me for the trial. I'll warn her to look out for it and to put it in a safe place."

"I can't get it until the lab opens, so it'll be mid-afternoon by the time I can get to you."

"That's fine. That gives me time to find out what lab we're sending it to."

"Perfect."

"Cameron, this is amazing. Great work."

"Not yet, it isn't. But we're getting there. Talk to you tomorrow."

When they hung up, Mason stared at the phone, then took quick notes of what he had to do on a pad:

Tell Peter dead body theory.

Contact sheriff to arrange DNA testing.

Tell Melody to expect tooth.

As he wrote, he realized they were going to need DNA to compare it to, so then he wrote— *Kevin Corwin DNA sample.*

He didn't know how Peter would react that he'd gone this far without telling him. He wasn't sure if Sheriff Sizemore would move quickly, or at all, on the DNA testing. He knew he could count on Melody to get the tooth from Cameron. And he didn't know how they were going to get the DNA from Kevin Corwin—if they'd have to subpoena him or if he'd do it voluntarily. And he actually didn't know that the body in the pier was Kent Corwin.

But the tooth, along with the unusable leather and the Naval Academy ring, was enough to make him believe that a body had been in there, whoever it was. And that was enough to go on.

It took another hour before Mason could get focused back on his cross-examinations and another two hours after that before he could go to sleep.

~

KYLE STEWART LEANED CLOSER to his computer screen, listening to the audio he had turned all the way up. His software glitch was fixed, so he listened to Pierce's side of the conversation again, and again.

A tooth. They'd found a tooth in the concrete and it was getting delivered to Pierce's office tomorrow.

Pierce had proof that there was a body in the concrete. Baggman needed to know. And he knew what Baggman would want.

So Kyle Stewart made plans of his own.

64

Mason wasn't sure how Peter Freid would react to the investigation that had been taking place after he'd specifically told Mason to stop. As Mason sat in Peter's office the next morning, explaining everything that had happened, culminating in the discovery of the tooth the night before, Peter didn't react. He just listened, face intent, until Mason finished.

When Mason was done, Peter sat there for a moment before he said, "Did you call the sheriff yet?"

"I did, but he's not expected in until eight."

"And the tooth?"

"Should be delivered here sometime this afternoon. Should we test it through his office or on our own?"

"Sable County doesn't have its own lab. He'll probably send it to the Michigan State Police lab down in Grayling. It might be slow, but I don't know if that matters." Peter tapped a finger, then grinned. "Because we're going to be able to argue there was a body in there no matter what. Whether it's this Corwin guy or not really doesn't matter." He cackled. "We're going to shove this right up Baggman's ass."

"You mean Olsen's?"

Peter blinked then waved. "Right, right, Olsen too. But this is going to make it a lot harder for Baggman to get his cash. Good work, Pierce!"

"Sorry I didn't tell you earlier, but until we got the tooth, I didn't think we had enough to go on."

"Omelets and eggs, Pierce, omelets and eggs. We wouldn't have wanted to push this into the open unless we knew we had something. Now we do, so we will. Call Sheriff Sizemore before we start this morning and let him know what we have coming and what we're going to ask him to do. Have Melody ready for it and have her take it over to him as soon as we receive it."

"Done."

"Are you ready for your witnesses today?"

Mason nodded.

"All right. Let's get moving."

Mason went back to his office. He studied his cross-examination outline until, at exactly eight o'clock, he called the sheriff's office and was put through when he told the dispatcher it was urgent. Mason had spoken to Sheriff Sizemore often when he worked for Judge Roderick, so he wasn't surprised that the sheriff took his call.

"Aren't you due in court, Mason?" Sheriff Sizemore said.

"In a little bit. I needed to talk to you first."

"What about?"

"Evidence of a body. From the Stone Street Cider Mill."

"There were a lot of those, Mason. That's why you're in court."

"Not from the collapse, Sheriff. I think it's an old one."

A pause, then, "What do you mean?"

"I think a body might have been hidden there."

"You found one? Why didn't you call me right away?"

"No. Not a whole one. I found a tooth. Some other evidence I found leads me to believe it might be from Kent Corwin."

The next pause was longer. "We talked about this. Kent died in a fishing accident."

"My understanding is that his body was never recovered."

"His boat was."

"Right. Our lab discovered the tooth encased in concrete. I should receive it later today. My thought was that I'd get it to you so that you can have DNA run on it—"

"—You bet your ass you're going to give it to me. I'll send a man over right now."

"It's in transit. I'll get it to you as soon as we receive it. If you're willing to test it."

"Of course I'll test it. What's this other evidence you're talking about?"

"I don't want to say."

"That's not how this works, Mason."

"It's all things that are available to everyone from the case. I'll be more specific when we're done."

"Here's my cell number," said Sheriff Sizemore. "Call me when you have the tooth, and we can meet."

"I will. How long will it take to test?"

"No promises, but the boys in Grayling owe me one. They'll move it along."

"Okay. Thanks."

They hung up, Mason collected his things, and hurried to court.

~

NORTHLAKE WAS the biggest town in Sable County, so the citizens of Northlake occupied most of Sheriff Sean Sizemore's time. For that same reason, the citizens of Northlake were also the primary well of Sheriff Sizemore's campaign contributions.

Sheriff Sean Sizemore had a complicated view on preferential treatment from law enforcement. Once he became involved in a case, the good citizens of Sable County could rely on the fact that Sheriff Sizemore would investigate and pursue a case by the book without regard to race, color, creed, or contribution. He took great pride in the fact that no one would ever be able to find the slightest hint of favoritism or cronyism or any of the other old-boy-isms in any of his cases. Once he became involved.

An ocean of gray existed, however, in the time *before* he became involved in a case. It might take some time, for perfectly appropriate and above-board reasons, to arrive in response to certain calls. Or a confidential investigation might become public knowledge, not because of a leak, but through actions that were apparent to anyone paying attention, like say a call for information from the public. Or, on very rare special occasions for a select few, a warning might be given that a by the book investigation was about to start. Of course, to someone listening to Sheriff Sizemore, it wouldn't sound like a warning at all.

Sheriff Sean Sizemore picked up the phone.

"Hey, good news, we may have a break in the investigation into Kent Corwin's death…I thought so too, but I just received a call from Mason Pierce telling me that he's found a tooth that he thinks belonged to Corwin… Apparently, this patio collapse case dug it up…Yes, the Pierce kid is something else…There's apparently some other evidence too, but I haven't seen it yet. It sounds to me like the tooth is the big thing…No, I don't have it, but when I do, you can be sure I'm going to send it down to Grayling right away and have DNA testing done…It's on the way to Pierce right now. He expects it by the end of the day…I'm as surprised as you, but I know you were good friends, so I wanted to let you know that, as soon as I have the tooth, I'll get to work on identifying it...Yes, you too."

Sheriff Sean Sizemore hung up his phone, pulled his aviators out of his shirt pocket with a smile, and cleaned the already spotless mirrored surface with a handkerchief he kept for just such an activity. Anyone who heard that conversation—and let's face it, in today's world somebody was always watching or listening—would have heard a concerned sheriff keeping an affected party apprised of investigative developments. And two years from now, when he was running for re-election again, that concerned party would donate, heavily, to the re-elect Sheriff Sean Sizemore campaign.

Sheriff Sizemore would never mention what just happened, and he wouldn't mention a donation for months and months, long after anyone would think to make a connection. He wouldn't write it down either, since writing lists of favors and amounts was an express ticket to Baraga Maximum Correctional. No, he would remember, because remembering and discretion was what he was good at.

When the imaginary spots of satisfaction were gone, Sheriff Sizemore put his aviators back in his shirt pocket and placed a call to the Grayling forensic science lab of the Michigan State Police to call in a favor for an expedited DNA review of potential evidence in a cold case.

Assuming he received the evidence soon.

65

That morning, trial played out exactly as Peter Freid had predicted. Astrid Olsen called a series of witnesses to establish that the Cider Mill was crowded and that the collapse was horrific.

Peter handled the first two witnesses. The first, a snow-bro who thought the Dune Sled was a blast if you were stuck east of the Rockies and went on for some time about how it was wall to wall to get the t-shirt and a High Noon, admitted that he never made it out to the patio and certainly didn't count the people who were there. The second, a nurse who'd finally had a night off only to find herself rendering on the spot first aid to people who'd been injured in the collapse, admitted she didn't have any idea what had caused it.

So, with a nod from Peter, Mason took the third witness, a guy in his late twenties who'd gone to every Dune Sled since he was fifteen and had never seen snow that deep or crowds that big. His testimony ended when Mason got him to admit that he hadn't counted, but that there definitely could have been less than two hundred and forty-seven people in Cider Mill that night. And Mason got the fourth witness, a guy who had a premonition and brought his girlfriend in from the patio right before it fell, to admit that he hadn't seen anything wrong with the patio himself and that he had, in fact, had similar gut feelings that were totally correct about the deaths of at least four rock band lead singers.

As that witness left, with at least two jurors hiding their mouths behind their hands, Judge Roderick said, "Next witness, Ms. Olsen."

Astrid Olsen was leaning over the rail listening to Jerome Baggman, who was whispering furiously.

"Ms. Olsen?"

Astrid straightened. "Yes, Your Honor. The State calls Terri Wozniak."

A paralegal sitting by the door opened it, spoke into the hallway, and a moment later, Terri Wozniak strode in. She was in her forties with short brown hair that was sprayed in place so that it didn't move as she met the gaze of every person on the way down the aisle, including Mason.

When she was seated and sworn in, Terri Wozniak introduced herself to the jury as a lifelong resident of Northlake who had spent the last ten years as a full-time mom after they were finally blessed with a child long after they hadn't thought it was in the cards for them.

"So, Mrs. Wozniak," said Astrid. "Actually, do you mind if I call you Terri?"

Terri Wozniak smiled. "I wish you would."

"You were at the Dune Sled that day?"

"We were. Our son, Jeremiah, was nine, and my husband insisted that it was time to take him."

"What did you do?"

"Why we sledded, of course. I have to say my husband was right—it was the most snow either of us had ever seen on the Big Dune."

"The most you'd ever seen as a lifelong resident?"

"Oh yes. I've probably gone, oh, twenty times or so at least."

"I see. And what did you do after?"

"Well, Jeremiah had a sleepover that night at the Prescotts, so after we dropped him off, my husband said that he'd heard the Cider Mill was having a big event with t-shirts and hot cider and the like, and I do like hot cider, so I said why not? He and I rarely get to go out alone anymore with Jeremiah's travel ball, so we did."

"What did you see when you got to the Cider Mill, Terri?"

"A line." She shook her head. "First of cars and then of people waiting to get in the door."

"What did you do next?"

"I had second thoughts, but my husband really wanted to get Jeremiah a Dune Sled t-shirt, and I must admit the thought of a hot cider sounded pretty good to me. And, if I'm being honest, I thought that maybe I was just getting old since I wasn't used to going out so much anymore. So we went in. Or I should say, we waited in line to get in."

"Did you eventually make it inside?"

"We did. It must've taken twenty minutes at least."

"What happened next, Terri?"

"We split up. My husband waited in line to get a t-shirt, and I went to the bar to try to get us a couple of ciders. So he waited and I waited, and I got to the front of my line first and ordered our ciders."

"Then what did you do?"

"Why I took a drink!"

The jury laughed.

Astrid smiled. "What did you do after you took a drink?"

"I tried to get out of line, which was almost as hard as getting to the front. I saw my husband was still a few people back, so I caught his eye and waved toward the patio, and he gave me a thumbs up."

"How did you decide to go to the patio?"

"I thought it might be less crowded. And the bartender told me they were serving drinks out there too."

"You're sure it was the bartender who told you to go to the patio?"

"He handed me my drinks and took my card. I don't know if he had a different title."

"What happened next?"

"I went out there, and there was more room, for a little while, anyway. So I sipped my cider and waited for my husband."

"What happened next?"

"Some girls, not girls, young women, invited me to join them by one of the heaters, so I did."

"Did you know them?"

"No. But I won't forget them."

"Why's that?"

Terri Wozniak paused, cleared her throat, then said, "Because their pictures were all over the news. Two of them anyway."

A picture appeared on the screen.

"Was this one of the women, Terri?"

"Yes. That was Molly."

Another picture. "And this young lady?"

"That's Sophia. There were two more, I'm sorry I don't remember their names because they weren't in the paper so much, but that's them back there."

The whole courtroom turned to the back row where one young woman sat on the last seat of the row, holding the hand of another young woman who was sitting in the aisle, in a wheelchair.

"You're indicating Ashley Trent and Carly Franklin?"

Terri Wozniak's eyes filled as she said, "Yes. Hi, girls."

Carly and Ashley gave very small, very serious waves.

"They were very kind to include me," said Terri Wozniak.

"What happened next?" said Astrid.

"My husband finally got through the line, so I thanked the girls and excused myself, and my husband and I found the last two-top table and shared a drink. His cider had gotten cold by then, so we bought two more at one of the cider stands they had set up out on the patio."

"Was there a line there too?"

"A little bit of one, but we'd timed it right—the line got really long behind us."

"What happened next?"

"The patio gradually got just as crowded as the inside. Pretty soon we were getting jostled even at our two-top and then"—Terri Wozniak smiled—"and then I found out that I *am* getting old because I asked by husband if we could go."

"Why did you want to go, Terri?"

"I was tired from the sledding, and I was cold and it was too crowded and getting home under a comforter suddenly seemed like a better plan. And..." she hesitated.

"And what, Terri?" said Astrid.

"And I got scared. Not scared, that's not fair. I got nervous."

"Why?"

Terri smiled, but she looked down. "I have a thing about exits."

"What do you mean by 'a thing'?"

"I mean, I need to be able to see a clear path to one when I'm someplace."

"Why's that?"

"It's just..." She looked up. "I was in a situation once where I needed one and couldn't get to it, and now it sort of freaks me out when I can't see one."

"Could you see one that night on the patio at the Cider Mill?"

"There was a sign, but it was so crowded there was no way I could get there, or anywhere really, in a hurry."

"It was too crowded?"

"It was too crowded. My husband is pretty good about it. He can tell when it's starting to bother me, and he did that night. He didn't even finish his drink. He set it down, said, 'Let's go home,' and so we did."

"How long did it take you to leave the patio?"

"I'm not sure, a while. It was harder to leave than it was to go out onto it."

"Why?"

"Because people were still streaming in, and the dining room was even more crowded than the patio."

"You eventually left, though?"

"We did."

"What was the last thing you saw when you left?"

Terri Wozniak cleared her throat. "The girls. They waved at me. I waved back, then we went home."

"Thanks, Terri," said Astrid Olsen. "No further questions, Your Honor."

Mason walked around the table and stood in front of Terri Wozniak.

"Good morning, Ms. Wozniak."

"Good morning."

"You testified that you believed the patio was too crowded that night, right?"

"That's right."

"And that's because you have what you described as 'a thing' about exits?"

"That's true."

"You felt that it was too crowded for you?"

"That's correct."

"You're not telling the jury that it was too crowded from a legal standpoint, are you?"

"I'm telling the jury that it was too crowded for me."

"That was a bad question, Mrs. Wozniak, sorry. One of the issues in the case is the maximum occupancy of the patio. You're not saying that the patio was over its maximum occupancy, are you?"

"I don't know what its maximum occupancy was, so no. I'm just saying it was too crowded."

"For you."

"For me."

"You didn't actually count the number of people on the patio, did you?"

"Count the people? Why would I count the people?"

"Exactly. You didn't count the people on the patio while you were talking to the girls or your husband, did you?"

"No, of course not."

"So you're not telling the jury that there was a specific number of people on the patio, are you?"

"No, I'm not."

Astrid Olsen stood. "Your Honor, could you please direct counsel to stop intimidating the witness?"

Mason turned, blinked.

"What do you mean, Ms. Olsen?" said Judge Roderick.

"He's looming over her with his aggressive questioning."

Mason noticed several things at once. Astrid Olsen wouldn't look at him. Jerome Baggman was smiling behind her. And when he turned back around, Terri Wozniak was leaning back in the witness chair.

Mason had been this big since he was fourteen. Projection, misinterpretation, and accusations came with his size, and he knew from experience that he needed to defuse it right away, but when he started to speak, Judge Roderick held up a hand and said, "Let the record reflect that Mr. Pierce's voice was not raised during his cross-examination and that the Court finds the questions to be relevant and within the scope of Mr. Pierce's representation of the defendant. Mrs. Wozniak, this is a court of law, and Mr. Pierce is permitted to question you and any of your assumptions. Do you understand that?"

She lowered her head. "Yes, Your Honor."

"Still, this can be taxing. Would you like a break?"

She kept her head down. "No, Your Honor."

"Very well, Mr. Pierce, you may proceed."

It was a disaster. First, Astrid had accused him of intimidating Terri Wozniak, then Judge Roderick had jumped in to defend him and appeared to have come down on her some more. He didn't need to look at the jury's expressions to know what they saw.

Mason took a step back. "Mrs. Wozniak, did you feel intimidated by the way I was questioning you?"

"No," she said, but her head stayed down.

"You can say."

"Maybe a little."

"Was I too close?"

"It felt like it."

"I forget what I look like sometimes, Mrs. Wozniak. I'm sorry."

Terri Wozniak's head snapped up. "I didn't mean that."

Mason smiled as he moved back to the defense counsel table and sat against the front edge. "I know you didn't. Is this better?"

"It's fine. Really."

Mason waved a hand. "No, you warned us when you testified on direct. You have a thing with knowing where the exits are, right?"

"I do."

He crossed his arms. "And I was a little too close for your comfort, wasn't I?"

"I'm sorry. You were."

"So I was making you feel a bit trapped?"

"Yes."

"That's how you felt that night at the Cider Mill, isn't it?"

"It is."

"There were a lot of people at the Cider Mill, right?"

"There were."

"And that made you uncomfortable?"

"It did. Very."

"The way I, by myself, made you feel?"

"Similar, yes."

"And that was enough to make you feel uncomfortable and want to leave?"

"Yes."

"Now Mrs. Wozniak, one of the State's exhibits is this." Mason held up a black three-ring binder. "It's a collection of affidavits from people who were on the patio that night."

"Okay."

Mason thumbed to a tab and opened it. "I'm going to hand you...actually, I'll stay back here. Ms. Gorman, would you mind handing this binder to Mrs. Wozniak?"

Holly Gorman's eyes widened at her name, but when the judge nodded, she came through her gate and took the binder over to Terri Wozniak while Mason stayed put, leaning back on his table.

"Thanks, Ms. Gorman," said Mason. "Mrs. Wozniak, I've opened that binder to State's compound Exhibit 30-142. Do you see it?"

"I do."

"Is that your affidavit and signature?"

"It is."

"In it you attest that you were on the patio the night of the collapse, right?"

Terri Wozniak scanned the document, nodded. "I did."

"If I understand the timeline of your testimony, though, you weren't on the patio *when* it collapsed, right?"

"No, that's what I said."

"Right, you said you left an hour before."

"Yes, that's right."

"Mrs. Wozniak, there are one hundred and seventy-eight affidavits in that binder you're holding of people who said they were on the patio that night."

"Okay?"

"We know you weren't on the patio when it collapsed, right?"

"Right."

"And of course, your husband wasn't, was he?"

"No, he was with me."

"And as we sit here today, you don't know how many other people who filled out affidavits like you weren't on the patio when it fell, right?"

Terri Wozniak frowned. "No. I don't know how I would."

"Thanks, Mrs. Wozniak. That's all the questions I have, Judge."

Astrid Olsen stood. "Terri, you do know some people who were on the patio at the time of the collapse, don't you?"

"Yes, Ms. Olsen." Terri Wozniak looked to the back of the courtroom. "I know of four."

Astrid turned to where Carly and Ashley sat.

"That would be Molly, Sophia, Carly, and Ashley?"

"Yes."

"Thank you."

Mason thought, then stood. "I'm sorry, Mrs. Wozniak, but did you mean three?"

Terri Wozniak thought. "No, I meant the four girls."

"Right, but Ashley wasn't on the patio when it collapsed. She was inside getting t-shirts."

"Oh, oh, I'm sorry, then three."

"That's all right. It's hard to keep track of, isn't it?"

"It is."

"Thank you, Mrs. Wozniak."

When Astrid Olsen shook her head, Judge Roderick dismissed the jury for lunch. As the judge left himself, Mason turned on his phone.

"Good work there," said Peter. "We'll split them again this afternoon—"

Mason had four missed calls from his dad.

The last time that had happened, his dad had been trapped under a truck in a snowbank.

"Excuse me, Peter," Mason said, and hurried into the hall.

66

The second Mason stepped into the hall, he said, "Dad, are you okay?"

"I've been trying to call you," said Jackson Pierce.

"I know. Are you okay?"

"I'm fine. Do you still have my angle grinder?"

It took a moment for that sentence to compute. "What?"

"My angle grinder. I have some rust starting on the passenger door of my truck that I need to get out, but my angle grinder is gone. Do you still have it?"

Mason exhaled and looked at the ceiling. "I do."

"Could you drop it by this afternoon?"

"Dad, I'm in court."

"No problem, I'll just head over to your house and look around—"

"No, Dad, stay put. I just remembered Austin borrowed it from me. I'll have him drop it off."

"Okay. If it's not too much trouble."

"It's not."

"I'd like to get on it tonight. Can't let that rust take hold."

Peter came out of the courtroom, scowling.

"Right. Dad, I have to go."

"All right, Son. I'll look for Austin."

Mason hung up. As Peter walked over, a text came in from his dad. *Don't forget the wire wheel.*

"Can you give me just a minute, Peter?" said Mason.

"Is it about the too—," Peter stopped, looked around, then said, "about the evidence we talked about?"

"No, sorry, just a thing I have to take care of."

"A thing?"

"Two seconds."

Mason walked away as he texted his dad *I won't forget*. Then he texted Austin. *Hey, can you do me a favor and run an angle grinder over to my dad?*

His phone buzzed a moment later.

"Where is it?" said Austin.

"In my garage, I think on the back tool bench."

"Aren't you in trial?"

"Yes, but there's been a rust emergency."

Austin laughed.

"And I can't have him driving over and then rooting around in there. Oh, and he needs the wire wheel too."

"Obviously. No worries, Mace. How's the trial going?"

Mason glanced over as Peter stood there, arms crossed.

"Doing some grinding myself."

"This law thing sounds fun. I get off at 3:30 today. Don't sweat it."

"Thanks, Austin. I owe you."

"You do. Next Loon's on you."

"Done."

They hung up, and Mason apologized again before he and Peter planned their strategy for the afternoon's witnesses.

Red Gibson had more resources than one would expect for a Chief Construction Officer of a company. He called one now.

"What do you have?" Red said.

"Two carriers came to the office today. We've been able to get both packages."

"How'd you manage that?"

"A suit and a helpful offer to save a trip inside do wonders."

"And?"

"No package from Cameron Thomas."

"Keep waiting."

"Will do."

"She might bring it personally. Blond, tall, in her thirties."

A pause. "I assume you want the package, no matter what."

"I do. Unopened."

"Done."

Red Gibson hung up. Though he had more resources than you would expect, those resources, and his trust in them, weren't unlimited.

That's why he was going to check the other place the package could go.

Chicago to Northlake was one of those weird limbo distances where driving the five hours was about the same time you would spend in the airport, so Cameron had decided to drive. She was about halfway to Northlake when she received the notification of an email from Mason.

She had the car read it to her.

Hey, change of plan. Please drop the tooth off at my house, I'm taking it to the sheriff personally. Key is in the fake rock to the right of the front steps. Thanks. Mason.

Because Mason was in trial and she was driving, Cameron simply replied, *Will do.*

Then she paid attention as she merged onto the highway that would take her around Grand Rapids.

KYLE STEWART WAS SCRAMBLING, a situation that wasn't helped by the fact that his credit limit on the betting site was exhausted. He'd had an impossibly bad run in cricket, badminton, and basketball and took absolutely no consolation from the fact that that sentence had probably never been uttered before. The bottom line, though, was that he had nothing left to bet, making his bonus on the Cider Mill case more important than ever. And right now his surveillance made it clear that there was a torpedo headed straight for that win in the form of a tooth.

He had trouble concentrating without a score ticker, so it had taken him a little longer than usual to figure out a plan, but in the end he had, and now it was time to put that plan into motion.

So Kyle Stewart glanced at his phone, remembered for the fourteenth time that he didn't have any bets running, then got into his car to take care of business.

67

Peter and Mason took turns handling witnesses in the afternoon. Mason had made a little headway with Teresa Wozniak by showing the one hundred and seventy-eight number from the prosecutor had some fluff in it, but Astrid Olsen was too good a lawyer to let the same thing happen again.

Every one of the thirteen witnesses she called that afternoon said the patio was crowded, though none could say exactly how many people there had been.

And every one of them had been on the patio when it collapsed.

IT WAS ABOUT three-thirty when Cameron Thomas turned onto the gravel road that led to Mason's house. She drove through the trees, past a couple of driveways through which no house could be seen, to Mason's cottage. She found herself smiling when she saw it, thinking of the big man in that little place.

She parked and grabbed the small square shipping box off her front seat, which contained a second evidence box marked with the lab it had come from and describing its contents as "One (1) tooth—incisor." She grabbed it and walked up the old wooden steps.

Cameron tried the door, found it was locked, and then remembered Mason's email. She went back down the steps and searched for a moment before she saw the fake rock behind the boxwood bush. She picked it up and shook it, smiling as she heard the rattle of a key. She turned it over, slid it open, and used the key to unlock the front door.

The main room was how she'd seen it last, with a kitchen table off to one side. Cameron went to set the box on the table and stopped. Even though she was in his house, she had sudden unease about setting such important evidence right there by the front door, so she went into his spare bedroom, the one he used as an office, put the tooth-box squarely in the middle of his desk, and inexplicably felt better.

She stopped at the back porch, because the day was sunny and the view to the lake clear. She had a little extra time, so Cameron thought about going back to the wooden deck on the bluff for a quick peek but, after her early morning and long drive, she decided to go check-in to her hotel instead.

She left, locked the front door, and replaced the key. When she got back in her car, she texted Mason. *Package delivered. Talk to you after court.*

Then she drove back out the gravel drive to the hotel in downtown Northlake that would be her home for the rest of the trial.

Austin Pierce was singing his favorite country song, which was, not so coincidentally, Hardy's Favorite Country Song. And on that particular afternoon as Austin drove to his cousin's house, he thought that if rolling along with your windows open on a sunny day didn't make you want to sing about the sounds of the country, then you just weren't ever going to want to.

As he pulled down Mason's road, Austin noticed that Mason's neighbor, Mrs. Roth, must have been having work done since there was a truck in the drive. He was glad to see it because the place had been falling apart ever since Mr. Roth had passed.

He parked in Mason's driveway in front of the stand-alone garage and got out, noting again that he had to get after Mason to let him put a new roof on it this summer. He yanked open the garage door to the mishmash of tools and mowers and general equipment that prevented Mason from parking his truck inside. He stepped around the mower, past the truck-mount snowplow that was set aside for the summer, to the workbench where, after only a modest search, he found the angle grinder and the infamous wire wheel brush.

He pulled the garage door back down and noted the fact that it was unseasonably warm, pleasantly sunny, and that he was doing a favor for his closest cousin who would unquestionably want him to enjoy a beer by the lake, not in payment, but in appreciation.

So Austin Pierce set the angle grinder and the wire wheel brush in his truck, then headed up the stairs to Mason's house to hit the fridge.

~

Everything was going to plan for the man until he heard the truck.

The sound of wheels on gravel travels farther than you'd

think, especially in the quiet of the country, so he thought there was a chance that it was just passing by. But then he heard the unmistakable crunch of tires on stone, the blare of a man singing on the radio about crickets and creek-side choirs, then the off-key driver continuing the tune after he turned off the engine.

The man considered slipping out the back, but he didn't have what he came for yet and he had to have it, so he ducked back into the kitchen and watched out the window as a burly man with a beard and a pushed back cap slammed open the garage door and went in, still singing.

The burly man came out a couple of minutes later, holding a tool and singing something about whippoorwills at the top of his off-key lungs. When the burly man tossed the tool through the passenger-side window of the truck, the man in the house thought he'd made it. But then the burly man paused, belted out a note that had little to do with the harmony he sang of, and headed for the front stairs.

The man ducked into what looked to be a spare room. As the front door opened, the hiding man saw the box on the desk.

~

AUSTIN WALKED through the family room to the kitchen, opened the fridge, and bent down to grab his favorite beer, which his cousin had thoughtfully stocked for just such an occasion. Austin straightened, knocked the cap off the bottle on the edge of the counter, and took a long drink. He glanced at the back kitchen door, which led outside to the lake, and grinned. Then he took another long pull from the beer and said, "I don't know what you're doing back there in my cousin's spare room, but I think we're gonna scrap."

Austin had spent his young life working heavy machinery

and listening to loud music, so he didn't hear the man rush up behind him until the last second. He also possessed a deep, cheerful, abiding belief that everything would work out because, in his three decades of experience, it always had.

So it never occurred to Austin that the man had a hammer.

68

It was close to five-thirty when Mason and Peter arrived back at the office after court that day. Peter closed his door, already on his cell phone reporting the day's events to the Firm, while Mason made a beeline straight for Melody, who was still there.

"Thanks for staying late," Mason said.

"Of course."

"So Cameron dropped off a package for me?"

Melody frowned. "No. I haven't seen Dr. Thomas today. She's in town, though. She called to tell us that she's checked in to her hotel and is available if you need to talk to her about the case tonight."

"But she texted me that she dropped off the package."

Melody shook her head. "I've been here all day. What time did she say she did it?"

Mason pulled out his phone and showed her the text. "About three-thirty."

"I was here then, Mason. She wasn't."

"Do we have a drop box or anything?"

"No. Our mail and deliveries come in here."

"You're sure?"

Melody looked irritated for the first time. "Mason."

"Right, sorry. I'll call her."

"That would probably be best."

He did. Cameron didn't answer, so he texted. *Cameron, Melody said she didn't get the package. Where did you drop it?*

Nothing.

"What would it look like?" asked Melody.

Mason realized he had no idea. "A small box, I'd guess. I'm going to go take a look in the lobby area."

Melody was a good enough receptionist to let him go see for himself.

Mason had made one lap around the entrance to their building, it really was quite small, when his phone buzzed. Mason answered without looking. "Cameron, Melody hasn't seen it."

"Mace."

Mason looked at his phone, then put it back to his ear. "Dad?"

Jackson Pierce spoke, but Mason couldn't make it out.

"Dad? Are you outside? I can't hear you with the wind."

"Get home! Now!"

"Dad, I can't I'm in the middle—"

"I think he's dead, goddamit!"

"Who?"

"Austin. Hurry!"

Mason blinked. What his dad said wasn't making any sense.

"Where are you?" Mason said.

"Your dune stairs. By the lake."

"Call 911. I'll be right there."

Mason hung up and sprinted out the door to his truck.

As he hopped in, he received a text notification from Cameron.

I dropped it off at your house.

THE MAN KNEW that there was no scenario in which the person he worked for wanted the tooth to ever be found again. It could make everything collapse, and the man didn't apologize to himself for the pun because it was true.

He put the tooth in a Ziplock bag, then put the bag inside another one, then laid a towel over them both so no fragments could escape. Then he took a hammer—yes, the same one—and hit the tooth over and over and over until it was pulverized.

After inspecting the plastic bag to make sure it hadn't broken (it hadn't) and the tooth to make sure it was powdered fragments (it was), he went for a drive along county roads towards the Big Dune on Lake Michigan. The hammer, fully wiped and cleaned, ended up in a quiet inland lake along the way.

When he arrived at the Big Dune, he climbed to the top, admiring the lowering sun like so many others. When he was halfway down, he emptied the bag, kicking the tiny pieces into the loose sand and scrub.

There was a trash can at the bottom of the dune. He dropped the plastic bag and towel in with it, shoving them among the water bottles and food wrappers that filled it.

The man looked at the lake for a short time to catch his breath, drank from a water bottle he'd brought for that purpose, then headed back up with the others to see the sunset from the top.

WHEN MASON PULLED up to his house, two sheriff vehicles and a fire department rescue squad were parked in his drive. He skidded to a stop and ran inside, but no one was there. He saw uniforms on his deck and ran outside.

A deputy turned to face him at the top of the dune stair. "Wait, sir, who—"

Mason barreled past him and down the stair, taking them two at a time. A body lay at the bottom.

It was covered with a blanket.

"No no no no no no." Mason didn't know he said it.

Sheriff Sizemore turned around, looked up. When he saw what was coming, he yanked a deputy over and the two of them caught Mason, then staggered back under his weight.

The deputy flew backwards into the sand. Sheriff Sizemore stayed upright by hanging on to Mason's arm with both hands.

"Stop! Mason, stop!" said Sheriff Sizemore.

"Who is it, Sean?!"

"Mason wait! Perkins, put that thing away!"

Mason jerked around and saw the deputy lying flat on his back in the sand, pointing a taser at him. Mason ignored him and whirled back to the body, pulling against Sheriff Sizemore's hands. "Who is it, Sean?!"

"Wait, Mason." Sheriff Sizemore didn't let go. "Drop it now, Perkins! Everybody just calm down!"

"WHO THE FUCK IS IT?"

"It's Austin, Son," said Jackson Pierce. "He's dead."

Mason saw his father sitting off to the side on a weathered wooden bench for the first time. His elbows were on his knees, his canes set to the side, as he stared out from beneath that long hair at the blue lake.

His father's voice cut through all of it. Mason stopped, nodded to Sheriff Sizemore, who let him go, which appeared to be enough to make Perkins holster his electricity.

"I need to see him," Mason said.

Sheriff Sizemore nodded. Mason knelt in the sand and pulled back the ambulance blanket.

It was Austin, his eyes unseeing, his ever-present smile

pulled tight with rictus, blood covering the side of his face and beard.

"Your dad found him," Sheriff Sizemore said. "Any idea why he was here?"

"I asked him to come get my dad's angle grinder."

"I thought you said he had it?" said Jackson Pierce.

"I didn't want you to have to come get it. So I asked Austin to."

Jackson Pierce nodded.

"What happened?" Mason asked his dad.

"I saw his truck in the drive with the angle grinder in it, so I looked for him. I found..." Jackson pointed.

"There was a beer bottle alongside the stairs," said Sheriff Sizemore. "Near as we can tell, he slipped and fell down the stairs. The wound on his head is pretty bad."

Mason looked at Austin's body, thinking it would sit up and laugh at any moment. A sudden suspicion hit Mason.

"Have you looked at anything else?"

"Do we need to?" said the sheriff.

"I need to check something. Dad, you want to come up?"

"I go when he goes," said Jackson, staring at the water again.

Mason looked at Sheriff Sizemore.

"We're going to be a little while yet."

Mason went up the stairs two at a time. When he got to the back door, he checked the second text he'd received from Cameron on the way over. *It was about 3:30. I left it on the desk in the spare room.*

Mason sprinted to the spare room.

There was no box on the desk.

He quickly searched the rest of the room. Nothing.

He looked in his bedroom, in the main room, in the kitchen.

Nothing.

He went back to the top of the dune stairs. "Sheriff! I need you."

Sheriff Sizemore gestured to the deputy and to the two EMTs who were standing by. As he climbed the stairs, Mason worked out what to tell him.

He decided to get his attention with the truth.

"What is it, Mason?"

"Something's been stolen."

"What do you mean?"

"Something's been stolen from my house."

"Today?"

"At about the same time as Austin's fall."

Though the sun had been setting, Sheriff Sizemore had been wearing his aviators. He took them off now and said, "How can you know that?"

So Mason told him that Cameron Thomas had delivered a package to him at 3:30 p.m., that Austin had left work at 3:30 and come straight here to get the angle grinder, and that the package, which had been inside the house, was no longer there.

"What was in the package?" asked Sheriff Sizemore.

"The tooth that we found in the support pier of the Cider Mill that we believe belonged to Kent Corwin."

"The one you told me about?"

"Yes." Mason pointed. "I think my house might be a crime scene."

Sheriff Sizemore stared at Mason, then stared at his house. "I'd better check."

~

When the deputy had finished processing the scene on the beach, the EMTs loaded Austin onto the gurney and started to take him up the steep stairs. They struggled.

"I don't need your help!" Jackson Pierce snapped. "He does."

Mason left his father's side where he'd been trying to help him traverse the sand with his canes, and went over to the EMTs.

"You two take the top," Mason said.

"The weight will all be at the bottom," one said.

"Right."

When they were configured, Mason supported the bottom end and walked Austin up the stairs, slowed only by the two struggling EMTs at the top end. When they reached the landing, the EMTs thanked him and took their normal positions to wheel Austin across the grass.

Mason raced back down the stairs to where his dad was a quarter of the way up. He offered his arm, which his dad refused, then dipped under one arm, supporting part of his weight, which his father, though he could curse, could not resist.

When they came to the top, Jackson was huffing hard, sweat making his long hair lank. When he'd recovered his breath enough to speak, he said, "We need to tell my brother."

The words hit Mason like a shovel. Then he nodded and said, "I'll go tell the sheriff."

There was police tape over Mason's back door. "Sheriff!" he said.

Sheriff Sizemore appeared.

"My father and I want to tell Austin's family."

"I'll need to interview them."

"I know. But the news should come from us."

"When?"

"Now?"

"Fine. Tell them I'll be over later tonight."

"Okay. Did you find anything?"

Sheriff Sizemore hesitated. "I'm not sure yet. But maybe blood. Can you stay somewhere else tonight?"

"Let me get a suit for court tomorrow."

"Fine, go in the front."

Mason raised an eyebrow.

"If there's blood, it's back here."

Mason packed a bag, took a suit for court, then went out front to meet his father.

Jackson Pierce was putting the angle grinder in the front seat of his truck. When he saw Mason, he nodded, and the two of them caravanned to Uncle Troy and Aunt Linda's.

~

SHERIFF SIZEMORE HAD BEEN sheriff long enough to know blood when he saw it, and what was smeared on the fridge door sure wasn't ketchup. Someone had made a hasty attempt to wipe up, but they'd missed a few spots, and Sheriff Sizemore was certain it was blood and that it would match Austin Pierce's.

They'd have to do an autopsy to see if they could identify the weapon from the wound. He really had thought that the head wound had been from falling down the stairs, and if it hadn't been for Mason's information about the theft, he'd have assumed that Austin Pierce had taken a drunken spill.

Now though, a murder had fallen into his lap, so he'd investigate it and follow the evidence wherever it led him.

But he'd only follow the evidence he found.

He hoped whoever had done it had covered their tracks.

~

MASON FOLLOWED his dad into Uncle Troy's circular driveway and stopped in front of the door. It took his dad a while to get out with the canes and all, which gave Uncle Troy plenty of time to build up a head of steam and come roaring out.

"If you think you're going to patch this up by dragging him

into this, you're even stupider than you look, Mace. And that's pretty stupid."

"It's not about that, Uncle Troy," said Mason.

Troy Pierce turned to Jackson. "Your son tried to torpedo my business; did he tell you that?"

The metal of Jackson's canes clanked off the concrete one, two, three times as he dragged himself forward. "This isn't about my son, Troy."

"The hell it isn't! He wanted to blame me—"

"It's about yours."

The fact that Mason and Jackson were standing in his driveway seemed to hit Troy Pierce. "What about Austin?"

Jackson Pierce dragged himself in front of his brother, gripping his canes so tight his hands were white.

"Austin's dead."

Uncle Troy's eyes widened. He looked at Mason.

Mason nodded.

Troy Pierce dropped to the stone steps and sat, staring.

Jackson Pierce dragged himself closer.

"I found him."

Jackson's voice broke.

"I stayed with him."

Jackson's tears hit the pavers at Troy's feet.

"And I'm here to take you to him."

Troy Pierce cried out, then grabbed the shaft of a cane in each hand. Jackson bent forward, toward his brother, squeezing the canes tight, holding both of them up.

Mason watched his uncle's back heave once, then tremble. Then it stopped, and Troy Pierce raised his face to his brother and said, "We have to tell his mother."

When Jackson nodded, Troy Pierce reached up, put his hands over Jackson's, and pulled himself up on Jackson's canes. Then the three remaining Pierce boys went into the house.

PART VIII

69

Kyle Stewart had a problem. A big one. Which pissed him off because otherwise his plan had worked perfectly.

The fake email he'd sent to Cameron Thomas had worked just as he thought it would. She'd been busy driving and Pierce had been busy at trial, so it had been no problem to divert her delivery to Pierce's house, and she'd responded to his email with an email back to the same fake account, just as he guessed she would.

Then it was a simple matter of listening and watching remotely until he knew she'd entered the house, dropped off the package, and left. As soon as he knew the Thomas woman was gone, he'd driven over, figuring he had plenty of time to pick up the tooth before Pierce came home from trial.

Then, once he was in Pierce's house, everything had turned to shit.

He'd gotten out of there as fast as he could and raced back to his apartment to see what the camera and microphones had captured.

What he saw put him in a panic. It was all right there. And his own camera put him at the scene.

Kyle wished he'd taken the camera and mics out of the house when he fled, but after what happened, all he'd thought about was getting out of there as fast as he could. There was no going back for it now, so Kyle started cleaning up his already pristine electronic trail. He made sure nothing was in the cloud. He deleted programs. He made sure all of his systems that hid who and where he was were still in place.

He was deciding what to do with the recordings themselves when his news alerts started going off. He'd set them to highlight any news of the trial or Mason Pierce or the Stone Street Cider Mill, and they started pinging now. He followed them.

It was being reported that Austin Pierce had been found dead at the home of Mason Pierce, his cousin, who was the defense attorney on the Stone Street Cider Mill collapse case.

Kyle Stewart broke into a sweat. The theft of a box with a twenty-three-year-old tooth in it was one thing. A murder was another.

Bonus or not, Kyle Stewart had to get the hell out of Northlake.

Kyle fumbled at his laptop to delete the video and audio when it hit him. The video might be the key to saving his bonus. Maybe.

He copied the video onto two thumb drives. Then he wiped it from his laptop.

He sent a disappearing message to Baggman on an encrypted app. He told him the package had been disposed of, that he'd be leaving town, and that he expected his bonus in the usual manner. He also told him that everything was locked down and that he might have some additional information he'd find useful, but that he'd contact him later about it.

Then Kyle put the phone he'd just used and his laptop into a bag to be destroyed. He wished again that he had the equipment from the house too, but this wasn't the first time he'd have to leave something like that behind; he knew that nothing about the devices was traceable back to him.

Kyle Stewart was out of the apartment for good twenty minutes later.

~

POLICE WORK HAD CHANGED a lot over the last twenty years. It seemed like everyone now had phones and cameras and smart devices that could control damn near anything in their house. Sheriff Sizemore had found that those things could make a sheriff's investigation a hell of a lot easier.

So one thing that Sheriff Sizemore did now anytime he was investigating a crime scene, particularly in a house, was use one of those gadgets that let you know whether there were any hidden cameras in the place. Why, just last winter, they'd found one of those nanny camera thingies in a sock monkey (a sock monkey!), which would have been hilarious if it hadn't also caught Sammy Merchant smacking his wife. The all-seeing sock-monkey had turned a "he-said, she-said" into a nice long jail sentence.

Sheriff Sizemore didn't hold out much hope that Mason Pierce had such a thing; the house seemed old, the appliances outdated, and the furnishings decidedly primitive, but still, he had Deputy Perkins fire up the whatsit that would tell him if any of the hidden do-hickeys were there, just in case.

He was surprised when Deputy Perkins called him into the spare room. By the time Sheriff Sizemore walked in, his deputy was pulling a small camera out of a smoke detector.

"What have we here?" said Sheriff Sizemore.

"I got a hit with the radio frequency detector, but then it disappeared, so I broke out the optical lens finder and—"

Sheriff Sizemore waved a hand.

"I found a camera in the smoke detector," said Deputy Perkins, handing it to the sheriff. "It's been disabled."

Sheriff Sizemore looked from the smoke detector to the desk.

"Doesn't seem likely that a lawyer would set up a camera to show the back of his head and his computer monitor, does it."

"No, sir," said Deputy Perkins.

"I'll ask Pierce, but I think we know the answer."

"Yes, sir."

"Any more of these things around?"

"Not that I've found."

"Interesting. Are we going to be able to see where it was broadcasting to?"

"Doubtful."

"We just know it's here, then?"

"Yes."

"Do everything you can."

"I will."

Sheriff Sizemore knew he would. He was also relieved his deputy would probably come up empty.

70

Cameron Thomas waited off to the side while Mason checked in at the hotel after he arrived late that night. He looked exhausted.

He gave her a faint smile as he came over, thanked her for making sure there was a room available. She said she was sorry and asked how his family was holding up. He told her how he'd gone to tell Lily and Bronson before they'd all gone back to his aunt and uncle's and that they were all doing their best, but that it was all too fresh to be anything but awful.

She invited him up to her room to figure things out and to eat. Mason said he wasn't hungry, and he didn't look it, but when they sat down in her economy suite, he tore into the Chipotle as if he hadn't eaten in days.

As she started her own, Cameron said, "I left the tooth in your house on your desk at 3:30."

Mason nodded, chewing.

When he didn't say anything, she said, "You really didn't send me the email?"

Mason shook his head. "I was expecting you to drop it at the office."

"So whoever took it diverted me there. Why?"

"I imagine it's a lot harder to steal from my office than from my empty house." He winced. "My supposed to be empty house."

"I'll give my email to the sheriff," said Cameron. "Hopefully, it leads him somewhere."

"I doubt it. The person had to know that the sheriff would get the email eventually."

"For a theft. Not for a murder."

"Maybe."

Mason unwrapped the second burrito.

Cameron hadn't been sure but was glad now that she'd bought it.

"It does let us know one thing," he said.

"What?"

"There was definitely a body in that pier."

Cameron nodded. "And someone doesn't want anyone to know who it was."

"Or at least not be able to confirm it." Mason took another bite. "Will you be able to testify that the body was enough to destabilize the pier?"

"Definitely. The air pocket it caused, combined with the lack of rebar is more than enough to cause a collapse after twenty-three years of settling."

Cameron pushed around at her chicken burrito bowl. "I don't want to sound callous, but will I be allowed to testify that a body was in there? Without the tooth?"

Mason looked at her, and the combination of coldness and anger in his gaze shocked her.

"They killed my cousin over it. So yes."

They didn't talk much more then. He finished his meal, thanked her, and told her they'd prepare for her testimony after court tomorrow.

She put one hand on his arm at the door.

He nodded, said, "I'll be fine," and left.

When Cameron closed the door, she wasn't at all sure.

~

"RESPECTFULLY, you've got to be kidding me, Your Honor," said Peter Freid.

"It's fine, Peter," said Mason.

"The hell it is. Excuse me, Your Honor, I forgot we were on the record, let me make sure the court reporter hears that—*the hell it is*!"

Judge Roderick sat behind his desk in chambers. Peter, Mason, Astrid, and Jerome Baggman were sitting in chairs in front of him with Holly Gorman off to the side. A court reporter was typing.

"You're new to our court, Mr. Freid, but Mr. Pierce is not," said Judge Roderick. "He's aware of our local practice."

"What local practice?" said Peter.

Judge Roderick raised his chin. "No continuances for funerals unless it is for a parent, child, sibling, or grandparent."

"Judge, his cousin died at his house yesterday!"

"Mr. Freid, you will recall that Mr. Pierce was a coworker of mine too. For longer than he has been with you. I am just as upset at this development for Mr. Pierce as you, probably more, but the court has found that expanding it beyond those relations causes one delay after another."

"Oh, I'm sorry if the death of Pierce's family member is inconvenient for the court."

"Mr. Freid! That's enough. Your latitude is gone."

Peter Freid didn't say anything, but the effort made his face twist.

Judge Roderick shook his head. "The fact is we already have

a jury seated, and we're not going to risk a mistrial with a delay. Who are you calling, Ms. Olsen?"

"Our expert Barry Wasmeuller, then some family members."

"Judge," said Mason.

All eyes turned to him.

"Could we have a continuance until this afternoon?"

"Why's that?"

"I'm conducting Wasmeuller's cross."

Judge Roderick thought for a moment, then said, "Ms. Olsen, will the state consent to switch the family witnesses to this morning and Dr. Wasmeuller to the afternoon?"

"Yes," said Astrid immediately.

"No," said Jerome Baggman.

Judge Roderick glared at Baggman. "Since the State consents to that switch, that's what we'll do. We'll start in fifteen. Thanks for coming in early."

As the attorneys stood, Judge Roderick said, "Again, my condolences to your family, Mason. It sounds like it was a terrible accident."

"It was more," said Mason.

Astrid and Baggman turned back. "What do you mean?"

"More than an accident. Sheriff Sizemore is looking into it."

"Why would that be?"

"I'll let the Court," Mason turned to look at Astrid and Baggman, "and counsel know if I hear something."

Astrid and Baggman both scowled.

Judge Roderick frowned. "I expect you to advise the Court of any developments, Mason."

"Count on it, Judge."

71

With Peter handling the morning witnesses, Mason decided to head up to a spot in the Northlake Law Library that he'd often used when he was working for Judge Roderick. He found the service door tucked away in a corner of the hallway and climbed the narrow stair to a landing with a small door. He was grateful that it was unlocked since he'd turned in his key when he left.

Mason was on the second level of the library, directly under the dome where the light streamed in through arched windows and stone columns rose like silent friends. A small circular table, the one he'd used so often, still sat in a nook between two columns.

Mason's great-grandfather had helped erect the stonework in this courthouse. When he first started practicing for the judge, he'd taken comfort from those columns, from the fact that he was practicing in a place his family had helped build, meaning that no matter how little he knew or what mistake he made, no one had more right to learn here, *to practice*, than he did.

Now he pulled a different comfort from that stone. Now, he used those columns to pull his mind away from the great-grandson of the man who had set them, to focus on the job at hand.

Mason patted the cool stone a last time, settled into the familiar chair that was far too small for him, and prepared to cross-examine the state's expert, Barry Wasmeuller.

PETER TEXTED Mason when the morning session was done and said to meet him in a client consultation room. Now.

Mason collected his things, hurried down the stairs, and flung the door open to the consultation room harder than he meant. Hyde Warren was sitting in a chair, his face flushed red, his eyes bloodshot and watering, his nose running unwiped down his face. His wife, Jessica, was sitting next to him, rubbing his shoulder. Peter stood on the other side of the table, looking exasperated.

"How could they say that!" said Hyde Warren. "She worked for me for eight years!"

Peter glanced at Mason before he said, "They lost her, Hyde. Don't take it personally."

Hyde turned on Mason. "They said I killed her!"

"Who, Hyde?" said Mason.

"The Portmans. They said I killed Callie."

"We knew this was going to happen, Hyde," said Jessica Warren, rubbing his shoulder. "We knew the Portmans and the Danvers would be especially hard."

His wife's voice seemed to soothe him. "It's different to hear it, Jess."

Mason sat next to Hyde on the other side from his wife and leaned forward. "There's going to be more of this, Hyde. Their expert is about to say everything they're accusing you of doing wrong—of being careless. And greedy."

Hyde's eyes snapped up. "But I wasn't—"

"—I didn't say it was true, Hyde, I said you're going to hear it. And you need to keep a straight face, and listen, and be sympathetic to the families."

"I am sympathetic!"

"I know. So show it."

"That's easy for you to say! You didn't have friends, good friends, die at your place!"

Mason stiffened. But he didn't say a word.

Jessica Warren went white.

Hyde looked at his wife, who was squeezing his shoulder. "What?" He saw his wife's face, looked confused, then went pale himself.

"Mason! Mason, I'm sorry, I didn't mean—"

"You're right, Hyde," Mason said as he rose and now, on purpose, loomed. "I didn't lose a friend yesterday. I lost family. And I'm going to do my job today with a straight, sympathetic face. Do the same."

Then Mason walked out, leaving Jessica and Peter to sort Hyde out.

He had an expert to cross.

72

Dr. Barry Wasmeuller was an older man with wispy gray hair that was grown long on top and combed back in the way of a man who hadn't accepted the fact that he was losing it. He wore thick tan pants, unscuffed tan work boots, a red felt shirt, and a pressed tweed jacket as he moved swiftly down the aisle and took his seat on the witness stand.

Astrid Olsen took him through the long list of engineering credentials he'd acquired and the structural projects he'd worked on and the companies he'd consulted with before admitting that, because of his well-known expertise, he had been consulted as an expert by numerous lawyers in general and by Jerome Baggman in particular, although he'd never had the great pleasure to work with Astrid Olsen or Sable County before. But he was sad—no, devastated—by the circumstances that had brought him here.

Then Astrid Olsen dove into it. "Dr. Wasmeuller, do you have an opinion on what caused the collapse of the Cider Mill patio?"

"I do."

"What is that opinion?"

"An excessive amount of weight was brought to bear on the patio in general, and on the northwest corner in particular, causing the support pier to collapse."

"What do you mean by excessive?"

"An amount of weight that exceeded the bearing capacity of the pier."

"What caused the excessive weight?"

"There were two components. An excessive amount of people on the patio and an excessive amount of snow on the roof. Together, those two things created a load that was more than the structure could bear. With tragic consequences."

"Can you demonstrate that for us mathematically?"

"I can."

Barry Wasmeuller then spent the next hour doing math. He took the number of people and calculated a minimum weight and took the snowfall for the previous two months and calculated its weight and had a neat moving graphic of the bearing capacity of the support pier and showed how, mathematically, the concrete support pier had failed.

Mason was watching the jury. They followed closely for the first five minutes, fidgeted for the next ten, then checked out until the animation of the pier's collapse at the end, which seemed to grab their attention and hold it.

After the cartoon pier had collapsed, Astrid said, "You mentioned that there were too many people on the patio?"

"I did, and there were."

"How did you arrive at that conclusion?"

"It's my understanding that there were at least fifty percent more people on the patio than was permitted by the occupancy permit."

"Is that dangerous?"

"That's why they have occupancy permits! It's incredibly

dangerous to overfill a structure. They're put in place to prevent events exactly like this from happening."

"Is there a way to prevent that? Going over the occupancy limit?"

"Of course! You just have to put patron safety above profits."

"How?"

"The patio had two doors from the dining room. Put someone there and manage how many people go in. All you have to do is count!"

"That's pretty difficult, isn't it?"

Barry Wasmeuller rolled his eyes. "Even if we haven't been to one, we've all seen TV shows or movies where people are waiting between velvet ropes to get into a club, right?"

"Sure."

"That's all they're doing! Sure, they might be managing who goes in, but they're also obeying their occupancy permit. That's literally all there is to it!"

"Who's responsible for that?"

"The owner. He might try to delegate it, but the owner is the one responsible for running a safe establishment."

Astrid Olsen nodded. "You also mentioned snow. Surely the owner can't do anything to stop snow from falling on his place?"

"No, no, I'm not suggesting that. What I am suggesting is that he manage the snowfall. Clearing a roof is no different than plowing a parking lot; it's something a responsible owner does."

"You're not suggesting you plow a roof, are you?"

"No. You rake it."

"What do you mean?"

"Before I came here today, I took the liberty of looking up three companies right here in Northlake that offer snow clearing services for your roof. They come out with long rakes and pull it down so that it doesn't harm your roof or, as in this case, cause a collapse. It costs money, of course, but, again, a responsible business owner must take steps to protect his patrons even if it costs him a few dollars more."

"Dr. Wasmeuller, having reviewed the evidence and determined the cause of the collapse, do you have an opinion as to whether anyone's actions directly led to the collapse of the Cider Mill patio?"

"I do."

"What is that opinion?"

"As the owner of the Stone Street Cider Mill, Hyde Warren had a duty to ensure that it complied with the occupancy permit for its operations and to maintain the premises free of hazards such as excessive snow. He utterly failed in this regard. His failure to comply with these duties directly caused the patio collapse, which killed seven people."

"I see. Do you have any other opinions?"

"I do. Hyde Warren's failure to comply with these duties showed a reckless and conscious disregard for the safety of his patrons and created a substantial risk of great bodily harm and, I'm afraid, death."

"Thank you, Dr. Wasmeuller. No further questions."

Mason came around and leaned back against the defense counsel table. "Dr. Wasmeuller, you're saying the support pier collapsed because the defendant put too much weight on the patio, right?"

"Essentially, yes."

"And you're saying the weight consisted of too many people on the patio and too much snow on the roof, right?"

"I'm glad you were paying attention, Mr. Pierce. Yes."

"That animation you played for the jury assumed that there were one hundred seventy-eight people on the patio when it collapsed, didn't it?"

Dr. Wasmeuller shook his head. "I'm aware of the testimony of Mrs. Wozniak and that there is testimony that the total number was less than that, but it was too late to change the animation. I based my animation on the affidavits submitted by the state. Further, as I said, a crowd of fifty percent over the capacity limit, or one hundred and fifty people, would have been sufficient to trigger the collapse."

Mason nodded. "Whew. That was a lot. But, again, the animation you showed the jury assumed one hundred seventy-eight people were on the patio, right?"

"I just explained—"

Mason raised a hand. "Tell you what, why don't you just play it for the jury again and put your little laser pointer there on the number that you put in the lower left corner of your cartoon."

Dr. Wasmeuller looked from Mason to Astrid to the jury. "Yes, the animation assumed there were one hundred seventy-eight people, but it was too late to change it."

"It was too late to change it because we all just learned yesterday that number was wrong, true?"

"That's true."

"But if I understand you correctly, you're saying the fact that the number that you told to the jury is wrong doesn't matter because the number of people on the patio, whatever it was, far exceeded the occupancy limit, correct?"

Dr. Wasmeuller nodded. "Exactly!"

"We can agree that no one knows the exact number, right?"

He hesitated, but then said, "That's right."

"We can agree the occupancy limit for the patio was one hundred?"

"We certainly can."

"Dr. Wasmeuller, the primary factor in occupancy limits is related to fire exits, isn't it?"

Dr. Wasmeuller blinked. "Excuse me?"

"I mean the occupancy capacity of an area, in this case the

patio, is primarily determined by the number of fire exits, not its structural strength, right?"

Dr. Wasmeuller glanced at the jury. "Both are factors."

"But the available fire exits are the primary factor, aren't they?"

"Both are important."

"The occupancy inspector made Mr. Warren add a fire stair, didn't he?"

"I seem to recall that."

"At a significant expense?"

"I don't know what it cost."

"That indicates the inspector was focusing on fire exits, doesn't it?"

"It indicates that it was a focus certainly. Not the only one."

"A sound support pier could withstand the weight of one hundred fifty people, couldn't it?"

"Clearly not."

"Doesn't the math, your math, show that a sound support pier could bear that load?"

Dr. Wasmeuller smiled and sat back. "Not with the additional weight of the snow, no."

"Yes, let's talk about the snow. You made an assumption about the weight of the snow on the roof, right?"

"I made a calculation based on the snowfall documented to have occurred in the months leading up to the collapse, yes."

"Yes, you spent a great deal of time walking us all through the math of it. So the jury understands, you didn't go up and measure how much snow was on the roof, did you?"

Dr. Wasmeuller sneered. "The roof had partially collapsed along with the patio, Mr. Pierce."

"Correct. So you didn't measure the snow, right?"

"I couldn't"

"You estimated it."

"Using National Weather Service data, yes."

"Did you take into account melt days, when the temperature was above freezing?"

Dr. Wasmeuller smiled. "That would just create ice, which would be even heavier. I'm being conservative by just assuming it was snow."

"The pitch of the roof has an effect on whether all that snow stays on the roof, doesn't it?"

Dr. Wasmeuller nodded. "My understanding is that this roof had a 3:12 pitch, which isn't as steep as you would like to shed snow in this part of the state."

Mason nodded, leaned back a little more on the table, and crossed his arms. "Let's talk to the jury about friction, Dr. Wasmeuller."

"What about it?"

"The Cider Mill patio had a metal roof, didn't it?"

"Of course it did, we've already shown the jury pictures..." Dr. Wasmueller's eyes widened, then he glanced at Astrid, who was staring straight ahead.

Mason smiled, nodded. "Snow slides more easily off metal roofs than shingle roofs, doesn't it?"

Dr. Wasmeuller's eyes darted. "Yes."

"You already agreed with me that there were days when the temperature was above freezing, right? Because you said that would form ice?"

He hesitated, looked at the jury, then said, "Yes."

"And you assumed that none of that snow slid off the patio's metal roof on any of those sunny days, didn't you?"

Dr. Wasmeuller didn't answer.

"I mean, I suppose we could go back through your math again, and you could show us where you took that into account—"

"I assumed all the snow stayed on the roof."

"Good, I'd rather not go through all that again, too. Finally, last assumption. You're assuming that the concrete support pier that collapsed was structurally sound, aren't you?"

Astrid Olsen stood. "Objection, Your Honor."

"Overruled for the reasons stated in denying your motion in limine, Ms. Olsen," said Judge Roderick without looking up from whatever he was doing.

Astrid Olsen stayed standing, which Mason found curious, as Dr. Wasmeuller said, "I did, although I would add that given the strength of modern-day concrete, even the absence of rebar would not be enough to cause the pier to collapse without an excessive weight load."

Mason smiled. "You guessed my question, Dr. Wasmeuller, but let's back up a bit so the jury understands what you're saying. You agree that there was no rebar in the support pier that collapsed, right?"

"None was found, yes."

"Good construction practice required rebar to be used in that pier, didn't it?"

"That would be ideal, yes."

"It would be standard, good construction practice, right?"

"It would be the best practice."

"Mr. Warren, as the owner, was not the one who would check for that, was he?"

"Not usually, no."

"So that pier was defective in a way that Mr. Warren could not have known, wasn't it?"

"I think defective is too strong a word, Mr. Pierce. Even without rebar, the concrete of that pier was more than strong enough to withstand normal loads."

"You're assuming that the concrete was poured properly in a standard manner, aren't you?"

"Your Honor," said Astrid Olsen. "May we approach?"

Judge Roderick waved them up.

"Your Honor," Astrid said, "we object to this line of questioning."

"And I've overruled your objection," said Judge Roderick. "You've preserved your record, Ms. Olsen. Mr. Pierce is entitled to question your construction expert on the construction of the pier."

Astrid Olsen hesitated, then said, "Your Honor, we believe defense counsel is going to do more than that, and once he does, this trial will be prejudiced."

Judge Roderick scowled. "Explain."

Astrid hesitated again, then said, "We believe defense counsel is going to argue that the structural weakness in the pier was caused by a body."

Judge Roderick stared at her, then stared at her some more. Mason had to hand it to him; the jury would not see any evidence that he was talking about anything unusual as Judge Roderick turned to Mason and said, "Is that true?"

"I'd be more interested in knowing how Ms. Olsen came to that conclusion, Judge."

"Are you going to turn my courtroom into a circus, Mr. Pierce?"

"No, Judge."

"So Ms. Olsen is wrong?"

"No, Judge. She's not wrong. There was a body in there, and it caused the pier to collapse."

"Do you have evidence of this?"

Now Mason hesitated. "Some."

Judge Roderick sat back. "We're going to have to have a proffer hearing on that before I let it in."

"Your Honor, we've already delayed Dr. Wasmeuller until this afternoon," said Astrid. "He needs to leave for another engagement."

Mason shook his head. "I have to question him on this, Judge."

Judge Roderick thought for a moment. "What's your theory on how this weakened the pier?"

"The body created an air pocket that weakened the structure."

Judge Roderick nodded. "You can ask a hypothetical question about air pockets and construction. You will not, under any circumstances, mention a body until we've had a hearing."

"But Your Honor—" said Astrid.

"Doesn't your expert have a flight to catch, Ms. Olsen?"

"Yes, Your Honor."

As they returned to their places, Peter looked a question. Mason nodded and went back to leaning back on the defense table.

"Dr. Wasmeuller, back to my question, you've assumed that the concrete for the pier was poured properly, in a standard manner, haven't you?"

"That's correct. And that it was strong enough to withstand normal loads."

"I see."

"With or without rebar."

"Got it. Dr. Wasmeuller, I'm going to ask you a hypothetical question."

He frowned. "Okay."

"I want you to assume that there was an air pocket in the middle of the concrete pier that was five to six feet tall and around two feet wide."

His frowned deepened. "Why would that be there?"

"That's not important for our purposes right now. I want you to assume the existence of that air pocket for the purposes of my question."

Dr. Wasmeuller looked at the judge.

"Please respond to Mr. Pierce, Dr. Wasmeuller."

Dr. Wasmeuller shrugged. "Okay."

"If an air pocket like I've described existed in the concrete of the pier, that pier would be prone to collapse, wouldn't it?"

"I don't know if I'd go that far. It would certainly weaken it."

"It would *significantly* weaken it, wouldn't it?"

Dr. Wasmeuller hesitated, then said, "It would weaken it, though I can't say how much without knowing how the air pocket was created and what its exact dimensions were."

"Thank you, Dr. Wasmeuller. No further questions, Your Honor."

Mason thought Astrid would re-direct so was surprised that she indicated she was done. Once she did, Judge Roderick excused Barry Wasmeuller, excused the jury for the day, then looked at Mason and said, "Counsel, in chambers."

They went—Peter, Mason, Astrid, Baggman, all followed Holly Gorman and the judge into his office.

Judge Roderick sat down and said, "Now tell me what this is all about, Pierce."

73

Mason told Judge Roderick what they knew for sure—that Kent Corwin had disappeared during the construction of the patio, that they'd found his naval academy ring in the wreckage, and that they'd subsequently found a tooth embedded in the concrete sample.

"What does the DNA show?" asked the judge.

"It was taken before we could perform a DNA test," said Mason.

"Isn't that convenient," said Jerome Baggman.

"Actually, it's not."

"Anything else?"

Mason knew the judge wouldn't buy that Austin had been killed during the theft of the tooth, not yet, but there was one fact he thought the judge might find significant. "We found chisel marks, like from a jackhammer, on some of the concrete fragments."

Jerome Baggman shook his head. "Probably from the rescue of survivors."

"And a section of the concrete pier is missing. A significant section."

"Somebody sneak it out in their pocket?"

"Mr. Baggman!" said Judge Roderick. "You are in here as a courtesy. Ms. Olsen will address any arguments for the state."

"It affects my case too, Judge."

"And when we're dealing with your case, the Court will entertain your arguments."

Jerome Baggman raised his hands and shut his mouth. For the moment.

"I assume you object?" Judge Roderick said to Astrid.

"One hundred percent, Your Honor."

Judge Roderick shook his head. "You sure don't bring the easy ones, Ms. Olsen."

"It seems clear to me this has to be excluded, Your Honor," she said.

"Well not to me. And it seems that the three of us—you, me, and Pierce here—recently learned the dangers of not allowing defense counsel to fully explore the prosecution's case."

Astrid Olsen winced. Mason knew she was remembering how they'd all gone down the wrong path on a case involving the death of a toddler and a firefighter and almost convicted an innocent teenager of murder.

The judge rapped his desk with his knuckles. "All right, my preliminary, *very* preliminary, ruling is that I'm going to allow the defense a narrow window to explore this. They can mention everything they found—the ring, the tooth, the chisel marks, the missing concrete. They cannot mention Kent Corwin or anyone else without more."

"Judge, I admire the creativity of Mr. Pierce and his expert, I really do," said Baggman. "I can't imagine how many late nights it took for them to come up with it. But how can they say there was a body in there if they don't have one?"

Judge Roderick looked to Mason. "I assume you have evidence that you in fact found a tooth in the concrete?"

"I do, Your Honor," said Mason.

"Then the defense can raise an inference that there was a body in there. And the state is free to cross-examine or bring other evidence to show that inference is incorrect."

Judge Roderick pointed. "I'm warning both of you—this is a narrow window. I can widen it or slam it shut depending on how the evidence progresses. And how you both behave."

A chorus of "Yes, Your Honor's" from which Jerome Baggman notably refrained.

"All right, get out of here. See you tomorrow."

As they were filing out, Mason whispered to Astrid, "How did you know?"

She looked at him for a moment, then said, "You weren't going to tell me until you sprung it on me in court, were you?"

Mason stared, then shook his head. "No."

"Then I don't see a reason for us to have this conversation."

Her face softened then. "Given what's going on in the case, I don't think I should come to your cousin's service. But give your aunt and uncle my condolences?"

"I will. Thanks."

Baggman was in Astrid's ear as Peter tapped Mason's elbow, guiding him away.

"I stowed Hyde in that consultation room again," Peter said. "Let's go tell him what's happening."

MASON EXPLAINED the body theory for the first time to Hyde and Jessica Warren, then said, "So the good news is that the judge will let us argue to the jury that there was a body in there which weakened the support pier. We can't go much farther than that, but, combined with what happened today, we think that's a good development.

Hyde didn't react how Mason expected at all. His face went white, then it went red, and then he said, "The judge is going to let you do that?

"It looks that way."

"You can't!"

Mason looked at Hyde, looked at Peter, then said, "Mrs. Warren, I'm sorry, but I think you'd better excuse us."

Mason was not at all reassured when Jessica Warren left without question.

When the door closed, Mason said, "Tell me you didn't put a body in the pier, Hyde."

Hyde looked confused, then said, "No! No, of course not."

"Then why not?"

"You saw the records! You know who handled that project!"

Mason frowned. "Corwin Concrete. Kent Corwin."

"That's who started it! You know who finished it."

"His son, Kevin."

"That's who owned the company. Who was running the project? Jesus, why didn't you tell me you were digging into this?"

"What? Wasn't Red Gibson the foreman?"

"Exactly!"

Mason was still confused. "And?"

"Jesus, Mason, you've lived your whole life here and worked construction besides. Who does Red work for now?"

"Warhelm Industrial Services. You hired them for the salvage and rebuild."

"And who owns Warhelm Industrial Services?"

"John Warhelm, I imagine."

"Of course it's John Warhelm! And Red doesn't just work for Warhelm; he's his chief construction officer. And how do you think he rose through the ranks at Warhelm Industrial?"

"I have no idea."

"He started by running a small company that Warhelm ultimately acquired. Corwin Concrete."

"You're kidding."

"How can you not know this?"

"The corporate documents were murky."

"Forget the corporate documents. How could you not know the history?"

"I was in elementary school when it happened, Hyde."

"Listen, we all knew old man Corwin died in a fishing accident. God rest him, the Lord and Lake Michigan work in mysterious ways, and I've never, until today, thought twice about it. But if you're telling me now that there was a body buried on my site and that body was Kent Corwin? Mason, Red was on the site then and he's on the site now, but now he's Warhelm's right-hand man! You can't bring this up!"

"Hyde, your life could depend on this."

"That life won't be worth anything if I'm crosswise with John Warhelm."

"I have to use it."

"The hell you do. Whatever you found was meant to stay buried, and I'm not going to be the face of digging it up."

"No, Hyde, I will be."

"I'll be blamed more than you, Mason. I should know better."

"But—"

"No 'but's, Mason. You don't bring up the body. Not under any circumstances. Or I'll complain to the Bar."

Mason looked at Peter, who shrugged.

"We have a couple of days until Cameron testifies," Peter said. "That gives us time to think about it."

"There's nothing to think about! This is closed. No one talks about a body!"

With that, Hyde got up, straightened his gold glasses, and hurried out the door.

Peter Freid smiled. “As you know, I’m new around these parts.”

“Yes.”

“Is this John Warhelm really that scary?”

Mason thought, then said, “Yes.”

74

When Mason pulled into his drive, he was surprised to see a sheriff's department vehicle still there. He was even more surprised when Sheriff Sizemore walked out his front door.

"Still working?" Mason asked.

"Just wrapped up. It's all yours."

"Find anything interesting?"

Sheriff Sizemore pursed his lips, put his hands on his hips, looked back into the house, and said, "You didn't have a security camera in your spare room by any chance, did you?"

"No."

"Didn't think so."

"Why?"

"Because we found one. Hidden in your smoke detector."

"Show me."

Mason's mind raced as he followed Sheriff Sizemore into his spare room. The sheriff showed Mason a baggie with a small camera in it, then pointed to the smoke detector behind his desk.

Mason looked back and forth. "That would have a clear view of my monitor."

Sheriff Sizemore nodded. "I noticed the same thing."

"That's the desk where the tooth was."

"So you mentioned. Any ex-girlfriends? Someone who would be snooping on you domestically?"

Mason shook his head. "My ex was more...direct in getting what she wanted. This isn't her style."

"Any other—"

Mason raised a hand. "Sheriff, I'm only doing one thing that's worth spying on me for."

Sheriff Sizemore looked away again, nodded. "I thought as much."

"Can you tell where it fed to?"

Sheriff Sizemore shook his head. "It's disabled. Nothing in the hardware itself will tell us."

"Sheriff, if there's video, it would show us who killed my cousin."

"That would be the easy way. Unfortunately, there's no way to see it."

"Did you find anything else?"

Sheriff Sizemore paused, nodded, and motioned for Mason to follow. They went into the kitchen, and the sheriff opened the fridge.

"You stocked Two Hearted IPA?"

Mason nodded. "It was his favorite."

"How many?"

Mason bent down, looked. "There was a twelve-pack in there."

"There are eleven now. And one by the stairs."

"Hardly enough for a drunken fall," said Mason.

"That theory's out."

"Why?"

Sheriff Sizemore shut the fridge door and pointed at it. "We found blood specks here and on the back door. Someone tried to clean up, but they missed a few spots. And I'm no medical examiner, but I can tell you that your cousin's head wound isn't from falling down the stairs."

"Can you tell what caused it?"

"A blunt instrument. The M.E. might be able to tell us what kind."

"Where does this all lead, Sheriff?"

"I can't tell yet, Mason. The camera's a dead end. There were no witnesses here. I'm betting the blood is Austin's, and we haven't found any fingerprints or DNA yet to indicate someone else. They'll check for other DNA at the autopsy, but there weren't any signs of a struggle."

"Seems to me Austin interrupted a theft."

"That's possible."

"C'mon, Sheriff, it's likely. We know Cameron dropped the tooth off at 3:30. Austin left work at 3:30 to come here, and now the tooth is gone, and Austin is dead."

"I'm not going to haul the County Prosecutor in for questioning without more."

"She's not the only one who's interested in that tooth. Jerome Baggman's on the civil case. He has about ten million more reasons to be interested."

"That much?"

"He probably thinks so. He has an interest in knowing what I'm doing."

A couple of things clicked into place for Mason. The objection to the body before he mentioned it. Baggman's comment about Mason and Cameron—*I can't imagine how many late nights it took for them to come up with it.*

"And it certainly seems as if he has."

Sheriff Sizemore kept staring in the other direction. "I still need more than that before I accuse the prosecutor and the families' attorney of something like this."

Mason ground his teeth. He understood Sheriff Sizemore's reluctance, but reluctance wasn't going to find who killed his cousin. "You can't just mail it in because the prosecutor might—the email!"

Sheriff Sizemore's eyes narrowed. "Watch yourself, Mason."

"No, what? Sorry, never mind. We have another lead. The email to Cameron—it said it was from me, but I never sent it. It's probably from the thief and the killer."

"Assuming they're the same. Do you have it?"

Cameron had forwarded it to him, so Mason pulled out his phone and forwarded it to the Sheriff, who read it on his.

"I'll need her device."

"She's at the hotel here in town."

Sheriff Sizemore nodded. "I may have to get the state boys involved on the computer forensics on this."

"Given the suspects, you probably need to anyway."

Sheriff Sizemore snapped him a look, then went thoughtful. "That's probably not a bad idea. We may need to get them all the way in this, to avoid the appearance of impropriety. If there's something here."

"My cousin's dead body is here, Sheriff."

"So it was." He waved his phone. "You've given me a lot to work on. I'll keep you updated."

"There's another possibility, Sheriff."

Sheriff Sizemore stared. "What's that?"

"If you don't think it's likely that Astrid or Baggman spied on me and killed my cousin to win their case, then whoever hid a body in a concrete pier might be your next best choice."

"Who'd want to do that?"

"Whoever wanted Kent Corwin dead."

Sheriff Sizemore shook his head. "That case was long since closed, Mason."

"Doesn't seem like it, Sheriff."

"I guess without the tooth we won't know."

"We also have his naval academy ring. And the date of his disappearance."

Sheriff Sizemore scowled. "That's the other evidence you talked about?"

Mason nodded. "We think it shows Kent Corwin was in the pier."

"That was what, twenty-three years ago? That trail's going to be pretty cold."

Mason pointed at his door, where his cousin's blood had been. "Seems pretty hot to me. And to my client too."

"What's Hyde have to do with this?"

"He's scared as hell that I'm going to mention this body in court."

Sheriff Sizemore frowned. "Why?"

"Because Red Gibson took over the patio project after Kent Corwin disappeared twenty-three years ago. And he knows who Red works for now."

"What are you going to do?" asked Sheriff Sizemore.

"Defend him. What are you going to do?"

"My job. I appear to have some new leads. Keep me informed if you find out anything else?"

"Yes. Same?" Mason held out his hand.

Sheriff Sizemore shook it. "Your cousin deserves it."

~

SHERIFF SIZEMORE HAD a new square corner to turn. He picked up his phone, made a call, and said, "Have you heard about Austin Pierce?...He was murdered...Yes, it is terrible...Happened out at Mason Pierce's place...Your name has come up...I'm going to need to ask you a few questions...No, thank you, I can come there...Now, is convenient, yes...I'll see you in twenty minutes."

Sheriff Sean Sizemore hung up. No one could ever accuse him of not doing his duty.

75

After the Sheriff left, Mason had intended to eat, then work from home. But when he looked at the outside of the fridge, which was now clean of blood, and the inside, which was now missing one Two Hearted IPA, he found that he couldn't do it. So he picked up the phone, called the two people who were going through the same thing, and agreed to meet at The Loon.

In the same way that his father had felt compelled to tell his brother, Mason had gone to the home of Lily and Bronson Stone to deliver the news to Lily that her brother Austin was dead. They'd spent time together there before going back to Uncle Troy and Aunt Linda's house so that the family could be together, and that was where Mason had left them when he went home to get a few hours of sleep before trial the next day.

So when Mason, Lily, and Bronson met at The Loon that night for dinner, they didn't have to go through all of those things people go through the first time they see each other after a horrific loss—they'd done it. Instead, Mason gave Lily a hug that was a little longer than usual, and Bronson slapped Mason's shoulder with one hand and held it a little longer than normal before the three of them sat at their table.

The same wasn't true of Brenda, of course, and it was a true measure of the depth of her sorrow that she came out from behind the bar and over to the table and gave each one of them a silent hug before taking their orders, which she said she would bring over.

"Wow," said Lily as Brenda left. "We must really look bad."

"Speak for yourself," said Bronson.

Mason and Lily looked at him, surprised at the uncharacteristic remark.

Bronson shrugged. "Austin would have said it."

Lily smiled, a little. "He would."

Mason knew he couldn't go too far down that road right now, so he said, "I talked to the Sheriff today."

"Again? How long does it take to investigate a slip?"

Last night hadn't seemed like the time to voice his suspicions, not when things about Austin's death weren't clear yet. But after his meeting with the sheriff, things were different. Now was that time.

"It wasn't a slip. Austin was murdered."

It took a moment for the statement to register with Lily before she said, "When they said his death was suspicious, I thought that meant they were investigating the slip on the stairs."

Bronson became dark with attention. "What happened?" he said.

"First," said Mason, "I have to tell you about my case."

So Mason laid it all out: the support pier and what they'd found in it, the theft of the tooth, and Mason's suspicion that Austin had interrupted the theft.

"The Sheriff assumed Austin had slipped, and that's all my dad heard. I only had suspicions last night, but it's pretty clear now that the thief killed him and tried to make it look like an accident."

The Dean came out then with four skillets and put one in front of each of them and one at the empty place. "These go on Austin's tab."

Lily looked stricken. "Dean, he's not going to be here."

The Dean nodded. "Then I'll just hold it for him."

It was the most Mason had heard The Dean speak in years.

It took Mason a moment to recover from that, but when he did, he told them about the leads the sheriff was tracking down.

The more he told them, the more his cousin and his best friend tensed up. Mason could feel the anger building in both of them. It was never hard to tell what Lily was feeling; it welled up and shot out more often than not without any censoring along the way. Bronson was different; his default was quiet, but his expression grew darker and darker as Mason felt each word coiling him like a spring.

"Okay," Lily said. "That's what the sheriff is doing. What are we going to do about it?"

"The email and the autopsy are the best leads right now," said Mason. "I don't know if we can add to that."

"Do your dads know?" said Bronson.

"Not yet."

"We can't just sit here," said Lily.

"Which one do you think it is?" said Bronson.

"What do you mean?"

"It sounds like it's either the people on the other side of your case or whoever hid the body."

"I can't believe it's Atti Olsen," Mason said. "It could be Baggman."

"Or Red Gibson," said Bronson.

Mason thought. "Baggman makes more sense. He's more likely to have set up surveillance on me than anyone."

Bronson nodded. "It sounds like we need to pay a visit to Mr. Baggman."

"You can't do that right now, Bronson. Not during the trial."

"No, *you* can't do that, Mace. Lily and I can do whatever we want."

"Anything you do is going to be imputed to me. He's going to say I sent you over to interfere with the case. Let the sheriff handle it for now."

"That's not how a unit handles its business."

"Just be patient. For a little bit."

Bronson's look, and Lily's, promised no such thing.

Mason's phone buzzed.

It was Amber.

Normally, he wouldn't pick up, but normally his cousin hadn't just died. Amber had lived with Mason for long enough to get to know Austin pretty well. She deserved to know.

"Hi, Amber."

"Mason, thank God you picked up. I'm scared."

That was not at all what Mason was expecting, so he just said, "What do you mean?"

"The man, he's here."

"Where's here?"

"Chicago. At my club."

"What man?"

"The man who paid me to spy on Peter about your case."

76

Mason got up and walked away from the table so he could hear.

"Talk to me, Amber."

The story tumbled out—how she'd been mad at Mason about not buying the lot, how she'd met a guy at a bar who was very interested in Mason's office, and how she knew Peter was very interested in her.

"So he said he'd set me up with some clubs here in Chicago that needed some influencers and I'd pass along anything I learned from Peter about the case," she finished.

"Why are you calling me now?"

"Because the last time I saw him, he was interested in anything Peter knew about the Cider Mill patio, and he specifically asked me about a body. I didn't know anything about that, and I decided I'd had about enough of him and of Peter and was headed back to Chicago. But then I saw on social last night that Austin died at your house, and I was just devastated. I was crying all night, he was just such a good man and we were so close—"

"—Amber."

"What? You think your family couldn't love me too?"

"Then what happened?"

"I could barely pull myself together today, but I did because the club was counting on me, so I came in tonight and I thought I was imagining it when I saw him waiting outside, but then the doors opened and he's here."

"This Kyle guy?"

"Yes."

"Are you with friends?"

"The clubs like to have at least three of us posting together."

"Stay with them. And stay there."

"But I'm supposed to go to—"

"Stay in the club. Don't leave. I'm on my way."

"To Chicago?"

"What's the club?"

"Echelon."

"Stay put. I'll be there before close."

"But—"

Mason hung up.

He went back to Lily and Bronson, sat down.

"What did Miss Model want?" said Lily.

"She's in trouble."

"Shocking."

"A man who was spying on me, about the case, followed her back to Chicago."

He had their attention.

"Coincidence?" said Lily.

"He asked her whether we'd found a body at the patio."

Bronson nodded, stood.

Mason raised an eyebrow.

"We're going to Chicago, aren't we?"

Mason stood. "Didn't want to ask."

As Lily stood with them, she said, "Don't even think about trying to talk me out of it."

Bronson scowled. "Why would we want to take it easy on him?"

She shook her head, smiled, and said, "I do love you."

THERE WAS no question that Lily had the best truck, so she drove. Mason was cleaning empty energy drink cans out of the passenger seat while they waited for Bronson to emerge from The Loon.

"Where is he?" said Lily.

"He was talking to The Dean."

"What's that about?"

Mason was pretty sure he knew but said, "How many of these do you drink?"

"As many as it takes. Forget what a working life is like?"

"Apparently."

Bronson emerged.

"Ready, Princess?" said Lily.

"Let's go," Bronson said, and climbed in.

THE BEAUTY of a four-and-a-half-hour drive is that you're not exactly going off half-cocked. The time allowed each of them to make arrangements on the way.

Bronson was a corporal in the National Guard, 1436th Engineer Company of the 507th Engineer Battalion. They specialized in construction-related projects, and he'd been deployed often, including a one-year stint to the Middle East a little while back.

That meant Bronson was used to making plans when the

heat was on, and that's what he did right then. He called a couple of members of his company who lived in Chicago, and they knew a couple of more soldiers from other companies of the 507th that worked there too, and soon Bronson had received the no-questions-asked assistance the three of them needed for what they were planning to do.

Mason had a little more ground to cover. He wasn't due to take any witnesses the next day, but he needed to lay groundwork with a message to Peter that he was following up on some case developments that may make him late to court.

Then he turned his attention to this Kyle guy that Amber was dealing with. As far as Mason was concerned, there were two pools of suspects on his surveillance and Austin's death—the lawyers and Red Gibson. He had no idea which one it was. He remembered a conversation with his dad about Red not too long ago and decided to give him a call.

"Hello, Son."

"Hi Dad, where are you?"

"At Troy and Linda's."

"Good. How are they doing?"

"Like you'd expect. Are you coming over tonight?"

"No, sorry, working on the case."

"Oh, right. I'll tell them."

"Can you talk?"

"I am."

Mason smiled. "You are. Do you remember when you warned me to watch my terms with Red Gibson?"

A pause, then, "I do."

"Why?"

"Do we need to talk about this now?"

"We do."

"Why?"

"I think it might be related to Austin."

"Really." It wasn't a question.

"Yes."

He could hear his dad moving, and when Jackson Pierce spoke again, it was softer. "Red's an exacting son of a bitch. He got it from old man Corwin."

"And?"

"Why does there have to be an 'and?'"

"Because I've worked for an exacting son of a bitch from the time I was eight, so I don't think that's why you'd warn me."

A pause, then, "He's tangled up with people it's better not to be tangled up with."

"Warhelm."

"What makes you say that?"

"My client about had a heart attack because he thought our case might be connected to Warhelm in some way."

"Is it?"

"That's what I'm trying to find out."

"Does that mean he might be connected to Austin?"

"I'm trying to find that out too."

"I wouldn't look too close, Son."

"What's that supposed to mean?"

"What I said."

"That tells me what I need to know."

"I mean it, Mace."

"I know, Dad."

Lily made a gesture to him.

"Oh, Dad, tell Uncle Troy and Aunt Linda that Lily and Bronson won't be over tonight."

"Don't tell me they're with you."

"Okay, I won't.

"Mason—"

"Bye, Dad."

Mason hung up. "You might not want to answer any texts from your mom and dad."

"Thanks," Lily turned on her blinker. "I'm going to stop here for gas and energy drinks. Load 'em up. We're halfway there."

77

Jackson Pierce pressed the button on the speaker in front of the wrought-iron gate.

"Yes?" came the tinny voice.

"Jackson Pierce to see John Warhelm."

A pause, then, "I'm sorry, Mr. Pierce, Mr. Warhelm isn't in."

"Yes, he is. Tell him it's urgent."

A pause. "I'm sorry, but he's not in, Mr. Pierce."

"Tell him it's about Red Gibson and the Cider Mill patio."

A longer pause, then, "Like I said, Mr. Pierce, Mr. Warhelm isn't in. I suggest you call his office tomorrow and make an appointment."

Jackson Pierce climbed out of his truck then. It always took him a while, but this time it took even longer as he fumbled with his canes, once, twice, and again. When he finally had them, he took a few steps forward, looked up at the closed-circuit camera, and pressed the button again.

"There's no need to get out, Mr. Pierce. I can hear you just fine."

"I'm sure you both can." He caned forward a couple of steps. "My nephew was killed yesterday. My son is the lawyer on the

Cider Mill case. He, my son, thinks those two things might be related."

Jackson Pierce pushed up on his canes, flipped his long hair out of his eyes, and stared up at the camera as he said, "My son shouldn't have to clean up that kind of mess when he's just doing his job."

His face screwed into a twisted grin that held no joy. "People should do their goddam jobs!" Jackson Pierce banged his canes together with a metallic clang.

He glared for another moment at the camera, then slumped, the angry energy gone. Slowly, he climbed back into his truck.

When he was in and he'd slammed his door shut, the tinny voice said, "Like I said, Mr. Pierce, please make an appointment tomorrow."

"I don't think so," Jackson Pierce said, and backed out of the drive.

~

PEOPLE MAKE things harder than they have to be. They put mental limits on themselves, tell themselves something can't be done, then convince themselves that because they couldn't do it, no one else could either.

Mason had built cinderblock walls with his bare hands since he was eight.

Lily raised seawalls, fighting the violent, frigid waters of Lake Michigan every day.

Bronson had been deployed over and over again to construct barriers against floods, hurricanes, and enemy fire.

For them, driving to Chicago and finding the bar was easy.

So was making the preparations on the way.

PART IX

78

Kyle Stewart didn't feel like he could wait much longer. Amber would notice him soon, and then things would go south.

He hadn't come to Chicago to find her; he'd come to Chicago to get the hell out of Northlake and keep going to parts unknown. He'd planned on stopping at the club to see if Fergus could loan him a couple of thousand until his case came in—they went way back and the club business was cash based, so it was never too hard. Kyle had been shocked at his luck though, when he saw Amber and two other women get out of a car and go straight in. Kyle knew then it was a sign—always ride a hot streak.

Echelon was a big club, so Kyle had made his way to the second level where he could see Amber at a bottle service table without being seen himself. That made it easier to keep an eye on her but that much harder to get past the velvet ropes and casually brush by.

Because that's what he needed to do. Once he knew she was here, he guessed she was here to "influence" for the night, so he'd risked running back to his apartment to pick up some chemical persuaders to make her more amiable to leaving with him. His heart was racing that he might have lost her, but her socials let him know that she was still at the club and even exactly where to look for her when he returned. He needn't have worried.

But now he was worried; it was getting later, and he still hadn't gotten close, and the thinner the crowds became, the harder it would be to slip off with her. So once Amber's girlfriends left, one to the dance floor and one to the bar, Kyle moved.

He was halfway there when Amber headed for the bathroom. Kyle smiled, palmed the small needle in his hand, and followed.

When Amber turned a corner, Kyle hurried so as not to lose her. He passed a service door then rounded the corner himself.

He froze. Amber was under a neon pink *Powder Room* sign, hugging a woman with blond hair that stuck out all over the place. When the woman looked at him over Amber's shoulder, her eyes narrowed. It took Kyle a moment to place her because she was out of context.

Northlake. Mason's cousin, the seawall builder.

Shit.

The builder woman pushed Amber behind her and headed toward him. Kyle backed up into someone. "Sorry," he said and turned.

"No problem," said a voice.

Kyle turned and felt a flash of panic. It was the other guy from the seawall crew. The not-dead one.

The not-dead guy grabbed his arm.

Kyle jammed the persuader needle into the man's arm, broke his grip, and ran.

"That's him?" said Lily.

Amber nodded her head.

"Stay in the club," said Lily, and ran after him.

"He jabbed me with something," Bronson said as she passed.

"Stay with Amber," said Lily and kept going.

Lily followed Kyle through the service door. Fortunately, there were no choices—the dark service hall ran in a straight line to a fire door that Kyle was banging through.

Lily hoped Mason had chosen the right door.

~

Mason stood at a corner between the main street and an alley so he could watch the main entrance and a side door at the same time. He wasn't happy about it, but their argument outside the club had been short-lived. Lily pointed out, correctly, that the jolly green giant wasn't going to be sneaking up on anybody inside the club and that the best bet was for Mason to stand outside one of the doors in case Lily and Bronson missed the guy inside.

So he was standing there, attracting a lot of looks, as always, but no one was bothering him, which was usually the case too.

His phone buzzed. A text from Bronson.

Service door.

Mason ran down the alley and up an eight-foot flight of stairs to a concrete platform and pulled on the handle of a steel door. He cursed.

It was locked.

~

Kyle ran down the hall to the fire door, pounded open the long push bar with both hands, and charged through.

Right into a brick wall.

Two arms went around him and suddenly he couldn't breathe.

Pierce.

That bald, broken-nosed son of a bitch was looking down on him, squeezing him in a bear hug. Kyle tried to push the needle into Pierce, but his arms were pinned to his sides. Then he tried to headbutt him, but his head only hit the ogre's chest.

He started to see stars. He couldn't breathe.

"Mace!" yelled a woman's voice. "Stop!"

Kyle felt a snap in his ribs, cried out.

Then another snap. He tried to cry out again, but there was no air.

His vision blackened around the edges, then narrowed to a tunnel.

"MACE! STOP!"

Mason heard his cousin, but he didn't care. He kept squeezing, and the piece of shit who'd killed his cousin kept squirming.

"If he's dead, we can't learn anything," Lily said as she ran up.

"I know," said Mason and kept squeezing until Kyle Stewart's lights went out.

79

Kyle Stewart woke up in darkness. And to voices.

"Jesus H., Mace!" A woman's voice. "How hard did you squeeze him?"

"Not that hard."

"Is he still out?"

"I think he's pretending to be."

Kyle felt around. Darkness turned out to be four wooden walls. Ten feet above him, he saw a night sky lit by an electric glow. A big bald head was silhouetted against it.

"Why did you send Amber to spy on Peter?" Pierce said.

Kyle's head ached and his ribs hurt. "Get bent," he said.

Kyle's eyes were adjusted enough to see Pierce's broken nose turn to the side. "Bring it closer," Pierce said to someone, Kyle guessed the woman.

"Where are you going, beautiful?" came a third voice, a man.

A woman's laugh. "I'll be right back, baby, don't you worry. Ask him for more of whatever was in that needle while you're at it, Mace."

Pierce looked back down into wherever Kyle was. "What did you hit my friend with?"

Kyle shook his head. "Just a persuader. He'll be fine. Now get me out of here."

"Last chance, why did you send Amber to spy on Peter?"

Kyle tried to clear his head but was having trouble. Still, he said, "You're really screwing yourself here, Pierce."

"How so?"

"You just lost your ticket, pal. You know you're on thin ice with the Bar Examiners. Word of this gets to them, and your license is gone."

The third man's voice again. "Lily, come back!"

"I miss you too, baby," said Lily.

Pierce didn't stop staring down into the hole. "So you did research on me too?"

"It's all public record, pal."

"That research include my house?"

Kyle realized he'd overstepped and shifted. "Get me out of here now, and I won't file a complaint."

"If you were the one watching me, then odds are you're the one who killed my cousin."

"I don't know what you're talking about."

Pierce nodded, looked to the side. "Swing the chute around, Lily."

Kyle realized he'd been hearing the rumble of a truck in the background.

"What are you doing?"

Pierce didn't answer.

"Let me out!"

Pierce reached out, and there was a clank as a semi-circle was silhouetted against the opening.

"I'm going to bury you, Pierce!"

"I doubt it. You might want to cover your nose. And mouth."

Pierce waved, and there was a rumble before something wet and heavy splashed out of the chute. Kyle ducked as it hit his shoulder, then shifted as the wet, heavy sludge piled at his feet.

Concrete.

Kyle screamed.

Pierce waved, and the concrete from what Kyle now knew was a concrete mixer truck, stopped.

"What are you doing? This is murder!"

"You would know."

"I haven't killed anybody!

"So you say."

"They'll put you away!"

Pierce smiled. "If they find out, maybe. But I think we know this column will keep our secret for years." He waved, and the concrete poured out again.

Kyle covered his nose and his mouth and bowed his head away from the stream that pooled around his legs. When it reached his mid-shin, he banged on the sides of the walls.

Pierce waved. The concrete stopped.

"My cousin's dead," Pierce said. "So I have no problem filling this column up. And if I feel that way, imagine how his sister feels."

"I didn't kill him!"

"Doubtful." He turned. "Go ahead, Lily!"

"I can prove it wasn't me!"

Mason raised a hand. "How?"

"I have video."

Mason stared. "From my house?"

"Yes, yes, now get me out of here."

"Of the person who did it?"

"Of the person who stole the tooth!"

"That wasn't you?"

"No, I tried, but I got there afterwards, goddammit. Now let me out and I'll show you."

"Tried to get it for who?"

"For Baggman! I worked for Baggman!"

Mason nodded. "Where's the video?"

"At my apartment, I'll take you!"

"I don't think so. If it shows what you say, we'll let you go. If it doesn't, Lily will fire away."

"It does, for chrissakes!"

"We'll see. Where?"

Kyle gave him the address.

"Keys."

Kyle tossed him the keys.

"How's the video stored?"

"There's a drive in my bag, next to the bed. Now let me out!"

Mason shook his head. "I'd march in place if I were you. You don't want your feet to get stuck in there."

Mason's head disappeared. Kyle yelled for help. When he kept yelling, the rumble of the concrete mixer grew louder. He quieted down.

The rumble kept going.

IT TOOK Mason half an hour to get to Kyle's apartment and another ten minutes to find the gym bag. He chuckled when he found not one, but two drives.

He went back to Lily's truck, pulled out his laptop, and loaded the video.

It wasn't long. It had a wide-screen shot of Mason's spare room. It picked up at 3:41 p.m. when a man jumped in and hid behind the doorway. The man stood there, crouched, back to the camera for several minutes. Then he slowly slid a hammer out of his tool belt, gathered himself, and rushed out.

The video cut off thirty seconds later.

The video came back on at 3:55 p.m. when Red Gibson, face now full on to the camera, walked in, took the box off Mason's desk, and left.

Mason picked up his phone and called Lily. "It wasn't him."

~

Kyle wasn't sure how long he'd been down there, but it seemed like hours. His ankles and shins were burning in reaction from the concrete. He kept trying to pull his feet out of the muck, but it hadn't hardened enough for him to stay on top, so he'd kept marching in place, terrified that his feet would get stuck.

When the rumble of the concrete mixer stopped, Kyle screamed for help. He heard the sounds of the city, but nothing loud, nothing that sounded like it was nearby, so he kept marching and shouted some more.

When he heard a siren nearby, Kyle screamed louder, voice cracking. The siren stopped, and he screamed some more. A flashlight shone down on his face.

"What are you doing down there?" said a voice.

"Thank God, who's that?" Kyle said.

"Chicago PD and paramedics. We had a 911 call that someone heard screaming. What happened?"

Kyle was exhausted, but he'd made plenty of bets when he was exhausted, and the key was keeping your cool. He had only one shot at Baggman's bonus, and it didn't involve spending hours answering questions. "I had a little too much to drink, I guess. I fell. Thank God you found me."

"We're going to have to ask you some questions."

"No problem, Officer. But first, I'm going to want to talk to my lawyer."

80

Lily hung up. "There, the rescue squad's been called too. Are you happy?"

"He kept his end of the deal," Mason said.

"I still should have emptied the mixer on him."

"Except that he didn't kill Austin."

Lily stared at the road, looking no happier now than she had when he'd talked her out of it. "What about what he said? About calling the State Bar on you?"

"He's not reporting anything."

"I suppose that would be dumb."

"It would. We're going to have trouble using the video for the same reason."

Lily scowled. "Why?"

"Hi, Sheriff Sizemore, this is the video we took from a man we beat unconscious. He gave it to us after we poured concrete on him."

She shook her head. "It'll only burn his legs a little. But I see your point."

"We're going to use it. I just have to figure out how."

"We don't need to use it."

"Why not?"

"Because I'm going to kill Red," said Lily, quietly.

Mason knew his cousin meant it. "Let me handle it first."

"I don't know that I want you to."

"Taking on Red is different than surprising Kyle. And I can't lose another cousin."

"They'll never convict me."

"They might. And that's not necessarily what I'm talking about."

Miles rolled on. Bronson kept snoring in the back seat. Lily checked the rearview and laughed. "I really do have to find out what the asshole used. He hasn't stirred since we left."

Another mile rolled by.

"He'll be as hard to control as me, you know," Lily said.

"I know. I need you to give me time."

Lily glanced at Mason, the headlights of a car behind them bouncing off the mirror into her eyes. "I'll be distracted until the funeral. No promises after that."

"Deal," Mason said.

But he wasn't at all sure what he was going to do.

Hundreds of miles later, Mason wasn't any closer to an answer. The drive back had been quiet—Bronson sleeping the sweet sleep of the drugged, Lily thinking about Austin, and Mason trying to figure out what to do with what he'd learned.

One thing he did know was that he didn't have much time. Word of what they'd done would get back to Baggman and Gibson, if it hadn't already, and Lily had pretty much said she was going to go off as soon as they put Austin in the ground.

And he still had to handle Cameron's testimony to defend Hyde.

They were all exhausted when they pulled into The Loon;

well, all of them except Bronson, who'd woken up as soon as they'd hit the Northlake city limits in an annoyingly chipper fashion. Mason thanked them both and climbed into his own truck so he could go home and get a couple of hours of sleep before trial.

81

John Warhelm loved two things—quiet and solutions. He'd figured out long ago that one begets the other and so cultivated both of those things in equal measure.

Northlake was quiet, and the location of his house quieter still, nestled as it was on a wooded hill with views of Lake Michigan and Lake Lacache. It was the quiet that had drawn him here in the first place, away from the blare and noise of Chicago, and when he discovered that Lake Lacache was the Americanized version of le Lac Caché, the Hidden Lake, he knew he'd found home.

Red Gibson was one of the people who brought him the solutions that allowed him to maintain the quiet, and it was that ability that had kept Red in his position for so long. Still, when one had warning, it was always best to put solutions in place in advance, so John Warhelm summoned one of his solution providers and commissioned him to fix one of two problems.

He'd let him know soon which problem that would be.

Then he went back to the quiet, staring at the patterns on his zebrawood floor.

82

Mason made it to court on time and presentable and was fortunately scheduled for no witnesses that day. While Astrid called chain of custody witnesses and the occupancy inspector, Mason thought about how best to utilize the two thumb drives he still had in his pocket, having learned the hard way that nothing was safe to leave back at his home.

He noticed absently that Peter was masterful. For all of his faults, Peter had an easy way in the courtroom of picking up points, of having witnesses agree with him, as if it were the easiest thing in the world. Even the occupancy expert, the very man who had issued the permit for the patio, admitted that the number allowed on the patio had more to do with the number of seats, square footage, and fire exits available rather than the structural integrity of the patio itself.

It was the afternoon break, and Astrid Olsen was preparing for her last witness when Mason wandered over.

"Atti."

"We still have a case based on Wasmeuller's testimony, Mason," she said without looking up. "And the occupancy guy still confirmed that it was unsafe for your guy to be over the occupancy limit."

"What?" said Mason. "Oh, right, the last guy. That's not what I wanted to ask you."

"I'm a little busy."

"I know. One question—did you ever authorize surveillance on me?"

She barely looked up. "Of course not."

"No secret warrants? To be looking inside my house?"

Now he had her attention. She stared at him. "Have you committed a crime?"

Mason chose to interpret that question as, "Have you committed a crime that I would be investigating?"

"No," he said.

"Then I wouldn't have a basis for a warrant, would I? What's this about?"

"Nothing. Well, something that came up in Sheriff Sizemore's search of my house. When he was checking it after Austin died."

Astrid's face immediately softened. "No, Mason. Nothing he found in there would have been from me."

"Thanks, Atti."

"Astrid?" said Jerome Baggman. "Carly's here."

"Thanks, Jerry." She nodded to Mason, and the two went back to their tables.

~

THE LAST WITNESS of the prosecution's case was Carly Franklin. She wheeled down the aisle and found when she arrived at the witness stand that it was not wheelchair accessible. She said she'd be happy to sit in front of the stand, that she didn't want to be a fuss, but Jerome Baggman was there to take the handles, tilt her backwards, and place her on the raised stand facing the jury.

Carly described the last day she and Sophia Kern and Ashley Trent and Molly Danvers had been together. She described the Dune Sled, and she talked about how she and Ashley had pushed Sophia and Molly to go to the Cider Mill, and how the two had had a great time despite themselves. Then she described the last decisions they'd made. How Ashley had gone back into the dining room to get Dune Sled t-shirts and so had survived. How Carly had gone to get drinks at the stand on the patio next to the dining room so had been spared the worst of the collapse and was fortunate to have been left with ruined legs. How Molly and Sophia had stayed in the northwest corner, in the corner where the support pier had collapsed, and so had died. And how none of their lives—neither Carly's nor Ashley's, and certainly not Molly's or Sophia's, or any of their parents—would ever be the same.

Astrid knew what she was doing. Her questions were brief, and the impact of Carly's testimony was massive.

It was Peter's turn. Suddenly, Mason knew what he had to do.

He reached out, put a hand on Peter's arm, pointed at Carly and then himself.

Peter raised an eyebrow but nodded.

Mason stood, staying right in front of his chair on the far side of the defense table. "I'm sorry you've gone through all of that, Ms. Franklin."

"Thank you, sir," she said.

"Do you think whoever caused that pier to collapse should pay?"

Tears leaked from the corners of Carly's eyes. "I do."

Mason nodded. "So do I."

Then Mason sat.

His words hung in the courtroom.

"Is that all, Mr. Pierce?" said Judge Roderick.

"It is, Your Honor."

"Ms. Olsen?"

Astrid stared at Mason as she said, "No further questions, Judge."

Judge Roderick told the jury that they were done for the day and that the defense case would start tomorrow.

When he was gone, Peter chuckled, leaned over, and whispered so Hyde wouldn't hear, "I see we brought the large onions this afternoon. Something you want to tell me?"

Mason thought, then said, "Not yet."

"Fine," said Peter. "But soon. And before you put Dr. Thomas on."

Mason nodded. "I have to go. Can I skip the Hyde debrief today?"

Peter was still smiling. "Do you care what I say?"

Mason gave him a quick grin. "I'd prefer you say 'Yes.'"

"Yes. And call me. Any hour."

"Done. And thanks."

Peter waved. "Go."

Mason hurried to his truck.

He made two calls on the way.

No one picked up on the first call, but he expected that and left a message.

The second was picked up right away.

"I thought I'd hear from you sooner, Big Boy."

"We need to meet, Jerome."

Jerome Baggman chuckled. "If I say no, are you going to shower me in concrete?"

"No, because your video cameras would record it."

"I don't know what you're talking about."

"Neither do I."

"Oh, but I think you do. And I think the Chicago PD does too."

"We need to meet."

"I'm not meeting anywhere with you, Big Boy."

"I'm going to text you a time and a place later tonight. When I do, I think you'll agree."

"I doubt that."

"Up to you. But it'll be in your best interest. Especially if you want to avoid being an accomplice to murder."

Mason hung up. It would work or it wouldn't.

He wasn't sure where to wait and decided on The Loon.

Because he'd been talking on the phone, he didn't notice the truck following him or the fact that it went by The Loon, circled back around, then parked at the closed butcher shop next door.

~

Brenda was a good enough friend that she didn't ask what had happened the night before and didn't ask what the hell he was doing drinking club soda at her bar. Instead, she poured him the club soda, added a lime, and patted his arm as she walked away to corral three propane drivers from next door.

Mason hadn't finished the soda when he received a text from a number he didn't recognize.

Yes. 7:00 p.m. Buzz in.

Mason passed the information on to Jerome Baggman. Then, since he had an hour to kill, he ordered a skillet.

He was starving.

83

Mason had never been there but, like everyone else in Northlake, he knew exactly where the house was so, at five minutes to seven, he hit the button on the intercom in front of the wrought-iron gate.

"Mason Pierce to see John Warhelm."

“Welcome, Mr. Pierce,” came a voice, and the gate opened.

The grounds and the house weren’t what was on his mind just then, so he was left with impressions rather than details. An exclusive section of the Bluffs all to himself, manicured grounds in front of a big brick home looking down at Lake Michigan. His dusty truck sticking out like an eyesore on the circular drive.

A man, not Mason’s size but close, greeted him and said that Mr. Warhelm was expecting him. Then he led Mason to a large study, which was more like a small library, with a wall of windows open to the view of dunes and blue water. His guide left, and Mason was in the room with the man himself.

“Good evening, Mason.”

“Hello, Mr. Warhelm.”

John Warhelm made no effort to get up from behind his desk. He looked to be in his late fifties, wearing summer country club clothes that looked light and well-tailored. His hair was full, short, and swept back, his features sharp, and his eyes clear as he put all of his focus on Mason for a moment. There was no way to describe that focus except to say that Mason felt John Warhelm was THERE and peering right through him.

Then John Warhelm turned back to the vista, and the effect was gone. He gestured. "Have a seat. I think we should wait for Mr. Baggman."

Mason took a seat with his back to the sunset, which he knew would just get lower and brighter as they talked. He was quiet for a minute, which gave him time to notice the floor.

"Is this the zebrawood?" Mason said.

John Warhelm's full attention came back to Mason. "You know wood?"

"I remember cases."

John Warhelm smiled. "That's right. You were there when the sheriff discovered Tommy Chase stole the first batch. What ever happened to him?"

Mason knew that they both knew that Tommy Chase had been sent to prison. "He ended up with life for the arson and murders that went along with it."

"Good. I hope it's hard time."

Mason also knew that they both knew that Tommy Chase had been beaten almost to death the day after he arrived in prison. And if Mason had to guess, he would say that it was for the theft, not the murders.

A minute later, Jerome Baggman arrived. "Hell of a place here, Warhelm." The lawyer strode across the zebrawood floor, extending a hand. "Jerome Baggman."

John Warhelm didn't get up and ignored the hand. "Hello, Jerome."

"Jerry, please." He left the hand out there a moment longer before he flopped, unphased, into a seat facing the sunset.

"What are we doing here, Big Boy? You've got a case to lose tomorrow."

"I thought the three of us should talk," Mason said.

"Why the three of us?" said Warhelm.

"Because Mr. Baggman has done something that affects me, Mr. Warhelm—"

Baggman snorted. "If by affects you, you mean beating the brakes off of you in court, then yes."

"—but also reflects on your company."

Warhelm didn't twitch. "What's that, Mason?"

"Yes, please, *Mason*, tell us what I did!" said Baggman.

"How much do you know about the Cider Mill patio case, Mr. Warhelm?"

Warhelm stared. "I'm aware of it."

"Both the criminal case the prosecutor has brought and the civil case Mr. Baggman has brought?"

Warhelm nodded.

"During our investigation, I discovered evidence that a body had been buried in the support pier that collapsed. That's what caused it to be unstable."

"So you say," said Baggman.

Warhelm ignored him. "What evidence was that?"

"A ring. And a tooth."

"Interesting."

"We also found that a section of the pier had been jack-hammered open, and that some of the concrete never made it to the airport hangar where the evidence was kept."

"Where did it go?" Warhelm said without apparent interest.

"That's not clear."

Warhelm nodded his head.

"Tall, desperate tales," said Baggman.

Warhelm ignored Baggman again. "I'm still not sure why you've involved me in this, Mason."

"Because Mr. Baggman arranged for surveillance of my house—"

"Scurrilous lies!" Baggman said with a smile.

"And he captured video of a man stealing the tooth off of my desk."

"And?"

"And the man was Red Gibson."

"Who's Red Gibson?" said Baggman.

"My chief of construction operations," said Warhelm. "Why would Red do that?"

"Red Gibson was a foreman for Kent Corwin when the old man had his fishing accident."

"I remember that," said Warhelm. "Didn't Corwin drown in the Big Lake?"

"That's what was reported. And what's been listed in the court proceedings declaring his death."

"Seems pretty conclusive."

"I thought so too. But then we found Corwin's 1970 Naval Academy ring in the concrete. Along with the tooth."

"I see."

"And later I remembered that Red was the one who tested the Cider Mill site the night before the wreckage removal started so he could declare the site safe for workers. Which would seem like the perfect opportunity to jackhammer and remove some concrete before everyone else showed up. Even better, no one would blink if they saw Red with a body; they'd just assume it was another casualty, if they didn't look too close. Which no one did."

"That seems like a lot of guesses, Mason."

"It was, Mr. Warhelm, until I found the video last night of Red stealing the tooth from my house. And drawing the hammer that killed my cousin, Austin."

Warhelm was still. "Is that on video too?"

"Only his preparation. But I'd bet Sheriff Sizemore will find that a hammer put the dent in my cousin's skull."

Warhelm nodded. "I appreciate you telling me this, Mason, but it seems like you should be telling it to Sheriff Sizemore."

"I will. Unless you want to."

"Why would I do that? You have the evidence."

"It occurred to me that you might want to be the one who turns Red in to Sheriff Sizemore."

"Why would you think that?"

"While there's certainly no traceable connection between Red's purchase of Corwin Concrete years ago and your company today—not that I could find, anyway—Red is currently your Chief Construction Officer. Turning him in distances your company from him."

"My company had nothing to do with Red's actions."

"I agree. But turning him in would make that even more clear."

"Why wouldn't you do it?"

Mason shrugged. "I'd rather not tell the sheriff how I got the video."

Baggman chuckled. "You don't want to talk about kidnapping and concrete? I think the State Bar might. Especially with your past."

"I think they might too. I also think they'll want to know about a lawyer bugging and tapping and videoing opposing counsel's house."

"I don't know anything about that."

"Then how do you know about the kidnapping and concrete?"

Baggman shrugged and waved, but he fell silent.

Warhelm looked thoughtful. "It seems there's a reason for this discussion then. Do you have a proposed solution?"

"I do."

Warhelm gestured.

"You turn in Red with the video." Mason placed a thumb drive on the desk.

Warhelm didn't touch it. "Is that it?"

"That's one of two that I have. I'll give you the other if you think this is a good idea."

"Are there more?"

"Ask him." Mason pointed at Baggman.

Warhelm looked at Baggman.

Baggman thought, then said, "No."

"Why would I have this video?" said Warhelm.

"You became suspicious of Red and wanted to know what I had learned."

"So I committed the crime of surveilling you?"

"I would never press charges against the man who caught my cousin's killer."

Warhelm thought. "Why can't this just be your own home security footage? Like from a nanny cam? And you brought it to me because he was my employee?"

Mason shook his head. "I've already told Sheriff Sizemore the camera wasn't mine."

"Perhaps you forgot."

"I don't think he'd buy that."

Warhelm nodded. "So you want me to turn in Red."

Mason didn't tell Warhelm the most important thing he was counting on Warhelm to do. Instead, he just nodded.

"Interesting," said Warhelm. "What would you do?"

"I put on evidence in court tomorrow that there was a body in the pier that destabilized it."

"Uh-uh, no way," said Baggman. "That blows my whole case. You're forgetting about the families."

"No, I'm not. Because the second part of what I do is negotiate the families' cases right now."

Baggman scowled. "What do you mean we negotiate that right now?"

"The three of us resolve the families' cases," Mason said. "Tonight."

"Why would all three of us be involved in that?" said Warhelm in a quieter voice than Mason liked.

"The criminal case isn't the end of things. If this keeps going as a civil case, I'll have all sorts of time to prove there was a body in there and keep the story in the headlines. I might even find more DNA evidence. If the civil case is settled though, all of that stops."

"I see," said Warhelm. "And since we're negotiating, what are you offering to Mr. Baggman?"

"I can offer Mr. Baggman the limits of my client's insurance for the accident. In turn, Mr. Baggman would agree that he won't try to collect from my client personally."

Baggman laughed outright. "Two million dollars? Split thirty-four ways? Get out of here, Pierce."

"That does seem low, Mason," said Warhelm. "Why would he do that?"

Mason kept his eyes on Warhelm. "Because a company that's in the chain of title from Corwin Concrete, say twenty years back or so, could then pay some remaining amount to the families that the two of you would agree on."

"I thought you haven't connected that company to one of mine?" said Warhelm.

"True. *I* haven't."

Warhelm looked thoughtful. "And what amount would that be?"

"That would be for the two of you to decide."

Warhelm turned to Baggman.

Baggman laughed. "Okay, I'll bite." He named a number with a whole lot of zeros.

"That's not really pursuing a solution, Jerome."

"I don't see why I would go lower than that. Not when Pierce is about to lose his case and guarantee my recovery."

"I'm the only one here who isn't a lawyer, but I think you mean you'd be guaranteed a judgment, not a recovery."

"Same thing."

Warhelm shook his head. "Not really. Judgments take a long time to collect. Who knows what can happen in the meantime?"

"Right, right, the world could end tomorrow, but I'm betting that it doesn't."

"Nothing so drastic, Jerome. No, I was thinking how unstable the economy is. You never know when a chain of metro radiology clinics could go under."

Baggman's smile faded.

"Physical therapy clinics too. Medical care is so volatile these days."

Baggman went white.

Warhelm kept his eyes on Baggman as he said, "Mason, would you excuse us for a moment, please? Jerome and I are going to negotiate our end of this."

Mason stood and walked out.

"There's a bar in the main room. Help yourself."

Mason closed the door behind him and walked down the hall, also zebrawood, to a room whose only purpose seemed to be the bar and a view of Lake Lacache. He took a club soda out of the glass-front fridge, sipped, and watched the shadow of John Warhelm's house grow longer over Lake Lacache as the sun set behind it.

Far sooner than he expected, Jerome Baggman opened the door and waved him in. He didn't meet Mason's eyes as he took his seat.

"We appear to have reached an agreement," said John Warhelm. "I will advise the sheriff of my suspicions about Red

Gibson and provide him with the video. You will advise your client to settle the case with the survivors and those injured for the limits of his insurance. A company to be named later will agree to pay an additional amount for its residual liability for the faulty support pier. And Mr. Baggman will accept that amount. Is that correct, Jerome?"

Baggman nodded.

"Mason?"

"Agreed."

Warhelm nodded. "Good. We all seem to have an interest in this agreement, which makes it a good solution for our mutual issues."

"Good."

"There is one thing though, Mason."

Mason didn't like the sound of that. Still, he smiled. "It's always the last screw that's stripped."

"What?" said Baggman.

But Warhelm smiled. "Indeed. Mr. Baggman advises me that the probate court must approve settlements involving wrongful death and minors."

"That's true."

"So the only way the settlement Mr. Baggman and I have agreed to will get approved is if you win the criminal case."

"How so?"

"Liability must be in doubt to justify the amount."

Mason understood. "Which won't be true if there's a criminal conviction. Got it."

"So, we're agreed?"

Mason nodded. So did Baggman.

"Then I think we're done."

Baggman rose and left without a word.

Mason stood and faced John Warhelm. "Thank you, Mr. Warhelm."

Warhelm stood, came around the desk, and extended his hand. "Call me John."

"Thanks, John." Mason shook his hand and almost smiled when he found it was as battered as his own. But he didn't.

"I appreciate you coming to me with a solution," John Warhelm said.

"I'll have the other drive to you first thing."

"I know. And I'm serious, about winning. Things might...fall apart if you don't."

"I know," Mason said, and he left.

He had an expert examination to fine-tune.

84

Kyle Stewart was tired, hungry, and angry. He'd spent almost twenty-four hours with the Chicago PD, and the only thing he'd had to drink was a cup of coffee from "the good cop" when he'd been trying to get Kyle to change his story. Kyle hadn't budged though, and when he kept saying he'd been drunk and wandered into a form of concrete because it had seemed like a good idea at the time, they'd eventually left him to cool his heels alone.

He'd had two calls with Jerome Baggman in that time. The first had been early in the morning, his "one call" shortly after his "detention." Kyle had told Baggman about the theft of the tooth, about the video, and about what Pierce had done to him. He'd had to be careful, the police were listening in after all, but Baggman had seemed positively delighted, both at the disappearance of the tooth and his new leverage over Pierce.

The second call had been just now, just before midnight after Kyle had finally been released and had access to his own phone again. Now that they could talk freely outside the police station, Kyle had expected more questions about the video or about what Pierce had done, but Baggman hadn't asked about that at all. No, Baggman had sounded strange, deflated somehow, even though he had insisted nothing was wrong, and his questions took Kyle in an unexpected direction—Baggman had wondered how secure, and how secret, their arrangements were with the radiology clinics.

Kyle had blinked, not sure why Baggman would suddenly be concerned about the dozen or so radiology clinics scattered around the metro area that would, in exchange for a discreet percentage of the recovery, always find an auto accident injury in the shadows of an MRI regardless of whether it was there. Kyle had reassured Baggman that their arrangements with the radiology clinics, and the PT clinics too, were undiscoverable and airtight, but he could hear it—Baggman didn't believe him.

When Kyle brought their conversation back around to the patio case, Baggman had reassured Kyle that his bonus was coming and that he shouldn't worry. Then Baggman had hung up with an excuse of trial the next day, and Kyle found that he didn't believe Baggman any more than Baggman believed him.

There were things in play in Northlake, things Kyle didn't know because he wasn't there, and now that there was a death involved, Kyle wasn't at all sure there wouldn't be another.

He took a rideshare back to Echelon, found his car, and got in.

85

"Could you introduce yourself to the jury, please?" said Mason.

"Dr. Cameron Thomas."

"Dr. Thomas, what are you going to tell the jury about today?"

"I'm going to explain why the concrete support pier failed."

"Could you give us a preview?"

"Yes. The support pier failed because it was structurally unsound."

"Why was it structurally unsound?"

"Because there was no rebar in it to support it and because there was a big air pocket in the center."

"Why was there an air pocket?"

"Because there was a body in it."

There wasn't a gasp, but the jury, and the rest of the courtroom collectively sat up. Astrid Olsen and Jerome Baggman stayed stone-faced.

Hyde Warren looked terrified.

That gave Mason a brief window to walk Cameron through

her expert credentials to talk about the strength of structures. When they were done, Mason still had the jury's attention and came back around to the pier.

"Dr. Thomas, the State hired an expert, Dr. Wasmeuller, to talk to the jury. Are you aware of what he told them?"

"Yes, he said the pier collapsed because there was too much weight on it."

"Too many people and too much snow?"

"That's correct."

"Was he right?"

"No."

"Why not?"

"Properly constructed, the patio piers would have been more than strong enough to hold the weight that night. In fact, they would have been able to hold a great deal more."

"Can you show us how?"

"I'd be happy too."

Then it was Cameron's turn to take the jury through an animation to illustrate the math that supported her opinions. When she was done, she said, "I've run the simulation by adding at least three times the occupancy limit for the patio and, with the proper support piers, it always held."

"But Dr. Thomas, the state has made a point of saying the occupancy limit is there to promote safety?"

"It is. But in this case, the occupancy limit's primary purpose was to mitigate fire risk, to allow for proper evacuation. It wasn't related to the integrity of the structure."

"So if excess weight didn't cause the collapse, what did?"

"Shoddy craftsmanship."

"What do you mean?"

"I mean, the concrete pier wasn't built properly. Worse, it was used for an unintended purpose, which dramatically weakened it."

"What was the purpose?"

"To hide a body."

"You'd better walk us through that, Dr. Thomas."

"I examined the concrete that was part of the failed pier. There was no rebar in it."

"What's rebar?"

"Bars of steel that are placed in a concrete form to help support it and give it additional strength."

"And there wasn't any rebar in the pier that failed?"

"There was not."

"Was there rebar in the other piers?"

"There was."

"Curious. What effect would the lack of rebar have?"

"The pier wouldn't be as strong."

"Is rebar standard in this type of support pier?"

"It is."

"What else did you find in the pier that failed?"

"I took samples from the concrete of the failed pier. In doing so, I found a ring."

"Dr. Thomas, I'm handing you what's been marked as Defendant's Exhibit 29. Can you identify it?"

"It's the 1970 Naval Academy ring that I found in the concrete."

"Did that cause you to draw any conclusions?"

"Not at that time."

"What did you do next?"

"I sent samples of the concrete to the lab."

"What did you find?"

"Nothing abnormal about the makeup of the concrete. But the lab did find a tooth embedded in the concrete itself."

"A tooth?"

"Yes."

"I'm handing you copies of Defendant's Exhibits 33 and 34. Can you identify those?"

"Yes. The first is a report from the lab indicating the presence of a tooth, an incisor, in the concrete, and the second is a receipt indicating that it had been packaged and given to me."

"Dr. Thomas, let me stop you for a second. Did you actually see the tooth?"

Cameron nodded. "I did. When I went to pick it up from the lab, they showed it to me before they packaged it up."

"So why did you take the tooth?"

"To have DNA testing done."

"Did you wind up having any DNA testing done?"

"No."

"Why not?"

"Because the tooth was stolen before the testing occurred."

"I see."

Judge Roderick had been very clear in his ruling that morning—Cameron could talk about everything she had personally seen and done, but she was not to mention Austin's death or the potential identity of the victim as Kent Corwin, so Mason moved on.

"Did you arrive at any opinions based on these facts, Dr. Thomas?"

"I did."

"What are those opinions?"

"The rebar forms a lattice, a kind of crisscross inside the form that would make it difficult to fit a body in there. We know that the rebar was either removed or never put into the form for that pier. The presence of the ring and the tooth leads me to believe that a body was in the pier. As the body decayed, it would have left a void, an air bubble in the concrete. This would weaken the pier over years until it collapsed, as happened here.

Would you like to see a simulation based on the size of an average man?"

"Certainly."

She ran it, complete with pulling rebar out and leaving a man-sized hole, followed by the pier cracking and falling over.

"Dr. Thomas, who built the patio?"

"Corwin Concrete."

"Did Mr. Warren?"

"No, he hired Corwin Concrete."

"Would you expect an owner to inspect inside the piers?"

"No. That's why they hire experts."

"Did Mr. Warren have a right to rely on Corwin Concrete to do a good and workmanlike job?"

"Sure, we all do when we hire experts to do something. That's why we hire them."

"No further questions, Your Honor."

Astrid Olsen strode right up in front of Cameron Thomas.

"You never found a body, did you, Dr. Thomas?"

"I found a tooth."

"You didn't find the head it was from, did you?"

"No. A great deal of—"

"—No, is sufficient, Dr. Thomas. Rings fall off fingers, don't they, Dr. Thomas?"

"That's pretty rare, Ms. Olsen."

"It's possible, isn't it?"

"It's doubtful."

"People take rings off, don't they?"

"I don't know that a person would take off a naval academy ring at a worksite and leave it lying around."

"You don't know that they didn't, do you?"

"I don't."

"Dr. Thomas, you're aware that seven people died in the collapse, aren't you?"

"I am."

"You know twenty-seven were injured?"

"I do."

"It's possible that one of them had a tooth knocked out in this horrific event, isn't it?"

"I'm sure they did, but—"

"But we can't check the DNA on that tooth to see if it matches a victim of the collapse because you say it was stolen, right?"

"I don't say it was stolen. Sheriff Sizemore does."

"Convenient."

"Not at all."

"We could waste a lot of time going through the math of your simulation, but let's cut right to it for the jury. For your collapse theory to be valid, there had to have been a body in the pier, do I have that right?"

"Yes."

"A body we don't have."

"We had a tooth."

"But you don't have one anymore, that you can actually show the jury."

"That's right."

"No further questions, Your Honor."

Mason stood. "Dr. Thomas, Ms. Olsen didn't let you finish one of your answers. Were you going to explain why you didn't find a body?"

"I was trying to, yes."

"Please go ahead."

"A great deal of the concrete pier was missing."

"Missing? What do you mean?"

"I mean it was gone, so that I could not examine it."

"Gone? Are you sure?"

"Positive."

"I also found sections that had been jackhammered open."

"That would be Defense Exhibits 9 and 10?"

Pictures popped up on the screen.

"Yes. Those are chisel marks there and there and there, indicating the pier had been split open."

"Dr. Thomas, Ms. Olsen also cut you off when you were talking about the tooth."

"She did."

"Did you have something else to say?"

"Yes. We know the tooth wasn't from a victim of the patio collapse."

"How?"

"Because this tooth was actually embedded in the concrete. The lab only found it when it split a piece of concrete apart. It got in there when the concrete was wet. A tooth from someone involved in the collapse would have been loose on the ground."

"Is there any other reason to believe the tooth came from inside the pier?"

"Yes."

"What is that?"

"It was stolen."

"No further questions."

Astrid Olsen stood. "So, Dr. Thomas, you would have the jury believe that some mystery person put a body in the pier back when it was built, then came back some twenty-three years later and spirited that body away from a mass casualty scene and stole a tooth from you to cover his tracks?"

"Yes, I would."

"Why in the world would someone do such a thing?"

"I don't know."

When she looked at him and continued to speak, Mason

shot to his feet, scared Cameron was going to name Red Gibson, afraid that the whole thing he'd worked for was going to be blown apart, but before he could stop her, Cameron Thomas gave Mason a small smile and said, "You'd have to ask someone from Corwin Concrete."

He sat back down.

86

When Red saw the number, he picked up right away. "Hi, John."

"Hi, Red. Are you working today?"

"Yeah, I'm down at the Pine Road site."

"Oh, my mistake, I thought you said you had a dentist appointment."

Red looked out at the pine woods beyond the lot they were working on. "No, I had a toothache, but it cleared up."

"Ah, good. Gone completely then?"

"Can't feel a thing. Even had a caramel this morning. I'm a sucker for candy. I'm glad you called, though; we had some tools go missing from the job site last night. I had to buy the boys some replacements this morning."

"What was taken?"

"Not too much. Just a couple of circular saws and a hammer. Do you want me to let the sheriff know?"

"No, not for something that small. How's the job going?"

"Good. Right on schedule."

"Sounds like you have everything under control then."

"You can count on me, John."

"I know, Red. Thanks."

"You bet."

Red hung up, put the phone in his pocket, and stared at the pines. John Warhelm had never, in the decades they'd worked together, called to see if he was on site.

Red Gibson waved to his foreman and pointed to his truck that he was leaving. The foreman waved goodbye.

87

Once the talk of a body in the pier had started, Hyde Warren had freaked all the way out. During the break after Cameron's examination, they'd taken him back to the conference room where Jessica Warren gave him "a nerve pill" and Peter had told his friend to nut up enough to see that the case was breaking their way, so that the last thing they needed was a delay while the defendant found his spine.

Then Peter turned to Mason and told him they were going to rest their case and he, Mason, was going to close. Mason didn't protest, but his look must have said it because Peter then said, "They believe the body theory or they don't. You're the only one who can sell them on it."

Mason agreed. He'd felt the momentum in the courtroom the same as Peter; he didn't know if it was enough, but their best chance was to strike now, and he agreed that he was the one to do it. More importantly, though Peter didn't know it, the sooner the case was over, the less time there was for the deal with Warhelm and Baggman to fall apart.

So Mason excused himself, went up to his seat among the

stone columns in the tower of the library, and spent twenty minutes preparing for closing.

He was almost completely successful in pushing aside thoughts that it was his first.

ASTRID OLSEN STOOD before the jury and said, "This case is about responsibility. Hyde Warren was responsible for everything at the Stone Street Cider Mill. Distilling, advertising, stocking food and drink, staffing, layout, all of it. Every witness who testified said that Hyde Warren was a hands-on owner who was invested in every aspect of his Cider Mill.

"That extended to special events. You heard testimony and saw evidence that Hyde Warren was in charge of the biggest Dune Sled event the Cider Mill ever held. He ordered t-shirts, he brought in extra staff, and, when the weekend looked like a hit, he set the patio up with extra bar stations and gas heaters. Hyde Warren was in charge of making sure his patrons had fun."

Astrid Olsen paused and let it sit there for a moment, then said, "He was also in charge of his patrons' safety. He was in charge of making sure safety rules were followed. He was in charge of making sure he engaged in safe maintenance practices. And he was responsible if he failed to do it.

"You had witness after witness testify to how crowded it was on the patio. We've also assembled one hundred and seventy-six affidavits from people who testified that they were on the patio that night. One hundred and seventy-six when the patio was only allowed to hold one hundred." She held up a three-ring binder. "They're all in here." She dropped it with a thud onto the table. "I encourage you to count them all for yourself. The same way that Hyde Warren should have counted the people that night.

"There's something that you won't find in the evidence. I wish you would, but you won't. You won't find an invoice for clearing the snow off the roof of the patio. During a winter with one of the highest snowfalls on record, Hyde Warren just let it pile up, let the snow pile up on the roof just like he let the people pile up on the patio, and eventually it was too much. The patio collapsed. And when it did, it took Callie Portman, his hostess for many years. It took Sophia Kern and Molly Danvers and four more just like them. It left Carly Franklin in a wheelchair she might never climb out of. When you return a conviction, you're going to hear from every single victim of Hyde Warren who can still speak and from the family members of those who can't. You can make Hyde Warren face them all and take responsibility for his actions because that's something he still hasn't done."

Astrid Olsen shook her head. "His lawyers haven't even tried to deny that the patio was overcrowded. They haven't come up here and argued that Hyde Warren complied with his responsibilities. No, they've just invented a story about a disappearing body and air pockets and rebar. It's just one more way that Hyde Warren is trying to avoid his responsibility. Don't let him. Don't let him shirk his responsibility now the way he did on the night the patio of the Stone Creek Cider Mill collapsed."

Astrid Olsen straightened. "Hyde Warren displayed a conscious disregard for the safety of his patrons when he loaded up his patio with people and let his roof stay loaded with snow. He caused the patio to collapse. His reckless, conscious disregard for the safety of others directly caused their deaths, the deaths of seven people. For that reason, we are asking you to find Hyde Warren guilty of seven counts of involuntary manslaughter. We ask that you make him acknowledge, finally, his responsibility for those deaths. Thank you."

As Astrid Olsen sat, Jerome Baggman kept watch from the

first row, his eyes boring in on Mason. Mason met his stare directly, then stood and walked over to the jury, being sure to stand a good six feet farther back than Astrid had.

"The collapse at the Stone Street Cider Mill is one of the worst things that's ever happened in Northlake," he said. "It's hard to find someone who hasn't been affected; nearly everyone in town knew someone or was related to someone who was hurt, or killed, in that terrible accident. That includes Hyde Warren, who lost Callie Portman, who he'd worked with for eight years, ever since she was in high school.

"We all wonder why something like this happened, why people our community knew and loved were hurt or killed. People look for someone to blame, and that's what the State has done here. It's decided to blame Hyde Warren. It's decided to accuse him of a crime, to accuse Hyde Warren of causing those unimaginable deaths. So now it's up to the State and Ms. Olsen to back up what they've said with proof beyond a reasonable doubt that Hyde Warren caused those deaths. And they just haven't done that.

"The State relies on two things for its theory—the number of people and the weight of the snow. Yet they can't tell you how many pounds of either of them were on the patio that night. Ms. Olsen showed you this binder of affidavits." He picked it up. "They could have called anyone they wanted out of this book, and they called Terri Wozniak. Ms. Wozniak was there that night, but she wasn't there when the patio collapsed. You heard her say she left an hour before. Who knows how many other people left or were in the bathroom or were in the dining room or simply were not on the patio when it fell. They needed to prove it to you; they needed to prove it beyond a reasonable doubt, and they failed.

"The same is true of the snow. Barry Wasmeuller sat right there and told you that we had a record amount of snow this winter, but he couldn't tell you how much of it was on the roof that night. In fact, he even admitted that he didn't even account for the patio's metal roof! How many times have you seen it? How many times have you seen snow slide off a metal roof on a warm day? Dr. Wasmeuller admitted that was true and admitted he didn't know how much snow was there the night the patio went down."

Mason shook his head. "They needed to prove to you what those weights were to support Dr. Wasmeuller's theory of why the patio collapsed. The fact is, neither he nor Ms. Olsen knows how many people were on the patio, and neither he nor Ms. Olsen knows how much snow was on the roof, so neither he nor Ms. Olsen can prove that's why the patio collapsed. They're just guessing. And that's not allowed under the law. They have to prove it."

"The fact is, even if you assume their numbers are true, which you shouldn't, the piers should have been strong enough to support that weight. A properly constructed concrete pier would have supported far more weight than might have been on the patio that night. But what we've proven to you is that the pier *wasn't* properly constructed. And that's why it failed."

"First, we proved to you that there was no rebar in the pier. There should have been. There was rebar in all of the other piers but not in this one. The absence of rebar is a *fact* that the State does not contest."

"We've also shown for a fact that there was evidence that a body was in that pier. Dr. Thomas found a Naval Academy ring from 1970. Regardless of what Ms. Olsen said, rings don't just fall off fingers. And I ask you to use your own experience—how many of you would put an academy ring like that somewhere it can get knocked into wet concrete? A cupholder in a car, on a nightstand, that's different. On the edge of wet concrete? I don't think so."

"Then there's the tooth. A tooth that was embedded in the concrete, a tooth that can only be embedded in the concrete if it was in there when it was being poured. The judge is going to talk to you about inferences, that you're allowed to infer things from the existence of evidence. The presence of that embedded tooth and that embedded ring in the concrete allow you to make the only logical inference—there was a body in that pier. And that inference explains why there was no rebar—so the body would fit."

Mason stepped back a little. "Ms. Olsen's right, we don't have the body. We've found evidence that concrete was taken from the site and evidence that someone chiseled the fractured pier open but we can't say for sure what happened to the body—but we know, for sure, that there was no rebar, and we know for sure, that there was a tooth and a ring, and we know for sure, that an air pocket the size of a man would cause the concrete pier to eventually fail."

Mason shook his head. "We only know about the rebar and the air pocket now because the pier collapsed, because we could look inside. There's no way Hyde Warren could've known those things back when the patio was built. The fact is that the State hasn't proved its case beyond a reasonable doubt. The fact is the State can't say Hyde Warren recklessly overloaded the patio because the State doesn't even know how much weight was on the patio. The fact is that we do know that the concrete pier wasn't built right. It wasn't reinforced, and it had something in it that caused an air pocket, most likely a body. The only ones who know for sure are the people at Corwin Concrete, and they're not the ones on trial here. Hyde Warren is."

"Hyde Warren didn't kill seven people. He didn't construct a faulty pier. The folks at Corwin Concrete did. The State has not proven its case; the case *it* has the burden of carrying. For that reason, we ask that you find Hyde Warren not guilty. Thank you."

Mason sat. As Judge Roderick started reading the jury instructions, Peter nodded. Hyde touched his arm and whispered thanks. Jerome Baggman stared, and Astrid Olsen followed along with the instructions to make sure the judge read them right.

Then the judge finished, and the jury was sent to deliberate, and Peter, Mason, Hyde, and Jessica went back to the conference room to wait.

88

They had been waiting for an hour and a half in the conference room when Mason and Peter received a text from Holly Gorman, the judge's civil bailiff.

The jury has a question.

Mason and Peter told Hyde and Jessica to sit tight and went back into the courtroom.

Holly was sitting at her desk. "We'll go back in chambers as soon as Astrid gets here."

"Sure," said Mason.

"Are those glasses a new print?" said Peter.

Holly nodded, smiled. "Cheetah."

"Nice."

Astrid Olsen walked in. Jerome Baggman followed.

Peter scowled. "Holly, given all that's happened, I don't know if it's appropriate if Mr. Baggman—"

Mason reached out and touched his arm. "Let him."

Peter tilted his head.

"I'll explain after."

Peter hesitated, then nodded.

"What's happening, Holly?" said Astrid as she walked up.

"You're screwed," blurted Holly, then cursed.

Astrid flushed. Baggman slumped.

"I mean, the judge wants to consult with all of you to answer the jury's question."

Holly went first, then the four of them—Mason, Peter, Astrid, and Jerome—followed.

When they were all seated and the court reporter was ready, Judge Roderick said, "We have a question from the jury. Holly, will you read it into the record, please?"

"Yes, Judge," she said, and unfolded a piece of paper.

"The jury's question is, '*Do we need to know who the body was to find that it was there*?'"

Judge Roderick nodded. "Thank you, Holly. Counsel, I assume we can all agree on the answer?"

~

SHERIFF SIZEMORE WAS WALKING out of the gas station with a fresh coffee when his county-issued sheriff's department phone buzzed. It didn't identify the caller because this caller had never tried to reach him on his public phone before, but Sheriff Sizemore still answered right away because he recognized the number.

"Sheriff Sizemore," he answered.

"Sean, it's John Warhelm."

"How can I help you, John?"

"I've received some information related to the Austin Pierce killing. It's most distressing."

"What is it?"

"I think it's better if you saw it. Can you come over?"

"Right away."

Sheriff Sizemore hopped into his car. He didn't turn on his flashers, but he sped the whole way.

JEROME BAGGMAN TRIED to reach Kyle Stewart. There was no answer. There hadn't been for some time.

Jerome Baggman believed in redundant systems. He called Kyle's counterpart and told him what to do.

WHEN KYLE STEWART saw the fifth call from Jerome Baggman, he decided it was time to destroy his phone. He didn't think Baggman could trace him, not really, but he was becoming convinced that the odds against him getting out of this alive were becoming very short.

Baggman knew Kyle had been spying on Pierce for him, and he knew Kyle had stumbled on evidence of the murder as part of it. That was all part of their ongoing business arrangement as far as Kyle was concerned. But Baggman's sudden question about the radiology clinics, about the under-the-table payout arrangements for recruiting clients and supporting claims which had formed the basis of Baggman's practice so many years ago could only mean that there was a problem.

Kyle had helped set up those arrangements; arrangements that could cost Baggman his license and destroy his practice.

Kyle Stewart knew Jerome Baggman. He'd bet anything that Baggman was taking steps right now to reduce the risk of discovery of those practice-destroying facts, and Kyle bet that dealing with him was part of it.

So Kyle Stewart tapped his fifth and final emergency fund, the one fund he'd had the discipline to maintain his entire career, his "Go" fund, then destroyed his phone.

The jury found Hyde Warren not guilty forty-five minutes after they asked their question. It had only taken so long because they had to fill out seven different sets of forms, one for each death. Hyde just stood there blinking, not seeming to take any of it in. Mason motioned to Jessica, who came up and guided Hyde back down to his seat as Mason and Peter made sure all the final technicalities were followed that would allow their client to walk free.

Mason, then Peter, shook Astrid's hand and exchanged mutual compliments on a case well-fought before Astrid went to speak with the Danvers and the Kerns.

Three of the jurors were willing to speak with Mason about the verdict. They wanted to know what was going to be done about Corwin Concrete and who would be held accountable for the collapse and the original murder. When Mason explained that would be up to the sheriff and Ms. Olsen, they didn't seem particularly satisfied, and one woman said she'd be calling Sheriff Sizemore to make sure he knew about all that had happened here. She even asked again what year the Naval Academy ring had been from, and Mason knew that some internet sleuthing was about to begin.

When he found his way back to the defense table, Peter was saying to Hyde, "We have a little paperwork to complete with your bond, but then you'll be free to go."

The words still didn't seem to be registering with Hyde, so Jessica, rubbing his back, said, "That's great, Peter. Hear that Hyde, just a little bit more and then we'll go."

Hyde stared straight ahead.

"Actually, Peter, we need to talk," said Mason. "All of us. Let's go back to the conference room."

Jessica looked concerned. Hyde stared straight ahead.

Peter said, "What are you talking about, Pierce?"

"There've been some developments."

~

Sheriff Sizemore pounded on the door. "Red? Red, it's Sean Sizemore, open up. We need to talk."

Nothing.

"Don't make me break this down, Red. You need to come down with me to the station."

No answer at all.

"Red?!"

Not a sound.

Sheriff Sizemore gathered himself to kick in the door, then rethought and tried it first.

It was unlocked.

He smiled. That's why he got paid the big bucks.

Sheriff Sizemore went in, one hand on the butt of his gun, still holstered.

It didn't take long to walk around the house to see.

Red Gibson was gone.

~

Mason explained to Hyde that Kramer Burns had settled all of the civil cases against him.

Hyde stared straight ahead.

"What do you mean, Mason?" said Jessica Warren.

"Explain the whole thing to them," said Peter, who didn't show a hint of surprise regarding the settlement he knew nothing about.

So Mason did. He told them that they'd made a deal so that Baggman would only seek to recover from Hyde's insurance policies against him.

Hyde blinked. "But that's not nearly enough."

"No, it's not. But he's reached a deal with one of the successor companies of Corwin Concrete for the rest."

Peter nodded. "Tell him why the company would do that, Mason."

"They don't want to be painted as having anything to do with the collapse, but you saw how this went today—if this case stays in the news, people will keep talking about their poor workmanship."

Peter nodded, the light on. "And the body."

"And the body."

Hyde focused on Mason for the first time. "So our house, our retirement, all those things?"

Mason shook his head. "Baggman won't come after them. It'll take some arm twisting with the insurance company, but it's going to see pretty quickly that it's better off paying a relatively small amount to get out from under that many claims."

Hyde shook his head. "Why would Baggman do that?"

"Winning today put Baggman's case in doubt. And now that there's a second pot of money, there's enough for the plaintiffs to get their money now instead of years from now. It may take a little doing, but it'll get done."

Mason had seen Baggman's face. He had no doubt he'd get it done.

"So it's over?" said Hyde.

"We have a deal. It'll take some time to finalize it, but you've spent your last day in court."

Hyde put his hand over his wife's. "She's safe?"

Mason nodded. "She is."

Then Hyde Warren wept as the weight of broken concrete and twisted steel fell from his shoulders.

A short time later, Hyde and Jessica Warren left the conference room. Mason and Peter followed.

"You're going to have to tell me how you pulled that off," Peter whispered.

"That's probably not a good idea," said Mason.

Peter stared at him, then grinned and slapped his shoulder. "You're probably right."

They hadn't gone more than a few feet when Peter started to laugh.

"What?" said Mason.

Peter kept laughing. "Mother Burns is going to shit itself."

89

Two days later, Red Gibson sat on his back deck, drinking his Kentucky bourbon. His house was on a hill, but unlike so many who chased views of the Big Lake and watched it eat yards of shoreline every year, Red had opted for a quieter place, still on a hill, but looking out at rolling miles of woods and vineyards.

No, a house in the woods was far more practical than a house on the lake. Practicality was Red Gibson's strength, and practical solutions his gift. It's what had brought him into John Warhelm's orbit in the first place and what had kept him there all those years.

His first boss, Kent Corwin, hadn't been that way. He'd been a by-the-book military man, abiding by military standards and ideals that often weren't related to the real world at all, hanging on and hanging on and hanging on in hopes of passing on his company to a son who didn't want it.

When John Warhelm had approached Kent Corwin about buying the Corwin Concrete operation and merging it into his growing family of companies, it was more of the same, with the old man focused on nothing but procedures and an exorbitant price that was "fair value" for the "good will" he professed to have built up in the community, rather than seeing it for the opportunity for expansion, and money, that it was. That, combined with John Warhelm's sudden arrival in town from Chicago, was enough for Kent Corwin to pooch the deal and turn it down. Which wasn't a practical result for anyone, not Kent Corwin, not his son the wanna-be veterinarian, and certainly not for Red himself.

It had taken almost no planning. Just a concrete form with the rebar taken out, a hammer, and a mix truck running and ready to go. A call for the old man to take a look at a problem with the concrete forms for the piers had brought him running, like it always did since, in his mind, the old man was the only one who knew how to fix it. Then a pop and a drop and a fill of the form. A pier was born.

The fishing accident hadn't been his idea, but it was a good one. Red had taken the keys to the boat, which the old man always carried and no longer needed, and had driven it out into the lake. Lake Michigan took boats on the best of days, so he hadn't been worried about that part, but the incoming storm had been an added bonus, so he'd headed straight out into the teeth of it for a couple of miles, cut the engine, and jumped off at the spot where John Warhelm's boat was waiting to pick him up.

Red smiled because he could admit, now, that the old man would have known that a body and a lack of rebar would make the pier weak. But Red had been new and hungry then and didn't have the experience he'd develop over the years, experience that had only sharpened his instinct for practicality and solutions.

He really hadn't been worried about the discovery of the death of the old man. Regardless of what had happened over the last couple of weeks, of the attention that had been turned to it, there was no body anymore, there was no tooth, there was no evidence. It might be a little uncomfortable, but it wasn't much of a problem.

No, the problem was the death of the Pierce boy, and for that there was only one solution, one made all the more elegant by the fact that it actually was the solution to two.

Unlike Commander Corwin, Red Gibson embraced the practical and didn't shy away from solutions. It had taken him two days to make sure that his estranged daughter was taken care of and that his ex-wife wouldn't see a lick, and, when he had that squared away, he'd come home, straight through town, so he wasn't surprised when he heard the knock at the front door and Sheriff Sizemore shouting to let him in.

Red Gibson took a last sip of his bourbon, then went to meet him.

~

JEROME BAGGMAN HUNG up the phone. His redundant system had failed to find Kyle Stewart. The man was gone. So Baggman would have to hedge.

Once he received the settlement from Warhelm and the insurance company, Baggman would pay Stewart's fee, with the bonus, into the usual account. He hoped that would keep Stewart gone and, if he stayed gone, that would be the end of it.

If he came back, well, a trial lawyer has to be prepared.

So he told the redundant system to keep an eye out for him.

~

SHERIFF SIZEMORE HOLSTERED his weapon before he walked through the acrid smell of gunpowder to approach the body. He bent down, felt for a pulse, but it was obvious that Red Gibson was dead. Fourteen rounds from a sheriff and two deputies will do that.

He nudged the weapon out of Red's hand that had been pointed at them a moment before, a Glock by the look of it.

"Should we call the ambulance?" said one deputy.

"No, call dispatch for the M.E. He's dead."

"A round wasn't chambered," said the other deputy, examining the Glock.

Sheriff Sizemore nodded. "Must have jammed. Lucky us. Process everything here by the book, boys. We need to put this Austin Pierce murder to bed."

The deputies donned gloves and started processing the scene. Sheriff Sizemore stepped back outside, satisfied that he had followed every lead to its conclusion, leaving no doubt that the trail ended right here.

For two murders.

He stepped a little farther away out of earshot of the deputies and made a call.

"We got him."

~

Mason Pierce hung up his phone, then walked from his truck through the grass to the graveside. Uncle Troy and Aunt Linda sat in front, Jackson sitting on the other side of his brother, resting his hands on the tops of his canes. Mason walked up to stand next to Lily, nodded to Bronson watching from the other side.

"It's nice to see our dads together," Lily said.

"It is," Mason said. "Hope it lasts."

"Who knows?" She stared at the hole. "Nothing's guaranteed."

Mason nodded, and the three just stood there, waiting for the pastor to do his thing.

"I said I'd wait 'til today," Lily said. "We're going after him tonight. Are you coming?"

"No."

She scowled. "Worried about your license?"

"No. Red Gibson is dead."

Lily looked up. "How?"

"Shootout when they went to pick him up. Sheriff Sizemore just told me."

Lily still stared at him.

Mason put one arm around his cousin, pulled her close, and kissed her temple.

Lily rested her head on his shoulder for a moment as Bronson caught Mason's eye and nodded.

When Lily straightened, she said, "We're doing something for him tonight, one way or the other."

"How about The Loon then, after we take care of your parents?" said Bronson.

Mason nodded as the pastor began to speak about divine plans. In that moment, Mason couldn't fathom what plan required his cousin's death to work. But he was grateful that the unspoken part of his own plan, that John Warhelm would suffer no loose ends, had.

~

PETER FREID WAS ALONE in the office when the call came in. Melody had gone to the service for Pierce's cousin, of course, but funerals just weren't his thing, so he was by himself when he picked up.

"What does the head of Mother Burns desire of her humble servant?"

"Peter," said Jax Wilbane. "You've been busy."

"We in the hinterlands are eager to serve."

"Congratulations on the win."

"It was nothing."

"I understand you passed off the closing."

"The kid was on a roll."

"We're split here over whether you were inspired or trying to cover your ass if the case went south."

"Who's to say, Jax?"

"And a settlement too? Very industrious."

"Always."

"Of course, by settling so soon, you've cost us years of billable litigation."

"Ah, you know these insurance cocksuckers, it'll take them a while to see the light. We'll make it up."

"That's why I was calling. To compliment you on the plan to make it up."

"You know me, always looking out for the Mother Ship."

"I do know you, Peter. That's why I was so surprised."

"About what?"

"That you would share credit with an associate for a deal you made."

"More than enough credit to go around."

"True. I think this new account will more than make up for the hours you lost on the patio settlement. We may even have to send you more help."

"I don't know if that's necessary."

"I do. You and Mason can hardly service the Warhelm Industrial account by yourselves."

Peter blinked, then said, "Oh, did Warhelm contact you directly?"

"He did."

"Good. That cuts through the red tape that way."

"Yes. And the bullshit."

"That can be annoying."

"It can. Congratulations. You'll both be getting a quarterly bonus when the retainer comes in."

"Glad to hear it."

"Of course, since you're a partner, you'll be able to see everyone's, so I wanted you to hear it from me directly."

"Hear what?"

"Pierce's bonus will be bigger."

Peter gripped the phone. "Makes sense. He's a big guy."

"Oh, it wasn't our doing. It was Warhelm."

"He *is* the client."

"He is. And he wants Mason Pierce to be his lead counsel."

"Money in the door is money in the door."

"It certainly is. Congratulations again, Peter. You've done an excellent job of mentoring."

Then Jax Wilbane hung up.

Peter sat there for a moment, regrouped, then decided it was too good a day to spend sulking, so he closed the office and went looking for company.

DR. CAMERON THOMAS was the last one to arrive at The Loon. Lily and Bronson sat on one side of the table, Mason alone on the other.

She stopped at the bar, ordered two more pitchers from Brenda, then took them over.

"Dr. Cammie," said Bronson and smiled.

"He'd be glad you're here," said Lily.

"We all are," said Mason.

Mason and Lily poured, refilling theirs and filling

Cameron's, and the four raised their glasses without saying more.

Cameron hadn't had a chance to say it, but felt like she had to, had felt like it all the way on the drive from Chicago. "You guys, I'm so sorry. If I hadn't fallen for that email, this never—"

"—No," said Bronson.

"Absolutely not," said Lily.

"It's been taken care of," said Mason, his eyes as cold, and then as warm as she'd seen them.

And that was it. That was all they'd hear of it.

They talked about Austin then, with Cameron mostly listening. At one point, a group of tourists found their way in, proclaiming themselves loudly in a downstate sort of way.

"We could get in a scrap in his honor," said Lily, smiling.

"He did like a good scrap," said Mason.

"I suppose that's frowned upon on the day of his funeral," said Bronson.

Mason nodded. "True. A plate of mini-tacos then?"

"Four, I think," said Lily.

Bronson looked at Cameron. "You know the rules."

She did. So Cameron, as the last one there, picked up the check when The Loon closed that night.

NEXT MASON PIERCE NOVEL

The Cinderblock Associate is the next book in the Mason Pierce Series. Click here if you'd like to order it or look for it on Amazon.

NEWSLETTER

If you want to know when the next Mason Pierce book is coming, sign up for my newsletter here or at https://michael stagg.com/newsletter/ . That's the first place I'll announce any major information about any of my series, including when the next book is on the way.

ABOUT THE AUTHOR

Michael Stagg was a civil trial lawyer for more than twenty-five years. He has tried cases to juries, so he's won and he's lost and he's argued about it in the court of appeals after. Michael was still practicing law when his first legal thrillers were published so he wrote them under a pen name. He writes full-time now and no longer practices, but the pen name has stuck.

Michael and his wife live in the Midwest. Their sons are grown so time that used to be spent at football games and band concerts now goes to writing. He enjoys sports of all sorts, reading, and grilling, with the order depending on the day.

You can contact him on Facebook or at mikestaggbooks@gmail.com.

ALSO BY MICHAEL STAGG

The Mason Pierce Series

The Concrete Alibi
The Cinderblock Associate

The Nate Shepherd Series

Lethal Defense
True Intent
Blind Conviction
False Oath
Just Plea
Lost Proof
Swift Judgment
Cruel Sentence

Printed in Dunstable, United Kingdom

70555771R00290